Till Death Do Us

Part...

BOOKS BY

C.M. STUNICH

ROMANCE NOVELS

HARD ROCK ROOTS SERIES
Real Ugly
Get Bent
Tough Luck
Bad Day
Born Wrong
Hard Rock Roots Box Set (1-5)
Dead Serious
Doll Face
Heart Broke
Get Hitched
Screw Up

TASTING NEVER SERIES
Tasting Never
Finding Never
Keeping Never
Tasting, Finding, Keeping
Never Can Tell
Never Let Go
Never Did Say
Never Could Stop

ROCK-HARD BEAUTIFUL
Groupie
Roadie
Moxie

THE BAD NANNY TRILOGY
Bad Nanny
Good Boyfriend
Great Husband

TRIPLE M SERIES
Losing Me, Finding You
Loving Me, Trusting You
Needing Me, Wanting You
Craving Me, Desiring You

A DUET
Paint Me Beautiful
Color Me Pretty

FIVE FORGOTTEN SOULS
Beautiful Survivors
Alluring Outcasts

MAFIA QUEEN
Lure
Lavish
Luxe

DEATH BY DAYBREAK MC
I Was Born Ruined
I Am Dressed in Sin

STAND-ALONE NOVELS
Baby Girl
All for 1
Blizzards and Bastards
Fuck Valentine's Day
Broken Pasts
Crushing Summer
Taboo Unchained
Taming Her Boss
Kicked

BAD BOYS MC TRILOGY
Raw and Dirty
Risky and Wild
Savage and Racy

HERS TO KEEP TRILOGY
Biker Rockstar Billionaire CEO Alpha
Biker Rockstar Billionaire CEO Dom
Biker Rockstar Billionaire CEO Boss

BAD BOYS OF BURBERRY PREP
Filthy Rich Boys
Bad, Bad BlueBloods
The Envy of Idols
In the Arms of the Elite

STAND-ALONE
Football Dick
Stepbrother Inked
Glacier

BOOKS BY
C.M. STUNICH

FANTASY NOVELS

THE SEVEN MATES OF ZARA WOLF
Pack Ebon Red
Pack Violet Shadow
Pack Obsidian Gold
Pack Ivory Emerald
Pack Amber Ash
Pack Azure Frost
Pack Crimson Dusk

ACADEMY OF SPIRITS AND SHADOWS
Spirited
Haunted
Shadowed

TEN CATS PARANORMAL SOCIETY
Possessed

TRUST NO EVIL
See No Devils
Hear No Demons
Speak No Curses

THE SEVEN WICKED SERIES
Seven Wicked Creatures
Six Wicked Beasts
Five Wicked Monsters
Four Wicked Fiends

THE WICKED WIZARDS OF OZ
Very Bad Wizards

HOWLING HOLIDAYS
Werewolf Kisses

OTHER FANTASY NOVELS
Gray and Graves
Indigo & Iris
She Lies Twisted
Hell Inc.
DeadBorn
Chryer's Crest
Stiltz

SIRENS OF A SINFUL SEA TRILOGY
Under the Wild Waves

CO-WRITTEN
(With Tate James)

HIJINKS HAREM
Elements of Mischief
Elements of Ruin
Elements of Desire

THE WILD HUNT MOTORCYCLE CLUB
Dark Glitter

FOXFIRE BURNING
The Nine
Tail Game

OTHER
And Today I Die

UNDERCOVER SINNERS
Altered By Fire
Altered By Lead

UNDERGROUND TUNNEL & SEWER SYSTEMS

UNDERGROUND CHURCH

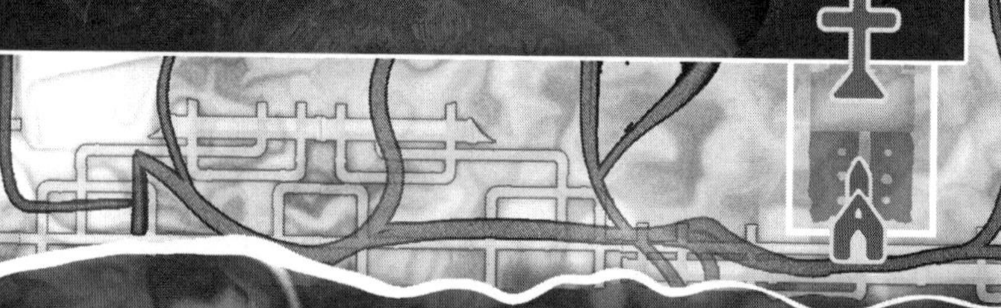

ABOVE GROUND

ALL-BOYS

CHURCH MAP

MAP KEY

 THE FOUNTAIN

 BELOW GROUND SEWER ENTRANCE

 ABOVE GROUND SEWER EXIT

 THE BALLROOM

 THE CLEARING

 THE UNDERGROUND CHURCH ENTRANCE

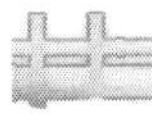 UNDERGROUND SEWER PATHS

 UNDERGROUND TUNNELS

 ALTER

The Forever Crew

C.M. STUNICH
INTERNATIONAL BESTSELLING AUTHOR

The Forever Crew

ISBN: 9798604254660 (pbk.)

For information address:
Sarian Royal, 89365 Old Mohawk Road, Springfield, OR 97478

Contact the authors at
www.cmstunich.com

this book is dedicated to Marmie.

you were here when I started this, gone when I finished.

I'll miss you forever.

AUTHOR'S NOTE

*****Possible Spoilers*****

The Forever Crew (*Adamson All-Boys Academy* #3) is a reverse harem, high school, murder mystery romance. What does that mean exactly? It means our female main character, Charlotte Carson, will end up with at least three love interests by the end of the series. There isn't any bullying in this book, not from the love interests anyway. This story in no way condones bullying, nor does it romanticize it. The love interests in this sequel are actually pretty damn nice (especially when compared to my boys in *The Rich Boys of Burberry Prep* series).

Any kissing/sexual scenes featuring Charlotte aka Chuck are consensual. This book might be about high school students, but it is not what I would consider young adult. The characters are quirky, the emotions real, the f-word in prolific use. There's some underage drinking, sexual situations, mention of a side character's possible suicide, and other adult scenarios although this remains a fairly lighthearted read.

Charlotte starts off as a bit of a brat, but I hope you enjoy the character growth in this series. ;)

None of the main characters is under the age of seventeen. This story will have a happy ending in the third and final book, but if you want to follow the Student Council into college, I'll be writing a fourth book follow-up that crosses over with characters from *Filthy Rich Boys,* titled *Orientation.*

READING ORDER:

***Adamson All-Boys Academy* Series**

1. *The Secret Girl*
2. *The Ruthless Boys*
3. *The Forever Crew*

***Bonus**:*

Orientation, a Burberry Prep x Adamson All-Boys Academy crossover novel

CHAPTER ONE

Drip, drip, drip.

That's the sound the blood makes as it slithers down the dead student's arm, a crimson pool forming below the fingers of his outstretched hand. It's the only noise I can hear above the rushing surge of my pulse and the ragged, frantic inhales of my breath.

"Chuck."

I turn around and find Spencer standing there, dressed in a black hoodie and smelling like cigarettes.

A black hoodie.

Why the hell is he wearing a black hoodie?!

"I saw you running—" he starts as I scramble away and find my feet. It's like, way early in the morning, and Spencer is out here smoking? It doesn't make sense. Add in the black hoodie, and Church with the knife, and … "What the fuck is that?!" He chokes out, pointing behind me in the direction of the shrine.

"I …" There's not enough time for me to get a single sentence out before two of the killers come crashing through the bushes.

Two killers … and Spencer Hargrove in a hoodie, awake at an hour he never is.

No. No. This is my forever crew; these are my friends.

"Spencer, run!" I scream, grabbing his hand and jerking him along with me in the way I should've grabbed Church. Why did I leave him there? *The killer was waiting for me in the hallway, that's why.* But I can't get past the feelings of fear and guilt that choke me as we sprint into the woods, and towards the other hot springs pool.

Branches slap my face as I run, my feet bleeding from the rocks and sticks and brambles that line the forest floor. Spencer stays right beside me, matching me stride for stride. That's when we come around the corner and run into several adults wearing masks.

Masks.

Like something out of a fucking horror movie.

They look like foxes, these wily, grinning things

that bring chills up across my skin.

"Holy shit," I murmur, but Spencer doesn't pause even long enough to take notice. He shoves me to the left, and then takes off with my hand in his, dragging me along with him. Within a few seconds, we're emerging out of the trees and stumbling over the rocks that line the pool.

Together, we fall into the warm water, exploding through the surface with ragged breaths.

"Swim, Chuck," Spencer urges, making sure I've got a head start before he takes off for the shore. We're barely out of the water before huge hands are grabbing onto my shoulders and yanking me up the rest of the way.

It's Church.

There's blood everywhere, all over his hands, on his face, his yukata stained and hanging off one, smooth porcelain shoulder.

Now, there's even blood on me.

"Let go of me!" I shout, freeing myself from the hands of the Student Council President. Spencer slides in front of me, arms out on either side, ready to fight.

"Don't fucking touch her!" he snaps, glancing over his shoulder in the direction of the woods. But there's nobody there, just the boy who gave me an engagement ring … and then put a knife through our teacher.

"I need you both to calm down," Church says calmly, swiping his palms down the front of his yukata and leaving crimson streaks.

"I saw you stab Mr. Dave," I whisper, pointing at him, hand shaking. I want to believe it was self-defense. But then Spencer, and the hoodie, and … It occurs to me that this could be some sort of long game that the guys are playing, the ultimate exercise in bullying. Every incident I've suffered—the first knife chase that led me to Ranger, the twins discovering my secret right off the bat, the headless bird and candles—they've all been connected back to the guys somehow.

"You saw him *what?!*" Spencer chokes out, and his reaction is so genuine, it feels impossible to doubt him. And yet, some primal instinct in me remains wary. He rakes his fingers through his silver hair and glances back at me. The thing is, Church isn't the only one with some explaining to do.

"I wasn't stabbing him; I was removing the knife." Church stays absurdly calm, moving toward us with slow, easy footfalls, the slap of his bare feet on the patio the only sound besides the lapping of the water against the shore. Spencer blocks him, dripping from his soggy hoodie, the hoodie that makes him seem so damn guilty. "It wasn't deep—it hadn't hit anything vital—and he asked me to help."

"There's a dead kid in those woods," Spencer growls out, panting hard. He swipes his hand down his face and flicks the excess water aside. "There's blood everywhere, and then here you are, covered in it."

"Please, Spencer, don't make an ass out of yourself," Church says, his gaze fully trained on me. I feel like squirming, under that stare of his. I'm not sure what I'm supposed to be feeling here: guilt, relief, suspicion. All of the above, most like.

My gaze flicks toward Spencer as he glances back at me, turquoise eyes dark with emotion.

He could easily be the third hoodie-wearing asshole, couldn't he? His brother has all those academy maps, and he disappeared when Eugene was killed. He runs the school's underground with his business ventures, and he knows every little nook and cranny of Adamson.

A lump forms in my throat, and I find it suddenly hard to swallow.

"You have no reason to trust anyone, Chuck," Spencer says slowly, panting from our run through the woods. "In fact, considering everything that's happened to you, it would be better if you didn't."

"Stay away from me," I warn, backing up until the edge of my foot touches the water. I want to trust them both, believe them both, but I'm having a really hard time doing that when one was wearing a hoodie and waiting in the woods, and the other is covered in blood and our teacher is nowhere to be seen.

The sound of pounding footsteps precedes the twins as they squeeze out the side door together and come around the corner. Both are white as ghosts, and their green eyes widen in unison as they spot Church.

"Dude, what the fuck is that?" they ask together, pointing at him as Ranger shoves his way out, panting and furious. As soon as he sees we're all here, he sighs with relief and comes toward me.

"Wait!" I shout, holding up a hand, scooting back even further, so that my already wet yukata dips into the water. "Nobody come any closer."

"What the hell is going on out here?" Ranger asks, glancing toward Church. "When I woke up, Spencer was gone, and then I found your guys' room empty …" He trails off, studying the blood for a moment. "Whose blood is that?"

"Not mine," Church says easily. *He lies as easily as he breathes,* I remind myself, wrapping my arms tightly over my chest. The door opens a moment a later, and the twins step forward, putting their arms against the doorjamb the way they did last night.

"Student Council only," they say, shoving whoever it is back. The half-wall and cluster of bamboo that decorates the spot near the door keeps the person from noticing Church and his blood-stained clothing. A grumbling curse follows, and then we're alone again.

Birds chirp from the surrounding trees, but the only sound I can hear then is the thundering of my heart, the rushing of my pulse in my head.

"He stabbed Mr. Dave," I repeat as Spencer steps aside, creating a circle with Church opposite me, the twins to my left, and Ranger standing beside his best friend.

"What the fuck, Church?" Ranger asks, his voice hard but not accusatory, like he believes me … but also like he believes Church wouldn't do something like that unless he had to.

"Mr. Dave was bandaging his wound; I left to find Charlotte," Church says, throwing his hand out toward me and then running his fingers through his honeyed hair and leaving ruby streaks. He seems to notice too late what he's doing, and his jaw clenches in disgust. "I don't know where he is now."

"And you stabbed him, why?" Ranger repeats as the twins exchange a look, and then turn their attention to me and Spencer, both sopping wet.

"*I* didn't stab him. He came into the room to talk to me, and one of those psychos followed him in. They grabbed Charlotte's hunting knife from the bag, and put it through Mr. Dave before I could stop them."

"How would a stranger know I had the hunting knife at all?" I ask, panting hard, wanting to believe the guys, wishing with every breath that I could.

"I don't know," Church supplies, holding his palms up and out in a placating gesture. He sighs hard, like he's exhausted already. "I have no fucking clue."

"Why are you two wet?" the twins ask together, studying me and Spencer in our sopping clothes.

"Yes, do tell," Church agrees, and then he unties the sash from his yukata and lets it fall to the ground, striding past me, and diving into the water to wash off the blood. Ranger doesn't hesitate before bending down and bundling up the bloody clothes. My eyes stray from him to Church as the golden boy of Adamson Academy breaks the surface of the water, pushing back his wet hair with both hands and opening amber eyes to stare at me.

My heart flutters in the worst way, and I fist my hand in the wet fabric of my robe.

"I was trying to hide from the headmaster, smoking in the woods." Spencer ruffles up his hair and closes his turquoise eyes for a moment. "I saw Charlotte run past me, and …" He trails off and then tilts his head back, opening his eyes to look at the bright, sunny sky of early morning. "Someone was chasing her."

"Two someones," I correct, "in hoodies."

The twins and Ranger both turn to look at Spencer, and the latter cocks a brow.

"Seriously?" Spencer asks, redirecting his attention back to me. "You think I'm one of the killers?"

"I don't know anything," I whisper as he sighs and then turns back to Ranger.

"We were chased through the woods, and then we stumbled onto some psychos wearing masks. Oh, and by the way, there's a dead kid in those trees, on some sort of shrine. It's beyond fucked-up. I'm pretty sure it was Jason Lambert."

"Who?" I ask.

"You wouldn't know him," the twins say together. And then Micah adds, "He's been running against Church for Student Council President since freshman year."

"Gee, thanks, that really helps clear my suspicions," I grumble as Church stands up, the water just barely lapping at his glorious hips, the rest of his muscular body on full display. My cheeks heat, and I turn away.

"Let's find the headmaster," Ranger begins, exhaling. "And then maybe call the police." His blue eyes harden as he holds the bloodied clothes against his chest. "But first, let's find Mr. Dave and get rid of this."

"Are you—" I start, and then the heavy wetness of my too-big yukata causes it to slide down my shoulders and just sort of … drop. It splats on the ground, leaving me completely and utterly nude, and staring down four of the five guys in the Student Council. My eyes widen, and I move to step back, forgetting how close I am to the water's edge.

Instead, I splash right in, my naked body slamming against Church's and sending us both into the water. He manages to right himself fairly quickly, holding my nude form against his, back to front. I can feel his dick, too, and it's not as soft as I would've liked it to be in that moment.

"Careful, Charlotte Carson," he whispers near my ear, a muscled arm banded across my midsection.

That, of course, is when my father chooses to step outside. The twins move to block him in like always, but you know, he's the headmaster and that technique doesn't work so well.

"Student Council only—" they start, and then balk as Dad pushes his way outside, freezing like a deer in the headlights when he sees me, naked. Church, naked. Our nude bodies pressed together in a very compromising sort of way.

"Mr. Carson," Spencer blurts, drawing Dad's attention … to his wet hoodie.

Oh, and did I mention the fact that the twins are shirtless, dressed only in boxers?

"Chuck."

My dad's voice comes out in a low, menacing hiss.

And that's when I know I have more to worry about than just murderers.

I have a pissed-off father, and that's almost as bad.

CHAPTER TWO

"There was a dead body here," I insist, pointing at the bare surface of the shrine while Dad stands nearby and fumes, his nostrils flared, his face never quite recovering from that purple-red color it got when he saw me and Church together.

As I stand there, next to a shrine with no body, in a forest bereft of creepy people in masks, I wonder to myself: have I done it this time, have I finally made Archie Carson angry enough to explode, to shed that careful calm of his?

"Sir, I saw it, too," Spencer begins, now dressed in a dry yukata and flip-flips with wooden soles. I think they're supposed to be reminiscent of these raised-platform shoes from Japan called *geta* (the twins have been giving me a serious anime/manga education as of late). "There was a boy here, pretty sure it was Jason."

"Well, there's nothing here now, and no sign that there ever was." My dad puts his hand to his forehead as Mr. Murphy hovers nearby, frowning. I haven't forgotten his involvement, or the note he left. Speaking of, I stuffed it in my yukata pocket as I ran. I haven't exactly had the opportunity to look at it. Chances are, that purple ink ran when it got wet, and I won't be able to read a thing.

But I don't need to.

I know who 'Adam' is now.

I focus my glare on Mr. Murphy; he notices right away and swallows hard, a muscle in his jaw ticking.

"It was probably a prank or something," Dad continues, and I swear, if *he* isn't going to turn purple and blow up, then maybe *I* will.

"A prank? Do you still think I'm making all of this up?" I ask, taking a step toward him and clutching my hands together in front of my chest. "Because I need to hear you say you believe me."

"I'll check with the other staff members and make sure all students are accounted for. Mr. Murphy, if you wouldn't mind escorting Chuck back to my room."

"Your room?" I ask, blinking stupidly through the dirty lenses of my glasses. They could use a serious cleaning right about now. "Why your room?"

"Chuck Carson, I do not need to run every parenting decision I make past you. Please follow Mr. Murphy back to the lodge, and don't argue with me. You're in enough trouble as it is."

"In trouble for what?" I ask, managing to keep my voice even and low. "In trouble for having sex? Because we both know I'm having it now. I'm seventeen, and in four months, I'll be eighteen."

Archie turns and walks away, but I'm not done.

I follow after him, grabbing onto his arm. He pauses to look down at me, and there's a fury and maybe even a deep-seated fear burning in his eyes that I don't understand. If he'd only tell me, I'd get it. If he'd only make his point known in words instead of orders.

"Dad, please, talk to me."

He hesitates for the briefest of moments before tearing his arm from my grip and taking off in the direction of the lodge. A frown settles over my lips as I turn back to Spencer and Mr. Murphy. This could be a mistake, but … I'm going to do it anyway.

"We know it's you," I say, and Mr. Murphy blinks big, innocent blue eyes at me. He's always so fucking nice all the time. Figures there'd be something wrong with him. Maybe he's a psychopath who can fake his emotions, just like Church said. "You're Adam."

"Ex-excuse me?" Mr. Murphy chokes out as Spencer's brows go up. I didn't exactly have the opportunity to fill the guys in after Dad caught me naked-ass-to-dick with Church in the hot springs pool.

"You've been writing the notes, in purple ink. You're Adam," I state confidently, lifting my chin up. "I saw you pin a note to my door, just before the attack happened. The question is: are you one of the murderers, or are you playing a different game?"

"Jesus, Chuck," Spencer says, casting a wary look around the shadowed woods surrounding us. We're standing just past the ominous red arch of the *torii* gate. It's creepy as hell out here, I won't lie. There are little cement statues covered in moss, gazing at us from the underbrush, and a whispering breeze that brings chills up on the back of my neck.

"I'm sorry, I don't—" Mr. Murphy starts, but then I take a menacing step toward him and he pauses, his gaze locked with mine.

"Are you one of the killers, Lionel? Or what? Because I'm seriously tired of being in the dark. This shit has gone too far. We know you're involved, just not in what capacity."

"Mr. Carson," Mr. Murphy begins, his face tightening with anger. "I'm still a staff member, so please consider how you speak to me, or I'll be forced to have a word with your father."

"Go ahead. And by the way, when we're in private like this, you can call me Charlotte. We all know you know my secret." Mr. Murphy's face pales as I turn away and head back to the lodge. I'm not about to wait around for 'Adam' to be my escort. If he has a problem with me heading back to my room with Church, he can go find Archie and explain the notes he's been leaving me, too.

"You shouldn't have confronted him like that," Spencer says, jogging to catch up to me. "He could still be one of the killers."

"He's not," I say, and I can feel it in my gut that I'm right. Mr. Murphy is too skittish, too nervous. He could hardly hurt a fly. And I mean that, like, literally. One time, there was this huge horsefly buzzing around our English lit classroom, and instead of just swatting it, Mr. Murphy spent fifteen minutes trying to shoo it out an open window. "I don't know what he's up to, or what his end-game is, but he's not a killer."

Spencer frowns and exhales, tucking his hands into the pockets of his yukata as we head inside the breakfast room and past Mark's raucous table where all his heartless, annoying football friends howl and squeal, like Eugene was never there, like he was never one of them. I haven't seen them show any remorse. They didn't even light a remembrance candle for him on the little shrine near the front desk.

"You're that certain he's not a killer, so when are you going to be that certain about me?" Spencer asks, and as soon as we turn the corner away from the breakfast area, he pushes me against the wall with a hand on my shoulder. He leans his elbow on the wall above my head and stares down at me, eyes dark with frustration.

"You were outside wearing a hoodie, Spencer Hargrove," I say, wanting to cry but refusing to let myself shed tears. I can't decide if I'm upset because of the dead body, because of the chase … or because of the uncertainty. I'm frustrated with *myself* for not being able to trust the boys. And I'm frustrated with them for making it so hard to do it in the first place. "Right at the butt cheek of dawn."

"Butt cheek of dawn?" he asks, looking slightly perplexed. "That's not a phrase, Chuck."

"Sure it is. Why is butt crack of dawn a phrase, but not butt cheek? What's the difference?"

"It's *crack of dawn,* Chuck-let," he argues, but I shake my head and hold up a finger.

"I've heard butt crack of dawn used plenty of times."

"Yeah, by *you.*" Spencer shakes his head at me, and then sighs, pressing his forehead to mine. My eyes close of their own accord, and my hands lift to fist in the front of his yukata. That spark between us is heating up again, and even *with* my suspicions, I feel powerless to stop it.

"I was out smoking early because I couldn't sleep, Chuck. I couldn't sleep because I knew you were in there with Church, and I …" He exhales hard, and his warm breath feathers against my lips. My eyes crack open, and I find myself staring up at him, at those long, dark lashes lying against his cheeks. "I was jealous," he admits. Spencer opens his eyes and crooks a wily half-smile. "Doesn't look too good on me, does it? All this jealousy?"

"I'd be worried about you if you *weren't* jealous," I whisper back, wanting to kiss him so bad my lips hurt. "I mean, if you were dating another girl … let alone multiple girls—identical twins, no less—I'd lose my shit. I couldn't do it; it'd break me."

"Break you?" he says, and then chuckles, his cedar and hyssop smell taking over me. "It'd take a lot more than that to break you, Chuck-let."

I smack him in the chest with the back of one hand, and then grab the edge of his yukata.

"I don't care that you're jealous; I get it. I don't want to share you with anybody else." The words come out in a low whisper, so low that I'm afraid Spencer hasn't heard me, and I'll have to repeat myself. He leans down suddenly and takes my lips in that frustratingly perfect way of his, this sweetly domineering escapade that leaves me breathless and enthralled all at once.

"You don't have to share me," he promises, sucking on my lower lip, taking it prisoner before mercifully releasing it. "I'm just having trouble sharing *you.* That's what kept me up all night, got me up so early. I was just trying to smoke a few cigarettes and have a think in the damn woods." He leans back a bit and picks at the front of his yukata with his fingers. "That isn't even my hoodie; it's Micah's. I borrowed it last night when Ranger and I went to smoke. It gets cold here in …" Spencer looks around for a minute and frowns. "You know, wherever this is, Butt Cheek, Middle of Nowhere, yeah?"

A smile twitches on my lips, and then I groan and sag back against the wall.

"That was Micah's hoodie?" I ask, pointing over my shoulder to indicate the clothing line where the soggy hoodie in question now hangs. Spencer nods briefly before pausing and gives me a look.

"You don't think …" he starts as I scrub my hands down my face.

"I don't want to think he's a killer any more than I do you," I sigh, dropping my hands to my sides. Spencer reaches into his pocket and digs around for a pack of cigarettes and a lighter, drawing first one out and then the other. He pauses again, frowns, and then flips the lighter over, so we can see what's on the other side.

What he shows me … gives me serious fucking chills.

There are spatters of red wax all over the damn thing.

"Let me guess," I start, before Spencer can say anything else. "This is Micah's lighter, too?"

Spencer might not be one of the killers … but Micah could be.

"It's just a lighter," Micah starts, blinking big green eyes at me as I drop the offending item into his palm. He studies it for a moment, and then his face pales. Likely, he's doing the same thing I am, and recalling the red candles and the headless bird, the spatters of red wax left on the coffee table in the girls' dorm. "Ah, covered in red wax. But I can explain that."

"Dude, you sound guilty as fuck," Tobias murmurs, giving his brother a sidelong glance. "Even I don't know why you have a lighter covered in red wax in your hoodie pocket."

"I brought it to smoke weed with Spencer," Micah argues, lifting an arm and gesturing at his friend. He reaches up to ruffle his red-orange hair as Church and Ranger watch him, standing to the right of the door.

Somehow, I feel like I'm surrounded by sharks in this room.

Just … are they going to eat me or eat the fuckers who are trying to kill me?

"Listen up, Jaws," I start, only vaguely realizing that perhaps my *Jaws* movie reference only makes sense to me. "You better explain yourself and quick. All of you." My eyes flick over to Church as he exhales and closes his own eyes for a moment. I still have yet to see hide nor hair of Mr. Dave.

"I …" Micah starts, and then clenches his teeth like he knows he's been caught doing something he's not supposed to. He runs his tongue across his lower lip and glances over at his twin. "I wanted to do something nice for Charlotte. I brought some candles. Just figured we might have a romantic sort of moment together."

"You did what?" Tobias asks, his voice low and cold. I sense the tension between them pull taut, and my mind drifts to Amber, this mysterious girl I still know nothing about.

"Yeah, well, I …" Micah trails off and turns away, moving across the room and sliding his shoji screen door open, so we can all see the koi pond on the other side. He's shaking, like he knows he's been caught and sees no way out of it. "Even though I like sharing girls with you, sometimes I want to be my own person for five fucking seconds."

My mouth drops open, and I realize there's a whole other layer of drama here to sort through that I haven't even touched.

There are the murderers …

And then there are the guys.

It's a whole other shit show I'll have to eventually go through, but now isn't the time.

"Interpersonal drama aside," I begin, touching Tobias' arm, so that he doesn't think I'm trying to downplay his feelings at all. I get it: once upon a time, Micah cheated with his girlfriend, and here he is trying to get private moments with me without telling his brother. Not cool. "Why red candles? And how did you get wax all over the lighter?"

Micah glances over his shoulder, and I can't help but notice how full and pouty his lips are as he frowns, or how much I like the pointed, angular lines of his face. He looks sheepish, but not like he's been caught in the midst of a murder plot. No, he's just a boy who screwed up a little.

"You know the Adamson campus used to be home to a church and an abbey, right? There are candles and crosses and all sorts of random shit in the storage rooms. I swiped some the other day when Eddie was smoking a cigarette. Red just seemed sort of romantic to me." He shrugs one shoulder and leans his back against the doorjamb. "And you try lighting dozens of candles in an enclosed space without knocking any over." He narrows his eyes briefly, and then flips Mark off when he sees him hitting on a server girl across the way. The football player dickhead actually flips him off right back, and the boys bristle. "That turd sandwich needs an extra helping of *ass kicking* on the side, don't you think Tobias?"

His twin doesn't answer, pursing his lips and crossing his arms over his chest. For several minutes, the room is quiet. I'm stuck standing near the door with

Spencer on my right, Tobias on my left; Ranger is right in front of me, and I can hardly look at Church.

"Where exactly did you set up all the candles?" I ask, and Tobias grimaces like I've slapped him. Micah gestures loosely in the direction of the staff cabins and shakes his head, like he's happy to explain later but not right now.

"I've lit them three times, but I hadn't figured out the best way to ask you over there."

"You mean ask her over there without me knowing about it?" Tobias quips, and I bite back a grimace of my own.

Ranger, bless his heart, seems to realize that we're in desperate need of a subject change.

"How did it go with the headmaster?" he asks, breaking the tension briefly as he lifts sapphire eyes to mine. There's something almost desperate in his gaze that makes me squirm, but I just don't feel like I'm in the right mindset to figure it out.

There was a dead kid in those woods.

I was almost a dead kid in those woods.

Church Montague, my pretend fiancé, stabbed our teacher.

"There was no body, no blood, no sign of anything. Pretty sure my dad either thinks I'm crazy or that I'm making it up." I rub my hands over my face, and then pause when I see him striding across the yard with the owner of the hot springs lodge by his side. He pauses briefly near the lobby entrance to glare at me, and then continues on inside.

So at least he knows I deliberately disobeyed him at this point.

Guess I have to wait to find out what he plans on doing about it.

"Did you try calling the police?" I ask, glancing back at Ranger.

"I did. Your dad already called them, and they said they've got a patrol on the way. But I think you're right, I don't think they believe us." Ranger tucks his phone back in his sweatpants.

"We have, what, four nights left here?" I ask, trying and failing to run my fingers through my hair. It's too matted and curly to do much with at this point. Spencer helps me untangle myself from my own hair and gives my hand a squeeze. "I can't even imagine."

"Five. Not that it matters," Church supplies, and the smooth, easy sound of his voice gives me the chills. "These people, whoever they are, very clearly have an agenda they're willing to carry out, regardless of locale."

"Where is Mr. Dave, Church?" I ask, and he frowns at me, shaking his head slightly.

"I don't know. I removed the knife and left him there to go after you. You were being chased, Charlotte." Church pushes off the wall and moves over to me. Despite an initial spark of fear, I hold my ground and look up at him. He gets close, close enough that I can smell that signature lilac and rosemary scent of his, the scent we share because we use the same damn shampoo. Even when I left Adamson to head back to Santa Cruz, I took a bunch with me, just so I could keep smelling it.

I told myself it was because I just like the damn stuff, and it's luxe as hell, something I definitely couldn't afford on my own … but maybe it was because it made me think of him? *Gah, I'm such a girly, romance-obsessed weirdo!* If I ever get to that point where I'm smelling sweaty t-shirts, so help me …

"I didn't stab the librarian. If I did, you would know. I would tell you that I'd done it, and why I did it." Church reaches up and pushes a loose curl from my forehead. It might be sexy, if my hair wasn't all gross and tangled from rolling around in my sleep. "I'm not sure where he went, but he very clearly came in to tell me something important. I think he's working with Lionel Murphy."

"That son of a bitch," Ranger grumbles under his breath. Before we questioned Micah, I gave a quick rundown of my side of the story. Everyone is now officially filled in on all the goings-on from this morning. The first thing the twins and Spencer suggested was that we 'kick his ass', but beating up a teacher is sort of worst case scenario stuff.

"You think Mr. Dave is a good guy?" I ask as

Church runs his long fingers down the side of my face, and then gently tucks his fingertips beneath my chin. It's a firm but gentle command to look up at him, and even though my first response is to be ornery and turn away with a scowl, I end up looking into his eyes regardless.

"Neutral, maybe. The only good guys are standing in this room. No matter how the evidence looks, do you believe that?" I start to respond, but Church cuts me off by leaning down and capturing my lips in a torturous kiss that's equal parts reassuring and terrifying.

The sweet, sharp taste of danger lingers on his lips, but I find myself falling for it anyway. A great kiss does not a trustworthy person make, and yet …

"What are we going to do if we get stuck here for five nights?" I ask instead, because even *if* we're right, and the dead student is an Adamson boy who just happens to be missing, that doesn't mean my father or the police will believe us. I mean, why should they? It sounds far-fetched, like some weird Japanese anime episode. *Murder at the Oishii Onsen Lodge, Part I.*

I shiver as Church steps away from me, trying not to catch the gazes of any of the other guys. Kissing one in front of the others is just … well, weird. Not sure I'll ever get used to it. *Although I wish this was a thing, a group relationship. I mean polyamory is real, so why not?*

Only, wouldn't polyamory imply they could date

other girls? And I'm just not cool with that. Seriously, I couldn't do that. They're all braver than I am.

"We'll be okay," Church says, glancing over at Ranger. "I'm assuming you took care of the clothes?"

"They're gone," Ranger says, and the flat, dark way in which he says it both relaxes and terrifies me. These guys work as a unit, a team. It's seamless. "Let's get some breakfast." He pushes up from the wall and pauses near me, offering up an arm.

After a small moment of hesitation, I take it, and let him lead me downstairs to the dining area. I notice he can barely keep his azure gaze off of me, like he's afraid I might disappear if he isn't vigilant enough. I'll admit, it's a bit sexy, the overprotective thing. Or like, maybe a lot sexy.

Dad is near the reception desk, talking with other Adamson staff members, and employees of the resort. He ignores us while we sit down and order, but right at about the time the bowl of edamame arrives, there he is, standing beside me.

I look up.

"Jason Lambert is unaccounted for," he says, voice gruff as his eyes scan the other boys. "When you're finished eating, I want to speak with you and Spencer again." I nod, but he's not done, dropping those blue eyes back to my face. "After I get your story, you can explain to me why you're not in the room like I requested."

He spins on his heel and takes off as I sigh.

This is going to be a long week, isn't it?

"Chuck Carson, I am not the bad guy," Dad says, his face etched with a deep frown. We stare at each other, standing outside on the bridge that spans the length of the koi pond. "Do you think I make up rules just to torture you?"

"Sometimes," I admit, and the look he gives me is pure hell. "What? You could try explaining things to me once in a while. Instead, all you do is give vague orders that I'm supposed to follow like a soldier."

Archie sighs and moves over to the edge of the bridge, staring down at the shiny scaled backs of the fish. They dart from shadows, gold tails flashing.

"You must've gotten that stubbornness from me. Your mother's always been an agreeable sort of person."

"She's dating Mr. Dave," I say, unsure as to why I've kept that from him for so long. Hell, maybe he already knows? *If he doesn't, he's going to be devastated,* I think as I watch the muscles in his upper back and shoulders tighten. "Did you know that?"

"I didn't," Dad says carefully, lifting his head up to look at me. He and Mom are eighteen years apart. I've always thought of that as a pretty big age gap. It makes me wonder if he ever considered this might happen, if she might decide she wanted a different life one day. "How do you know about this?"

"She took me to dinner with him in LA. Don't you think that's odd that they'd meet up like that?" I swallow hard as Archie sighs, rising to his full height, a muscle in the side of his jaw ticking. "And also, that's pretty messed-up that she didn't tell you."

"Chuck." Archie glances my way, mouth pressed into a thin line. "You know your behavior lately has been out of control. What is going on with you and those boys?"

"I'm … we just like each other." It's all I can think to say. And it's true. That's all that happened, isn't it? We just sort of started getting along.

"First you claim you're dating Spencer Hargrove, then you announce you're dating twins." Dad scoffs and runs his fingers through his thinning hair, dropping his voice to a whisper. "I find a morning-after pill in your things, and then you fake an engagement to get the Montagues to throw their weight around. Does this sound reasonable to you? Because I raised you better than that."

I just stare at him and then lift my palms in a helpless gesture.

"Being in a healthy, happy relationship with more than one person doesn't make me a bad human being," I say, and my voice sounds soft and mature, most definitely a new Charlotte sort of a thing to do.

"Watching my daught—*son* go after and bed five different boys is not something I'm interested in. This is not the sort of behavior anyone would condone for a seventeen-year-old." He pushes his glasses up his face, and inhales deeply, like he's trying to keep it all together. "It isn't right."

"But why? I'm not doing anything wrong. What do you care who I sleep with as long as I'm happy? My grades are better than ever, and for the first time in my life, I'm actually thinking about college. I even started filling out a couple applications. Shouldn't you be happy about that?"

"Sir." It's Church, standing not too far off from us, dressed in a fresh yukata, and looking as chipper as well, someone who didn't stab their teacher just hours prior. "There's a police officer at the front gate who'd like to speak with you about Jason."

Archie stares at him in a completely new way, all of that shiny joy at being around the best student in school wiped clean. Frankly, Dad looks like he hates him now.

"Thank you. If you could please stay with Chuck while I'm otherwise occupied. I don't particularly like the idea of you two being alone, but I like the idea of him being by himself even less." Archie takes off in full headmaster mode, moving down the path toward the front entrance.

Church and I exchange a look.

"You don't really think he's involved, do you?" I ask, because the thought that my dad would turn against me is impossible to fathom. We've always butted heads, but then we've always been together, too.

"In some capacity, I do," Church says, amber eyes dark. "But I don't think he's trying to kill you. More like he's involved with Mr. Murphy and Mr. Dave somehow. He knows more than he's letting on."

He holds out a hand, and I hesitate just a split-second before taking it.

An enigmatic smile curves over Church's lips, his eyes sparkling.

"Come, Chuck. I don't bite—not unless you want me to."

Tentatively, I place my hand in his, and he yanks me forward. I nearly trip over the edge of my yukata, stumbling into his arms, and finding myself gazing up into that handsome face and wondering what it'd really be like to be engaged to someone so perfect. Church Montague is smart, accomplished, handsome, and a member of one of the richest families in America. Basically, he's a dream.

A dream … who stabbed someone that's now currently missing.

Trusting him is a gamble.

Not trusting him, that could cost me something even greater: a friendship. Or even a romance. A relationship that could last for life.

"You're still afraid of me," he says, but not like he's angry, more like that's expected.

"I'm not," I protest, but maybe I am. Just a little. "But it would be the ultimate prank, to draw me in, and then finish me off after I already, you know, sort of like you guys and stuff."

"Sort of?" Church asks, and then he leans down and hovers his lips just above mine, that lilac and rosemary scent we share mingling in the cool air. His breath is minty and fresh, and I realize that as much coffee as he drinks, he never has coffee breath. Never. See, he really is perfect.

Almost too perfect though, right? Is there such a thing?

"Wow, look the faggot has a harem of gays all to himself." Mark sneers as he walks by, and Church's face flashes with this dark energy. He pulls a fan from his pocket, one that's all folded up, and then he chucks it with two fingers hard enough to hit Mark right in the throat. The idiot gags and starts choking, grabbing at his neck. "Did you seriously just throw that at me?!"

"Prove it," Church says with a dreadful looking smile. "You've been uppity lately, Mark. Tell me: are you up to something the Student Council should know about?"

"Eat some dick. Clearly that's your thing, right?" Mark storms off, rubbing at his neck, and Church releases me, sauntering over to pick up the fan and tucking it back into his pocket.

"Come, let's try to enjoy the rest of the trip." He turns and heads back in the direction of the lodge and, with a deep breath, I follow along behind him.

CHAPTER THREE

Later that night, I'm sitting in the room I share with Church. Dad and I had another fight about where I'd be sleeping tonight, but the stress of the day must really have gotten to him because he gave up without a win for once.

So here I am, with my assigned roommate, in the room where he stabbed our teacher …

A lantern flickers on the low table near the door as I sit cross-legged on my sleeping mat, surreptitiously watching Church as he browses on his phone. After a moment, he looks up at me.

"You don't have to take a turn on watch, you know. Just wake Ranger up." Church pokes his friend with a bare toe, and our favorite naked baker grumbles in his sleep. They're all in here, by the way, the entire Student Council.

The twins started off bickering, but now that they're asleep, somehow Micah's arm is over Tobias. It's pretty cute actually. Spencer is all tangled up in his sheets, and Ranger is curled up, like he's trying to protect something.

"I'm fine taking a watch," I say, shrugging a shoulder, all nice and casual like. Church pauses and sets his phone down on the table, next to a pot of tea and a set of cups with saucers.

"Are you worried? Sleeping in here with all of us?"

"If I were, I would've just let Dad win the argument and padded over to his room." I scoot over to the table and pour myself some tea. It's still warm, the steam rising in a white cloud. "So, where do you think Mr. Dave went?"

"No clue," Church says, relaxing back against the shoji screen and watching me as I bring the tea to my lips. It's some sort of green tea, very earthy, with a grassy kind of smell. I'm surprised to find that I actually like it. "Maybe he is guilty, and he made a run for it?"

There's a long pause as we both consider that. It's a possibility, that's for sure.

"I'm sorry I ran away," I repeat, and Church lifts his head, golden hair feathering across his forehead and catching the light. He's absolutely stunning in that yukata, with the fabric sliding down one shoulder and exposing his skin to the candlelight.

I wonder if he's wearing any underwear beneath his robe?

I facepalm for even thinking that.

When I look up, Church is raising a single, skeptical brow at me.

"Did you just literally facepalm to your own thoughts?" he asks, and I grimace. I have a bad habit of wearing my heart on my sleeve. He smiles at me before I get a chance to respond and sets his teacup aside, leaning forward and putting a hand between my legs. My robe catches under his palm, giving me absolutely zero chance of escaping. "I love how animated you are, Mr. Carson."

"Animated is one way of putting it," I hedge as he leans in even closer, and I smell that familiar lilac-rosemary scent we both share. I've just been using the cherry blossom stuff they stock the bathroom with here, but I'm pretty sure Church must've brought some of the Adamson stuff with him. That, or I'm just, like, super attuned to his scent. My cheeks flush red, but I refuse to accept that last idea as fact.

Church's smile gets a little wider, just enough that the emotion finally glints back at me from his beautiful amber eyes.

"See what I mean?" he whispers, leaning in close

enough that I think he's going to kiss me again. Instead, he moves past my mouth and plants a kiss on the side of my jaw instead. "You're blushing. Pray tell: what thought's just skittered through that pretty little head of yours?"

"Pretty little head ... that's kinda sexist, don't you think?" I murmur, flushing even harder, and Church laughs again. It's a low, soft sound, almost dangerous. I can't believe I ever thought he was a sociopath (or psychopath, whatever, I can't remember the difference). He's just bottled up, full of emotion he refuses to submit to. Me, I'm a slave to my emotions.

Church just pulls back slightly, leaning over and turning the gas down on the lantern, plunging the room into darkness. My breath catches, and I have to throw a lasso around my heart to keep it from beating so furiously that it escapes out of my gently parted lips.

"You don't have to apologize for running. You saw me with my hands on a bloodied knife; you had a killer staring at you from down the hall. I'm glad you ran. I'm not sure I could handle it if anything happened to you, *Chuck.*"

My palms are sweaty when I lift them up and lay them on Church's muscular upper arms, surprised yet again that the coffee-obsessed prince of the school is so buff beneath his uniform and cultured exterior. *Pleasantly surprised,* my brain reminds me, and I'm glad the lights are now off so he can't see exactly how red I'm getting.

Our mouths brush, just the slightest touch of lips, and a sea of butterflies takes off in my belly, making me feel dizzy. *We can't have a full-on make out session with the other guys in the room, now can we,* I tell myself, but it's hard to figure out group dating etiquette when, you know, there really isn't any available.

The hot, slick tip of Church's tongue teases along my lower lip, and I shiver, curling my fingers around his biceps. He presses further as I gently open my mouth and welcome him in; it's impossible to miss the fact that his hand is sliding ever closer to the sweet spot between my thighs.

Unfortunately, that's also the same moment that I notice movement behind Church's shoulder and glance up to see a shadow looming on the other side of the shoji screen. There's the faint outline of a person peering in at us, and my breath catches—but for completely different reasons than before.

Church stiffens up and glances over his shoulder. Before I can even think about how to handle the situation, he's pushing up to his feet and heading for the door. The person on the other side takes off as he slides the screen open.

"Wake the others up!" he hisses, and then he takes off running.

"Fuck," I grumble, shoving up to my bare feet before using one to kick at Ranger's shoulder. "Get up, trouble!"

He snaps awake in an instant, but I'm already taking off after Church. I ran away from him before; I won't let him chase down a murderer by himself.

My naked feet slap against the wood planks outside as I chase after Church and the shadow, fireflies dancing in the air around the courtyard. The shadow person rounds the corner first, but Church isn't far behind.

By the time I catch up, panting and huffing, I see Church grabbing the person by their shoulder and shoving them into the wall. He tears the hood of their gray sweater over their head and reveals a face I never expected to see here.

"Selena?" I ask, choking and coughing as I come to a stop beside the pair of them. Her brown eyes glare down at me as she struggles to catch her breath, blond hair stuck to her sweaty forehead. We only met once, at the Everly All-Girls Academy Valentine's Day dance, but how could I forget the girl who gave me her dress, a wig, and some makeup when I really needed it? "You're one of the killers?"

"What?" Selena asks, blinking back at me like I'm a crazy person. "Is that what he calls his groupies now?"

"Groupies?" I echo, exchanging a look with Church. "Whose groupies?"

"Mark," she replies with a huff, pushing Church's hands off her shoulders and rubbing at them like she might have bruises later. I'm not surprised: Church has a disturbingly strong grip, at odds with his president of the academy appearance.

"Mark has groupies?" I blurt, and there must be some level of abject horror in my voice because Selena turns her glare on me. Church, on the other hand, doesn't look particularly shocked.

"They call themselves the foot-bra-lers which, really, doesn't make any sense at all."

"Mark, the douche-canoe-ass-pig has groupies who call themselves … what? Like, footballers but … brawlers?" I'm just having trouble making the connection. Mark is nowhere near cool enough to have groupies.

"Please don't call my boyfriend a douche … wait, did you say ass pig?" Selena asks, giving me a special sort of look. I know my insults are unconventional, okay? But since when is creativity a bad thing? Some paint with oils, others with acrylics, and me … with juvenile quips that make no sense. We all have our mediums.

"Bra-lers, like brassiere, no W," Church corrects, his shrewd gaze locked on Selena's face. She seems innocent enough, but she *was* lurking around in the dark, wasn't she? And besides, she goes to Everly, not Adamson, so what the hell is she doing here at all?

"What the fuck is going on?" Ranger snaps, coming around the corner shirtless and glorious and sexy and

… I swipe the imaginary drool off my face and try to remember what we're doing out here. Spencer and the twins aren't far behind, and I almost choke when Tobias reaches out to fix my yukata. It's fallen so low that the bindings on my breasts are showing.

"I got you, Chuck," he whispers as he adjusts my robe and then turns a green-eyed glare on Selena. "The hell is going on out here?"

"We have an Everly girl sneaking around the shadows," Church says as Selena huffs and crosses her arms over her chest. Crickets chirp and moonlight dances on the koi pond in the front courtyard, but it's far from serene out here. I swear, I can taste the metallic bite of blood in the air.

"Aren't you the girl from the dance?" Spencer asks, cocking his head to one side. I notice as he runs his fingers through his hair that his hand is shaking. I also notice that Tobias has put some distance between himself and Micah, not good. I feel like I've upset their careful twin balance. "We smoked weed on the dock with this chick."

"*This chick* has a name," Selena barks, lifting her chin defiantly. I can't unsee her and Mark grinding on each other outside Church's parents' party. Gross. Not an image I wanted burned into my brain, thank you very much. "Selena McConnell, and before you lose your ever-loving shit on me again, don't worry: I'm not here for you." Spencer and Tobias exchange a look as

Ranger narrows his sapphire eyes on her, and Church leans one shoulder against the wall, deceptively casual. Micah sidles up to stand beside me and we trade a skeptical look of our own. "I'm looking for my boyfriend, Mark."

"Why on earth would you come all this way looking for your boyfriend?" Church asks, a dangerous edge to his stoic face and smooth voice.

"I don't owe you an explanation," Selena grinds out, but then she must realize how ridiculous this all seems, so she sighs and continues on, tucking some hair behind her ear. "He's been acting really weird lately." She looks my way, as if seeking some female solidarity. "Sneaking around, lying about where he's been, and he's been spending *way* too much time with miss goody two-shoes." Selena rolls her brown eyes again. "Aster even followed him here, so why shouldn't I?" Selena's face darkens as my own eyes widen in time with Micah's.

"Who's Aster?" Micah asks, but even if he doesn't remember who she is, I do. She's the curvy redhead who danced with both me *and* Ross during the Valentine's Day dance. But maybe he doesn't need to remember who she is to be weirded out that not one but *two* girls from Everly have shown up at the Oishii Onsen right after a murder occurred.

"Yeah," Selena snaps, her face coloring. "She's here, and she's probably in the middle of riding my boyfriend's—"

"I know where Mark's room is," Church says casually, cutting her off midsentence and staring at her with those honey-amber eyes of his. "Do you want us to show you?"

The tone of his voice says that's not a request.

Selena glances around at the group of us, narrowing her eyes slightly with an understandable amount of suspicion.

"Maybe. Why were you guys on my ass like that?" she asks, looking back at me again, the only other girl in a circle of dick. "The Adamson Student Council, and the headmaster's daught—"

"Son," I choke out, just in case anyone can overhear us. Selena cocks a brow and sighs, but she doesn't contradict me. "And we weren't on your ass, we just …"

"Chuck and I were about to get hot and heavy, and you interrupted us," Church finishes before I can stop him. My cheeks flame as the other four boys in the Student Council glance my direction. Uh-oh. "We don't particularly like being watched."

"She said *killers*," Selena hedges, but I am beyond done with this conversation. I step forward and grab her arm, plastering on a fake smile.

"Come with me, and we'll find Mark, okay?" I say, and although I'm pretty sure Selena thinks we're full of shit, she lets me guide her down the walkway in the direction of her boyfriend's room. When we get there, she wastes no time in wrenching the shoji screen door open.

The room is empty.

Mark isn't in it, and neither is Aster.

Selena's face heats up as I step back and bump back to front into Ranger, reminding me that not all that long ago, we were nude but for our aprons, and in a position much more compromising than this. He puts his hands on my hips in an almost possessive sort of way, and I find myself shivering.

"You're sure this is his room?" Selena asks, her voice dark and thick with suspicion as she glances back at me. Church steps forward to take control of the situation like he always does though.

"I'm sure," he says, and Selena frowns. I wonder where she's staying? Or how she got into the resort after-hours. Then again, when you have money, pretty much anything is possible, isn't it? She could've bribed any number of people to let her in.

"Thank you," she quips, tossing her hair and stepping into the room. "I'll take it from here."

Without another word, she turns and slides the screen door shut.

Ranger's big, hot hands are still sitting heavy on my hips, and when I turn around, thinking he'll step back, he doesn't move. Instead, it's just his sapphire eyes glaring into mine.

"Next time, an explanation would be nice when you kick me awake in the middle of the night," he grumbles, his voice gruff but oh-so-sexy. I swallow hard, but I nod anyway, and he grabs me by the hand, dragging me back toward the room I share with Church. The rest of the boys follow, and we reconvene in the dim light of the gas lantern.

"I can't be the only one who's suspicious as fuck," Spencer whispers, sitting cross-legged on a *tatami* mat and leaning back on his palms. The way he looks at me and Church though, I'm sure he's thinking about more than just Selena, Mark, and the dead body I'm positive we didn't hallucinate. "She came all the way down to Butt-fuck, Nowhere, North Carolina to see if her boyfriend was cheating on her?"

"People have done stranger things in regard to possible affairs," Micah says, his voice strained. Tobias scoffs, crosses his arms over his chest, and looks away. We're still on about the candles and lighter apparently.

I sigh and rub at my forehead with the heel of my hand. My other is still captured in one of Ranger's, and he doesn't seem at all ready to let go. Church takes his seat on the pillow next to the low-set table and picks up his discarded teacup, sipping it and clearly wishing it were coffee instead.

"So, you buy her story then?" Spencer asks, cocking a dark brow. Sometimes, when I look at him, I get all giddy and weird on the inside. Like, he was my first time, and I'll never be able to forget that. Scratch it: I wouldn't *want* to forget that. But I'm also aware that dating five guys isn't a super realistic life choice. *At some point, I'm going to have to choose between them, huh?* The thought flitters through my mind like a moth, and I brush it away to the dark recesses of my brain.

"Not exactly," Micah replies, carefully glancing over at his brother. I'm already missing their twin thing, and they've only been 'fighting' for all of half a day. "I'm just saying that maybe *she* isn't the suspicious one. Like, where the fuck is Mark? And who the hell is this Aster chick?"

"Aster was at the dance," I say, feeling my palm sweat against Ranger's. His is dry and warm, and I can only hope he isn't squicked out by my moistness. I mean, the moistness in my palm that is. Like, I'm sure he wouldn't mind moistness elsewhere … I bet he'd mind the word *moist* though. He seems like the type to get peeved over a word. "She danced with me and Ross …" I trail off, because that's not particularly helpful information. No offense to her or anything, she was a nice enough girl, but our interactions were fairly forgettable.

"Aster, huh?" Ranger says, narrowing his eyes to slits. He squeezes my hand in his and then finally lets go, glancing my way. "You said you were sure one of the attackers was female?"

"Positive," I reply, letting my mind follow his train

of thought. "You think Aster could be one of the murderers? Or even Selena?"

"Either one would make sense, considering how suspicious Mark is," Spencer adds as Church sits in quiet, contemplative thought. I can see the wheels in his head turning.

"Mark is guilty; we've known that since forever ago," Micah says with a scoff, sitting down near Spencer and giving his twin some space. That particular sentence, I think it was meant to come out in unison. Glancing over at Tobias though, it's quite obvious that he has no intention of playing along. "But seriously, what sort of guy could string his best friend up in a tree like that?"

"Mark *is* a serious cum wad," I point out, and all five boys give their agreement in murmurs, nods, or shrugs. *Also, note to self: don't say* cum *around all five of your boyfriends, Chuck. It takes on a less gross and more, um, sensual sort of tone.* Luckily, nobody notices my embarrassment in the dim light. "Honestly, finding out that he murdered his bestie would be less surprising than learning he has"—dramatic eye twitch —"*groupies*. Total vom moment."

"But why?" Church says, breaking his silence as he looks up. "We're missing a motive here. Do I believe Mark could be dark, broken, and stupid enough to kill his best friend? Sure. But *why?* Why would Aster or Selena come after our Chuck?"

Our Chuck? I think, licking my lips as I take a seat near the table. Glancing around the room, I realize I kind of like that idea, of being their Chuck. Weird, huh? I mean, they used to crack eggs down my shirt and dump jars of spiders on me, give me swirlies and lock me out of the dining room at Culinary Club. And now, these Student Council Boys feel like they could be my forever crew.

“Maybe we should set up some sort of surveillance, see when Mark comes back and who with?” Tobias suggests. “I could take the first watch.”

“I'll go with you,” Micah adds, standing up, but Tobias gives him a tight smile.

“I'd rather go with Spencer, but thanks anyway.” Tobias heads for the door and lets himself out while Spencer groans and grumbles under his breath about lack of sleep. On his way out, he comes over and blesses me with a kiss to the forehead before leaving.

Micah's crestfallen face on the other hand, that haunts me well into my dreams. In it, he's looking at the dead body of his brother on the shrine’s stone altar, instead of the stranger that Spence and I saw.

It feels like a warning to me, and I don't like that.

I don't want to lose one of my crew, not now or ever.

And I really, really don't want to choose.

CHAPTER FOUR

The next morning, I wake up in a puddle of drool with my hair stuck to my face, just like Anna in fucking *Frozen.* Unlike Anna in fucking *Frozen*, I have Micah McCarthy grinning at me and taking pictures with his phone.

"If any of those end up on social media, I swear, I will destroy you."

"Already posted to Insta," he says with a dark grin as I reach out to swat him.

"Boner wizard," I mumble in the most insulting way possible, pushing myself up into a sitting position and finding the rest of the room empty. The boys have rolled up their futons, folded their blankets, and stored their pillows in the closet. "Where is everybody? Did Mark ever come back last night?"

"Yup," he says, tucking his phone away and leaning back. His red-orange hair falls into his face as he studies me with moss green eyes. It isn't lost on me that the reason he's fighting with his brother is because of me. Because he wanted to do something romantic for me. I bite my lower lip against a rush of guilt. "But Spence and Toby bailed when he and Selena started fu —"

"Okay, okay, enough. I don't need to rinse my ears out with bleach this early in the morning." I stand up on shaky legs and yawn, trying to forget that I actually screwed both McCarthy twins on a Disneyland ride. As if I have a right to be prudish. "So, Mark came back, and not with Aster?"

"Yup. But who knows what he was up to before then? He told Selena he was hanging with the guys, but when Spencer and Tobias left, they checked all their rooms and it seemed like everyone else was fast asleep and had been for a while. Could be wrong though." He shrugs his shoulders, and his yukata slides down just enough that I can see the rose tattoo on his shoulder. "Everyone else is at breakfast. Jason Lambert is missing, and your dad is starting to freak."

"Any sign of Mr. Dave?" I ask, and Micah shakes his head. "Mr. Murphy?"

"He's acting like nothing's wrong," he says, exhaling and reaching up to run his fingers through his hair. His eyes track my movements as I pad over to my bag and heft it up by the handle. I'm in desperate need of a shower, some toothpaste, and a fresh set of bindings for my breasts.

I also know I can't go to the bathroom without an escort. Hell, none of us should be going anywhere without an escort. The last thing I want is for my nightmare from last night to come true.

"Hey, I was thinking ..." Micah starts, pulling his wax-covered lighter from his pocket and flicking the wheel absently. His eyes, though, they stay locked on mine. "You deserve to know about Amber."

"I don't want to do anything that might put more distance between you and Tobias," I blurt, and Micah smiles, standing up and reaching out to open the door for me. We both take a moment to scan the hallway for knife-wielding psychos, but there's not a soul to be seen, just the distant laughter from the dining room.

"I asked him if I could tell you, and he said it was okay, so long as I told you the truth." Micah walks me down the hall and into one of the bathrooms. This place is set up a bit like a hostel. There are only a few shared bathrooms, but they're spacious and clean, with both a chain lock and a deadbolt on the inside.

Instead of waiting outside for me after checking around for any lurkers, Micah closes the door and locks it, making my breath catch.

"You can wait outside, you know," I whisper, and he

grins at me, making my heart race.

"I'd rather wait in here." He takes a step forward and leans down like he's planning on kissing me. Unfortunately for him, I have the worst morning breath, so I backpedal and end up plastered against the glass door of the shower. Micah just chuckles and takes a seat on the bench near the door, kicking off his shoes and resting his feet against the pebbled floor. He pauses for just a moment and glances up at me. "I mean, provided you're cool with it?"

"I'm cool with it—as long as you get naked first," I say, and Micah grins at me. It's one of those cocksure little grins of his, and it gives me chills all over. *Did I just invite a dude to get naked in a communal bathroom, surrounded by classmates, and with my dad prowling the halls?*

Yes, yep, I totally did, and I'm not ashamed of it.

He stands up again and reaches for the tie on his robe, cocking a brow in my direction.

"You sure you don't want to talk about Amber first?"

"Talk about a girl you dated before me? Not really. Do it after or I might kick you out of here instead." I step back into the shower and then just sorta freeze there. I'd intended on stripping and being all sexy and shit, but now that Micah's starting to strip off his own yukata, I find myself frozen in fear. Micah pauses, noticing my discomfort, and comes over to stand in front of me. When he puts his hands on my shoulders, I relax a little.

"I don't want to pressure you," he says, gently sweeping hair back from my face. "I'll step outside and —"

"No," I say, because I can tell he's misinterpreting my emotions. I'm not afraid *of* him, I'm just afraid I'll make an ass out of myself. "Don't go. I'm just … I don't want to mess this up."

"Mess what up?" Micah asks. I gesture randomly between us.

"You, Tobias, me, the Student Council, any of it." I look up at him and he sighs heavily, putting his arms around me and pulling me in for a hug that I wasn't expecting. Slowly, I lift my arms and hug him back. It feels good, to just hug somebody. As well as we've all been taking the shit that's been thrown at us, it isn't easy to see a dead body, or have nobody believe you when you talk about it. I feel distant from my mom, my dad, but at least I have the Student Council.

"You are not screwing anything up, Chuck Carson," Micah says with a little laugh. There's a nervous warble to it that I've never heard before. I'm used to him being the confident, cocky one. Slowly, I pull back and look up into his face. There's a confession resting there that I know I need to hear. Instead of pressing for it though, I just wait. Sometimes people need to come to you in their own time. "It was me that screwed things up with

Tobias. He's never gotten over the Amber thing."

Micah takes a step back, and I realize that we're not going to have sex, not right now. He needs to talk. I move over to the sink, brush my teeth while he chuckles at me, and then slap him in the chest.

"Stop that. I'm super self-conscious of my breath, okay? Nobody wants to kiss a morning mouth or a coffee mouth or—" Micah steps forward and eloquently sweeps one arm around my waist, cupping the back of my head with his other hand. He cuts me off midsentence with a kiss that I can feel down to my toes. They curl against the pebbled floor as I grab onto the front of his robe and bunch the fabric up in quaking fingers. He tastes like peppermint and cherries.

"Exactly why I had Church and Ranger watch over you while I snuck into the bathroom this morning to clean up." He chuckles against my lips, and I grin back at him. "You're not the only one who's worried morning breath might fuck this up." Micah pauses suddenly and pulls back, grabbing my hand and taking me with him.

He opens the bathroom door and … there's my fucking Dad, standing there and staring at me with one of his eyebrows twitching.

"Chuck. Carson." The two words are ground out between his teeth as I blink back at him in shock. What are the chances, people? No, for real, like what are the chances he'd appear outside the bathroom at this exact moment?! The author of my life must hate me. "Would you like to explain to me what the two of you were doing in the restroom together?"

I was going to seduce Micah, but then I got all nervous, and he wants to confess something to me, so …

"Brushing our teeth?" I blurt, but it's almost a question and not particularly convincing. I am so going to get it. Between the fake engagement, the dead body, me pressed naked against Church, and now this? How long until I turn eighteen again? Christ on a cracker.

"And you needed to do that together because …?" Dad continues, trailing off and then pausing as Mr. Murphy approaches on his left side and leans in to whisper something. Dad's face tightens up and he nods, looking me and Micah over with an expression of bewilderment. "I'm quickly running low on patience with you, Chuck."

I purse my lips, but keep my hand clamped around Micah's as Dad takes off down the hall and Mr. Murphy scuttles after. He looks terrified to be in my vicinity, so when he passes, I flip him off and take delight in the fact that he cringes. "No way he's one of the killers," I murmur, but still, I can't figure out his motivation. Church is right: that's our problem. We have a lot of clues but without a motive, it's impossible to put them together.

I could never blame myself for not knowing sooner, what we were dealing with was so much more than I ever could've imagined.

"Come on," Micah says, leading me back to my room and through it, out the opposite door that leads to the front courtyard. I grab my sandals on the way, and we stroll down the curving paths near the koi pond. The air is crisp and clean, and the scene around us is so peaceful, it's hard to remember that I saw people wearing fox masks in the woods just yesterday. "After I tell you this story, you might hate me for it."

"Impossible," I say, exhaling and glancing over at him. I'm starting to learn that just because people make mistakes, it doesn't make them disposable. Even if the mistakes are big. If there's love there, and you care enough about another person, you work through it and you both become better people. I don't mean keeping toxic or abusive people in your life, but … Micah is human. Whatever he did to Tobias, he's a good person now, and that's what matters. Our past isn't an anchor that keeps us tied to a shipwreck beneath the sea; it's the sail that we can collect wind in so that we can soar.

"You know that during freshman year, Tobias and I went to a private academy in Santa Cruz, right?" I raise my eyebrows as Micah stops and turns toward me, the wind teasing the loose strands of his red-orange hair around his face. We've paused on the decking that overlooks the koi pond. Micah steps forward and crosses his arms on the railing, leaning over and looking across the property.

"Actually, I didn't," I say, coming up to stand beside him and leaning my butt against the railing. He smiles, but the expression is tight, and I get the idea that this memory hurts him as much as it does Tobias.

"Well, we did. And while we were there, we met a girl named Amber Muse." He smiles a bit more, but it's a sad expression that doesn't quite reach his eyes. "She lived with her mom in a shitty trailer on her grandfather's property." He pauses and looks my way with a small quirk teasing the edge of his mouth. "Anyway, Tobias and I were both really into her, but, uh …" He trails off again and sighs, leaning forward and putting his forehead against his forearms. "As usual, she preferred Tobias over me."

One of my brows goes up, and I lean down, trying to get at eye level with Micah McCarthy.

"What do you mean, *as usual*?" I ask, and then one of the koi fish slaps its tail on the surface of the water and splashes the tops of my feet, making me squeal. Micah grins and chuckles as he lifts his head up.

"It's been like this forever," he says, shrugging his shoulders like he doesn't care. I can tell that he does. "Our parents, our friends, girls. What do you do when there are two twins? You pick one. Tobias has always been the nicer of the two of us, the more relatable." He lifts a brow and then glances my way. "Even you were attracted to him first."

I open my mouth to argue but then snap it shut.

Micah's right. Tobias has a gentler demeanor, but I have to admit, there's something about Micah's sharp edges that I like. I don't prefer his twin over him. Hell, I don't prefer any of the Adamson Student Council boys over the others, and I have a feeling that by the end of the year, that could be a problem.

"Anyway, Tobias and Amber started dating, and I admit, I was jealous. I ..." He sighs and stands up the rest of the way, putting his palms on the railing and looking past the koi pond toward the gate. There's a cop car without its sirens on, followed by a plain black SUV, and they're both pulling onto the property.

Micah and I exchange a look, but it doesn't take a genius to figure out what they're doing here.

"You were jealous," I repeat, looking him over and seeing this vulnerable side to him that I never expected. "And then what?" Micah's green eyes slide over to the uniformed police officers and detectives climbing out of their cars before flicking back to me.

"Amber's mom went into rehab," he says, and my heart clenches, thinking of my own mother and her struggles with addiction and rehab. "And neither of us could stand the thought of her living alone in that crappy trailer by herself. We invited her to live with us —our parents barely cared since they're never around." Micah gives a self-deprecating sort of smile, and I feel like I can see his layers peeling away to reveal the real McCarthy boy underneath. "That room, the one with the ocean view and the balcony, we moved out of it and gave it to her."

Micah pushes away from the railing as the petals come loose from one of the trees. I lift my hand up and catch some, like pink snow on the surface of my palm. The petals are soft and delicate; I think they're cherry blossoms.

"She lived there for three months before …" Micah stops and bites at his lower lip for a moment, reaching out to pluck a petal from my hair. "Tobias was gone one night, at some MMA thing that I bowed out of. I told him I was sick, but I lied; I just didn't want to see him with Amber. I had no idea she was staying home that night, too."

"So, you were alone with her?" I clarify, and he nods, reaching up to run his hand down his face.

"I stole some of my dad's stupid craft beers, and lit some candles, and we just hung out and talked all night. Just before Tobias got home, we …" Micah shrugs his shoulders again, and I feel the dark snake of jealousy rear its ugly head inside of me. "That was my first time," he admits, biting his lower lip and looking me over like he's waiting to see a particular emotion. I must surprise him a bit because his brows go up. "Anyway, we kept our affair ongoing for a while. Almost two months. One day, Tobias walked in on us and everything fell apart."

"How do you mean?" I ask, imagining the pain from

both sides. What Micah did was wrong, but I can see the progression, how he got there. I don't think he ever meant to hurt his twin.

"Tobias went on a fucking bender. He was drinking and smoking; he totaled three cars."

My brows shoot up, and my lips part in shock. I can't imagine Tobias McCarthy doing any of those things. I mean, he smokes a little pot, drinks socially, but … not like that. "Our parents didn't like what was happening between us, so they shipped us off to Adamson. Our dad went there as a kid, so it made sense."

Micah sighs again and the smile slips from his face.

"What happened to Amber?" I'm almost afraid to ask, but at this point, I have to know how the story ends.

"School shooting," he whispers, closing his eyes for a moment. Fuck. I don't need to ask any other questions about that. Growing up, we've all gotten used to fearing for our lives when we go to school. It's a sad, sick part of life as a member of Gen Z. "Her mother moved to Santa Clarita just after we left for Connecticut, and Amber only ended up doing half a semester there before it happened." Micah's eyes water, and I remember how he wept when he thought first Tobias, then Ranger, and then Spencer were dead. He really does have big feelings. "I think in some small way, Tobias blames me for her death. Like, if I hadn't slept with her, and we hadn't left for Adamson, maybe she wouldn't have moved with her mom after rehab."

"You can't know that," I whisper, feeling my own eyes water. "But it's understandable to wonder what-if. You just can't let it destroy you. We make choices every day that don't seem important. Usually, they're not. But every once in a while, something big happens. It's impossible to predict; you'll drive yourself crazy if you try."

The corner of Micah's lip twitches, but there's too much sadness weighing down his expression for him to smile.

"When did you get so wise and shit, Chuck the Micropenis?"

"When did you get so melancholy?" I retort, stepping forward and putting my arms around him again. He stiffens up slightly, but after a moment, his hand falls to my back and he relaxes a little. I'm pretty sure he expected me to judge him, to hate him, to blame him. But I don't feel any of those things. The only thing I feel is empathy for him, and sadness for Amber. The little spark of jealousy is gone.

"We hide it well, huh?" Micah asks as I breathe in his cherry and vetiver scent. I like how he says *we*, even though I'm only talking to him. "Are you sure you don't want to dump my ass and just date Tobias? I'd understand if you did."

I snort and bury my face in his robe.

"You're being stupid right now," I murmur, watching the cherry blossom petals skirt around in the breeze. Lifting my head, I glance up at him and find his green eyes on mine. "You guys share girls now, remember?" This time, it's his turn to snort back at me. "Well, not girls. Girl. Singular. One. Just me, Chuck the Micropenis." Micah finally smiles as I take a step back. There doesn't seem to be anyone around, but if they overhear me refer to myself as a girl then so what. Screw them. This secret is getting old anyway.

"Do you know why we decided to share girls?" he asks. "Because we didn't want anyone or anything to come between us ever again. And yet, here we are. Me, fucking up and ruining everything yet again." Micah pauses and lifts his gaze up to look over my shoulder. When I glance back, I see Tobias standing there, watching us with narrowed eyes.

"What did he tell you?" he demands, coming over to stand on my other side, arms crossed over his chest. His eyes are dark with old anger, turning them hunter green in the sunlight. I don't think it was truly the fact that Micah brought candles to woo me that pissed him off; it was their past coming back to haunt them both.

"That he fucked up, he loves you, and he's sorry," I say, and Micah groans from behind me.

"Not verbatim," he mumbles, but I can already see Tobias softening slightly toward his twin. The way he looks at me, I can tell he's searching for the same thing that Micah was. But whatever anger or hate or pain he thought he might see, there's none of that. If I can forgive Monica for what she did, then I can certainly accept Micah, despite his prior mistakes.

"He admitted that he messed up, and he said if I wanted to date just you, he'd understand." I test the waters to see Tobias' reaction, and he frowns.

"No." Just that one word as he lifts his face up to glare at his brother. "That is not an option. You're not getting out of this so easily. Apologize and admit you screwed up, and maybe I can apologize, too, and admit that I overreacted."

I flick my gaze between the two of them and then carefully and quietly try to back away to give them some space. Instead, they both flash matching grins at me.

"Oh, no you don't, Chuck Carson," they say, grabbing me by the arms and dragging me forward. I end up with a kiss on both cheeks and matching feral grins. "You're not getting away that easily."

They drag me by the arms over to a utility closet on the far side of the courtyard, toss me inside, and then close the door. I get a mad sense of déjà vu from that day in the Jaw Flapper when they first discovered my secret. The pair of them standing over me, resting their forearms on the wall behind my head.

"Are you guys okay?" I ask skeptically, and Tobias pauses, glancing over at his brother. There's a bit of tension between them, but it fizzles out pretty quick.

"Losing Amber was awful. Thinking Spencer was dead just about killed me. Life is too short, too weird, and too shitty to stay pissed at my brother for wanting to woo our girlfriend." Tobias puts his forehead against mine and closes his eyes. It's too cute a move and statement for me to resist biting my lower lip in a flirtatious sort of way. "Where are those candles, by the way?" There's a bit of a teasing note in Tobias' voice when he says that, making me think he already knows. He cracks his green eyes and grins, a glitter of mischief in his gaze.

"Funny you should ask," Micah begins, taking his arm off the wall and pulling the lighter from his pocket. He flicks the wheel and proceeds to move around the room, lighting a dozen red candles placed in various locales: on top of an old wheelbarrow, on a rusty metal shelf, on the head of a weird concrete statue that looks a bit like a gremlin. "What a coincidence, don't you think, Chuck?"

"I think there's a murderer on campus," I grumble, but the set-up is cute anyway.

"Exactly," Tobias says, pushing up off the wall and standing in front of me in a black and red yukata. "Like I said, life is short." He moves over to a futon on the floor in the corner and flops down on it, grabbing a bottle of saké, and a plate of rice balls that are perched on a small red table next to it. "So let's not waste any of it, shall we?"

With a grin, I bounce over and join the twins, grabbing a rice ball in two hands and biting into it. It's wrapped in seaweed and stuffed with salted plums. Yeah, I was skeptical, too, when I first heard about it, but I have to admit: this shit is next level.

"My dad caught me and Micah coming out of the bathroom this morning," I say with a small grimace, swigging some of the saké with my right hand. Meanwhile, Micah is downing some plum wine and snacking on edamame that they must've stolen from the dining room. "Pretty sure he thinks we were ..." I trail off and make that cringe-y face that Monica always teases me about, the one she bought me an emoji umbrella for.

"Were you?" Tobias asks casually, looking down at the rice ball—it's called *onigiri* in Japan, y'all—and studying it a little more intensely than one might normally look at their food. "Fucking, I mean."

I choke on my food as Micah smiles softly.

"We weren't, but we almost, sort of did," he starts, exhaling. "Is that a problem?"

Tobias lifts his head up and shakes it slowly.

"No. Not a problem. I think ... we both need to be okay with spending time with Charlotte alone." He glances my way, swimming in my oversized robe, my glasses sliding down my nose, my hair all mussed up, and the tip of a new rice ball tucked between my lips. I just stare back at him, and I'm not sure what to say to that.

"You said you two shared. How many girls have you shared, exactly?" The twins exchange a look and then shrug in unison.

"Not many," they reply, and then they both cringe at the same time.

"We've only, uh, ever shared one girl. As in, we've only ever slept with one girl at the same time … once." Tobias looks sheepish as hell, swiping his hand over his red-orange hair. "We just *decided* that we'd share girls after the thing with Amber. We work better as a unit."

"Not better," I say, dropping my hands and the onigiri into my lap. "You're great as a unit, but I like you both individually, too." I pause for a moment, and then cock my head to one side, finally processing what they've been saying. "One girl. You mean … us, the Pirates of the Caribbean …"

"Just that," Micah murmurs, shoving a full rice ball in his mouth so he doesn't have to keep talking. He looks up at the ceiling as I cock a brow.

"Your bad boy façade is starting to crumple like tissue paper," I snort, flicking a bit of rice his way. It hits him right in the chest as he turns that sharp little face of his my way and grins, reaching up a thumb to swipe a bit of plum wine from the edge of his mouth after taking another swig.

"Bad boy façade? No way, I never pretended to be a bad boy." Micah grabs the rice ball from my hand and sets it back on the tray, reaching down to undo the belt at his waist.

"The matching yellow Lambos? The drag racing? Running over my ex-boyfriend with your car? The tattoos? Stealing the staff's keys? Fighting in illegal MMA fights?"

"Whoa, whoa, whoa, first of all, it was *Tobias* that ran that cum stain Cody over with his car. Second … uh, second …" Micah flicks his belt aside and then reaches up to rub at his chin, eyes flashing with amusement. "Yeah, okay, fine, the bad boy label was fair."

"We *share girls*," I tease, dropping my voice to this comical boom that sounds nothing at all like the twins. "What you meant was that in reality, you'd each only ever slept with one girl and not at the same time anyhow. I've pretty much ruined you both, corrupted you and all that. You'll never look at Disneyland the same way again."

"We corrupted *you*," they respond together, and then Micah pushes his robe over his shoulders and reveals that long, lean, chiseled body of his. He's completely and utterly nude underneath it all. My breath catches as he fishes out a handful of condoms from the pocket of his robe and drops them in front of me, ignoring my flaming cheeks.

"And speaking of corruption," Tobias continues, casually slouching with a smirk on his face, one elbow on his knee, his bare, muscular calves showing from beneath his robe. "If you're going to claim that title, don't you think we should do it more than just once?"

"It was a good just once!" I blurt, cheeks flushing as Tobias reaches up with one hand to work on the belt of his own robe. Meanwhile, my eyes slide over to Micah and find his cock, already hard and impossible to miss in the flickering candlelight.

Tobias stands up, tossing his own belt aside, and then moves around the room, blowing out every candle save one. The room falls into a soft darkness, the flickering flame casting more shadows than it dispels.

He drops down beside me, his robe fluttering around him in a pool of cotton fabric. One elbow rests on his knee, his beautiful face propped against his knuckles.

"So, Chuck, what would you say to another kissing tutorial?"

"I don't need anymore kissing tutorials," I mumble as both twins chuckle, and my skin heats up, fingers fisting in the fabric of my own yukata. "I've done plenty of kissing since—"

Tobias leans in, capturing my mouth before I can finish my protest. His tongue slides across my bottom lip, encouraging me to open up as I inhale with a sigh of pleasure, his sweet and tart cherry scent making my heart flutter.

"Lesson one: less talking, more kissing," he says, his mouth still pressed close up against mine.

"Lesson two: learn to share," Micah adds, crawling toward us and putting his right arm on my left side, tangled up with his brother's. He leans in close, skimming his lips across mine and then pressing them against the side of my jaw instead. "And lesson three is, kissing doesn't just have to happen on the mouth."

"I well remember where else kissing can happen," I murmur weakly, remembering our little restroom break during that restaurant dinner with Mom. The twins kissed a whole lot of other spots on my body that didn't involve mouths or cheeks or even necks. Speaking of which … Tobias is kissing his way down the side of my throat, pressing his hot mouth to my shoulder as I sigh.

Together, they reach up and untie the sash on my robe as a small moan escapes my lips. The flickering candlelight adds a sense of whimsy to the moment, making me forget for the briefest of instances where we are and what happened yesterday.

"We don't always have to do it together," I whisper, and they both laugh in unison.

"We know," they say. And then Micah adds, "we won't. But just for today."

The sash comes off, and Tobias tosses it aside as the two of them reach up with perfectly coordinated movements and push the robe down my shoulders.

"Glasses off," Tobias murmurs against my clavicle,

reaching up and plucking them off my face. He sets them reverently aside before returning his mouth to my skin. Meanwhile, Micah curls his fingers beneath my chin and takes my lips for his own, using his right palm to cover his brother's left.

They push me back into the futon as I wrap one arm around the back of each of their necks, fingers tickling that spiky red-orange hair of theirs. *I've got identical twins on either side of me!* I think with a little internal squeal, biting my lip as they both move down my chest and toward the bindings on my breasts. *Two fit, tall, gorgeous, rich, funny* ... I cut myself off, so the list of adjectives doesn't get too ridiculous, but come on? How is this not every girl's dream?

"Lesson four: stop thinking so hard," Micah chastises, reaching up and pulling off the little metal pin I use to keep the bindings taut. He flicks it aside and then pulls the first layer off, letting Tobias tug from the other side. I lift my back so the cotton strip can slide more easily underneath me, and then giggle as Tobias tosses the end to his brother, and they start the process over again.

"I was only thinking about you two," I say, coming to my own defense as my breasts are finally exposed to the cool air, nipples taut and pink. I'm breathing just a little too fast, a little too hard.

"Shush," Tobias whispers, cupping my left breast in a warm palm. "Let us take care of you." He puts his mouth over my nipple, shattering my self-control to pieces. His hand slides down my belly, underneath my panties, and cups the wetness between my thighs that promises I'm most definitely not a boy. No, I'm a secret girl, with my ruthless boys … my forever crew.

A sigh slips from my lips as Micah mimics his brother's movements on my other side, kissing my right breast, and then slipping his hand down to join Tobias'.

In the distance, I can hear the shouts of the other Adamson students enjoying the hot springs, but I don't care. We're in our own little bubble in here, and I'm loving it too much to care about any possible consequences.

The boys tease me, slicking fingers across my aching body while they use their mouths on my breasts, collarbone, and neck, taking turns capturing my lips. A shocked gasp escapes me when they both put a single finger in, using that incredible unity they share to their advantage.

"You're so fucking tight, Chuck," Micah whispers in my ear while on the other side, Tobias says, "Your lips taste like candy, Chuck." Just a little sneak peek into their personalities, similar, but different enough that I couldn't imagine giving up either.

My hands drop down, searching for the hard, warm shaft of each twin, fingers curling around their identical bodies.

"Oh, I see how it is," Micah whispers, thrusting into my grip as he bites my ear. Tobias tries to push my hand away, but I won't let him, taking a firmer grip on his body and working him until he's doing the same thing as his twin.

"Condoms," I murmur, and Tobias scrambles up to grab them, coming back over with two packages in his hand. He flicks one at Micah, hitting him in the chest, and then proceeds to put his own on.

Micah moves his hand away from the hot warmth between my thighs as I grab Tobias by the hair and bring his mouth down to mine for a kiss. While we're kissing, Micah slides my panties down my legs and tosses them aside.

"C'mere, Chuck," Tobias whispers, pulling me toward him and smoothing my hair back as he grins. "Do you know how many dirty, rotten things I want to do to you right now?"

"Um, I can take a wild guess based on how many dirty, rotten things I want to do right back to you," I murmur as he slides one of his legs between mine. He takes my mouth again, maneuvering his body between my thighs and pressing me down into the futon with his weight.

"However many things that is," Micah whispers, lying down beside me and licking the shell of my ear. "Double it."

His twin chuckles, reaching down to cup my ass

with one hand and keeping himself propped up with the other. With the shadows from the dancing candle flame, Tobias' face takes on a sharp edge, making him look more like Micah. Our gazes meet and he thrusts in deep, groaning and kneading my ass with strong fingers. The moans escaping my own lips are verging on the edge of a scream, but I've already had a door kicked down on me once mid-coitus. Not happening again, not when my dad's wandering around the grounds in a mood.

Tobias rolls onto his back with me on top as Micah carefully slides his hand over my mouth to shush me, chuckling against the back of my neck.

"How dirty do you want to get, Chuck?" he whispers, kneeling behind me and reaching between me and Tobias to find my clit with his other hand. He works me slowly, kissing my throat, and then finally releasing my mouth when I seem to have my breathing under control. "Do you want to go a little further?"

"Micah ..." Tobias warns, but his own breathing is uneven, and he's not fully in control of himself, setting his hands on my hips.

"How ... dirty can we get?" I ask, and the boys exchange a brief look.

"Stand up," Micah tells me, and I balk. We've only just gotten started and I'm not ready for this to be over. But at a nod from Tobias, I take Micah's hand and stand, letting him turn me around by the shoulders.

Gently, he pushes me back down and Tobias helps angle himself to enter me again. With a groan, I sink down, facing toward Tobias' legs instead of his face. When Micah stands up at the edge of the futon and puts the heavy weight of his cock near my lips, I know where we're going with this.

My fingers curl around the base of his shaft, and I slowly, carefully put my mouth around him.

For a first-time blow job, I don't feel like I do too shabby.

Tobias' fingers squeeze my hips, urging me to move my pelvis while at the same time, Micah gently encourages me with soft fingers in my hair. The former twin is the first to reach his climax, shuddering beneath me, his moans in chorus with his brother's. After he finishes, he stays right where he is, leaving me to work my clit with my fingers and continue using my mouth on Micah.

"I'm close," he warns, massaging my scalp. "Do you want me to move?"

I pull back slightly and shake my head before continuing, enjoying the way his breathing speeds up just before he finishes. His fingers tighten against my scalp, and I can tell he's struggling not to thrust, letting me control the interaction. But he wants to. And maybe, one day, I'll let him get just a little more intense.

"Holy crap, Chuck, you're hardcore," Micah says as

I swallow, my own body panting and shaking with need. I'm a bit impressed with myself for taking such a leap, but I'll have to wait for some good girlfriend time with Monica to high five her, smirk, and be all *I swallowed, first time, you know.*

Carefully, Micah and Tobias lay me down on the futon between them and use their hands to bring me my own orgasm, carefully covering my mouth when I get a little too loud.

Afterward, we stay there together, all cuddled up, each boy with one leg over my own, and we drink plum wine and saké until the single red candle burns its way out.

There aren't a lot of perfect moments in life, but this, this is one of them.

"I take it you've all made up?" Spencer asks, turquoise eyes taking the three of us in as we move up the single step to the wooden walkway that runs along the side of the main lodge building. He's leaning against the wall with his arms crossed over his chest, dressed in the same navy-blue yukata from earlier. A cocksure smirk rests on his face, but I can see the smallest hint of jealousy glittering in his beautiful gaze. He does, however, do an admirable job of controlling it.

"If you can call it that," Micah says, lips splitting into a naughty little grin. He slouches against one of the columns, all boneless and languid. Both twins have this look of pure male satisfaction on their faces that makes me want to be contrary. I flick Tobias in the nipple just for good measure and he chuckles at me.

"Huh." Spencer pushes off the wall and comes to stand in front of me, putting his hands on either side of my face. When he leans down and kisses me, my tired body comes back to vibrant, arduous life. Ugh, at least girls don't have, like, refractory periods, you know? And by refractory periods, I mean that annoying time after dudes come where they can't get hard again. Come to think of it, it's almost like teenage boys don't have refractory periods either …

Spencer smiles at me as he pulls back, and then nods his chin in the direction of the dining room. "Figured I'd give you some sugar before I let you know that your dad's on the warpath."

"Um, and why is he on the warpath?" I venture, my lips still tingling from our kiss. Spencer drops his hands into his pockets and grimaces slightly before reaching one up to run his fingers through his silver-ash hair.

"The twins texted to let us know you were safe, but when your dad started asking, I just said you were on a nature walk … for the last six hours."

"We've been gone for six hours?!" I choke out, glancing over my shoulder at the darkening sky. There are strings of paper lanterns lit for the evening, as well as an array of decorative torches to ward off mosquitoes. "Crap, shit, *fuck*." I chew my bottom lip and wonder if I can't fit in a quick shower before I—

Oh, nope, wait, there he is.

Storming toward me.

Face is ... that funny purple-red color.

My mouth twitches.

"Char—" Dad catches himself, grits his teeth, and stops just a few feet from me. "Chuck Carson, where the *hell* have you been all day?" Wow. For Dad to use even a minor curse word must mean he's truly pissed off. Since he rarely shows much emotion, this is kind of a big deal. "And if you lie to me right here and now, not even your fake engagement to Mr. Montague is going to save you."

"Excuse me," Church says, appearing seemingly out of nowhere. I shiver, but also have to hold back a smile when I see him and Ranger waiting behind me, their faces severe, a pair of matching frowns in place. They've most definitely got my back, huh? Literally, in this case. "No offense intended, Headmaster Carson, but I really wish you wouldn't demean the validity of our relationship."

A group of students passes us by, whispering and snickering. Of *course* Mark Grandam is part of the crowd, sneering in our direction. My father's just essentially outed my engagement to Church to the whole school.

Archie's nostrils flare and his hands curl into fists by his sides. *Is this it, the moment he finally snaps?* I wonder. It might be hard to understand *why*, exactly, I'd want my father to go into a rage, but it's actually pretty simple. He rarely shows much emotion, so little that at times I wonder if he truly cares about me. But if he got mad, then I'd actually get to see that he has feelings, that he does love me.

Instead, he closes his eyes and reins it in, making my chest feel tight and my eyes sting.

"The twins and I stole some plum wine and saké from the restaurant, and drank it in a utility shed," I say, looking him straight in the eye. If he can't be honest about his own feelings, then why should I? "But the twins also slipped an extra hundred onto the counter to compensate the owner. We're sorry we did it."

"You're stealing alcohol and drinking in secret now?" Archie grinds out, looking at the two McCarthy boys like he'd truly enjoy wringing their necks. He turns his blue-eyed gaze back to me, clearly struggling with what to do, how to handle me. I'm at that questionable age that straddles childhood and adulthood. Archie wants to fall back on old habits and order me around, but he can't do that anymore. He'll have to use that admittedly intelligent mind of his to find a workaround. "How am I supposed to respond to that?"

"How do you want to respond to it?" I ask, enjoying the shield of protection my engagement to Church is granting me. I keep my voice calm, and for once in my life, I hold my temper in as Archie struggles to grab onto his.

He just stares back at me, surrounded by the Student Council, and then he snaps.

For the first time in his fucking life, Archibald Carson loses it.

He reaches out and snags me by the upper arm in a tight grip, making me cry out.

"No." That one word from Ranger, booming like a thundercloud. He steps between us, breaking my father's grip on me. "I won't allow you to touch her like that."

"Mr. Woodruff," Dad barks, but there must be something in Ranger's face that deters him from pressing much further. "You kids don't know what you're messing with," he hisses out, a flash of pain crossing his features. It only lasts a split-second before it's gone, and I'm left wondering if I imagined it. "If you think I'm going to stand back and watch while you drink and … and …"

"Make love?" I question, and Dad flips his lid.

"Chuck Carson, you are asking to be shipped off to

a military academy. Do you think I can't arrange that? Montagues or no, I am still your father, and until you're eighteen, you belong to me."

"Okay, boomer," I say, and this stillness settles over our little group. Dad's eyes darken and he steps back. Maybe that wasn't the best way to respond to him, but I'm getting tired of being yelled at, tired of the lies, and the secrets. Dad knows something, I can tell. Why else would he know what we're messing with? He withheld the information about Spencer and Eugene when he *knew* I was breaking. So why should I offer him any apologies or excuses right now? "There was a dead kid in those woods. There were people in fox masks. And Eugene Mathers did not hang himself. We all know those are facts. If you don't want to tell me anymore than that, fine, but don't expect me to rearrange my whole life to accommodate your needs."

A long moment of silence follows my statement.

"Jason Lambert is missing," Dad says, looking right at me, his face cooling to an impassive stone mask. "There are going to be hourly room checks tonight, and every night until this trip is over—maybe even after that. You might not want to listen to your father, but if you disobey your headmaster, I can and *will* expel you from this school."

Archie turns away, leaving me there with an outer calm, and a broken, shattered heart.

"He's serious about that, isn't he?" I whisper, and

it's Church that glances my way first.

"I have a bad feeling that he is."

Slowly, almost in a daze, I move over to my now-dry yukata, hanging on the clothesline, and pull the abandoned note from Mr. Murphy out of the pocket. As I'd expected, the ink's run, and only one word is still readable.

"*Run,*" I whisper, just before the wind snatches it away and blows the note over the garden wall and into the dark woods beyond.

CHAPTER FIVE

I throw my bags down on my new bed, the one that sits opposite Church Montague's. I've been moved (more like kicked out) from the headmaster's house to here, as his roommate. Spencer, Ranger, *and* Church got written up for switching rooms without permission, proving right out the gate that my dad is serious about his threats.

"You want to play a game with engagement? Fine. You can bunk with your future husband."

That's pretty much the only thing he's said to me since I *okay, boomer'd* him at the hot springs.

"Make yourself at home," Church says, lounging on his own bed, already dressed in his striped pajamas, the top fully buttoned to his throat, as per usual. He taps his long, elegant fingers on the surface of his bedspread as he watches me. "And don't forget that tomorrow, you should wear the ring."

"Are you sure about that?" I ask, flicking my gaze in the direction of the nightstand where the little velvet box sits. "Mark gossiping on social media is one thing, but do you really want to make this official?" I turn back to look at the Student Council President as he rises from the bed, unfolding that long, lean form of his in front of me.

"Are you ashamed?" he asks, reaching out to stroke some of my hair away from my forehead. "About being engaged to me?"

"Me?!" I choke out, lifting a brow and trying not to tremble under that blindingly brilliant amber gaze of his. "I figured you were the one who'd be ashamed. Wouldn't you be better off marrying some heiress or something?"

Church smirks and moves away from me, leaning down to pick up one of the boxes from the floor and setting it on my bed. The top flaps are open, leaving a clear view of the contents inside. On the very top, there's a female Adamson uniform zipped up in a plastic garment bag. Church lifts it out and examines the navy blazer and plaid skirt inside. It's a junior's uniform; starting Monday, seniors have to wear champagne colored jackets and blue ties, lucky us! The fact that the new uniforms were late has been yet another stressor on Archie's plate. Spencer said his mom—who's on the school board herself—told him some of the other members aren't pleased with my father's performance.

I finger the edge of the plastic garment bag and sigh. Dad bought this uniform for me last year and had it waiting in the hotel room the day we were supposed to fly out, like he thought I'd be excited about it or something.

After I'd finished throwing a fit about living in Connecticut, I demanded a boy's uniform, cut off all my hair, and well … the rest is history.

"This may come out as arrogant," Church says, and I cock a brow, crossing my arms over my chest.

"May come out as arrogant? Well, since most of the things you say are *peppered* with arrogance, I'm just going to assume that it's bad." I nod my chin and then gesture up at him. "Alright, go ahead and say it. Come on, Churchie."

"Churchie?" he asks, laying my abandoned girl's uniform out on the bed and stepping back to examine it. "Interesting choice of nickname." He lifts his honeyed gaze up to mine and smirks. "But considering you're my fiancée, I'll let you call me whatever you want." Church turns my way and crosses his arms over his own chest, mimicking my stubborn pose. "You asked if I'd be better off marrying an heiress."

"Yeah?" I prompt, feeling a tiny bead of sweat work its way down my spine. I'm nervous right now. Why am I nervous? I mean, this is just Church Montague, President of Adamson All-Boys Academy, and prince of the school, the richest person in Connecticut, and my future fake-husband. Hah. Hahahaha. Nothing at all to be nervous about.

"Well," he begins, lowering his voice and stepping forward. One of his cool, dry palms comes up to cup the side of my face as his eyes meet mine. "I don't *need* to marry an heiress. My family is wealthy beyond all reason." Church leans down toward me, and I feel myself start to tremble at the thought of him kissing me. *I mean, he's a damn good kisser.* My mind strays back to that night at his parents' house, the way his hands roamed up under my skirt, the heat of his lips against mine. "And what is money for, if not to provide some level of freedom and control over one's life?" He levels his gaze on mine, speaking directly against my lips. "You've met my parents. They don't believe in arranged marriages, or convenience marriages—they believe in true love. They're fanatical about it."

He releases me and steps back without actually following through with a kiss, and disappointment fills me the way that ice-cold water filled the tunnels beneath this creepy school.

Don't get embarrassed, Chuck, stick with the snark! That's our thing.

I flick some of my blond hair back from my forehead and give Church a saucy Monica-inspired look.

"Don't you think they'll freak when they find out?" I ask as Church lifts a few of the boxes marked *Miscellaneous Crap* from the floor to the top shelf in the closet. I'm too damn short to reach it.

"Find out about what?" he asks as he raises his arms up, and his pajama top climbs *just* high enough to show off the muscles in his lower back. I reach up to wipe drool from my lips, even though it's just a metaphorical move in the first place.

"That we're not actually …"

"In love?" he questions, looking back at me just before the door opens and Spencer appears, Ranger not far behind. Spence's hands are tucked in his pockets as he moves into the room and looks around like he's sizing up the place. Then his attention lands on the uniform lying across my bed, and his mouth twitches.

"In love?" he says, repeating Church's words back to him. "And with a schoolgirl uniform just waiting to be put on? Come on, what am I supposed to think about this?" At least he's smiling when he says it. Ranger, not so much.

"I can't believe we were written up during senior year. Your dad's an asshole."

"Yeah, sorry about that …" I say, tapping a finger against my lower lip. "Come to think of it, I really shouldn't have talked back to him like that. He's going to go out of his way to make this year a living hell for me." I pause as Spencer unzips the garment bag and fingers the pleats of the skirt, and Ranger steals a coffee from Church's little red mini-fridge. "And also, probably for you guys, too. Apologies in advance."

"Eh, you're worth every write-up," Spencer says, lifting his turquoise eyes from the uniform to my face. Heat strikes through me like lightning, and I find myself shifting nervously in front of him, suddenly self-conscious about my baggy *California Love* sweatshirt and matching sweats. The way Spence looks at me, you'd think I were wearing a ballgown and a full face of makeup. He coughs suddenly and turns away, back to the stupid uniform again. "You know, now that we've got a lead on Mr. Murphy for the notes and … Mr. Dave for … Church stabbing him …" Spencer trails off and Ranger makes a grunt of protest as he sits on the edge of his best friend's bed. "What I mean to say is," he lifts his head up to look at me, "why not just go as a girl now?"

"What?!" I blurt out as Church closes the closet and turns back around with that contemplative look on his face. *Where are the fucking twins anyway?* I wonder as all three guys stare at me like they're actually considering this nonsense. "I can't go as a girl! Newsflash: one of our teachers has been leaving me threatening notes, another one of our teachers got stabbed by someone in a hoodie, and there was a dead kid in the woods. Not to mention the creepy people in fox masks."

"Yeah, but it's pretty clear at this point that it isn't femicide," Ranger says, his blue-streaked black hair shiny and razored into an edgy rock star look. He puts *just* enough gel in, that one might think he spends zero time in the mirror. Now, I don't know for sure, but since the twins each spend an hour perfectly mussing their hair each morning, it wouldn't surprise me if Ranger did, too.

"Femicide?" Spencer asks, also snagging an iced coffee from the mini-fridge. Church snatches it right out of his hand, and he rolls his pretty turquoise eyes as he goes in for another.

"A sex-based hate crime," Ranger replies, leaning back on the bed, dressed in a tight black t-shirt and jeans. Tomorrow, he'll be back in his uniform, so I take a brief moment to enjoy the sight. "Meaning, I don't think Charlotte is being targeted for her gender."

"Yeah, but …" I start, thinking of all the reasons I didn't want to attend Adamson as a girl in the first place. I'm not going to lie: I was scared. It was scary to be a girl surrounded by unfamiliar guys, especially in a new school, a new state, on the opposite side of the country from everything I'd ever known. And then the notes started coming, and the boys were bullying me …

Things are different now though, aren't they?

But I'm still scared. Just for a different reason.

"It might actually make things easier," Church muses, leaning against the wall next to the closet. He's got that faraway look in his gaze again, like he's piecing together clues nobody else is even aware of. "You've got us now, and only a complete moron would bother the Student Council's girl."

"The Student Council's girl?" I say skeptically, but … it's pretty much true, isn't it?

"But it *would* get more eyes on you," Church continues, pushing off the wall to open the door for the twins. He must be, like, psychic or something, because they didn't even get a chance to knock.

"More eyes?" Tobias asks, lifting a red-orange brow in question as he and Micah fill up the narrow hallway space between us and the door.

"If Charlotte starts attending class as a girl, then the whole school will be talking about her, looking at her —"

"This is not a very compelling argument," I murmur, but Church just plows on.

"The more people that are looking at her, the more she stands out, the less she can be targeted in the shadows." He slides his palms down the lapels of his fancy pj shirt. "It's a solid idea, my darling."

"Your darling?" the twins echo, making faces and then sticking their tongues out. "Gross."

"It may be, *Churchie-poo*," I retort, and both Ranger

and Spencer join in in looking squicked out as I pick up the ring box and flick the lid open, examining the pink diamond inside. “But I'm not sure I'm ready to deal with attention from the entire school.”

“It's your decision to make,” Ranger says, narrowing his eyes to slits, like he's pissed off about something. He's probably not though. I've learned over the last year that he just always sort of looks like this. But it's also his fierce determination and overprotectiveness that make him likable. And also, lickable. Notice how those words are only one letter apart from each other. “We're here to back you up either way.”

There's a brief knock at the door before it opens up and Nathan the douche-canoe security guard is swinging the beam of his flashlight in all our faces.

“Curfew time, everyone to their own rooms,” he barks as the twins turn in unison, blocking Nathan's view of me in my pajamas. Hopefully they're baggy enough that he won't notice anything noteworthy, but the moment also makes me realize how much easier it'd be for us to hunt the murderers if we didn't have to worry about this secret on top of everything.

“You're supposed to knock first,” the twins snap, lifting their lips up in matching snarls as Nathan blinks bored eyes at us. His beard is sprinkled with Doritos crumbs again, and I can smell the Mountain Dew from here. How pleasant.

"I did knock," he says with a shrug, tucking his flashlight into his belt. "But, despite what you little shits think, I'm not on your orders. The Headmaster wants all students accounted for and in their own rooms by eight."

"This is ridiculous," Spencer growls out as Church's face goes ice-cold. He's looking at Nathan like he's almost certain he's one of the prime suspects. "Since when do you get to cuss students out?"

"Good question, Mr. Hargrove," Church says, watching as Nathan's eyes swing his way and stay there. The two of them stare at each other for a long, long moment before Nathan retreats, slamming the door behind him. He'll be back in thirty minutes to check on us. And then once every few hours after that. Thanks to Jason What's-His-Name's 'disappearance'—aka his *death*—we really are being subjected to nightly attendance checks. Guess dad just didn't mean at the hot springs resort, huh? *And there goes my new sex life,* I think, flushing a bit. "When *did* Nathan get so uppity?"

"He was looking at you funny, too," Spencer adds as the twins exchange a look and Ranger stares across the room at me.

Maybe he can tell I'm actually entertaining the ridiculous thought of attending Adamson in a skirt?

I must be slowly losing it.

CHAPTER SIX

Despite my father's desperate attempts to keep the gossip buzz to a minimum, the following Monday at Adamson is flooded with rumors about Jason and what might've happened to him.

"He was the only person on this campus who stood a chance running against Church and saving us from the shitty Student Council," Mark declares loudly as I take my seat in my English and literature class. Of course, he's timed his remarks in just such a way that the twins —my escorts for today—have already left for their own class. "Has anyone else noticed that all of this weird shit started happening after Chuck enrolled here?"

I ignore him, pulling out my academy-issued iPad

and using the eReader program to open my textbook. I'm determined to do well this year. I'll have to, if I want to get into college. The twins talked about Bornstead University like they were sure I could get in, if I really wanted to. And I do. For the first time in my life, I have a plan for my future—as tentative and unsure as it may be. In the past, I used to just fantasize about hanging out at the beach, surfing until the sun went down, and supplementing my income with something random like working at the Jamba Juice.

Yeah, I'm finally starting to figure out how silly that sounds.

"You have nothing to say for yourself, *Chuck*," Mark sneers, coming over to stand in front of my desk. He puts his palms on top of my iPad, smearing fingerprints across the screen. My lips twitch in irritation as I look up at him. "And then on top of everything, your skinny, pathetic ass is now engaged to the richest guy in school? What a crock. You're nothing but a gold-digging faggot."

I shove up from my seat, bristling with anger as the rest of the class turns to look at us. Mark's dark eyes twinkle with satisfaction, and the smirk working its way onto his face makes my fists itch with the threat of violence. I'd love to deck this ass pig, but what good would that do me? He could probably kick my ass in his sleep.

"You don't know anything about my relationship

with Church," I hiss, narrowing my blue eyes on him. "And besides, you're one to talk. Your best friend committed suicide, and you don't seem to give two fucks. I bet you tied that rope to the tree and hung him yourself."

Mark's faces flashes with barely suppressed rage as he reaches out and grabs me by the new blue tie I've got on. While juniors wear navy slacks and blazers with champagne colored ties, seniors get the reverse: champagne colored slacks and blazers with blue ties.

"Really? You're accusing me of helping my best friend commit suicide? I could just as easily ask you why the only guy in this school who's *ever* challenged Church Montague for his position in the Student Council is now missing. Seems pretty convenient, huh?"

The door to the classroom opens and Mr. Murphy walks in. Unfortunately for me, he teaches both junior *and* senior English. Most particularly, he teaches the non-AP classes which, obviously, I'm in.

So now I get to sit here and learn about classic literature from a guy who's been leaving me threatening notes. He glances my way and notices Mark's hand on my tie. The asshole releases me fairly quickly and saunters back to his seat, but not before tossing a look over his shoulder that says he isn't done with me just yet.

I take a seat and glare at Mr. Murphy for the

remainder of class. He pretends not to notice, but I know he does. His smile looks a little forced, and there's sweat on his forehead, despite the cool autumn temperature.

The rest of our first week back is like that, uneventful but a little weird, a little off. It's like the student body can sense that there's a murder-mystery brewing right beneath their noses. I'm actually surprised to reach the weekend unscathed.

Well, relatively unscathed. With the lockdown in full effect, Nathan breathing down our necks, and my dad treating me like a delinquent, it hasn't been a very exciting five day stretch.

"I swear, I could close my eyes and like, not wake up for an entire month." I flop down in Ross' old chair in the lobby of the Student Council room and lean my head back against the seat. His job is *so* much harder than I thought. Like, I had no idea how much I was padding onto my workload by accepting the job of personal assistant to the Student Council. It's a job I won't have much longer if we don't win the elections next week. Each guy has to run separately for his position, although based on what I hear of past years, there's absolutely zero competition.

You know, except for the recently deceased Jason.

"Remember the first year we did this," Ranger says to Church as the latter of the two starts some fresh coffee brewing on the table in the corner. "Before the twins transferred here. We had that idiot Gerald Mikel as secretary and his dumb-shit of a best friend as treasurer. What a nightmare."

"Gerald Mikel used to bring decaf coffee to meetings," Church says, narrowing his eyes in just such a way that says that's most definitely an unacceptable and inexcusable action. "I never liked him."

He turns around to look at me, an empty mug in hand, holding it out of habit maybe?

For the past five days, we've been dancing around the fact that we're one, technically engaged; two, sharing a room together; and three, dating. It's been a little awkward, but in a good way, in an *I have butterflies living in my belly* sort of way.

"Has anyone given you shit over our engagement?" Church asks as the door opens and Spencer and the twins come in, laden with Tupperware from yesterday's Culinary Club meeting. We're practicing for the bake-off against Everly All-Girls Academy in spring. You know, provided we're all still alive then.

"Not really," I start, rubbing my finger over the ring on my hand. Whenever I pass Dad on campus, I swear, his eyes dart right to it and he bristles in frustration. Hypocrite. Mom was nineteen when she had me, and by then, they'd already been married for months. Besides, Dad was in his *thirties* when he started dating my teenage mother. He really has no room to talk. "Mark called me a gold-digging faggot on Monday, does that count?"

"Let's beat him up," the twins say, and I smile. It's sort of their, like, motto or something.

"This is getting *way* out of control. Mark used to know how to toe the line, but now he just insults our girlfriend and gets away with it? I don't like that," Spencer says, tucking his hands together behind his head and frowning hard.

"Don't forget," the twins say, each lifting up a single finger in the air. "He's guilty. We're sure of it."

"So you've said before," Church murmurs, finally pouring a mug of coffee and then, contrary to his usual character, he douses it with cream and sugar before coming over to stand in front of me. He offers up the mug while the other four boys gape at us like we've just started having a wild rut in front of them. This time, when Church hands me the cup and tries to keep our fingers from touching, I thread mine through his and he goes completely still. Our eyes meet, and a hot cord of tension runs between us, invisible but powerful and potent anyway. "I've been thinking about him. Him, and all our other suspects, and here's what I've got."

Church releases the coffee into my hands and moves away as Spencer flips his tie over one shoulder and leans back against one of the walls, popping open the top on a Tupperware container and going for a freshly baked molasses cookie. Our food theme this week was *autumn fresh.* Bleh. Ranger made it up, can't you tell? He also made miniature fondant squirrels to stick on some cupcakes. Don't think I missed him blushing while he examined their cuteness.

P.S. They had sparkly tails, too.

"And?" Tobias asks, taking a seat on the bench and leaving his feet flat on the floor. When Micah sits beside him, he crosses his legs, and I smile. It's the little tells, right? "What's the verdict, Mr. President?" He takes an M&M cookie from a separate container, picks the blue M&Ms out and then gives them to his brother. Micah does the same, but passes the green ones to Tobias.

"Mark's family has attended Adamson since the very beginning," Church says as I sip my coffee, wishing I could take my bindings off but knowing that we've got student meetings today. It's my job to check each person in, mark down names and complaints into the computer system, and then lead them back to the boys for their meeting. Once they're finished, I have to add the resolution—if any—to the student's file, how long they were in the room, and then run any errands necessary. On Monday, I had to head out and reset the locker combinations on *five* different lockers. Of course, I can't go anywhere by myself, so Spencer went along with me and we may or may not have made out in an alcove on the way.

I'm a bit useless as an assistant right now, I suppose, but the boys want me here anyway, and I'm too selfish to say no.

"And, interestingly enough, so have Selena's *and* Aster's families." Church pours himself a cup of black coffee and turns around. "By the beginning, of course, I mean since the very first class was held on this campus. They all have ancestors who used to work at the abbey that was here before it was turned into a school."

"That's a hell of a coincidence," Micah says, polishing off his third cookie and heading for a fourth. Ranger just stands in the middle of the room, arms crossed, listening to the conversation. Things have been a little weird between us since the double naked baking incident. I've noticed he's been avoiding his frilly aprons a bit, too. Not cool. We need to work out all this tension. *And, really, I mean, there's only one way to work it out.*

"Truly. There are only two dozen students who've ever shared that sort of lineage in the history of the school."

"Between Everly and Adamson, is there anyone else that fits the bill?" Ranger asks, but Church just shakes his head. Damn.

"Other than Selena's brother, Gareth, no. Nobody else but you."

"Me?" Ranger asks, wrinkling up his nose. "That

shit must be from my dad's side of the family then. I feel like my mom would've mentioned it. Does that mean it's a dead lead?"

"Maybe." But Church doesn't sound entirely convinced.

"There are most definitely three attackers," I say, scrubbing my hands down my face. We only have about fifteen minutes before our first appointment of the day arrives, unfortunately, so this is our last chance to talk this over as a group today.

I feel a little niggle of frustration when I hear a knock on the door. It's still locked; we don't bother unlocking it until about five minutes before the first meeting. With a sigh, the boys brush the crumbs off their uniforms and disappear into the meeting room, leaving it cracked behind them, just in case.

What I don't expect to see when I open the door … is Aster Hayes smiling back at me.

"What is this crap about more girls coming to the school?" I snarl, storming into my dad's house without bothering to knock. He looks up from the dinner table with an almost bored facial expression, waiting until I come around the corner to see the rest of his dinner guests. "And postponing the Student Council elections just for them? That's total toilet water." *Should've said bullshit, pretty sure toilet water is not a commonly used phrase.*

Girls.

Three girls.

Aster being one of them.

She'd just stopped by the Student Council room to introduce herself today.

And to announce that she, too, was actually going to be running for Student Council President.

What. In. The. Actual. Fuck?

"When I told you that I'd be treating you as a headmaster would instead of a father—at your request, I might add—I was serious. Bursting into my home unannounced is worth a write-up, at the very least." I just stand there fuming, looking between the three confused faces sitting around my father's table while Ranger guards my back, waiting just outside the open front door. "Girls, this is my … *son*, Chuck Carson."

"Pleased to see you again, Chuck," Aster says, tucking a strand of curly red hair behind one of her ears. She glances down the length of the table toward my father, her other hand poised on a fork that's currently resting on a plate of tri-tip, mashed potatoes, and asparagus. That's, legit, like my favorite meal, and Dad could barely be bothered making it for me, but he can make it for three strangers?! Three new guinea pigs to do his bidding.

I'm furious.

"We met at the Valentine's Day dance, as well as in the Student Council room today," Aster explains, smiling prettily. The other girls smile at me, too, and one of them even blushes and bites her lower lip. Spencer and Ranger act like I make such an ugly guy, but apparently, I don't have a ton of trouble getting female attention.

"Ah," Dad says, eyeing me with no small amount of displeasure. "Well, you'll be sorry to learn then that Chuck is now engaged to our current Student Council President, Church Montague, and is presently off-limits." His voice is as dry as sand and twice as grating. We glare at each other for a moment before he pushes away from the table. "Excuse me for a moment, ladies."

Dad carefully folds his napkin and heads in the direction of his office, fully expecting me to follow. For once, I actually do. But mostly just so I can yell at him and try to get to the bottom of what's going on here.

I pause briefly to move over to the screen door and gesture for Ranger to step inside for a minute. The boys and I have been rotating partners, so that nobody is ever alone, not even when they're showering. I mean, nobody quite shares a shower stall the same way that Spencer and I did that one time, but …

Ranger moves into the dining room, and all three girls exchange looks. *Yeah, yeah, I know he's handsome, but he hates most people, and you wouldn't understand the naked baking thing the way I do.*

"Go talk to your dad, Chuck," Ranger whispers in my ear, this big, intimidating presence over my shoulder that I've come to really like. It's comforting, having him standing there, like I know I've truly got someone that's willing and able to watch my back. "And let me deal with the girls, okay? They're nowhere near as cute as you, and you know how much I like cute things."

My cheeks flush, but I refuse to give into the compliment.

"I thought you said I made an ugly guy," I whisper back as I turn to look at him, well-aware that the girls are staring right at us. Ranger's sapphire eyes sparkle, and the edge of his mouth quirks a bit. Not into anything as obscene as a full smile, but close enough for him. His sugar, vanilla, and leather scent wraps around me, briefly knocking the common sense straight from my head.

When he captures my chin and leans in close, the girls squeal.

"Oh my god, they're having an affair," one of them whispers, sounding far too excited about her discovery.

"While she's wearing the Student Council President's ring and everything!" another gushes, grabbing onto Aster's arm. Her green eyes twinkle excitedly as she grabs her friend right back.

"It's like a *yaoi* come to life," she breathes, and Ranger rolls his eyes. *Yaoi* is the name for a genre of Japanese comics and TV shows featuring guy-on-guy action, but intentionally made for women to enjoy.

"Our love isn't for the female gaze," Ranger snaps, and then he kisses me hard and fast, spins me around and pushes me in the direction of my father's office. It occurs to me as I stumble away that we've just had our first kiss. I feel drunk as I slip into the room and put my back to the door, pushing it closed.

"Did you come all the way up here just to act like a fool in front of my guests?" Dad asks, and it takes me several seconds of blinking to clear my head. *Ranger is ... such an unexpected treat, isn't he?* He always said I was ugly in my glasses and baggy uniform and mussy hair, but he thought I was fucking cute.

"Huh?" I ask, blinking again to clear my vision and staring at Dad, sitting behind his desk like he thinks the big, old wooden antique is some sort of shield against me and my ridiculousness. "No, I ... Why wouldn't you tell me you were planning on adding more girls to the school?"

"I've been working on this all summer, which, you might've known if you'd been willing to have a conversation with me. Everly and Adamson are working on an exchange program to test the waters.

We're sending three boys to them, and vice versa. But we can't bring the girls over until they have a proper place to stay. We plan on starting them here during the second quarter, after the girls' dorm is cleaned up and ready."

"I see." I can't decide if I should be angry, relieved, whatever. "What about Jason? What about Eugene? What about Jenica? I saw a dead body in those woods, Dad." I look him straight in the eyes, and for the first time, I realize what all his anger is about. He's *afraid* for me. "Where is Mr. Dave?" I decide to ask, and Dad blinks back at me a few times, like he's surprised by the question.

"He had the flu, but he'll be back on Monday," he says, and this time, it's my turn to look surprised.

"You've spoken with him recently?" I ask, because we haven't seen nor heard from Mr. Dave since the, err, stabbing incident. At this point, I've been *choosing* to trust Church, despite the evidence. I'd love to get Mr. Dave's point of view from that fateful morning. And isn't it interesting how he never reported the attack to anyone? Not my dad, not the police.

"Just this afternoon, why?" Dad asks, standing up from his desk. He's decidedly calmer today than he has been since I called him a boomer. Heh. I mean, he's technically Gen X—I think—but you can call anyone a boomer that's acting like an asshat. Every Millennial and Gen Zer worth their salt in online slang knows that.

"No reason." I pause, wondering if I should tell Dad about Mr. Murphy and the notes. But there's just something about the way he's been acting since we got to Adamson that makes me suspicious. I think about Ross' casual mention of Mr. Dave and Mr. Murphy praising my father for sending me back to California.

A thought forms in my mind, and I shift nervously in place.

"I have to go," I say, turning toward the door.

"Not until you sign this write-up," he says, and I groan. Three write-ups is suspension. Seven is expulsion. Not good. I take the stupid thing and head back to the dining room where Ranger's still waiting for me.

"I just need to grab something from upstairs," I murmur, bouncing up the steps and then creeping down the hall to my dad's room. His phone is where it always is, resting on the nightstand next to the bed, plugged in and charging. I could take it, but he'd know right away that it was me. Instead, I check to see if he still has the same pin code to get in and curse under my breath when it doesn't work. I try a few more combinations, including his birthday, my mom's birthday, their wedding anniversary. Nothing. Instead of wasting anymore time on it, I look through his closet real quick, his bathroom.

But there's nothing.

Some sleuth I am. In movies, don't characters like, have random revelations, and all the clues just fall into place? Why can't that happen for me?

Instead, I decide to quit while I'm ahead, moving into my room to grab a few extra jackets from my closet—stupid northeast autumn. It feels like it gets colder every damn day. When I step into the room, I see a set of girls' uniforms on the bed, three different styles with varying lengths of skirt, color combinations, and ties.

He must be trying to decide on a uniform for the new students, I think, stepping up next to my bed. The one thing they all have in common is a champagne colored blazer—meant for a senior. On a whim, I grab a uniform set, wrap it up in my coat, and then head downstairs and out the door before Dad can see or stop me.

I never wanted to attend Adamson as a girl.

But now that there are other girls preparing to come here?

It feels like a challenge.

Okay, that's it.

I'm going to do it.

I'm going to attend Adamson in a fucking skirt.

Wish me luck. I'm gonna need it.

CHAPTER SEVEN

"You're really going to do it then?" Ranger asks as he walks me back toward the dorms and I show him the uniform I just stole. It looks like it might be a bit tight in the chest, but compared to the bindings, I'm sure it'll feel like the girls are a'bobbling around in the wind. "Go as a girl?" He gets out a cigarette, cupping his hand around the flame of the lighter as he tries to get it burning.

"I … think I am," I say, furrowing my brow as I hold the garment bag up and then sling it over my arm. Ranger offers to take it for me, and I pass it over with a grin. "You're quite the gentleman today."

He snorts, but doesn't say much else as we follow

the curved path past the main building. It's dark out, but there are brand-new lights along the path that really help drive back the creepiness from the surrounding woods. Somewhere nearby, an owl hoots and I shiver.

"It's the least I can do, considering what I almost did to you in that kitchen," he growls, his sapphire eyes ringed with black liner, the top buttons on his uniform undone just enough that I can see the edges of his *Jenica* chest tattoo.

"Meaning what, exactly?" I whisper, crossing my arms over my chest and trying not to let the darkness freak me out. Even if the three attackers came on us now, I have a new container of pepper spray in my pocket, next to my replacement Taser (since my original one was lost in the tunnels). And, you know, I also have Ranger. Just the memory of him putting Cody in a chokehold brings me great joy.

"Meaning I was going to throw you over the counter, slap your ass and leave a flour handprint, and then probably fuck you in that apron." Ranger shivers and my mouth drops open, redness filling my cheeks as he stares down at me.

"I mean … that's not what I was asking!" I put my hands over my face as he lets out a deep, dark chuckle from beside me.

"You should be clearer next time then," he says, the slightest hint of a laugh in his voice. "Because I could've described my fantasies in a hell of a lot more detail than that."

"I was just wondering why you thought you needed to be a gentleman," I ask, dropping my hands down as we pause outside the boys' dorm. There are a few other guys out here, talking and smoking, so I make sure to cover up the uniform hanging over Ranger's arm with my jacket. "You didn't do anything wrong that day."

"It was wrong because we hadn't talked about it," he clarifies and then sighs, ashing his cigarette in the wind and then bending down to scrape the burning cherry against the sidewalk. He puts the butt carefully into the trashcan, his eyes distant in thought. When he turns to look back at me, my skin breaks out in goose bumps under that powerful gaze. "But I guess, since we *have* talked about it ... it wouldn't be so wrong."

"Are you saying you want to naked bake with me?" I whisper back, just before we hear the sound of footsteps on gravel and turn to see a boy that looks like an older version of Spencer Hargrove standing on the path nearby.

"Jack?" Ranger asks, a small flash of surprise taking over his face before he turns on that signature glare of his. That's when I remember that conversation Spencer and Ranger had during one of our video chats.

"Jack, huh?" Ranger had said suspiciously, just before Spencer gave him a look.

"Don't start on my brother, man."

Right. Because that whole week that Spencer was

missing, he was with his brother, former drug dealer at Adamson Academy, apparent asshole whose parents pay off cops, and holder of intimate Adamson geographic knowledge. He is most *definitely* a suspect, as far as I'm concerned.

Of course, I'm having trouble concentrating on all of that because I'm a romance addict who can't stop thinking about Ranger's-threats-that-should-be-promises. Flour handprint? Yes, please. *I've never been spanked before,* I think absently, fidgeting on the loose pebbles of the pathway.

"What are you doing here?" Ranger asks as Jack approaches us, his resemblance to his younger brother startling. They have the same face, although Jack's eyes are much lighter and bluer than Spencer's penetrating turquoise gaze. Jack's hair is a dark chocolate brown that I imagine must be Spencer's natural color, and he's also a good two inches shorter and forty pounds heavier than his brother.

"I was hoping I could talk to Spence real quick?" he says, eyes darting around nervously. Ranger notices. I mean, if my oblivious ass notices, then the dark, observant eyes of my new boyfriend definitely won't miss a move as obvious as that.

"Did you ever consider using a phone to call or text? Or hell, from what I remember, you pretty much live on your laptop. Facebook messenger? Insta DM? Send him a Snap or a Tweet? Post a fucking video on

TikTok? Come on, Jack, we both know you're not here just to chat."

My brows lift up as Ranger turns fully to face Jack, like he's squaring up for a fight or something. I curl my fingers around his arm, digging my short nails into the champagne color of his blazer. Ranger glances down at me, sapphire eyes dark, and then licks his lower lip before glancing back up at Jack. After a tense moment, he curls his arm around my waist.

"I'm not here to start trouble," Jack says, but he does look a bit sweaty and worse for wear. His baggy t-shirt is wrinkled and his jeans are streaked with dirt. "I just … want to talk to my brother, okay?"

"We'll get him for you," Ranger says, eyeing Jack like he's suddenly positive that he's one of the killers. He steers me away from Spencer's brother and inside, past a sneering Mark who's sitting on the couch, surrounded by some of his meathead friends.

"Wow, I've heard that fags like to sleep around, but Chuck puts the *uck* in fuck, am I right?" Mark snickers as Ranger freezes in place, turning his head around to look at the football playing dickhead. Last year, he was the wide receiver on the Adamson football team, but this year, he's the quarterback, taking Eugene's place like he was never there.

"As lame as that sentence is, I'm still going to kick your ass for it." Ranger pushes the jacket and uniform into my arms and then grabs Mark by his tie, choking him as he drags him over the back of the couch. Without skipping a beat, I whip my phone from my pocket and dial up Church.

"Ranger and Mark, lounge room," I say without waiting for his greeting.

The other football guys don't seem to know if they should get involved or stay back, giving Ranger enough time to put Mark on his back and throw a hard punch into his pretty little face. There's definitely a bit of blood on Ranger's knuckles, and the sound Mark makes … is kind of like a dying giraffe. I mean, not that I *know* what a dying giraffe sounds like, but it's high and keening and weird.

Guess that hurt.

"Make another homophobic joke, you prick. Piss me off a little more by insulting my boyfriend. See what happens."

"Tsk-tsk, Mr. Woodruff," Church says, appearing like a summoned specter at the bottom of the staircase. Like, he didn't even have to rush to get down here. "Violence isn't the answer, even when dealing with bigots, homophobes, and idiots."

Ranger pauses a moment as I rub my thumb against the band of my engagement ring, glancing between him and our fearless leader/president.

"You heard him, you psycho. Get the fuck off of me."

Luckily, the twins and Spencer appear at the bottom

of the steps, panting, and ready to fight, evening the odds a bit. Seven of them, six of us, although I'll be the first to admit that I'm a tad useless. I *do* however, have that pepper spray and Taser on me.

"Ranger," I say, because I wouldn't put it past Mark to mention this incident to my father, and I'm afraid that by pissing my dad off, I've put the guys in an awkward sort of spot. I don't know how I'd function if one of them was expelled. "Let him go. People who hate from a place of ignorance can't be beaten into submission; they need to be educated."

"Spoken like a prissy little girl," Mark spits, and Ranger just loses his shit, punching the asshole again. The two groups of boys come together in a raucous of flying fists, and for the first time ever, I get to see what Church can really do.

Eugene's taunts echo in my mind: *"Right. One of your cronies, but never you personally, huh? Are you scared to fight Church?"*

Two of the guys come our way and my hand reaches down to the weapons in my pockets. I don't get the chance to use them, however. In the blink of an eye, Church is moving between our would-be attackers, and then they're both lying on the floor holding their throats and coughing. What. in. the. actual. fuck?!

"Krav Maga," Church explains casually, naming a type of military self-defense from Israel, and turning to look back at my shocked face with a smile. "I've been taking lessons three times a week for years." He turns back to the fight in front of him and then heads for the brutal but unpracticed beatdown that Spencer's giving the team's new wide receiver. Church touches the guy's shoulder, and when the asshole throws an elbow back, Church steps to the side, blocks the blow with his forearm, and then hits him in the face with a punch that drops the kid to the floor.

"Oh, my poor, sweet ovaries," I murmur, because even though I *know* that violence isn't the answer to my problems, it's still pretty hot to see the guys I like kick serious ass. Within just a few minutes, the football dicks are lying on the ground, moaning and holding their heads, and the Student Council is standing above them.

It's pretty hot ... until the door opens and Archibald Carson walks in.

His eyes go from the collapsed boys and straight over to me.

Oh. Shit.

I'm in big trouble, aren't I?

"This is all your fault, Woodruff," Mark sneers, mucking the floor of the chicken coop as he glares at

Ranger's back. It's not technically our turn to help with the chickens or mind the organic vegetable garden that feeds the school, but … it is now. For the rest of the motherfucking semester.

"Shut your mouth, Grandam, or I'll shove chicken shit down your throat and smile while you choke on it." Ranger puts the last of the eggs in a basket, and then glances down at the little yellow chicks chirping near his boots. His cheeks flush for a moment, but when he sees me looking, he storms over and grabs my hand, putting the basket in it and taking the broom from me. "Go deliver these to the kitchen, and I'll finish this up."

"I can handle a little sweeping," I grumble, but Ranger's pushing me out the door anyway. "Don't think I didn't see you snuggling one of those chicks earlier," I murmur, but I *really* don't want Mark and his toxic masculine bullshit to hear, so I head off with the heavy basket.

Spencer joins me with his own basket, his split lip and slightly swollen and purple eye oddly charming.

"I totally ruined the season for Diego," he says with a sloppy bad boy grin, pausing as a pair of chickens waddles across the path in front of us. "You know what's coming, right? Why did the chicken cross the road …?"

"Noooo," I groan, bumping into his shoulder with mine. I almost lose an egg when it slips out the side of my basket, but Spencer grabs it in mid-air, spins it around on his finger, and deposits it into his own. “You think that made you look cool, huh?” I ask, and he grins, his silver hair falling across his forehead in just such a way that I feel my heart melt.

“Didn't it though?” he asks, and I roll my eyes. “By the way, Jack bailed and sent me some bullshit text about being out of town for a while.”

Ah, right. Jack ... I'd almost forgotten in all of the hubbub yesterday that Spencer's brother was there at all. By the time we were done being lectured by Archie, and all the boys had been patched up by the school nurse, he was gone.

“Did he say anything about what he wanted? Or why it was so important he couldn't text you?”

Spencer shrugs loosely and then pushes in the kitchen door with his shoulder to let me pass through, turquoise eyes dark. He doesn't want to believe his brother's involved anymore than I want him or Church to be. Not that I blame him. Wondering if my dad’s involved is killing me. But last night, I had a little revelation: I’m convinced that Dad, Mr. Murphy, and Mr. Dave know something about what’s happening on campus. I’m also convinced that, despite the evidence, they’re on our side. Based on the way Church reacted when I told him last night, I feel like he agrees.

I shift the heavy basket from one hand to the other and then turn to find Ian Freaking Dave standing in the kitchen waiting for us. *Speak of the devil.*

My mouth drops open, and I damn near drop the basket of eggs.

"What ... what are you doing in here?" I choke out, because it's only Saturday, and Dad said Mr. Dave wouldn't be back until Monday. Looking at him now, you'd never know that Church Montague helped him remove a hunting knife from his body just a few weeks ago.

"Mr. Carson, Mr. Hargrove," he says as Spencer grits his teeth for a moment, making a split-second decision. We could run, or we could stay here and see what the big, gruff man who just so happens to be dating my mother has to say. One of the kitchen staff members comes forward and collects our baskets, just before we hear a shout from the storeroom, and I realize with a small sigh of relief that we're not alone in here with Mr. Dave.

Even if he is one of the killers, he can't get us right now.

Spencer steps forward, letting the exterior door slam shut behind him, his gaze wholly focused on Ian Dave, the perfect shot at the shooting range, the asshole, the enigma who didn't like me snooping around in the library.

"What happened between you and Church?" is the first question Spencer asks, and I raise an eyebrow. I've made the decision to trust the mysterious, stoic amber-haired boy who put a ring on my finger, but I also haven't forgotten what the twins said in Disneyland, how Church was missing the week prior to my attack at Santa Cruz High. There's something going on with him, regardless of whether it has to do with Adam or the murders.

"Jesus," Mr. Dave grumbles, sneering like only a villain would. "You kids are idiots, you know that?"

"Church removed the knife for you," I say, repeating the story as I've heard it, waiting for surprise or shock to register on Mr. Dave's face. Instead, he just glares back at me with dark eyes and sighs, reaching up to run fingers through his thick head of hair. I imagine he's closer to Mom's age than Dad is. No thinning hair here. "Not a great medical decision, by the way, but I trust you had your reasons." I cough into my hand. "But who *actually* stabbed you?"

"Yes, Mr. Montague helped to remove the knife. I'm not at liberty to discuss who attacked me in the first place, but I *have* mentioned to Headmaster Carson on numerous occasions that letting you all traipse around campus like amateur detectives is a terrible idea."

"If you hadn't noticed, we're on chicken and garden duty," I snap back as Spencer reaches over and plucks a feather from my hair. "And if we are 'traipsing'"—I make snarky little quotes with my fingers—"it's only because the police and the administration are useless. Nobody believes us about what we saw in the woods."

"Just like they don't believe Eugene and Jenica were

murdered," Mr. Dave says with a long sigh. He looks so goddamn tired, I'm surprised he didn't ask for a few more days off. Spencer and I exchange a look before glancing back in his direction. "But I do. I believe you."

"You do?" Spencer blurts out, backpedaling a bit, like he's drowning in disbelief. I mean, after all the crap we've gotten from the adults around us lately, I'm not surprised. I turn back to Mr. Dave, surprising myself with my own inner calm. I'm not usually like this, you know, calm. It's a foreign thing for me.

"Yes, I do," Mr. Dave says, moving several steps closer to us and lowering his voice. "And that's why I'm asking you to *stay out of it.* Keep your heads low, stick together, and let me handle this."

"Like a librarian is anymore qualified to deal with this shit than we are," Spencer scoffs, folding his hands together behind his head while looking Mr. Dave over like he doesn't believe a word coming out of his mouth. "You're probably one of the masked creeps we saw in the woods. Like, seriously, we're supposed to believe you just happened on Charlotte's mom in the middle of Los Angeles?"

Mr. Dave closes his eyes for a moment, nostrils flaring, as his big, meaty hands work themselves in and out of fists. He's very clearly frustrated with us, but there's something going on between him, Mr. Murphy, and my dad. I'm sure of it.

"My relationship with Eloise is none of your business. I truly care about her, and I promise you, our ongoing communication has nothing to do with this case."

"This case? Um, like that's not at all creepy," Spencer says, putting a protective arm around my waist. A little thrill chases through me as I run my finger over the engagement ring again. For whatever reason, it's become a symbol of the whole Student Council, and not just Church. "Dude, you're just digging yourself an even deeper hole. Come on, Chuck."

He steers me away from Mr. Dave, but I pull back, turning to face the librarian one more time.

"I know Mr. Murphy's been writing me those notes," I say, and Mr. Dave's nostrils flare again, though he doesn't confirm or deny the accusation. "And I know that whatever he's up to, you and my dad are in on it."

We turn and leave the room, letting the door slam shut behind us, but I've got that little niggle of an idea in my head again, and there's no getting past it.

I know what I need to do.

CHAPTER EIGHT

On Monday, I break my usual routine of sleeping in, waking up too late to brush my hair, and rushing to class in rumpled clothes, skewed glasses, and a bad mood. Instead, I'm up as soon as Church starts the coffee brewing, lifting one perfect brow in my direction as I whisk open the closet doors and stare at the uniform I stole from Dad's house. I'm pretty sure he came down to the dorm the night of the fight to yell at me over it, but lost his train of thought when he saw the mess my boys had made of the football team.

So, now it's mine.

The choice is mine.

And I've made it.

"Are you sure about this?" Church asks, hiding a genuine sort of smile with his coffee mug. "This changes everything."

"I'm sure," I declare, unzipping the plastic garment bag and pulling the outfit out, so I can study it. "Positive."

Church helps me carry my makeup bag, nail polish, and blow dryer into the bathroom; the rest of the Student Council boys empty the room and guard the door, giving me time to shower and do my hair and makeup before they help me into a winter coat with a hood. It messes with my hair a bit, but oh well. I curled that shit into ringlets this morning.

"You take almost as long to get ready as we do," the twins say, pointing across at one another. "Being a girl is hard."

"Have you ever heard *The Sexy Getting Ready Song* from the show *Crazy Ex-Girlfriend*?" I ask, pursing my freshly glossed lips and giving the boys a look as I swirl a finger around indicating my face. "This is a bunch of patriarchal bullshit. *This* doesn't make me a girl. I just … it's like armor or something, okay? I feel calmer wearing it. I *want* to wear it. That's feminism right there: choice."

"No arguments here," Ranger says, his usually deep, calm voice a little ragged. When I squint, I swear I can see spots of color on his cheeks. He quickly grabs my shoulders and turns me around to face the door, his hands burning me, even through the thick wool of the jacket. *If we don't resolve our little sexual tension problem soon, we're both going to explode.* “But let's march out there and own that femininity, shall we?”

He pushes me out the door and into a sea of boys sneering and glaring, holding their dicks and bouncing up and down in anticipation of using the bathroom. Spencer and Church finally step aside and allow the horde into the bathroom.

“Fuck you guys,” Mark sneers, storming past us. He eyes me suspiciously as he goes, but I've got an entourage of Student Council members around me; I feel untouchable. We head back to my room, and I toss off the jacket, fixing my hair in a handheld mirror while all five guys stare at me.

“What?” I ask, popping my lips to even out my lip gloss. With a sigh, I put a fist on my hip, my pleated skirt swishing with the movement. “Come on, it's not like you guys haven't seen me all dolled up before.”

“No, but …” Spencer starts, lifting up a finger and then dropping his hand by his side. His dopey lovestruck grin fades into a smirk. “It's just, our little Chuck-let is all grown-up and tackling Adamson in a skirt. It's a proud, but scary moment for your harem.”

“My … what?!” I choke out as Ranger grits his teeth, Church raises a brow, and the twins grin.

“We're living a reverse harem,” they say in unison, nodding and then exchanging a look. Tobias reaches into his front pocket, pulls out a little *Ouran High School Host Club* button with all the characters on it, and attaches it to my own blazer pocket, right next to the Student Council pin.

"There," he says, his grin getting a little lopsided as he looks me over with those pretty green eyes of his. "Now everyone knows."

"And," Micah adds, lifting up a finger. "This gives us carte blanche to beat up anyone who says anything derogatory."

With a sigh, I shake out my arms and close my eyes. This isn't going to make things easier for me here at Adamson. No, it's going to make things harder. But I'm also fairly certain that this is the best way for me to get at the heart of this mystery.

"Alright, let's do this."

The boys check the hallway to make sure the coast is clear, and off we go, my fitted blazer buttoned beneath my breasts, the little blue ribbon tied into a bow at the throat of my fitted white button-down. The skirt is plaid, a mix of champagne, honey yellow, and navy blue that swishes around my legs as I walk. My knee-high socks are held up with garters (totally stole them from Monica when I was in Santa Cruz), and I've donned the same, plain shiny brown loafers I wore as a boy.

I'm pretty sure gender is just a ridiculous social construct, but also ... the world sometimes subscribes to social constructs, and I'm standing knee-deep in the middle of it.

All of a sudden, I'm finding it hard to breathe.

I stop on the path, the boys pausing around me, a glorious mix of champagne blazers and navy ties, and I close my eyes for a minute, listening to the wind in the trees, the hoots of those stupid short-eared owls. *Just breathe, we'll get through this,* I tell myself, opening my eyes again to find five concerned sets of eyes looking back at me.

"It's not too late to change your mind," Church says, crossing one arm over his chest and resting his chin in the palm of the other hand. "If you want to go back and change, nobody here will think less of you."

"No, I'm doing this," I state, lifting my chin and choosing to ignore the trembling in my hands. With another deep breath, I continue down the path, passing a few random students here and there who look up in shock. Pretty sure some of them are recording me with their phones, taking pictures and video, but I don't care.

Instead, I head right up to the double doors of the main building and throw them open with an unnecessary amount of force and dramatics. The twins catch them and hold them wide, leaving me silhouetted against the gray light from outside, my skirt billowing in the breeze, my chin held high.

Bet I look like a total badass, huh? I could be

Regina George in Mean Girls *or something, ruling this entire school and looking fab while doing it.*

"What the hell?" Mark asks, blinking at me as I move into the hall and pause, a good three dozen boys standing in the foyer, staring back at me. I scan the room, meeting as many pairs of eyes as I can.

Without a word, I strut forward and head straight for my locker, the presence of the Student Council deflecting any commentary or questions. At least for now. We manage to make it through an awkward breakfast in the cafeteria with everyone staring at me before my dad finally shows up, his face that funny purple-red color, eye twitching.

"Charlotte Carson," he warns as I push my breakfast tray forward and stand up, lifting my chin in defiance. Without a word, I leave the Student Council boys and exit the cafeteria to stand in the hallway with Archie. "Do you want to explain to me what this little stunt is about?"

"Stunt?" I ask, unintentionally taking on the snark tone without meaning to. It's just force of habit with Dad at this point. That, and I feel like he always comes at me on the offensive, making it ridiculously easy for me to fall into an aggressive defense. Why couldn't he just put his hand on my shoulder, smile softly, and say, *'is there a reason you decided to change the game plan without telling me, honey?'* Hah. Like that could ever happen. "This isn't a stunt. This is what you and the school board wanted all along, isn't it? I'm taking control of my own fate at this academy."

"Is this a cry for attention?" Dad asks, reaching up to adjust his round glasses. "Do you need something more from me?" He sounds almost desperate as he leans in, teeth gritted. "Because I've only ever done what I thought was right by you."

"Really? Like not telling me Spencer was alive. By refusing to believe me when I told you I saw Jason Lambert dead in the woods. That I saw a group of people wearing fox masks."

Dad's hand lashes out and he grabs me by the upper arm, dragging me down the hallway as I struggle against his grip. The cafeteria door opens a second later, and there are the boys, with Ranger in the lead. He looks about two seconds from tearing my dad's hand off my arm, but I wave him away and follow Archie outside.

Dad doesn't stop walking until we're standing at the edge of the woods, the shadows around us like a curtain of privacy. This time, when Dad looks me dead in the face, I see a hint of father and a whole lot less headmaster in his gaze.

"Charlotte, if you wanted to attend as a girl, that's fine. It doesn't make any difference to me, but there are things at this school that you don't understand."

I narrow my eyes and purse my glossed lips, tearing my arm from his grip and returning his panicked gaze with a glare of my own.

"Right, like Jenica, like Eugene, like Jason."

"Exactly like that," Dad whispers, eyes wide with fear. "And little publicity stunts like these don't help."

"Somebody wants to kill me," I blurt back at him, and he cringes. Cringes. *My* dad, Archibald Charlie Carson. It's enough to make me take a step back.

"Yes, Charlotte, somebody does."

A long pause follows with us staring at one another, my eye twitching in the same way his does. Nature or nurture, I got it from him.

"Wait, I'm sorry, what did you just say?" I ask, tugging on the little diamond stud in my ear, a fifteenth birthday present from Monica. "Pretty sure I just heard you agree with me."

"Charlotte," Dad starts with a sigh as the first bell rings, and I glance over to see the boys waiting for me at the front entrance to the school. We're all late now, but so what? This is bigger than class (although I really am trying this year since, you know, Tobias teased me with Bornstead University and all). I'd love to go to college with my boys.

My cheeks flush bright as I realize what I've just said.

My boys.

Mine.

Ugh.

Told ya I'd fall in love with every boy. I'm a sucker

for romance.

"I've already said too much. Get to class and we'll discuss this later." Dad stands up straight, glancing over at the school and the cluster of Student Council members with his mouth in a flat line. "Is this some sort of rebellion thing?" he asks me, and I realize after a moment that we've switched topics, from murder to boys. Based on my dad's face, I'm guessing they hold about the same weight in his mind. "Pretending to date them all like this."

"Uh, believe it or not, my dating them has nothing to do with you," I snap, frowning hard. "And don't think I'm just going to walk away and let this whole thing go. You know someone's trying to kill me, and you're not going to do anything about it?"

Dad looks back at me, and I can tell by the expression on his face that he's scared for me, really and truly terrified.

"I'd give my life to protect you, Charlotte," he says, and then he takes off in the direction of the administrative offices, leaving me standing there dumbfounded behind him.

"Are you alright?" Church asks as the boys join me near the woods, and I turn a worried face their direction.

"Pretty sure my dad just admitted that someone's trying to murder me," I hedge, and we all go quiet for a moment. It's one thing to suspect something, and it's another to have it confirmed. Fantastic. Senior year, in a skirt, five boyfriends, three murderers on my tail.

This should be fun.

I barely make it through two classes before Mark is schmoozing his way over to me with his football buddies in tow, cornering me just outside of math, the one class in the day where none of the boys are close by.

He cuts me off in the middle of the hallway, but I'm not concerned. I wasn't afraid of him while I was wearing pants, and I'm not afraid of him in a skirt.

"Well, well, who knew Chuck Carson was actually so fuckable underneath those ugly glasses?" He reaches out to touch my hair and I smack his hand away, making him and all of his stupid friends laugh. "What's the matter, Chuck? I thought you liked dick. You're already screwing five different guys, so what's one more?"

"Nice to know that you're a homophobe *and* a sexist pig," I snap back, narrowing my eyes. My fingers are just itching to pull out that pepper spray and let loose with it. "Now get the hell out of my way."

Mark just sneers at me again, this violent edge to

his behavior that's only getting worse by the day. He was insufferable last year. This year, he's a total nightmare. I'd love nothing more than to kick him in the balls—if he has any, that is.

"What if I don't want to get out of your way?" Mark asks, stepping closer to me, trying to intimidate me with his size. Too bad. I'm not afraid of him. Without even stopping to think, I reach out with both palms and shove him as hard as I can, knocking him back several steps and into his football buddies.

"Girl or not, I'm kicking your ass," he snarls, shoving off his friends and coming for me.

He doesn't make it very far.

Mr. Murphy steps between us, forcing Mark to stumble to the side to avoid doing whatever he planned for me, to our teacher.

"If I recall, you were just written up and put on garden duty for the rest of the semester, Mr. Grandam. It's senior year; I'd hate to have to write you up again." Instead of his usual soft, sweet smile, Mr. Murphy looks resigned, like actually writing someone up might set off an anxiety attack or something. At least he looks like he'd actually do it—it'd be his first time, by the way, ever writing a student up.

With a scowl, Mark takes off down the hall just as my boys come around the corner. Spencer's eyes go wide at the sight of our friend 'Adam' standing in front of me, and he exchanges a look with the twins. Church doesn't seem particularly surprised, but Ranger is *pissed.*

"What the fuck was Mark up to?" he asks, storming over to stand beside us, and then turning his glare on Mr. Murphy himself. "And how about you, Adam? Huh? You want to explain some shit to us?"

Lionel Murphy stares at Ranger for a long, quiet moment, and then hangs his head, almost in shame.

"Meet me after class in my office," he says, lifting his head, a deep sort of sadness resting in his pale blue gaze.

"Why? So you can admit what you've done?" Ranger continues, refusing to let up. He takes a step forward, but Mr. Murphy is already turning away and heading back into his classroom. Meanwhile, Mark's wasted most of my break, so instead of getting a snack, the bell rings, signaling that it's time to head for third period.

Surreptitiously, Ranger leans over and pushes one of his homemade granola bars into my hand, carefully wrapped in that reusable beeswax food covering he likes so much, and tied with a dainty pink ribbon. My cheeks turn about that same color as I clutch it to my chest. Church, meanwhile, hands over one of the two white chocolate mochas in his hands, the kind that Merinda only makes for him. I just barely resist the urge to hop up and down. Church can tell, I'm sure, and he smiles in that way only he can—like a smile means everything.

"What do you think that was all about?" the twins ask absently, watching the door of the classroom like some clue might jump out at them.

"I have no idea," Church replies, voice as smooth and stoic as always. "But I suppose we're going to soon find out."

After school, the six of us meet up outside the door to Mr. Murphy's office. He's already waiting for us, welcoming us in before he closes and locks the door, and lowers the shades on the window that faces the hallway.

While we stand there, in various states of awkwardness (me), anger (Ranger), and curiosity (everyone else), Mr. Murphy takes his sweet time preparing a cup of tea and then sitting down behind his desk. He looks exhausted, and like, ten years older than he did this morning.

"You ready to confess or what?" Ranger asks, pausing only when Church gives him a look that very clearly says *calm down, my friend.* Mr. Murphy cringes slightly, his cheeks turning a funny pink color, the way mine do when the boys tease me about sex stuff, or how Ranger's do when he sees a fluffy kitten.

"You asked me about Jenica before," Mr. Murphy begins, and very quickly, the room goes silent. Ranger's entire body tenses up as he curls his hands around the chair in front of him and leans forward, sapphire eyes glittering like the night sky. Our English teacher looks up with tears in his eyes, and Ranger rears back like he's been slapped, clenching his jaw in anger. Without thinking about it, I reach down and grab hold of his hand, giving it a squeeze. Almost immediately, I see a change in him, and a little flower of gladness opens up inside of me.

...

Flower of gladness?

Jesus, it's no wonder I'm no poet.

"You said you thought it looked like we might've dated ..." Mr. Murphy pulls a manila envelope from the top drawer of his desk and very carefully slides it over to us. He lets go, and the object sits enticingly between us and him. "You weren't wrong about that."

"Hah!" The word bursts out of my mouth, and my cheeks flush with the inappropriateness of my outburst. I'm not meaning to be disrespectful to Jenica or anything. But when Ranger glances my way, there's at least the ghost of a smile on his lips. It doesn't last long though. As soon as he turns back to Mr. Murphy, he's frowning again.

"She was afraid of Rick, and as much as it pains me

to admit it, so was I. We started seeing each other in private," he admits, a smile lighting his lips that's pretty damn similar to the one Ranger just gave me. *Oh my god, they totally did it!* I think, but I clamp my lips shut on the revelation. Hell, I could be wrong anyway, right? Ranger and I haven't done it … yet. Ahem. Cough. That time in his room when the tip slipped just barely inside doesn't count. Nope. Nope, nope, nope. "We also …" He trails off again as Ranger grabs the envelope and carefully, with his black painted fingernails, opens it up. What he slides out changes everything.

The missing pages from Jenica's journal flutter to the surface of the desk, drawings in black ink, slashed through with red. That's not all of them, surely, because I counted the torn pages as best I could. Even a conservative estimate gave me two dozen missing sheets, and we're only looking at about six.

"The rest of the pages are personal," Mr. Murphy says, looking down at the desk again. "I'd rather not share those, if you don't mind."

"You had access to her journal," Ranger says slowly, not yet looking at the few pages in his hand, or the ones that've fluttered down to the desk. His attention is fully focused on our kind-hearted English teacher, the one that's literally too nice to kill a fly. A literal fly. He works really hard to shoo them outside. As much as I dislike flies myself, you can't mock kindness in others, even if you feel it's too extreme. Kindness, provided it doesn't cause more harm than good, is never too extreme. "After she died."

"Yes, after she was killed," Mr. Murphy says, looking back up at us. "I shouldn't even be telling you any of this."

"Yeah," Spencer starts with a harsh laugh, "except Chuck caught you purple-handed, leaving that awful fucking note on her door. There's nowhere left to run, dude. Just fess up."

"I only wrote the notes because I was trying to protect her," he pleads, and the sincerity in his voice is convincing. Mr. Murphy stands up from his desk, wringing his hands, his face scrunched up in mental anguish. But I keep Church's words about psychopaths in mind, just in case.

"So you admit it then?" Church asks casually, a sharp thread of steel in his voice, well-disguised under his genteel manners.

"I admit it," Mr. Murphy whispers back, his eyes meeting mine as a chill washes over me. "I was just trying to get Chuck to leave Adamson. I didn't know they would follow."

"That who would follow?" Church asks as Ranger swaps one page out for the next, faster and faster, until he's back at the beginning again. His kohl lined gaze flicks up to Mr. Murphy, burning with an intensity that makes me squirm.

"A cult?" Ranger asks, his voice thick with disbelief. "You want me to believe that my sister was murdered … by a goddamn cult?"

Mr. Murphy stares right back at us, dead fucking serious.

"They've been at this school since the beginning, since it was St. Augustine's abbey. That's where the tunnels are from."

"And these?" Ranger asks, pulling the keys out from inside his shirt. It kills me that he wears them around his neck like that. There's something so sweet but so sad about it, like it should be his sister's arms holding him tight, not a pair of necklaces with ribbons that she carefully strung her keys from. "We know one opens her door in the girl's dorm, and that she was wearing it when she died. But what about this one, the gold one?"

"Where did you find that?" Mr. Murphy asks, biting at his lower lip and glancing in the direction of the door. The soft Enya music that's been playing this whole time—gag me with a spoon, definitely not my choice of tunes—gets turned up, like he's trying to drown out any listening ears from outside.

"In one of the posts on her bed," I supply, and Mr. Murphy sighs, rubbing a hand over his face.

"I've looked everywhere for that," he admits, this blanket of sadness making his shoulders slump. I'm still pissed about the evil notes he wrote me, but I'm not without sympathy. "That's how you got into the tunnels?"

"Somebody led us to the tunnels," Micah says, his voice sharp and hard, with that ruthless edge I've always noticed that sets him apart from Tobias. "On purpose. The rain might've been accidental, but locking us in was not."

Mr. Murphy sits back down at his desk and takes a careful sip of his tea as *Only Time* plays in the background. It doesn't quite set the right mood. We need something … ominous, scary, foreboding. I mean, did Ranger just say cult?

"I'm glad you have Jenica's room key; that'd make her happy, I think. She spent weeks looking for just the right ribbon …" His face softens with memories, and there's this long, awkward moment where he's clearly in another corner of time. When he looks up, the gentleness of those memories shifts into the coldness of fear. "The gold key we found in the woods. One of *them* dropped it."

"One of who?" Ranger snaps, slamming his fist down on the desk. He's shaking now, but I can't blame him. This is a lot to take in, even for someone like me who never met Jenica. "One of fucking *who*? Sorry if I don't just buy into this cult nonsense."

Mr. Murphy's face snaps up suddenly, alarm striking across his handsome features. "Oh, it's not nonsense. It's very much real, and it's why I tried to get Charlotte to leave Adamson. As soon as they chose her, I started leaving the notes."

"You're JR, aren't you?" I ask you, cocking my head to one side. "Junior. Jenica's suicide note, that was for you."

"It wasn't a suicide note," Lionel Murphy whispers, closing his eyes against the memory. "We were supposed to meet at the angel statues—"

"I fucking knew it!" Ranger roars, slamming his fist down on the table and then leaning forward to grab our teacher by the front of his pale blue button-down. He yanks him forward with enough force that Mr. Murphy's teeth rattle in his skull. I put my hand on Ranger's upper arm, warning him back from the edge of violence. He'll be eighteen in a few weeks, and the charges for physical assault are pretty damn serious. Although ... I guess his mom would probably pay off the cops the way Spencer's family does for Jack, huh? "And you said nothing? My mom's a devoutly religious woman. She believes her daughter went to hell. And you thought it was okay to keep this all a secret?"

"They'll kill me if they find out I've spoken to you," Mr. Murphy whispers, shaking. He really is too nice for this world. Well, unless he's a psychopath. Fuck! It's like, even finding out answers to some of my questions leaves *more* room for doubt. "And they'll kill you, too, if they know you know."

"Know what?!" Ranger snaps, shoving Mr. Murphy back and then raking his fingers through his hair. He moves away from all of us and puts his forehead up against the door. I decide to leave him alone for the time being, turning back to the skittish English teacher as Church steps forward and puts his palms flat on the desk. He looks so … aristocratic. And knowing that he's like, some badass martial arts expert? Be still my beating heart.

“You wrote the notes to Chuck?” he clarifies, and Mr. Murphy nods. “You let her out of the trunk the night I locked her in?”

“You let me out?” I ask, looking at Mr. Murphy with wide, disbelieving eyes.

“And you chased her with the knife,” Church clarifies, and Mr. Murphy groans, putting his face into his hands. “Presumably, to frighten her?”

“I wasn't going to hurt Chuck,” he moans. “I'm sorry I wrote those awful things. I didn't know how else to get her to leave the school.” He lifts his face up, expression drawn and tired.

“How did you get the keys to my dad's car?” I question, blinking through the confusion.

“The break room,” Mr. Murphy admits sheepishly, and my brows go up. Of course. Just like I'd planned on stealing *his* keys. Why the hell didn't I think of that until now?

“*Dear JR*,” Church begins, reciting the suicide note—or rather the *not* suicide note—from memory. “*I think they know about us. There's not much left I can do. If you want to meet me, you know where to find me. I'll be waiting with the angels. Love, J.* Explain it, please."

"The cult found out that Jenica knew about them, that she'd been watching them," Mr. Murphy says, shame coloring his words. "We weren't sure if they were aware of me, too. She was going to leave campus, but she needed Jack to give her a ride; she didn't want to risk calling a car. She thought … well, it doesn't matter what she thought."

"Jack?" Spencer says, his voice high and tight. I glance back in time to see a look of surprise cross his handsome features. The twins exchange a look behind him and step forward, like honor guards, taking up on either side of him. "Jack killed Jenica?"

"No, but I think he knows who did," Mr. Murphy says, standing up suddenly and reaching for the cord on his blinds. When he opens them, I can see that we're done here. He's told us all he's going to. He's a nice man, a kind man, but he's also a coward. That much is obvious. "Try not to be too hard on him. If he spoke up, he'd be dead, too. Now, go back to the dorms and stay together. It's almost over …" His voice trails off, and I exchange a look with Church.

What the crap is that supposed to be mean?

And is it a good thing, or a bad one?

CHAPTER NINE

Ranger slams a set of ceramic mixing bowls down on the counter, cracking one in half. He's positively fuming, anger-baking in a whirl of sugar, butter, and flour. His words from the other night—*slap your ass and leave a flour handprint*—flitter around my mind for a moment.

"Are you okay, man?" Tobias asks, trying to lightly touch his friend's shoulder. Ranger ignores him and continues to whip out all the ingredients necessary for a lemon meringue pie.

"A cult?" Ranger mumbles, but more like he's talking to himself than to any of us. "My sister was killed by a cult?"

Church pulls the pages from the manila envelope and

studies them as the rest of us peer around and try to get a glimpse for ourselves.

There's that symbol again, the one from the stone, next to Jenica's unique handwriting. No wonder Church claimed that it could only have been her who wrote the note; her handwriting is like a signature.

This is the symbol I saw, on the stone above Libby's bed. She snatched it back when I asked about it, and the bullying got worse. Way worse. I didn't think anything of it until I found that key. Until I saw them in the woods, wearing their robes and masks.

Adamson and Everly, two different schools, one history.

I don't like the way this looks—not for me, or anyone else who stumbles into this mess.

The danger here is very, very real.

Church turns the page without waiting to see if the rest of us are caught up reading along with him.

"Where the *fuck* are my lemons?!" Ranger roars, overturning a bowl of fruit. An apple rolls across the counter and bounces across the floor. I struggle for a moment to decide if I should go to him or if he needs a moment to himself, deciding on the latter when he smacks the wooden bowl off the counter with his forearm.

Besides, I feel like we all need to be caught up to understand what he's truly raging about here.

The next page shows a dark drawing done in charcoal that looks an awful lot like a door leading into a tunnel, like say, the one we stumbled down last year during spring break.

Lionel is the only thing that gives me joy anymore, the only person who takes the hurt away. When he's around, I don't need Jack's pills or Rick's overconfidence; I just need him. He holds my hand the way a boy should always hold a girl's hand—like he'd rather die than let her go, but also like he'd help lift her into the sky and say goodbye if she wanted him to.

I should never have taken him down those steps or into the woods.

This is my fault.

And I'm going to make certain that I'm the only one who pays for my mistake.

"This is getting dark, and quick," Spencer says as I tear my eyes away from the journal pages to look at his face. He's a bit sweaty right now, like he's lost in the moment, like he's just realizing that what happened to Jenica could so very easily happen to us.

I lick my lips as Church flips the pages again, taking Tobias' hand when he reaches down to grab mine. We exchange a look before turning back and finding ourselves face to face with a page full of that W-shaped rune, drawn in red, over and over and over again.

They know that we know.
The Fellowship of the Divine.

They heard us creeping around, and they know.

I thought if I went home for break, that I'd be safe there. But the way my father looks at me, I don't think that's true. Not anymore.

"Ranger," Church says, lifting his head up from the page to watch as his friend puts every ounce of anger and frustration he's feeling into a lemon meringue pie. He's whisking sugar, flour, cornstarch, and salt in a saucepan like it owes him money. Next, he'll have to stir in the lemon juice and zest, milk, and butter, then carefully add the hot mixture to some egg yolks without cooking them. It's hard as hell: trust me, I've messed up too many lemon meringues to count. Oh, and also been pegged in the face with a few of my zesty failures. "Are you alright?"

"No." Ranger turns around, his jaw ticking with anger, sapphire eyes an ebon black with rage. "No, I'm not alright." His attention flicks to me, and I swallow. He thought he'd scared me before? Nuh-uh. Maybe a little bit now though. *Yeah, and you're like, excited by it. Thirsty bitch.* "I need to get naked."

He's quivering now, and yet all I can think is: *how much can you love a guy who gets naked, dons frilly aprons, and bakes his anger out?* The answer being: *with everything you have.* I bite my lip.

"Is it okay if I get naked?" he asks, and it's Church who answers, gesturing elegantly in his friend's direction.

"Take it off, please," he says, and then he turns the page again.

I'm having trouble looking back down at the torn journal pages. One, because it's a bit heartbreaking to read. Two, because I'm maybe, sort of, just a little bit, freaked out by this cult idea. And three, because Ranger is throwing his apron aside and stripping right there in the middle of the kitchen.

Micah sneaks over and double-checks to make sure the door is locked before he rejoins us.

We have three pages left, three pages that Ranger's already seen, that are freaking him all the way out. I have to keep reading.

They only have two new recruits this year. Sometimes there are more. Sometimes there are none. But there's always an initiation.

There's always a bit of blood.

Dad knows. He's one of them. And I know the things he did.

I've been using the key to follow them around the tunnels. They speak freely down there about their blessings, their privileges, and the sacrifices they're more than happy to make to keep them. The Fellowship of the Divine is a cult, an old one, with origins tied back to the Catholic church.

And they scare me.
No, no, they terrify me.
The more I learn, the less I wish I knew.
My name comes up more often than I'd like it to.

Next page.

I'm honestly not surprised to see a drawing of the fox masks that Spencer and I spied in the woods.

Dear Diary, I wish I could tell you that I understood. But I don't. Sometimes people do things that make little sense to the rest of us. Sometimes the people we love betray us. It happens, and there isn't a damn thing we can do about it.

Today, I move my things into the girls' dorm.

On Sunday, when Jack comes back, I'm leaving. I'd go sooner, but I can't very well send for a car, now can I? Because he'll know.

And he'll never let me go.

Neither of them will.

They said to each other, "Catch for us the foxes, the little foxes that plunder the vineyards; for our vineyards are in blossom."

Deep breath. I look up and catch Micah's moss green eyes across the drawing as Church slowly switches to the last page. Jenica was such an interesting person, and she carried a lot of hurt. Reading these pages is killing me.

"Too bad she couldn't have been a little more direct," he says, and Ranger makes a growling sound that draws our collective attention … straight over to his cock. It's not erect currently, which is probably a good thing for me, but is he butt naked, and his muscles are, like, chiseled by the gods.

"Wipe the drool off," Tobias whispers, reaching up to dab at the corner of my mouth with the end of his blazer sleeve. I slap him away as Ranger swings a white apron with ruffles and an adorable lemon pattern over his neck. He turns, flashing that tight ass of his to the rest of us.

"Chuck, if you wouldn't mind …" he grinds out, as I blink in surprise at his glorious backside.

"I'm not touching your balls," I choke back, gesturing at the other boys. "Especially not in front of them."

"Oh god, Chuck-let," Spencer groans, running a hand down his face. Church and the twins just smile as my face turns a brilliant ruby red. "He wants you to tie his apron, my sweet little micropenis."

"But it's nice that you're thinking about my balls," Ranger deadpans, looking over his shoulder at me, eyes dark.

"I wasn't though," I murmur, even though my protests are a lost cause and I've already made a total ball sack … I mean ass out of myself. Carefully, so as not to touch his scorching skin, I start to tie the apron strings into a floppy bow. Ranger grabs my hands and pulls them around his waist, pressing my palms over the front of the apron. I can feel the hardness of his abs beneath it as I try to relax against his mostly bare back. *His skin smells like leather and sugar, and he's so goddamn warm.*

"Just ... stay there for a minute," he says, and I close my eyes, pressing my cheek into his skin and trying not to pass out from the dizzying gallop of my heart. My first day attending Adamson as a girl, my first time hugging Ranger Woodruff in the nude. Oh, and cults. Don't forget about the cult. What a day.

"I'll read the last page aloud then," Church says, exhaling like he's already glanced down at the page and knows what's coming. "*I'm meeting Jack at the angel statues, that glorious spot where Lionel and I had our first time.*"

Ranger makes a choking sound, but doesn't stop stirring the filling for the pie.

"*I'm going to ask Lionel to run with me; I don't know if he'll come. He's a good man, but a skittish one. A kind heart does not a warrior make. If he doesn't, that's okay; I'm not sure the Fellowship is aware he's been watching, too. I just want him to be safe. I just want to make it out of here. I just want to live.*"

Church stops reading, but when I move to step away from Ranger, he won't let me go. He presses one of his hands against my palms, keeping me still, keeping me pressed against him.

"You know what this means, right?" Ranger asks, the sound of his deep, angry voice rumbling through his body and into mine. If I'd been confused before about, what, exactly, our relationship was supposed to be, well, then, this clarifies a lot. I squeeze him a little tighter.

"It means we still don't know shit?" Spencer questions, and I hear the old pages rustle as, presumably, he takes them to look at. "So, we're supposed to believe there's a cult on this campus, preying on students?"

"It's fucking ridiculous," Ranger says, but when he finally lets go of me, and I peek around to get a look at his face, I can see that he's buried deep in his own thoughts. "But why would Jenica lie in her own journal? It was for her eyes only. There's nothing but harsh truths and sad realities in there." Ranger removes the boiling mixture from the hot burner, scooting it over to a cool one and putting the whisk in my hand, hot fingers caressing my skin as his eyes make startling contact with mine, sending a sharp thrill from my head down to my toes. "Keep stirring, don't let it burn." He switches over to a glass bowl with the egg whites in it, whipping them with strong, hard beats of his arms. He doesn't even bother to grab an electric mixture. I appreciate the dedication—and the view. "Did you see her mention my dad?" More whipping, the *clink, clink, clink* of the whisk against the side of the glass bowl speeding up in both intensity and volume. "That piece of shit."

"Your father was involved, clearly," Church begins, moving around to the opposite side of the island, so he can look at his best friend. His face is cold and dark, that seriousness that used to scare me so much rising to the surface. After meeting his family, though, it all makes a lot more sense. They're ruthless in business, ruthless in protecting the ones they love, but they're not evil or psychopathic or anything else. My heart thumps hard and I look back down at the bubbling yellow mixture in the saucepan. "So, what do you want to do?"

Ranger starts gradually adding sugar to the egg whites, turning the mixture into a peaked foam that'll sit pretty on top of the pie when it's done. The oven dings, and I scramble to slip on a pair of oven mitts in the shape of pink bear paws, flinging it open and removing the pastry shell Ranger started before it gets burned. Carefully, I pour the pie mixture into the shell, and Ranger steps close to spread the meringue across the top.

The twins and Spencer move around to stand beside Church, four gorgeous boys in matching uniforms that make my heart pitter-patter, all waiting to see what Ranger's going to say, how he wants us to proceed.

"I want you all to get out," he says carefully, watching like a hawk as I take the pie in my mittened hands and put it carefully back into the oven. He nods once, satisfied that I've at least learned something out of my time with the Culinary Club. Last time he let me grab an unfinished pie like this, I dropped it and spattered cherry filling on everyone.

"You want us to leave?" the twins ask in unison,

exchanging a look.

"If you need space, that's under—" I start, when Ranger grabs me around the wrist and yanks me toward him, looking down at my face with a searing heat that has my throat closing up and my pulse pounding. *Uh-oh. That's not a good look, not a good look at all.*

"Out," Ranger repeats, holding me close and giving the other boys one of his signature glares. "You can wait in the hall, if you want."

"Wait in the hall for what?" I choke out as Spencer sighs and rakes the fingers of both hands through his hair.

"Five for five," he murmurs under his breath, giving me a look that says *good luck, Chuck.* "I'd rather you guys didn't get murdered on the way back to the dorms, so we'll wait. Just don't take too long."

"Don't take too short either," Micah says with a bit of a smirk, excusing himself into the hallway. Tobias lags behind slightly, giving me a smile and then pulling out a handful of condoms from his pocket. He leaves them on the counter as the color drains from my face.

"Text me when you're ready for us to pick you up. We'll be in the library." Church moves toward the door, pausing just once to look back at us with amber eyes and a bright smile. "If you don't check in with me after an hour, I'm coming up to get you both."

"Might be longer than an hour," Ranger says as Church grins and then slips fully out the door, closing it behind him, and then locking it from the outside with the key. Slowly, carefully, I look up at Ranger, finding all of that dark anger locked into a fairly intimidating facial expression. He's not as scary as he looks though, cute-stuff-loving Ranger.

"Might be longer than an hour for what?" I ask, backing away slowly and entwining my fingers together behind my back. My skirt swishes around my thighs as he approaches, and I keep backing up, until I'm standing in front of the large stainless-steel doors of the sub-zero fridge, shivering as the cold metal touches the backs of my thighs.

"You know what," Ranger says, putting his forearm above my head, azure eyes swirling with hot-blooded intent. "Now get naked and put on an apron."

I shiver with delight as he goes to move away and then pauses, turning back just briefly to press a soft kiss to my forehead.

I notice that before he gets out the newest batch of ingredients, he pauses to put Tobias' proffered condoms into the pocket on his apron.

Holy crap, holy crap, holy crap, I get to do it with Ranger Woodruff! I think, biting my lip and then cringing when I draw the slightest tang of blood. Standing up and exhaling, I smooth back the perfect ringlets of my sandy blond hair, glad that I made the decision not to bleach or straighten it this year. I kinda like it the way it is.

"Are you sure you're okay?" I ask him, moving over to the cabinet with all the aprons in it and browsing through a few before I find a black one with pink cupcakes all over it, lace and ruffles galore at the pockets, hem, and neckline. There are even little jeweled hearts on the pockets that I suspect could easily be real diamonds. Fucking rich people. "This can't be easy for you, to learn all this stuff about Jenica and your dad." I lean my elbows on the edge of the counter as Ranger gets out an avocado, some honey, a banana … My eye twitches. I'm okay with trying kinky stuff, but maybe not that kinky.

"It's not easy," he says, looking over at me, quietly fuming. His blue-streaked black hair falls across his brow, his tattoos peeking out the edges of his apron. "But it's better to know the truth than be left wondering. Now stop stalling and get naked."

Pursing my lips, I step back and reach up to pull on the edges of the ribbon I'm wearing as a bowtie. It slithers off my neck and drops in a puddle of silk on the floor next to me. Ranger's watching, removing the lid to the blender as he studies me, my fingers shaking as I slip out of my champagne colored blazer and start to unbutton my shirt.

"Back at my mom's house, you couldn't wait to strip down and get naked. But now you're scared?" he asks, leaving the supplies on the counter to come over and help me, pushing my trembling hands aside and sliding his fingers down the bit of bare skin showing between the parted halves of my shirt.

Exhaling, I close my eyes and try to maintain some level of composure.

"I'm not scared," I say, which is true. "I mean, not of you."

Ranger pauses with his fingers on the lowest shirt buttons, hovering just above my belly button. I open my eyes to meet his sharp gaze, his leather and vanilla scent that perfect mix of bad boy and sweet thang. I want more of it.

"Of the cult?" he asks, and we both shudder at the mention. "We're going to get to the bottom of it, for you and Jenica both, I promise that." Ranger finishes unbuttoning my shirt and then pushes it off my shoulders. As soon as he sees the bright blue bra with the tiny pink bow that I'm wearing underneath, his cheeks heat up. "Fuck, that's adorable," he whispers, putting his hands on my sides and making me tremble with suppressed need.

This tension between us, it's been there from the very beginning, since I barreled into him at full speed, running from … Mr. Murphy with a knife. So weird. Anyway, it's finally coming to a peak, and I'm ready to tumble down the other side.

Ranger slides his hands up my sides, palming my breasts and making me shudder.

"The bra or the boobs?" I whisper, and a low,

throaty chuckle escapes from him.

"Both," he says, sliding his hands behind my back and undoing the clasp of the bra. As the cups fall forward, I reach up to cover my nipples, blushing furiously. Ranger sighs, but not in a bad way, in a longing sort of way. "You're so goddamn cute," he murmurs, turning my skirt around on my hips so that the zipper's in the front. "Even as a boy, with your dirty glasses, your floppy hair …" He unzips it and lets it fall to my feet, leaving my matching panties, garter belt, and knee-high socks exposed. "Jesus Christ."

"There you go with that word again," I choke out, but I'm finding it very hard to breathe.

"I've always liked cute things," he says, moving his hands down my sides, his gaze almost too intense to look at. And yet, I can't pull myself away either. "Soft, vulnerable things."

"I'm not soft or vulnerable," I huff as Ranger pushes the hair back from my face. His smile is lascivious, crafted in equal parts anger and lust. He's upset about what we've just discovered, but it's almost like looking at me soothes away some of that rage. I swallow a lump in my throat.

"It's okay to be soft and vulnerable sometimes. That's why I like that shit. It reminds me that I don't have to be on top of Mark Grandam, beating the shit out of him, to be happy. Life is balance, Chuck. Hard and soft. I'm too fucking hard sometimes; I need something to take the edge off."

He curls a single finger under the waistband of my panties, one on either side as I stand there motionless, transfixed with him, with the hard line of his jaw, the fullness of his lips, his gently slanted eyes, the dark blue color that reminds me of an endless galaxy.

"You put your panties on over your garter belt and thigh-highs," he remarks, his smile turning several levels away from cute and charming, and much closer to lascivious. "Only a naughty girl knows you put the panties on top, so you can take them off without removing the rest."

"I read it in a book somewhere!" I howl, but it's too late: Ranger is pushing them down my hips, dropping to his knees, so he can help me pull them over my shoes. After he got naked, he slipped his feet back into his boots, so at least we're both still wearing footwear.

He stands up and grabs the apron, tossing it over my head, and then turning me around to tie the back.

We've come full circle, haven't we? I think, remembering when I first stumbled onto his naked baking, how we almost had sex at his mother's house, how I couldn't forget this moment for the rest of my life, even if I tried.

"Let's make some dark chocolate avocado pudding," he says finally, and I swear to god, I've never heard a word come out as sexually as *pudding*. Pudding. Holy shit. My hands twist together in front of my apron as

Ranger moves back over to the counter, removing the lemon meringue pie from the oven and then grabbing a knife to cut the avocado in half. “Maybe some brownies, too.” He nods his chin in the direction of his discarded pants. “Check the back pocket—I think I have some weed in there. Wouldn’t say no to ‘special brownies’ right about now.”

I do as he asked, bending down to dig through the jeans when I realize that the room's gone completely silent.

Glancing over my shoulder, I see him staring at me with wide eyes and realize what I must look like.

Naked, wearing shiny shoes and thigh-highs, a frilly apron aaaaand … nothing else. The view must be, um, intense.

I barely have time to stand up and turn around before Ranger's there, pushing me up against the first island, his forehead to mine, his breathing harsh and ragged.

“Goddamn it, Chuck,” he murmurs, rubbing his face against mine. With a shudder, I close my eyes and grab onto the front of his apron. I'm not the only one trembling, apparently, and I can't get enough of this, of him.

“Oh, Ranger,” I whisper back, sliding my palms down the corded muscles in his arms. He responds with a shiver, putting his hands under my thighs and lifting me up to sit on the counter. Because of his height, and the height of the countertop, he's now settled comfortably between my thighs. I can feel the hardness beneath his apron, the same way I did that day in his mother's kitchen. "The twins and Church," I start, swallowing hard as Ranger grinds against that fervent heat between my legs, "they were afraid for you to find out my secret; they were afraid you'd turn me into your sister."

The laugh that escapes his throat is best described as bawdy, this dark sound that has my nipples tightening to hard points.

"Does it seem like I consider you a sister? Because if so, then I've either fucked up royally, or you've seen some kinky shit in your day."

I snort a laugh, but the sound is cut off when Ranger crushes his mouth to mine.

Holy mother of unicorns, I think, throwing my arms around his neck.

Ranger's mouth is a fervid, wild mess of heat and blind need, but underneath it all, in the careful way he touches me, in the frantic beat of his heart as he presses his body to mine … there's affection and tenderness there.

He likes me! My brain squeals as we gasp, coming up for air and looking right at each other.

"What did you say?" he asks me, as I blink stupidly back at him.

"Did I say that out loud?" I choke, flushing from

head to toe. "I did, didn't I? Oh my god, I'm so freaking embarrassed. Why am I always blurting out random shit?"

Ranger gives me a feral grin, capturing my lips with his, the faintest hint of lemons and sugar on his tongue.

"He does like you," Ranger growls out, sucking my lower lip between his teeth. "A *lot.* He's just hoping you like him back."

"I love him," I blurt, and then we both pause.

Swear to the God of Dark-Holes-For-Embarrassed-People-to-Crawl-Into, I better not have just messed this all up. But instead of pulling away from me or acting like I've just committed the worst cardinal sin known to man, Ranger takes it in stride.

"I love you, too, Chuck," he replies easily, the edge of his mouth turning up in a genuine smile. "I have since the moment you asked for that hug at the Valentine's Day dance." Ranger cups the back of my head, kissing me long and deep, his tongue swirling against mine, and then he pulls back to put his forehead to mine. "Now. Get off this counter and turn around. I'm slapping that ass, and fucking you in that apron—just like I promised. We'll finish our baking afterward."

My heart is beating so fast, my body flooded with happy hormones, pushing away the fear of the … whatever that stupid cult is calling themselves. Of Jenica's last sad, soft memories. I've got her brother now, and I'm not going to let him get hurt again.

Ranger pulls me off the counter and spins me around, putting his hands on my hips and then kissing his way down the side of my neck, leaving a trail of goose bumps in his wake. When he lets go of me briefly to retrieve the bag of flour from the island, my jaw drops open.

"I thought you were kidding," I whisper as he dumps some out on the counter and then powders his hands in white.

"I want to see all the places I've touched you." His voice is dark with a possessiveness that I'm not sure I'm going to like … until he touches me again, putting white handprints on my hips. When he pulls back and cracks me across the ass with his palm, my breath hitches, and my fingers curl against the surface of the stone countertop. "Jesus, I've been wanting to do that for an entire year. You're such a brat, Chuck. You needed a good spanking."

"Hey, I resent—" I start, but then he spanks me again, and I shiver, goose bumps breaking out across my skin. *We're on campus, in a classroom, naked.* That thought doesn't deter me from my course of action though. No way, no how. It only makes me want it *more.*

My skin tingles as Ranger runs a fingertip over the sweetly sore spot, sliding his palms up my body to cup my breasts through the front of the apron. He fondles them with a firm but gentle grip, teasing the nipples through the fabric.

Another crack on my ass surprises me, but I like it, shocking my own preconceived inhibitions.

Ranger pauses briefly to slip the condom on as I close my eyes, trying to control the wild, jittery feeling in my stomach. When he slips one palm around to lie flat against my belly, and whispers in my ear, I groan.

"Are you ready for this, Charlotte?" he asks, and the sound of my real name on his lips undoes everything inside of me. I've barely got the strength to nod, a moan falling from my lips as Ranger presses the hard tip of his cock to my opening. There's a brief moment there where he stills, and the only sound in the room is the synchronous rhythm of our breathing.

Ranger slides himself slowly inside of me, groaning under his breath as he fills me up with his body. "Holy fuck."

"Good?" I ask, because for some reason, I think that makes me seem cool. In reality, I was never that good at being 'cool'. No, that was Monica's thing. Actually, I preferred being nerdy, weird, blurt-y Chuck the Micropenis. With an exhale, I relax into Ranger's touch and close my eyes, changing the narrative. "Your touch makes me feel like I'm on fire."

"Beyond good, Charlotte," he whispers, and then he begins to move, the slickness of my own body making it easy for him to thrust, to create this beautiful friction between us that builds pleasure in my belly like a slow-burning fire. With each movement of his hips, the embers burn, and the flames climb higher. Just when I think I'm going to collapse and fall right over that edge, Ranger slows and bites the curve of my ear. "I want to see your face when you come."

"You're not serious," I choke out, because apparently, even in the throes of passion, I'm a dork. He pulls away from me and then gently turns me around by the shoulders, cupping my face in his warm hands.

"Deadly," he murmurs back, taking my mouth with his, his control a heady sort of aphrodisiac that I never expected to like. Vaguely, I remember that conversation I had with Ranger, back when Spencer didn't know my secret and thought his friend was topping me. I'd argued I could've easily been the one in charge. But nah. Nope. I don't think so. "Come here."

He lifts me up and onto the edge of the counter, pushing me back and then climbing up after me. My ass leaves cheek prints in the flour as I scoot back, throwing my arms around his neck again as Ranger kisses me down to the cold surface of the countertop.

This is most definitely not *sanitary,* I think, but then I also don't care. There's something about fearing for your life that really puts that kick in your step, makes you realize that tomorrow isn't guaranteed, and that it's okay to be happy *now.*

When he shoves my apron up, I gasp, our eyes

meeting as he thrusts into me again.

“Much better,” he murmurs with a smile, and I groan, closing my gaze against the intensity in his. “Oh come now, Chuck. We've been through too much to pretend this isn't happening.” He rubs a thumb across my brows, and I open my eyes again. We're both still wearing our aprons, our shoes, a whole hell of a lot of flour. “Here.” Ranger takes my hand and puts it between us, right over my clit, smirking at me as he does it.

He kisses me before I can chastise him, moving deep and slow, pushing me closer and closer to a climax. When it hits, it's a shock to my system, a wave of fire that burns through my inhibitions. My nails dig into Ranger's upper back, drawing blood, and my body locks down on his. A scream starts up that I can't control, one that he cuts short by kissing me fiercely and coming hard, his muscular body shuddering above mine.

Ranger takes off the condom, ties it up, and then slips it into his apron pocket to deal with later before lying down beside me, right on top of the stone counter. He throws one arm across his brow as we pant and stare up at the filigreed ceiling tiles above our heads. Does he even realize how lucky we are, how beautiful this place is? The ceilings at Santa Cruz High are drop ceilings, with ugly stained tiles and metal tracks.

"Holy fuck," Ranger murmurs, turning his head to glance over at me. He grins and I flush, still breathing hard, but I am proud of myself for managing to meet his gaze. "That was amazing."

"You think so?" I ask, and he raises a dark brow at me.

"You don't? Please tell me I'm better than Spencer, at the very least."

"Oh my god," I groan, rolling onto my side and putting my face on his chest, enjoying the wild rhythm of his heartbeat. "You guys are the worst, you know that?"

Ranger slides an arm underneath me and tucks me against his side, like he might very well hold me there forever, keep me safe from the monsters trolling our school.

"We really are, aren't we?" he murmurs, turning to press a kiss to my forehead. I realize then that he's truly putting himself out there, in a way he never has before. He's not letting the pain of Jenica hold him back anymore.

With a smile, I nuzzle into him, and then surreptitiously lean forward to take a little peek at his dick.

"What's that?" I ask, pointing at a small scar along one side of his shaft. He groans and slaps his right hand over his face in a rare moment of true chagrin.

"Candy making," he mumbles, "now can we change

the subject?"

I sit up a bit, covered in flour, my ass smarting, my lady parts—and by lady parts, I mean my vagina and clitoris, don't be a prude—singing, and give him a look. Candy making involves a lot of hot, boiling liquids by the way.

"Wait, wait, wait. You naked-baked some candy and burned your junk?" I ask, and then I howl with laughter. Ranger sneers at me, wrapping his arms around my body and pulling me on top of him.

The laughter only lasts so long as it takes him to kiss me.

CHAPTER TEN

"Okay," Tobias starts, standing shirtless and in low-slung sweats that do nothing to help me concentrate. "Arms up, let's try again."

I bend over in my PE outfit, panting and choking on my own saliva as Mark Grandam scowls at me from the other side of the gym. As promised, Archie's got me in PE with all the other guys, many of whom were, um, not super thrilled that I was wandering around the locker room during the physical fitness test. It's like, as excited as they were to see a girl in their midst, they all still hate me. Which, maybe, is a good thing? Like, they hated me as a guy, and they hate me as a girl, too? Equal opportunity dislike. Heh.

"Training that tit-less stick figure to fight, what a

joke," Mark guffaws, sauntering across the gym like he owns the place.

"Sexist pig," I growl back at him, standing up and swiping at my brow. The twins are both in PE with me, and every Wednesday and Friday, when we have self-defense training, they take turns going over some of their MMA—mixed martial arts—moves with me. Just in case. You can never be too prepared, right? Especially not when being chased by a cult.

A cult ... God. We're all still having trouble processing the information that Mr. Murphy and, posthumously, Jenica gave us.

"Sexist? Selena is ten times the woman you are," Mark growls, his face twisted up in disgust as Tobias' nostrils flare, and I get the feeling we're coming close to another brawl between the boys. "*She* could be trained. You? You're just a weak, little peasant that stumbled into a school where you don't belong."

"Why don't you stumble into this fist?" Micah says from my other side, eyeing Mr. Tribble (yes, that same PE teacher who unknowingly shoved me into the locker room that day, and who's apologized to me about fifty times for the incident) to make sure he's not looking. "You think you can insult our girl on a regular basis and walk? You only think Ranger turned your ugly face into a pulp. It could've been so much worse."

"Whatever, McCarthy," Mark sneers, backing up to rejoin his friends on a separate training mat. The twins watch him go and then exchange a look over my head.

"What?" I ask, looking between them and trying to pretend like I'm not so exhausted that I'm seeing stars in my vision. True story though. But I really need an exercise routine in Connecticut to replace all the surfing I did back home. Seemed like learning how to fight from the twins could kill two birds with one stone. Err, considering the headless bird we found on the day of Eugene's memorial, maybe that wasn't the best metaphor.

"He's such a pill," they say in unison, with matching sighs and shrugging shoulders. It's quite the performance. *'Sometimes I want to be my own person for five fucking seconds.'* I remember Micah's words from the onsen and tug on a blond ringlet in thought. "I just hope he's guilty, so I can beat him up," he adds, while Tobias stays silent.

Coach Tribble blows a whistle, signaling the end of class, and Tobias gives me a look.

"We're coming with you to change," he says, and I groan. Since there's no girls' locker room just yet, I've been changing in the bathrooms just outside the gym. The thing is, I kind of need the twins to watch over me, so the killers can't catch me with my pants down—literally speaking.

After we're back in our uniforms, we head to lunch with the rest of the Student Council.

Ranger pulls me onto his lap as soon as we get

there, and Spencer rolls his eyes.

"I know you two just did it for the first time, but come on, the lovesick puppy dog eyes are killing me."

"Jealous?" Ranger taunts, tapping the toe of his combat boot against the floor and watching the lunch crowd with narrowed eyes. "Because I'm pretty sure that I saw Charlotte sneaking out of our room on my way back from the shower."

My cheeks flush, but even though my mouth's hanging open like some sort of total derp, I have no response to that. It's true. Spencer and I did sneak some private time in this morning, but, like, we only did hand stuff. Although hand stuff is sex. If anyone tells you otherwise, they're either ignorant, delusional, or else they subscribe to a hetero-normative view of sex that's antiquated and weird.

Ahem.

"It's so weird that you guys are banging now," Tobias remarks, looking at the two of us like we're alien creatures with purple tentacles coming out of our crotches. He watches that kind of porn sometimes. Trust me, I know, I've seen it. I played the twin game and stole *their* key the other day, snuck back into the room to surprise Tobias when Micah was with Church, and caught him masturbating. That was fun.

"Maybe it's weirder that they're *not* banging," Micah adds, pointing between me and Church. My eyes go wide as Spencer and the twins chuckle a bit. I have to say, they've really embraced this whole group dating thing. Maybe it's because they were so close before I ever stumbled into their family? No matter what, I won't let myself break any of these bonds.

"We're waiting until marriage," Church deadpans, putting his chin in his hand, long, elegant fingers curled against the side of his face. I laugh, but only a little, because this is the second time he's made that joke, so … Anyway, he's not looking at us, staring across the sea of students like he's ruminating on something important. After a moment, he turns those amber eyes back in our direction, his honeyed hair smooth and straight, framing that elegant, aristocratic face of his. "I had a thought," he muses, changing the subject in an instant. He's a natural born leader, this one. "Why do you think the killers leave us alone for such long periods of time? Hmm? There are plenty of opportunities to strike and yet, it's been weeks since school started and there's no sign of them."

"Because they're fucking cowards is what," Spencer snorts, swinging his gray shoes up onto the bench and leaning back like he owns the place. He sort of does, in a way. Nobody gets weed on campus without going through him. That's why I'm not overly concerned with the upcoming debates. The boys are going to kill it, I just know they are.

Then again, they don't know what's coming.

None of us do.

"Mm, no, I don't think that's it," Church says, turning his attention back to us. "They're very clearly willing to attack in public places—like they did to Chuck in California. That, and they've obviously got an in with the police. So why? I've been asking myself that since we were at the onsen."

"And did you come up with an answer?" Ranger asks, squeezing me close and putting his face up against the side of my neck in just such a way that my toes curl inside my shiny new shoes. Dad sent over several boxes of Mary Janes with Adamson Academy logos on the heel. I'm not a huge fan of them, but they look better with my new uniform than the brown loafers I had on before.

"I did," Church says, flashing one of his high wattage smiles. "It's because at least one of them doesn't go to this school."

My brows go up as I scoot my lunch tray closer to the edge of the table, so I can reach my lemonade. They make lovely strawberry lemonade here, with little umbrellas, glass straws, and bits of candied fruit on the side of the glass. I'm also aware that Ranger is most definitely *not* letting me off of his lap, so I better get used to sitting here while I eat.

"Meaning?" the twins ask in unison, picking up a banana each and peeling it. They both immediately go for blow job miming jokes and I roll my eyes.

"Meaning that I think we should check out Jeff

Rabot, and the other holdouts in Nutmeg." Church pauses as the doors to the cafeteria swing open and several girls walk in.

The entire cafeteria goes quiet as Aster clasps her hands together in front of her champagne and honey colored plaid skirt and smiles at everyone.

"Hello boys," she says, beaming like crazy, her frizzy orange hair fluffed up around her face. "I hear today's the assembly where students announce they're running for Student Council?"

"Oh, shit," Spencer murmurs, paling a bit and reaching up with a single finger to loosen his tie.

Oh, shit. Oh, shit is right.

Because the only thing that could possibly convince the students to vote out their only party drug supplier … is a hot chick in a skirt.

"They can't do this," Spencer grumbles as we move through the dark shadows of the woods together. It's late, not obscenely late, but late enough that we're most definitely going to be missed during the nightly room checks. Nathan's going to be pissed. Micah suggested we bribe him, but Church just shook his head and the case was closed.

I feel like he knows something.

I feel like he's always known something.

Zipping up my sparkly hoodie with the rainbow on it (a gift from Ranger), I turn back to the trail we're following—one of Spence's secret trails, courtesy of his brother Jack—that lets out on the road that curves down the mountain, away from Adamson and toward the tiny little nothing town of Nutmeg, Connecticut.

"They can, and they are," Church muses, hands in his pockets, a black knit sweater on his lithe form, paired with jeans that probably cost more than my dad's wedding band—the one he's still wearing, by the way. Despite the divorce, despite the fact that Mom's dating Mr. Dave. "It's going to be tough, with the three girls running against us."

"And they put Mark on the ballot? I mean, that's just fucking insane," Spencer groans, picking up a stick and swinging it around like a sword. "Mark Grandam for secretary. The dude can't spell the word *idiot* to save his life. And then adding Gareth in as treasurer? What a joke. He can't even count the number of balls he doesn't have."

"Who's Gareth?" I ask, picking the long, reaching limb of a blackberry tendril off my black skinny jeans and then shrieking as Ranger lifts me up and carries me admirably through a mud puddle, not giving a shit about soaking his black combat boots. He sets me down on the other side, but not before pausing to look into my eyes.

"Gag, much?" Spencer asks as a stray shaft of moonlight catches on his silver hair. But he doesn't sound that mad about it, not anymore. He really reined in the jealousy after our talk, and the effort isn't lost on me. "Gareth McConnell," he continues, tossing his stick aside and then lighting up a cigarette before handing one over to Ranger. "Pretty sure he's related to Mark's girlfriend, What's-Her-Name."

"Selena?" I ask, raising a brow as we come out the other side of the trees and onto the road where the sleek, black length of the limo is waiting.

"Gareth used to sell weed with Eugene and Spencer," the twins supply, each one pointing across their chest at Spencer. "But he can't count with worth shit, and we're pretty sure he skims cash off the top."

"Either way, he's a terrible choice for treasurer." Spencer kicks a rock and then tucks his hands into the pockets of his blue jeans, glancing back at us with that fierce turquoise stare of his. "Why am I the only one freaking out about this? Were you guys at the same debate I was today?"

"I could really use the Student Council job for my college applications," I admit. I actually took the twins' advice and applied to Bornstead University in Colorado. There's not a snowball's chance in hell that I'm getting in, but at least I can say I tried. My second choice was UC Santa Cruz because I figured at least I'd be close to the twins' house. I shake my head and push away thoughts of college. It's still fall for crap's sake; I have months to worry about what life will be like when Adamson is over.

"We killed it with our speeches today," Micah mumbles, ruffling up his red-orange hair in a move that's adorably similar to his best friend.

"And yet nobody was listening to the actual words coming out of our mouths." Tobias picks an orange leaf off a low-hanging tree limb, tucking it behind my ear as Ranger opens the door and lets me slide into the backseat of the limo first. He's right though. Nobody was listening to the boys talk because they were all too busy checking out the new girls, laughing at Mark's stupid ass jokes, and gossiping about the official announcement my father made just before the debates started.

Integrated student body. Mixed gender population.

He looked pointedly in my direction at least three times during the speech, too.

"It's our fault," Spencer says, climbing over a grumbling Ranger first before he scales my lap and flops into the seat on my left side. "We took the only girl in school for our own, so she doesn't have as much sway over the student body as she should."

I snort, but that's pretty much the gist of it. During my first week in female form, the boys were a tad … vicious. How stupid is it that I like their ridiculous caveman behavior?

"And thus, we are all animals," I say aloud, and everyone turns to stare at me as I cough and choke into my hand and pretend I've got some level of social decorum. Church smiles, one of his big bright smiles that I realize was never actually fake, and then taps his knuckles against the glass of the window.

"Does it strike anyone as odd that Jason Lambert was murdered, and then here Aster Hayes is, campaigning against me?"

"Why not just kill *you* then?" Ranger asks, tapping his combat boot against the floor, blue-black hair razored and falling in glorious shimmering strands around his face. He notices me looking and then smirks in my direction, sapphire eyes bright. My body reacts instantly, and I have to suck in a sharp breath to keep my cool. "If this cult stuff is all true, and Jenica was killed because of it, then why not just off you? Or me?"

Spencer takes my hand, curling his fingers through mine, and sending goose bumps up along my skin. When I glance his way, at his turquoise eyes and silver hair, I feel my body react in the same way it did when I looked at Ranger. Yep. Yep. In love with every boy. My cheeks and ears heat up, and Spence raises a questioning brow.

"Maybe they tried, you know, when we were in the tunnels?" I suggest, looking away from him and back toward Church and the twins. The McCarthy boys are paying attention, but they're also absently entertaining a private thumb war together as well. Looks like Micah might win. "They lured us down there and locked us in, didn't they?"

"Mm," Church muses, but doesn't reply. Either he doesn't think I'm following the right train of thought, or else he doesn't know.

And that scares me.

Because if Church can't figure it out, then nobody can.

About an hour later, we're emerging from the darkness of the woods, the faint twinkle of the town's lights in the distance. Church rolls the window down between us and the driver and requests that he stop where we're at, leaving us with a good ten-minute walk to hit the first stop sign that leads into town.

"We're going full sleuth, huh?" Tobias asks, stretching his arms above his head and surveying the quiet town of Nutmeg with eyes that look like emeralds under the glow of the moon. "Like, true gumshoeing? I feel like we need hats, and little pipes, and then every time I make a brilliant deduction, I'll consult with dear Watson over here—"

"Bro, if either of us is Sherlock Holmes, it's me. And *you're* Watson," Micah announces, tucking his hands into the front pocket of his Adamson Academy hoodie. Tobias is wearing the same hoodie, just in navy blue instead of champagne.

"Bullshit. You might win at drag racing, but my grades are better than yours by far. Plus, I'm older by eight minutes. That makes *me* the detective, and you the sidekick."

"Remind me how many fights you've won versus how many *I've* won. I'm superior in the ring, and I'm better at sex. Even Charlotte thinks that. *I'm* Sherlock."

I roll my eyes, because they both know I think they're equally good at, um, well, you know. *Sex, Charlotte, say sex. If you're mature enough to do it, you're mature enough to say it.*

"Neither of you is Sherlock," Church says, pausing on the corner of Main and Adamson (yep, the road that goes up the hill to the school is that cleverly named), and looking down the long length of empty sidewalk at the pools of light cast by the streetlamps, ringed in ominous shadows. "I am Sherlock. Ranger is Watson. You'd both be lucky to be our faithful bloodhounds. Now shush."

Church pulls out a set of keys from his pocket and leads us across the street, and down a narrow alley behind the row of businesses. I recognize the bookstore right away, from the cute little bistro sets sitting on the outdoor patio. The weather's a bit too cold to sit outside right now, so they're chained together in stacks and pushed under the overhang. The lights, however, are still on.

I don't see anyone, but my heart is racing like crazy,

and my palms are soaked in sweat. I'm a terrible sleuth, that much I can promise.

"Come on," Church says, unlocking the back door to the business just next door. On the other side, there's a parking lot and the side entrance to the Jaw Flapper, the same one the twins dragged me through last year. He ushers us all in and locks the door behind us, his blond hair bright, even in the dark.

"What's the plan?" Spencer asks, picking up a glass clown and shuddering as he sets it aside. "No wonder I've never been in this store before," he adds under his breath.

"This is Closet and Trunk Antiques," Church says, not bothering to whisper, but not raising his voice either. "My father bought my mother's engagement ring from here when they were seventeen." He looks around, using what little light is trickling in from the orange streetlamp outside to see. Subconsciously, I rub at the ring on my finger and Church smiles. "And yes, that one, too."

"You bought a used ring?" Spencer asks, giving Church a look. "You? Of all people? How much was it?"

"In some instances—*rare* instances—tradition is more important than price." Church moves away from the door and toward a set of stairs with a chain across them, and an *Employees Only* sign dangling in the middle. He moves it out of his way as I stand there, short of breath, bathed in the shadows of the antique shop. It has a bit of a musty smell, but it's got a hominess to it that I like.

"I've never been in an antique shop at night," I whisper, even though it's obvious that we don't need to be quite so silent. "It's equal parts creepy and cool."

"You're only saying that because you don't know about the ghosts that haunt this place," the twins whisper, coming up on either side of me and parking their elbows on my shoulders.

"There's no such thing as ghosts," I snort, but they exchange a look over my head and then shrug.

"Only people who are truly afraid of ghosts say such things," Tobias continues, pretending to look around the looming shapes of old wardrobes and ancient rocking chairs, like he's on the lookout for something.

"Jenica wasn't the only person to be murdered in this town," Micah whispers, after a quick glance over his shoulder to see that Ranger's fully climbed the stairs after Church. "Back around that same time, there was a foreign exchange student who was found dead in the local park. There were no signs of trauma, no evidence of a struggle, but he was clutching the key to this very store, the store where he'd been working part-time."

"Okay, that's enough of that crap," Spencer says, yanking me away from the snickering redheaded demon assholes. "There was a kid who died in the park, but the coroner determined it was insulin shock. Ignore them." He takes my hand in his, squeezing it hard, and then tugs me up the steps to an office area. Antiques clutter this portion of the store, too, but it's clean and well-kempt. A stray shaft of moonlight highlights a ledger that's been carefully scribbled in. Looks like this store is in the red—big time. Maybe whoever runs it should try using a computer? I bite my lip and glance at the open door that leads to yet another set of stairs, these ones narrow and steep and most definitely not up to modern code requirements.

Spencer and I continue up, with the twins close behind us, and come up to an attic room with windows on all sides. We can see the whole of Main Street from the front window, the flat roof of the sporting goods store on one side, and the three-story building on the other that houses the bookstore. As far as I could tell, only the first floor is part of the business.

In the center of the room, there's a miniature replica of the antique store, complete with little people, furniture, and plants. The detail is absolutely stunning, even if it is hard to see in the dark.

"The woman who owned this store before my parents bought it—and who still runs it—made this with her miniatures club almost forty years ago." Church leans over beside me and peers into the top floor, looking at an exact miniature replica of the room where we're standing.

"She did a damn good job," I murmur, thinking of the numbers in red ink in the ledger. "Maybe a better job than she does running the business. Do your parents know how far in the red this place is?"

Church smiles at me again, an expression that's becoming a lot more frequent, and then stands up.

"I'll tell you the story later, Chuck. For now, we're collecting information."

"Are we just here on the off-chance that something happens, or do you have something specific in mind that you're looking for?" Ranger asks, just before the lights next door go on, flooding the second floor of the bookstore. From here, I can see a round table set with chairs, a kitchenette, and a fireplace on the far wall that's not currently lit.

Jeffrey Rabot walks in and sweeps over to it, using a Duraflame log to get a roaring fire going.

"There are only five businesses left in Nutmeg that my parents don't own," Church says as the boys and I fan out along the length of the window. Hopefully, it's too bright in there and too dark up here that he won't see us if he looks, but I still get that creepy feeling on the back of my neck, like somebody's watching me. "The business owners meet up with Jeff here, every week, like clockwork."

"So we're just hoping they do something suspicious?" Spencer asks, glancing in Church's direction. "Or did you plant some fancy recording equipment in there so we can actually hear what they're saying?"

Church's amber eyes watch the scene below as Jeff sets up what looks like a pretty nice charcuterie board for his guests.

"I did inquire if my parents' security team might be able to get in there and set up some surveillance."

"And?" Ranger prompts, waiting for the other shoe to drop. Because there always is one, when it comes to Church Montague.

"They couldn't get in. There's a team watching Jeff's business. All the businesses, actually, that my parents don't own. Now tell me: how do five struggling business owners afford a security team that rivals my parents'?" He turns toward Ranger, and even though I can't see his face, I can hear the coldness in his voice. "They don't. If there's a cult at Adamson, then it's run by some of the more powerful families, otherwise my parents would know all about it." He turns back to the window as Jeff opens the door and welcomes in a few new faces that I know I've never seen before. "And why on *earth* would these people refuse the overblown prices my parents have offered them for their businesses? Jeff's whiny complaints about not wanting to sell the store are bullshit. He hates it here, and he always has."

"So you think the business owners are part of the cult?" I ask, but Church doesn't respond, his face tightening in frustration. He's smart, but he hasn't figured that part of the equation out just yet.

“What about Jack?” Church turns to look at Spencer next, that cold gaze of his fixed firmly in place. One day, he's going to be too powerful for his own good. That is, unless he has someone around to keep him humble.

I shift in place and run my finger across the surface of the ring—my new nervous tick.

“You know how hard he is to track down, but I'll find him. He's always in town for the Halloween party.”

Church nods, and I feel a bit of FOMO coming on. Last year, I didn't get to leave campus on Halloween, while the guys were very clearly at this fabled party. This year, I better find myself with an invitation.

After a while, I get bored and wander over to the miniature with Spencer and the twins while Ranger and Church keep vigil over the meeting downstairs. Doesn't look like much of a business meeting to me. Mostly, Jeff and his guests of honor laugh and talk and eat, and then they break out a game of charades. Like who even plays charades anymore?

“This thing is pretty cool,” Spencer says, playing with the movable front door, and then pointing at a seam along the roof. “Does it open?”

“It does,” Church replies absently, a hint of frustration in his voice as he glances over his shoulder.

"Just don't break it or Magdalene will run you through with her cane. She once beat my sister for breaking an antique cat statue from the 1930s. Trust me: she isn't afraid of anyone."

Spencer snorts, but carefully grabs either side of the miniature, opening it like a dollhouse and giving us a much better view of all the rooms inside.

"Look," he says, pointing at the bookcase downstairs. "It's got your favorite book: *Moby Dick.*"

"Funny," I snort, making a face at him, and then reaching in to pull one of the tiny books off the shelf. That's how detailed this thing is; the books actually come off the shelf and open up. Inside, there are tiny pages with little scribbles of faux writing. Next to *Moby Dick,* we've got *Alice's Adventures in Wonderland, The Wonderful Wizard of Oz,* and even a copy of *A Study in Scarlet*—the first Sherlock Holmes book. When I reach to grab that one, I accidentally knock the bookcase loose from the wall.

"Nice one, Chuck-let," Spencer says as I try to put it back in place, only to see that it's actually connected to the wall with a hinge. Pushing it with my finger, I open it wider and find a faux doorway behind it, painted to look like a dark room with a set of steps.

Spence and I exchange a look.

"Hey guys, you might want to come see this …" he starts, just as Jeff says goodbye to the last of his friends, and the lights on the second floor flick off.

"Do you think everything about this miniature is true to life?" Ranger asks as soon as he sees what we're looking at, but Church just purses his lips and heads for the stairs, taking them two at a time. With his long legs, it's a struggle to catch up, but when we do, we find him sliding his hands along the side of the bookcase. A moment later, there's a click, and the twins move forward to help Church drag it open.

Behind the bookcase, there's another door, but this one's locked.

Church and Ranger exchange a look before the latter pulls the gold key out from inside his shirt, tries the lock, and gets the satisfying click of tumblers in return.

The door swings open.

"Bingo," Church says as we gaze down a set of stone steps and into a sea of blackness.

CHAPTER ELEVEN

The other girls aren't supposed to move in until next quarter, but that doesn't stop them from visiting the campus on the weekends to work on their campaign for the Student Council—especially Aster. Or hell, maybe she's just here to screw Mark under Selena's nose? What do I know?

"Do you really think Mark's cheating on Selena with Aster?" I ask Spencer, adjusting the floppy packer penis in my panties, and then turning around to grin at him. It makes a nice bulge under my skirt, and I chuckle. We're supposed to be working on our Halloween costumes, and I figured it'd be fun to do something with the infamous dick aka Ranger's 'prosthetic'. Mom still doesn't get the joke. The other day, when she called me, she inquired about his 'accident' yet again.

"I'm supposed to answer that question when you've got your hand down your panties?" Spencer asks, lounging on my bed and tossing a Hacky sack up in the air. He catches it as it comes down and then sits up, tossing his tie over one shoulder. The way his eyes take me in reminds me of that day when he walked in and saw me ass-up and bent over, trying to dig my phone out from behind the bed.

He's never looked at me any different—boy or girl, or after dating his friends.

"Um, yes." I put my hands on my hips and give them a little twist, swishing the skirt around my thighs and flopping the penis around with the motion. "Yes, you are."

"Well, then," he says, standing up from the bed, the scent of his Kenneth Cole Black fragrance filling the room and making my heart flutter. "The answer is hell fucking yes. You've never been to a party with Mark, have you?" I shake my head as Spencer moves a little closer, reaching down to cup my faux dick under my skirt and giving it a squeeze. "He'll sleep with any girl that'll have him. No wonder Selena's all up his ass."

Spencer leans down and brushes his lips to mine, sliding his hand up and under the waistband of my panties. Instead of going straight for the wet heat between my thighs, he strokes the packer penis like it's really a part of me.

"Church might be back soon," I murmur, loving the way Spencer's fingers feel as he slides them across the side of my neck and into my hair. I look up and find him smirking down at me, this cocksure little grin that reminds me why I fell for him in the first place. He acts like a total badass, but really, underneath it all, he's got the best heart.

"So?"

"So he might not like walking in to see you nailing his fiancée in his room."

Spencer chuckles, and removes his hand from my panties, dragging me over to the bed and pulling me down on top of it. He kisses me like he can't get enough, sliding his hands up and under my skirt to cup my ass. It's like, my ultimate naughty fantasy, to be fucked in my schoolgirl uniform. But we haven't exactly gotten there yet.

Just when I think we might, the sound of the door being unlocked causes Spencer to scramble off of me, cursing and grabbing a pillow to hide the erection in his slacks. He most definitely does not need a packer penis to pass the grab test.

Church walks in with the other boys on his heels and pauses, cocking his head to one side, an iced coffee in one hand and a long poster tube in the other.

"Are we interrupting something?" he asks, but both Spencer's and my sputtered nonsense that they aren't proves that they most definitely are.

Ranger rolls his eyes and takes a seat on Church's bed, crossing his arms over his chest and meeting my eyes from across the room. The twins aren't shy about stealing some of Church's canned coffee drinks from the mini-fridge and then making themselves comfortable on my bed.

"What's in the tube?" I ask as Church hands it over to Ranger, sucking on the straw of his coffee while his friend pulls out the papers inside.

Maps? I lean closer to get a better look and find blueprints instead. And not just of Adamson, but of the entire town of Nutmeg, too.

"With these, we can see where, exactly, the tunnels go," Church says, watching as Ranger unfolds the large sheets of paper on his friend's bed, weighing the corners down with the stack of mangas—Japanese anime comics—from Church's side table. "When they built Nutmeg, and expanded the Adamson campus, they were concerned about the possibility of the tunnels collapsing, so they mapped it all out."

"This is where we went in originally," Ranger says, pointing at a spot on the map and then tracing down the long length of tunnel. "And it's no wonder we couldn't find another way out. This one runs for miles before it branches off or offers up another exit. But look at this." Ranger points out the antique store on the map, and then draws his finger along the length of tunnel underneath it. The bookcase entrance we found leads not only to the entire underground network, but also to several of the other stores.

The stores that the Montagues *don't* own.

The only exception is the antique store itself.

"Church's family bought the antique store from my parents who bought it from Magdalene," Ranger explains. "My mom got it in the divorce, and I remember my dad was pissed." He looks up, nostrils flared, mouth tight. "And why would he be? Over a tiny little antique store run by an old lady? Mom sold it to the Montagues not long after that."

"So that means the businesses are involved with the cult somehow?" I ask, and Ranger exhales sharply through his nose.

"Maybe. You know what else it means? That my dad knows more than he should." Ranger pushes the maps aside and then reaches up to grab at the front of his shirt, clutching the keys through the fabric. "He wanted me to come see him during fall break. I just might."

"Not alone, you won't," Tobias says, sitting up behind me and crushing the coffee can in his hand. "If you go, we're coming."

Ranger grunts, but he doesn't argue, looking up and out the window at the sudden rainstorm.

"Where'd you get those things anyway?" Micah asks, reaching up a hand to play with my bra strap through my shirt. I slap his hand away, but we're both grinning like idiots.

"The library," Church says, and then very quickly adds, "the one in town. We went to the school library, but Mr. Dave wasn't exactly forthcoming." He pauses for a moment like he's thinking about something, and then shakes his head. "I suppose he wasn't exactly forthcoming with anyone about the stabbing either, so there's no surprise there."

"Did we mention there are other missing yearbooks?" Ranger says, kicking off his boots and leaning back into Church's pillows. They're all silky, luxe, and soft—a feathered pillow here, a satin pillow there, one with thick black faux fur. I've often wondered what it would feel like if Church were to lift me up there and lay my head down on one before he kissed me. "No pattern to the missing years, just one here or there."

"I'd say I could talk to Dad about it, but he's been even more close-mouthed than usual since that little confession of his." I sigh and reach up to push some curls away from my forehead. "I still think he's involved with Mr. Murphy and Mr. Dave. I just *hinted* the word cult when I stopped by yesterday, and he slammed his office door in my face."

"It would make sense," Spencer says, picking at a seam on my comforter. "The three of them working together to protect Chuck-let behind the scenes." He looks up, the skin around his mouth tight with worry.

"That's what I think Jack was doing, when he came to get me at the cabin—he was protecting me."

"Yeah?" Ranger retorts, and I feel the tension between them climb sky-high in an instant. There's quite a bit of contention about Jack, and his role in Jenica's death. Not that I blame either of them for the position they're taking, it's just hard to see them fight with each other. "Well then, if he's so damn worried about you, why show up out of the blue on campus, disappear at the slightest hint of contention, and then ghost the fuck out of you afterwards?"

"Jack isn't a bad person," Spencer says, and there's this sad but determined note in his voice that reminds me of that day in the hallway when he looked at me like I was a liar. Thinking about it makes my heart hurt, so I push the thought away. "He's just a coward. It's pretty clear to me that he's scared of this … Fellowship of the Divine or whatever the crap they're calling themselves. Rightfully so, I might add, considering the body count."

"Let's not grace them with a proper name," I suggest, trying to break the tension. "Let's call them … Fellowship of the Dirty Toilet Brushes."

"What *is* it with you and toilet brushes?" Micah asks, getting an elbow in the chest from me as payback. "Let's call them the Dick Cheese Initiates."

"Dude, I just ate," Tobias says, yanking on a tuft of his brother's hair. "Now be serious for a second here:

are we going back down in those tunnels?"

"No!" I shout at the same that Church says, "yes."

He looks over at me and smiles slightly.

"*You're* not, but I am."

"Have you lost your mind?!" Spencer snaps, dropping the pillow he was using to hide his erection and rising to his feet. "I know I wasn't there, but like, didn't you guys learn your lesson the first time? You all could've died."

"Send one of your parents' security lackeys down there to investigate," Ranger says, and Church sighs, like he expected this sort of response from his friends.

"This cult," he says, crossing his arms over his chest and finally sitting down on the end of his bed. "They're clearly made up of powerful families, families with resources that match my own."

"Nobody's resources match your own," the twins murmur behind me, but only loud enough so that I can hear.

"This is a game, can't you see it?" He looks up with this fierce determination burning in his amber gaze. "The people who are after Charlotte are young, inexperienced. They're not hitmen, they're not professionals. Think about it: the school board's denied our requests for extra security. Why? Because they *want* this to be challenge. Jenica wrote it down plain as day: this is an initiation." Church's nostrils flare, and I realize then just how fucking smart he really is. He could run circles around the rest of us if he wanted to. "Even that quote about the foxes, the one from the Bible: *Catch for us the foxes, the little foxes that plunder the vineyards; for our vineyards are in blossom.* It's a metaphor." He gestures in my direction. "Jenica, Eugene, Jason … Charlotte. They're the foxes. The vineyard is the interests of the cult—whatever those might be." Church stands up suddenly, clearly incensed over his speech, obviously frustrated that he hasn't solved the entire murder-mystery on his own. He is *way* too hard on himself. "These families, they've sent their own in to do the deed, and I intend on meeting that challenge." He moves over to the door, hand resting on the knob, and glances back, just once. "And if my parents taught me anything, it's to protect the ones you love—no matter what the cost."

Church disappears into the hallway and slams the door behind him.

I stand up to go after him, forgetting that I've still got the packer penis in my underwear. It flops out onto the floor and bounces over next to Church's bed, ruining the dramatics of the moment.

Without skipping a beat, Ranger reaches down, picks it up, and stuffs it into his pants before standing up and pointing at the rest of us.

"I'll go get him. You assholes finish your fucking Halloween costumes and stop dicking around."

"Lovely use of a pun," Tobias remarks before

Ranger flips him off and heads out to find his friend. It takes about two seconds for Spencer and the twins to devolve into raucous laughter. But me, I can't stop thinking about the way Church's eyes met mine when he said the word *love.*

I haven't needed much tutoring since school started, seeing as Church's help last year made a huge difference in the way I study and tackle problems. He was right: I had no foundation, and without that foundation, it was impossible for me to build anything new. But he gave that to me, and since then, I've had no trouble putting things together on my own.

"Do you really think I could get into college?" I ask Church as I set my books aside and look over at him, bathed in the dim light from the lamp next to his bed. We each have wall-mounted electric fireplaces on the walls at the end of our beds, burning cheerily to ward off the cold weather outside.

While I work on Mr. Murphy's stupid English assignment, Church has blown through his homework and moved onto Jenica's journal pages. He tackles them like he does everything else in life: like he's on a life or death mission. In this case, however, it's pretty damn literal.

"Name the college, and I'll see that you get in," he murmurs, circling things on the screen of his iPad. He's scanned all the pages in, so he can play around with them and make notes. The real ones are tucked back in Jenica's journal and stored in a small safe in Ranger and Spencer's room. Church pauses briefly to look up at me, sitting on my bed in my glasses and paint-spattered sweats. The boys keep trying to buy me new pajamas, but what they don't understand is that I *like* these ones. They're comfy, and they're lived-in. When I put them on, I think about my aunt Elisa, and how she lured me over to her house with pizza and light beer to get me to help paint her living room wall purple. Money can buy new pj's, but it can't give me a flood of happy memories the way these sweatpants can. "Provided, of course, that you keep your grades up."

"I don't want to buy my way in," I say, wondering what his plans are for graduation, wondering how it's going to feel to give back this ring and disappoint his parents, his sisters … myself. I exhale and stand up, moving over to sit down on the end of his bed. "Let me guess? You're going to Harvard or Stanford or Oxford or something. Old money, fancy school."

Church doesn't bother answering. Instead, he just gives me another one of those blinding smiles, the ones he learned from his family.

"Maybe. Why? Is that where you want to go? As

husband and wife, we should probably attend the same university."

I grab one of his discarded, fancy-pants pillows, and smack him with it.

"You're impossible, you know that?" I sigh and tuck the pillow close to my chest, eyeing the Jenica notes and wondering if there's anything new there that he hasn't told us. Sometimes, I get the idea that he tries to do a lot of things alone. "When are you going to tell them?"

"Tell who, and what? Do we need to talk about clarifying subjects, my darling?"

My eye twitches, but I'm not going to be phased by a little verbal whiplash.

"The boys. Your fellow Student Council members." *At least, Student Council members for now, maybe not at the end of the quarter, and after the stupid elections.* "When are you going to tell them about being adopted?"

"I wasn't planning on telling them at all," Church says, circling a name on the screen. *Libby.* Who the hell is Libby? I mean, besides the awful girl that carried around a stone with a cult symbol on it, and bullied poor Jenica. "You're the only one I want to tell. I love the boys, but there are just some things a man should share with his wife and no one else, don't you think?"

My cheeks flush, but in that small room, with the

roaring fireplaces, and the storm outside, it feels awfully cozy and intimate; if I give into my embarrassment, I may very well shrivel up and die. So I try humor as a deflection technique.

"If we're really going to be husband and wife, then why haven't you put the moves on me yet? I mean, we *are* sharing a room and all. The opportunities for seduction are ample."

Church sets his iPad aside for a moment and looks me over, studying me with such careful precision that I'm surprised he didn't figure my secret out sooner. He doesn't miss a damn thing.

"When your father was writing me up and, might I add, tarnishing my perfect academic record, he made sure to let me know that if I laid a finger on you, he'd expel me, and that he didn't care who my parents were." Church's mouth lifts into a smile. "He cares about you, you know that, right?"

"Then why is he such a goddamn dick all the time?" I groan, hiding my face in the pillow.

"He wants to protect you, but he doesn't know how. And I don't just mean with this cult thing, I mean in life." Church sighs and scrubs a hand over his face as I look up, reaching out to pull the iPad toward me.

Next to the circled *Libby*, is the last name McConnell.

It's a name I'm really, really starting to dislike hearing.

"Libby is Selena and Gareth's sister?" I ask, switching the subject the way Church usually does, from personal to business. He glances over at the iPad and frowns, that ice creeping back into his expression again.

"She is."

"So … could Selena be our female attacker then?" I venture, wondering if all the clues add up. "I mean, that's a lot of coincidences—her brother running for Student Council, her sister being mentioned in the journal, and her showing up at the hot springs."

"I'm leaning more toward Aster, to be honest with you." Church sits up, crossing his legs in front of him. My eyes rove a bit past his ankle to the bit of calf muscle showing beneath his pants, making me feel like some sort of Victorian pervert. *Dear me, I saw a flash of ankle! How scandalous.* "But mostly because they're both connected to Mark. The twins are right: he's guilty."

"Are we saying that because he's a total waste of life? Or because you know something you're not telling me?"

"It's just a hunch," Church says, reaching over and shutting the screen of the iPad off. After a brief pause, he leans in and brushes a gentle kiss across my forehead. "Now get to bed. We have a long day ahead of us tomorrow."

I slink back to my own bed, but not without

wondering what Church might do if I tried to crawl under the covers beside him.

I decide I'm too scared to risk rejection and end up falling asleep to dreams of amber eyes, aristocratic fingers, and smiles that are just for me.

CHAPTER TWELVE

Surprisingly, the boys end up getting their way, and the

"Girl," Ross starts, eyeing my costume with a twitching brow from his position on the other side of my phone screen. I decided after much thought that instead of going with the usual short skirt, crop top, racy Halloween garb I've worn in the past, that I'd rather go as Geralt of Rivia from *The Witcher.* Ross gestures up and down, indicating my padded shoulders, long gray wig, and faux beard with a quirked lip. "You had a dramatic coming out of the closet moment to go from boy to girl, and now you're all dressed up as a man with a big dick?" Ross leans in and squints at the screen, pointing in the general direction of my crotch where, of course, I've stuffed the packer penis. We're close now, me and this floppy silicone dick. "All I can say is—I *approve*."

He leans back and smirks at me, lips curved up beneath the red-brown hairs of a faux mustache. Ross McCubbin, former assistant to the Adamson Student Council boys, rainbow unicorn extraordinaire, and surprising new friend of mine. He graduated last year and is now going to school in California while dating his new online love match, Andrew Payson (who's actually still a senior in high school which totally makes Ross a perv).

They're living it up in SoCal, dressed up as Darryl Whitefeather and Josh Wilson (aka White Josh) from the TV show *Crazy Ex-Girlfriend* for Halloween. I accused Ross of making the costumes too easy—he's essentially wearing a suit and his boyfriend Andrew has on a tank top, board shorts, and flip-flops for crap's sake—but he shut me down quick and said their costumes were more about *character* than appearance.

"Right? I look hella badass, huh?" I say, flexing my fake biceps. "Toss a coin to your Witcher, peon!"

"Oh god, please stop, your Geralt voice is horrendous. You sound like you have strep throat or something. Don't insult Henry Cavill like that. Speaking of hottie hot men with silver hair, how's our Spencer doing?"

I roll my eyes at the insult and shrug one shoulder, glancing over to find Church sprawled on his bed, dressed as Fred Jones from *Scooby-Doo*. I won't lie, he looks pretty damn hot with his hair coifed back like that, wearing blue jeans and a white shirt with an orange ascot tie. The guys have a theme going on here, dressing up like the full cast of mystery solving teens: Ranger is going as Daphne (I cannot *wait* to see this in person), Spencer as Velma (okay, also really excited to see this transformation), with the twins going as Shaggy and Scooby. I'm the only outlier, as per usual.

"We'll get to see him in knee socks and an orange turtleneck if that helps?" I start, just before the door opens and I turn, bringing the phone with me to show off 'those meddling kids'. A snort escapes before I can stop it, and I clamp a hand over my mouth.

"Not a word," Ranger growls, dressed in heels, pink tights, and an orange wig. His makeup, however, is pretty damn flawless. Lots of sparkle around the lids. Spencer doesn't look any happier, wearing glasses with no lenses, a short brown wig, and a pleated red miniskirt. Tobias is outfitted with a faux goatee and brown bell bottoms while Micah is swimming in a big, furry Scooby-Doo costume.

My composure only lasts a moment before I'm howling with laughter.

"Give me that," Spencer growls, snatching the phone away from me. "It's not fair: I should've been Daphne."

"You can't walk in heels for shit," Ranger snarls,

scowling and looking my costume over with a raised brow. "Still think you should've gone as Scrappy." I stick my tongue out at him because, come on, nobody likes Scrappy-Doo anyway.

"We miss you, bro," Spencer says as the twins crowd up behind him, waving enthusiastically.

"How's that online stalker internet dick?" they ask, and this time, it's Ross' turn to roll his eyes. We were all fairly certain he was going to get murdered and turned into a lampshade by his online crush, but thankfully, it looks like they've actually got a strong romance going on over there.

I watch Ross' face to see if he has any reaction to seeing Spencer Hargrove, his former crush, on the screen, but instead, his new boyfriend Andrew steps up behind him. As soon as Andrew enters the picture, the rest of us might as well be invisible.

"It's fantastic," he says, looking back at us briefly as his boyfriend sheepishly waves back at the twins. "So fantastic, in fact, that I'm going to go and do a little pre-party partying. You guys have fun and be safe out there while you're sleuthing. If any one of you dies —even the ugly little mop-headed one"—he points distinctly in my direction—"it'll totally ruin my winter travel plans. Snow in Connecticut is only fun when it's blood free. *Byyyeeeee.*"

"*Byyyeeeee*," we all call back, waving as the video chat cuts off and Spencer hands my phone back to me. I can't help it—I reach over and cup his ass under that short skirt.

"Damn," I murmur, and he flashes a grin, reaching up to tug at a strand of my long, gray wig hair.

"Still think I would've made a hotter Daphne," he says, rolling his eyes and then snapping his fingers. "Oh! Before I forget, Jack texted and said he'll be at the party tonight."

"Excellent," Church says, standing up and sliding his palms down his white shirt. "Perhaps he can give us some extra insight into Jenica's notes."

"Or explain why he wasn't there to pick up my sister like he said he would," Ranger snaps, and Spencer bristles. The twins exchange a look, like they're afraid Spencer's loyalty to his brother and Ranger's loyalty to his sister might cause the two to clash. For whatever reason, I have a little more faith in the boys than that.

"Maybe he can tell us who, exactly, is after Charlotte?" Tobias muses, scratching at his glued-on goatee. "Because as soon as we know, it's no-holds barred. I will kick the shit out of some cultists."

"That's a good question," Spencer says, frowning hard, the expression almost comical with the big black-framed glasses sliding down his nose. "What happens when we do find out who these creeps are? Do we fight them? Turn them into the FBI? Kill them?"

"Kill them?!" I choke, making a face very similar to

the one on my emoji umbrella. "We're not killing anybody."

"If we have to kill to keep you safe …" Spencer starts, shrugging one shoulder. But there's a look in his turquoise eyes that says he's not fully comfortable with the idea. Church, on the other hand, doesn't look like he has any reservations at all.

I almost believe he *would* kill to keep me safe.

"Let's hit this party," Micah says, breaking the tension by flipping the head up on his Scooby-Doo costume. "After all, Charlotte hasn't seen the church before."

The church, apparently, is an old relic that used to be connected to the school via those crazy underground tunnels. It's much smaller than the church that used to be housed in the Adamson Academy main building, but still impressive. Or, I feel like it might've been if it was anything more than a pile of rubble.

There aren't any full walls standing, just these piles of old stone covered in teenagers wearing costumes. A DJ blasts music from a stage nearby, and the alcohol is flowing like water.

"If this party wasn't so amazing, we'd go to New

York instead," Micah says, pausing on the edge of the clearing, just under the canopy of trees. The limo took us to the southernmost part of Nutmeg and dropped us off at a busy trail, already covered in partygoers wearing Halloween costumes. Apparently, this old church isn't much of a secret to the locals.

"This is where you all were last year?" I ask, and he nods, grabbing my hand in one of his furry paws and dragging me into the fray. I'm nervous—I won't lie about that—but I keep telling myself it's impossible for these Fellowship freaks to get me in such a big crowd.

Although … that doesn't mean they're not watching.

The first thing I notice is that Mark is here with Selena, chugging beer from a keg as she cheers him on. I'm not exactly sure who they're supposed to be. I *think* Mark is meant to be some famous rapper while Selena's a popstar of some kind.

The music is made up of modern hits, the same sort of stuff I'd be listening to if I were partying at Monica's house with all our old friends. But there's definitely an edge of money and privilege here that I recognize from that party in the New York penthouse that the boys took me to. As much as I like my new life with the guys in Connecticut, this is one thing that I'm not sure I'll ever get used to.

There's food—obviously catered—plenty of drinks, drugs, and a sound system worth more than my dad's car. As soon as the crowd recognizes that it's Spencer in the wig and glasses, they cheer, and he grins, unloading the bag he brought with him onto one of the tables. There's enough weed there to get him thrown in federal prison.

"You want to dance?" Micah asks, giving me this lascivious look from under the hood of his costume that makes me grin.

"With a furry?" I retort, looking him up and down. "I don't know, man. You're pressing your luck."

"How about I promise not to proposition you for sex while I'm wearing this thing, and we'll settle on some grinding instead?"

"Deal." I take Micah's hand and let him pull me into the sweaty, gyrating group of dancers on the old, bowed, and grayed wood floors of the church. There are a few pews, pushed to either side of the space and filled with people talking, laughing, and snapping selfies. The majority of the rubble—including a broken stained-glass window—is gathered in the corners of the crumbling structure.

After a few songs, Tobias cuts in and takes Micah's place, smiling at me from above that scraggly goatee. I give it a little tug, laughing as he spins me around, our only source of light the full moon above the trees, and the colored spotlights sweeping across the crowd. It's interesting, to look up into eyes that are the same shape and color as Micah's, but at the same time, so different. The thought makes me smile, knowing that there's so much more to a person than what you see on the outside.

"College applications are due in November," Tobias whispers, leaning in close so that his mouth is near enough to my ear that I can hear him over the music. "I filled mine out for Bornstead U, and guess what?"

"What?" I whisper back, shivering as he nibbles my earlobe playfully.

"Spencer filled his out, too. Even though he said he wasn't interested in college. I think you're having a positive influence on us, Chuck." I smile, curving my arms around his neck as the music shifts into a slower, softer song. Half the crowd groans, sweating and booing, while the rest of us relax into the melody, swaying together. "We should hear back in December. Then we can decide."

"Decide what?" I ask, looking up, my heart pounding like crazy. College seems so far away, but in reality, I'll know whether I was accepted within a month, I'll be turning eighteen around the same time. And we're already almost two months into the schoolyear. It's a little scary, thinking about the future and all of its unknowns.

"If we're all going. You know we've always sort of planned to stick together, right?"

"I didn't, actually," I say, looking up into Tobias' eyes. There's a calmness there in his gaze that I grab hold of and cling to. I like the way he looks down at me, like he's more than happy to take care of me and Micah both. He's got a giving sort of heart.

"We never really decided if we wanted to travel or go to school first, but I like the idea of us all going to Colorado together, don't you?"

"I'm pretty sure that'd be a dream come true." I wrinkle my brows and then move my left hand between us, so I can stare at the pink Asscher cut diamond that Church gave me. "But how would it all work? I'm … just assuming that at some point, you're going to want me to choose?"

"Choose, what?" Tobias asks, but before I get the chance to answer, I see Spencer waving us over. Tobias and I exchange a look and then weave our way off the dance floor, over to where Spencer's frilly little red miniskirt is swishing away through the trees.

We follow him to a small clearing, occupied by a few hot and heavy couples that make my cheeks flush if I look at them too closely. Okay. Yep. Not my business. I refocus my attention on the brown-haired boy leaning against a tree, dressed similarly to how he was the last time we saw him: baggy t-shirt, loose fitting jeans, sneakers.

"Hey, Jack," Spencer says, slapping palms with his brother. "You didn't dress up?"

"Nah, I'm not staying," Jack says, looking past Spencer and over at the rest of us. Me, in particular. He flicks his blue eyes back to Spence's. "I was sort of hoping we might be able to talk in private?"

"Not a chance in hell," Ranger says, just as intimidating as always, even in a wig and lavender heels. He crosses muscular arms over his chest and waits, rather impatiently I might add, for Jack to continue. "Well? We know all about the Fellowship of the Divine now, so what can you tell us that we *don't* know?"

"Jesus Christ, man, keep your voice down," Jack hisses, looking around like he expects a monster to leap out at him at any moment. If one did, I mean, we're appropriately dressed. I've got on the Witcher costume, and the boys are prepped to tear off a mask so the villain can shout stuff about meddling kids. "Who told you that shit? And do they, by chance, have a freaking death wish?"

"Lionel Murphy," Church supplies easily, watching Jack carefully. It's the little tells, right?

"We saw the missing pages from Jenica's journal," Spencer says, and Jack just lifts an eyebrow. I'm guessing he's never seen or heard about this mysterious journal. "And man, I hate to say it, but it really makes you look guilty."

"Me?" Jack chokes, looking around again. I don't see anybody but the happy couples, sexing it up around the clearing. God, teenagers are sort of gross, huh? All hormone-y and shit. *Damn, Spencer's legs look fine in those knee socks.* I facepalm but nobody's paying any attention to me. "Jenica and I were friends."

"Yeah? So you sell your friends prescription drugs and cocaine, and you don't give a fuck what it does to their lives?" Ranger asks, stepping forward. Spencer stops him by putting an arm out, and the two exchange a long, studying look before Ranger finally steps back with a growl.

"I didn't kill her though, if that's what you're implying." Jack looks imploringly at his younger brother. "You know me. I wouldn't do that; I couldn't hurt her."

"Where were you when you were supposed to give her a ride that night, the night she died?" Spencer asks carefully, keeping his gaze trained on his brother's face. The twins move around our little group in slow circles, pushing away drunken revelers and leaving us with enough space to talk in private.

"When she didn't show and didn't answer her phone, I went looking for her," Jack says, and the way his breath catches, the way sweat beads on his forehead, that tells me right away that I'm not going to like this part of the story. "She was always meeting with Lionel at the clearing with the old angel statues. I went there, and … I saw things I didn't want to see, okay?"

"Like what?" Spencer asks, voice hardening. He's pretty intimidating, too, I have to admit—even in his, um, glorious Velma costume. "You can't possibly look anymore guilty than you do now, so spill it. That's what you wanted to talk to me about, isn't it?"

"I came to warn you, you idiot," Jack says, leaning in toward his brother's face. "Why the hell do you think I came all the way up here to get you that day? Did you ever wonder who locked you in that cabin and why?"

"The Fellowship," Church supplies, but Jack ignores him. Spencer's right: he doesn't seem like the villainous type, but he's most definitely selfish and most definitely a coward. The only person Jack cares about is himself, almost the polar opposite of his brother. Spencer was willing to rewrite his whole world view to make sure I fit into it, and Jack wasn't even willing to rearrange his schedule to meet with Spencer sooner.

"This cult, they're real, sure. I saw them drag Jenica into the clearing by her hair, barefoot and wearing her freaking nightgown." Ranger stiffens up at Jack's words, and I realize with a start that it all makes sense. Jenica wrote that note to Lionel in her journal and tore the page out, like she was in a hurry, choosing to tear up her book instead of finding a separate piece of paper. And the way she cut off that last journal entry mid-sentence? She could've been writing in it when she heard or saw something, panicked, and then … she never even got the chance to get dressed before they got her. "They were wearing masks, but I recognized

Rick's voice. I mean, he was always yelling at her, pushing her, grabbing her by the neck."

Mark and Selena stumble into the clearing behind us, making out and fumbling with each other's clothes. I roll my eyes because, unfortunately, I've seen this particular routine before, and I wasn't impressed. Mark's dick is even smaller than Cody's which, believe it or not, is smaller than any of the five boys in my … err, harem. Spencer, surprisingly, is the biggest.

Then again, I haven't gotten much of a look at Church …

"What happened, Jack?" Spencer asks, softening his voice just enough that he's being sympathetic, but not so much that Jack thinks this conversation is anywhere near over.

"They lit some candles, chanted some weird shit, and then they wrapped a rope around her neck and hung her from a tree."

Our entire group goes silent, our collective breath held, as we think about that, about Jenica being dragged across the wet forest floor in her nightgown. My mind strays to that awful moment in the woods at the Twilight Slumber Camp. That could very well have been my last night on earth.

"And you just let them do it?" Ranger asks, his voice like a shard of ice, digging its way into my heart. If I were Jack, I'd run, and not from the cult, but from the little brother of the girl I failed to save.

"If they find out that I know, they'll kill me," Jack whispers as the twins stand with their backs to the rest of us, keeping careful watch over Selena and Mark. Based on her moans, however, I get the idea that she's at least partway through faking an orgasm. "Besides, what was I supposed to do? Attack an entire group of psychos by myself? Call the police? They *own* the Nutmeg police. That, and the Fellowship has access to the whole campus, through the tunnels. They even have a *church* underneath the school. I've been all over that campus with a fine-toothed comb. Trust me, I know, I've seen some things I can never forget."

"That's some far-out shit, Jack," Spencer says, but he doesn't look entirely unconvinced.

"Half the school board and a good fourth of the staff is involved. Don't believe me? Fine. But I fucking *lived* in that school. I know every inch of it. The families that are involved are powerful, and I wasn't about to drag ours into that mess. Sorry, Ranger." Jack looks over at Jenica's brother with a small grimace and a flash of pain, and then quickly turns his attention to Church. "Maybe the Montagues have the resources to deal with this crap, but it wasn't worth it to me. I'd just as soon stay out of their way, thanks."

I scoot behind Spencer, so that I'm standing between him and Ranger, and then I take one of their hands in either of mine, joining them, and comforting them both in one fell swoop. It can't be easy for

Spencer to see his brother in this light, and I know it's not easy for Ranger to hear any of this.

"Why lock me in the cabin then?" Spencer asks, and Jack gives him a look.

"You're joking, right? They're after your fucking girlfriend. Each initiate *has* to get blood on their hands, and it *has* to be the person the cult's chosen. No exceptions. She's dangerous man, stay away from her. They only locked you in there to get you out of the way, but don't think they won't kill you, too, if it suits them. Pretty sure the only person they're scared to touch is that one." Jack flicks his hand in Church's direction and then shakes his head, tucking his hands in his pockets and pulling out a bag of pills. "Now take these and pretend we were meeting to talk shop—and don't say I've never gone out on a limb for you."

Spencer does as his brother's asked, but his face is pale, his mouth tight. I can tell that he's pissed. Hard to say what he's most upset about; we're sort of dealing with a lot here.

Jack gives his brother a hug, and then disappears into the woods like he was never there. Spencer looks down at the pills briefly, and then tucks them into his pocket.

"You guys are in danger because of me," I say, thinking on Jack's words for a moment. The boys might actually be better off if I left for good, huh?

"You're worth it, Chuck-let," Spencer says, looking

up and meeting my eyes. He turns his attention to Ranger, and the two boys spend a long moment studying each other. "Jenica's worth it."

Ranger nods, and we head back toward the party, leaving a groaning Selena and Mark in the darkness behind us.

CHAPTER THIRTEEN

Archibald Carson's been ignoring me, and I don't like it.

I mean, most seventeen-almost-eighteen-year olds *do* want to be ignored by their parents, but not after being told that, yes, they're pretty certain that someone's out to kill them. Dad knows things; Mr. Murphy knows things; Mr. Dave knows things.

Nathan, the annoying and seemingly useless night watchmen, has been following me around quite a bit lately at my dad's behest. That makes me wonder if he's a tad less creepy and a bit more on our side, but since I can't exactly go up to him and ask what he knows about a mysterious cult lurking in underground tunnels beneath the school, I'm resigned to his presence.

"We never get to talk anymore," Monica says, lying back on her bed with her dark hair trimmed short, her makeup relaxed and casual. This is a big turnaround for her, considering that in the past, she'd rather stay at home and miss a weekend of partying than be seen with a bit of bloating from her period.

"Um, I begged you to talk to me when I first got here, and you and Cody blew me off like nothing," I remind her, twirling a bit of blond hair around one of my fingers and realizing that I've already just slipped back into my Valley Girl accent.

Monica cringes, but I get no satisfaction out of her reaction. It's not fair for me to say that I forgive her, and then continue holding the Cody thing over her head. And honestly? She did me a favor. I'd take any *one* of my new beaus over Cody any day, let alone *five* deliciously rich assholes.

Wait.

Deliciously rich asshole? That sounds gross as fuck, like … a butthole covered in chocolate sauce or something. Gag. Vom.

"You're right," she says, sighing and closing her eyes for a moment. I know that she's over Cody, and she seems happy, but also, I'm pretty sure she liked him far more than I ever did. His betrayal hurts. "I have no right to complain, but I miss you. It was never the same after you left, like the magic went when you did."

I snort, and she lifts a lovely microbladed eyebrow at me.

"Please. The only magic I bring with me is an innate talent for pissing people off, a habit of blurting inappropriate things, and an obsession with romance. I've fallen in love with *every boy* on the Student Council." Speaking of … right after we get back from fall break, it's go time. A week of debates followed by election day.

They might not be Student Council boys anymore.

And for someone like Aster Hayes to be president? No, thank you. Church is the fucking prince of this school. He's on the brochures for crap's sake.

"Where is your gaggle of boyfriends anyway?" Monica asks as I sit up and stretch an arm over my head, using the other to keep my phone more or less focused on my face.

"Well, two of them are practicing martial arts moves in the gym, another one of them is baking in the buff while his best friend does calculus next to him, and the last one is waiting just outside the cracked door of this room."

"Sorry to ruin the gossip train," Spencer says, peeking his head in, and then moving into the room when I gesture his way. "If you need to talk shit about me, I understand. Just make sure you let her know that I do, in fact, have the biggest dick of all the guys."

"I haven't seen enough of Church's yet to know for sure," I blurt, and then I groan and fall back into the pillows. "Okay, I'm hanging up now. You bring out the ho in me."

"Every girl has a ho inside, waiting to liberate her from the puritanical shackles of our modesty-based society that shames women for having natural pleasure and dominion over their own bodies. Enjoy all that dick, and we'll talk soon!"

She ends the call, and I, in my infinite grace and poise, drop the phone right on my face by accident. Spencer's right there in an instant, pulling me up and into his arms, like I'm actually suffering much more than bruised pride.

"Ah, Chuck-let, you're bleeding," he says, reaching up with the edge of his blazer sleeve to wipe some of the red away. I try to slap his hand back, so he doesn't stain his uniform, but he ignores me and dabs the liquid away from my upper lip. "It's gonna be hard to kiss you now, babe."

"Babe?" I ask, lifting a skeptical brow in his direction. But he's impossible not to like, with those cocksure grins, vibrant eyes, and silver hair. His face is a bit more angular, like the twins', but he has a squarer jaw, closer to Ranger's. "That's a new one."

"I'm testing out extra nicknames, just so I've got fun things to call you from across the room. Babe seemed pretty tame, but knowing how much you love insults like condom face, ass pig, and toilet brush, I figure I'll get creative next time. I'm playing around with *my little slice of hot sauce toast*, in homage to your favorite breakfast food."

Aww, he remembers that I like to douse my French toast in hot sauce … Too freaking cute.

"You want to yell *hey, hot sauce toast!* across a crowded room, then that's your choice. Just don't expect me to answer." Spencer smirks and leans in, kissing a drop of ruby red blood away from the corner of my mouth. I smack him away again, but he just chuckles and burrows his face against the side of my neck. "Don't you know about, like diseases and stuff? Don't lick my blood, that's gross."

"Don't be so dramatic. What diseases could you possibly have?" He sits up and looks me over in my white-button down and plaid skirt like I'm the most beautiful woman he's ever seen. "I took your virginity, after all, and I'm clean as a whistle."

"Mm-hmm." I give him a look, but his expression is tender, and I know he's just being playful. "You know," I begin softly, looking down at my lap and forgetting about my split lip for a second. "I always wanted a boy who'd love me in a ballgown and a face full of makeup, but also love me just as much in sweatpants with a pimple on my nose."

"Like the one you have now?" Spencer says knowingly, and I balk at him.

"I do not have a pimple! What is wrong with you, Spencer Hargrove?" he grins at me, and then reaches up to brush back some of my hair. After that talk with Jack on Halloween, I was sure he was going to draw into himself. Spencer's always said he hates lies more than anything else, and Jack's clearly been lying to him for years. But instead of freaking out and running away, he's here, and he's dealing with it. I'm proud of him. "I'm trying to be poetic and romantic and—"

"I was getting ready to suck your dick, Charlotte Carson. I was looking up the ins and outs of anal sex, and if silicone lube was better than water-based—it is." He pauses and smiles at me in a way that breaks my fucking heart and sews it back together all in a single glance. "If you think that I wouldn't love you in sweatpants and pimples, then you're just not paying attention."

"Love me, huh?" I ask, and Spencer lifts a dark brow. My heart is beating out of my chest, thinking about Ranger's confession and wondering if I could be so lucky to hear that phrase twice.

"You know I love you, Chuck." He shrugs his shoulders again, like it's no big deal. But it is. It is a big deal. I lean forward, placing one of my hands on his legs, lips parted gently, waiting. "Shit, you can't look at me like that."

"Say it again," I tell him, leaning even farther forward, knowing that the top buttons on my shirt are undone, and that I'm sitting in *just* such a way that there's maximum cleavage going on.

"I'm not afraid of the L-word," he says, flashing a foxy smirk in my direction and then reaching up a single finger to brush down the side of my throat. "I love you, Chuck-let."

"Even if your love for me gets you killed?" I ask, pausing and glancing away, toward one of Church's coffee posters. Part of me wonders what would happen if I ran, if the cult would eventually give up. If I weren't here, would the boys be safer? Maybe they could just hire private security for me, and I could wait this out back in Santa Cruz? The thought is crushing, but now that we know what we're dealing with, I can't help but wonder.

Then again, if the families behind this are in the league of—or at least close to—the power and influence of the Montagues, then I don't imagine they'd let me go quite that easily.

"I'd rather die for love than live without knowing how bad it hurts," Spencer says, smiling. "Now say you love me back, and let's do it before those other assholes show up."

"I love you, Spencer Hargrove," I say, and I mean it, I do.

The thing is, I'm pretty sure I love all five of the boys. Equally.

What's a girl to do?

"My dad is never going to let me go," I say, sitting on the counter in my skirt and loving the power shift I feel in this kitchen. A year ago, I was remaking quiches and being locked out of the dining room while Ross sniveled and snickered next to Spencer. Now, I'm sitting here and being pampered by a horde of lovesick boys.

I tap my crossed ankles against the cabinet and think what a difference a skirt can make. Essentially, I'm a femme fatale now. I *own* these boys.

"Get off that fucking counter and finish this fruit tart," Ranger says, pointing at the freshly baked crust which is seriously bereft of fruit. "And make it cute. We need to up our game on Insta. Our feed is garbage."

With a roll of my eyes, I slide off the counter, and then duck like a damn ninja when the twins toss two chocolate chip cookies in my direction, like they're throwing-stars or something.

"You're getting better at that," they say in unison, like they're surprised about it. The thing is, they shouldn't be. I've been working really hard in the gym and doing my best to memorize everything they've taught me. I even have the sore muscles to prove it.

"What a shame."

"We *liked* pegging you in the face and back with food," Tobias remarks, parking his elbow on the counter and putting his chin in his hand. "It's just not the same, with you getting all badass on us and stuff."

Ranger grabs a clean spatula from the drawer beside the stove and swats Tobias in the ass with it.

"Get up and finish your cream puffs. The bake-off against Everly is going to be brutal this year, and I intend to win. I'm not letting lazy good-for-nothings ruin my chances—*especially* not after finding out Jenica was bullied at Everly because of some cult."

"Maybe you want to take that apron off, get naked, and finish the cream puffs yourself with some special sauce?" Tobias grins at his own joke, and then pales when Ranger turns a thundering look his direction.

"*Get back to work, you little pissant,*" he snarls, and Tobias scurries off to do as he's told. Church, on the other hand, has already finished his tiramisu, and is now sitting in one of the armchairs, working on his Jenica notes.

"Speaking of Libby and the stone," Church says, glancing up with amber eyes. He's got a small espresso on the arm of his chair, and a muffin with a chocolate-coated coffee bean on the top sitting on the plate next to it. "Her possession of it would indicate that she's a member of the Fellowship," he continues, staring at the screen of his iPad. "Which would make Selena our most likely candidate for the female attacker."

"Technically, yeah, but what about Ranger?" Spencer asks, pointing over at his friend. He's still working on some boiled bagels that smell heavenly. "If this shit is, like, passed down to everyone in a family, how could Ranger's dad be a part of it when Jenica and Ranger aren't?"

"That's what we're going to find out during fall break," Ranger says, determined to finish icing his three-layer pink cake with the fondant roses waiting to be put on it. "We'll snoop and dig and sleuth, and then if worse comes to worst, I'll confront his ass with the evidence."

"Like I said, my dad is never going to let me go," I repeat, restarting our conversation about fall break. Dad and I always spend Thanksgiving together, so the chance of him letting me out of the *country* for a weeklong trip is laughable. "Besides, I don't have a passport."

"You will not confront him," Church tells Ranger, ignoring me and putting the iPad aside as he rises to his feet to help Micah with some fairly fucked-up looking macarons. At least I'm not the only one who struggles in the kitchen sometimes. Church whips an apron over his hips and looks pointedly at Ranger. "Your father is no stranger to scandal. If he could get rid of Jenica, then surely he'd get rid of you, too."

"Yeah, except that Jenica wasn't his biological kid,"

Ranger says, and I pause. Pretty sure the other boys are just as shocked as I am by that statement. Flicking my attention over to Church, I catch a brief flare of hurt in his eyes before he shuts it down. "You know my mom was married to my dad's brother first, right? He died in a plane crash when Jenica was like, five, and Mom, in some like grief-induced haze married his kid brother that she'd never really liked."

"So you and Jenica are cousins *and* siblings?" Spencer asks, and Ranger gives him a look that could curdle milk. He very quickly holds up his hands in surrender.

"Don't make it weird. It's not like there was incest or anything. Chill out." Ranger turns back to his cake, focusing in on piping some frosting lace along the edges. He's doing it again, baking out all his frustrations. It's a pretty healthy outlet though, if you ask me. "I'm just saying, my dad's a petty, pathetic asshole. So maybe he figured he'd sell Jenica down the river?"

"But not recruit you into the Fellowship?" Micah asks, and the room goes quiet again. After a moment, Church comes over to where I'm standing, removes a small blue book from his pocket, and sets it on the counter next to me.

When I reach out to grab it, I see that it's a passport —with my name and picture on the inside.

My eye twitches.

"I see that when you asked me to stand against the white wall in our room, so you could get a headshot to sketch for art class, you were totally full of shit."

"Full of shit," Church agrees with a brisk nod. "So, pack your bags: you're going with us to London—whether Headmaster Carson likes it or not."

CHAPTER FOURTEEN

The way that Dad looks at me, I'm sure I've done it now. This is literally the last straw in our relationship, the lynchpin being pulled, the coup de grâce if you will.

"You are not going to London," he says, looking at me like I've lost my mind. "To stay at Eric Warren's house? Absolutely not." My face pales because I most definitely did not say anything about Eric Warren's house. We figured since dad's admission that he knows at least *something* about the cult which means he might also know about Eric's possible involvement. Instead, we spun some almost-lie about staying in Church's parents' flat in Hyde Park—that's one of the rich people parts of London—for the week.

"I've never been out of the country," I plead, folding my hands together like I'm six years old all over again. Yes, we're going to see Eric Warren née Woodruff (he changed his last name to his mother's following a political scandal) as part of our investigation, but … it's more than that. This is a chance for me to see another part of the world, a place I never thought I'd be able to go. "Hell, until we moved here, I'd never been out of California. This is the chance of a lifetime for me."

With a sigh, Dad puts his glasses aside and then pinches the bridge of his nose, leaning back in his chair like he's tired. And I don't just mean from the day, it looks like he's feeling his exhaustion bone-deep.

"Charlotte, do you think I want you to suffer?" he asks, dropping his hands in his lap and studying my face.

"Um, yes?"

"Charlotte Farren," he groans, looking like he'd rather take a long walk off a short pier than keep talking to me right now. "Eric Warren is a dangerous man, and you have no business traveling to a foreign country with a bunch of boys that you barely know—"

"I've known them for over a year," I correct, "and we've been through a lot together. We almost died in those tunnels; we all grieved Spencer together. They took me to *Disneyland.* Why can't you just accept that they're in my life and they probably will be for a long,

long time."

"Regardless of your relationship with these boys, I won't have you going to see Eric Warren."

"Because you know he's involved with the Fellowship of the Divine."

Silence.

You could hear a pin drop.

Speaking of pins, Dad sort of looks like he wants to shove one into my eye right now.

"Where did you hear that name?" he asks, and I grimace. Would giving Mr. Murphy away do me any good right now? Or would I just get him in trouble? Because I don't want that. He's a good person, even if he is a coward. He did care about Jenica, and he tried to protect me, too, in his own way.

"That doesn't matter right now," I say as Dad stands up and comes around the front of his desk, eyebrow twitching. I back up because I know at this point that I'm in pretty deep shit here. "The point is: I do know the name. And I know that *you* confirmed what I already thought: that someone's trying to kill me."

"Charlotte," he says, but there isn't a lot of heat in his voice anymore. For a second there, he just looks like a frazzled, middle-aged man who needs a vacation. "You are a child."

"Young adult, eighteen in a month," I murmur, but he isn't listening to me anymore than usual.

"It's not your job to search for the answers. Your

job is to go to school and listen to what I tell you. I'm not making things up just to make your life miserable. There are people looking into this, but those people are not you." He puts his hands on my shoulders and looks at me, really looks at me. "When I came to Adamson, I'll admit, I was ignorant. I didn't know what was going on, and maybe I didn't want to. But you're going to graduate at the end of the year, leave this place behind, and start a future. Until then, you have to abide by my rules. Don't you believe that I'd do anything to protect you?"

"Nothing will happen to me in London, Dad. The guys will be there, and really, it has to be safer than here, right?"

"Eric Warren is a leader in this 'cult' you're so fond of discussing, Charlotte. You're not going to his home —that's the end of this discussion."

"But—"

"But what?!" he screams, and I have to blink several times to make sense of what I'm seeing here. Dad. Breaking down. Turning purple. Losing control. "Do you want to wind up at the end of a noose like Eugene Mathers? Charlotte, I'm trying to protect you!"

My eyes water, but I'm not exactly sure why in that moment. So many emotions are tumbling through me that they seem impossible to make sense of. It's a storm inside of me, with a little bit of rain, some clouds, but some sunshine, too.

Dad cares. He just isn't good at showing it. He won't let me go to London. He's *afraid* for me.

I bite my lower lip.

"This is a very dangerous organization with centuries of history, influence, and power. You need to stay here, on this campus, where Ian and Nathan can watch you."

"Ian and Nathan?" I ask, giving my dad a look. "The librarian and the shitty security guard who smells like Mountain Dew?"

"Charlotte, I have a migraine, and I need to lie down. Please. Go back to the dorm and stay in your room. Between that write-up for bursting into my home, and the one you got for missing your room check on Halloween, you're creeping into dangerous academic territory here." Dad fails to mention that pretty much every student in the school got a write-up for missing curfew on Halloween, but thus is his way. "You're safest here. If I'd known what I know now, I never would've sent you to California."

"The boys can hire private security for me," I start, but Dad's not listening. We had a moment, but that moment's over. He walks away from me, out the door of his office, pausing just briefly to survey the five boys standing in his kitchen.

"Sir," Church begins carefully, but that shiny glitter that used to fill my father's eyes at the sight of our school's best student has faded away to a steely irritation known by any teen who's ever had an overprotective parent. It's this well-meaning stubbornness that sometimes defies logic and reality. "If it's Eric Warren that makes you uncomfortable, then perhaps we truly could stay at my parents' place."

"Son," Dad begins, and I know then that he's getting deadly serious. The word *son* usually only comes out of Headmaster Carson's mouth when he's in full disciplinary mode. Church is in trouble. "You put a ring on my daughter's finger without asking my permission—we are not friends."

"Oh my god, you're such a boomer!" I choke out, falling back into old patterns. With a deep breath, I settle myself and try to resist the flinty glare my father's just turned on me. "It's not 1605 anymore. I'm not your possession, and Church doesn't have to ask you. The only person he had to ask was me."

"Well, when's the wedding?" Dad asks, trying a different tactic as he turns on me. The twins, Spencer, and Ranger stand back, unsure where to interfere in this verbal tussle. At least I know that if Dad tries to grab me again, that they will step in. "Because at least when all this is over, you'll be forced to admit to your lies." He heads out the door, breezing past the boys and heading for the stairs as I stumble after him. "And by the way, you can't leave the country without a passport."

"I have a passport," I admit, pulling it from my

pocket as dad pauses with one foot on the bottom step. He looks over his shoulder with a mix of helplessness and fear. More than likely he's realizing that Church Montague's gotten me a passport without consulting him. Somehow, that means Church managed to get a hold of all the required documentation on his own. Admittedly, that's equal parts fascinating and terrifying to me, too. "What if I stayed with the Montagues? What if … I promised not to see Eric Warren or go anywhere near him?"

Before Archie can respond, there's a knock on the screen door.

"Hello? Is anyone home? It's okay, I'll come in. I'm coming in."

The door swings wide, opening in for a magnanimous woman with blond hair and blue eyes.

"Mother," Church starts, blinking rapidly in a rare moment of surprise. "What are you doing here?"

"To see you, silly," she says, planting a lavender kiss on both of Church's cheeks and leaving lipstick stains. The twins and Spencer snicker until she turns her attention to them, ruffling hair, and kissing faces. Even Ranger isn't exempt. Even *I'm* not exempt. "My future daughter-in-law!" she says, eyes tearing up as she yanks me close for a floral-scented hug, and then cups my face to kiss both my cheeks and my forehead.

Church's mom is impossible to miss, this radiant woman in a floppy white sunhat, gloves, and a dress that hugs her lithe form. She stands out like a sunbeam in the dark, sometimes dreary atmosphere of Adamson Academy.

"Mrs. Montague," Dad says, giving me a thunderous look. To be fair, I had no idea she'd be showing up here today. I hold my palms up and out in apologetic surrender. "How may I help you? The academy encourages parents to call before stopping by for a visit or a tour."

"Oh, don't be ridiculous," she says, waving her gloved hand around dismissively, a garment bag draped over her other arm. "I was in Nutmeg to work on a little business project and thought I'd come up to give Charlotte a present. Was is this I hear about staying with us? Charlotte is always welcome in our family."

"Mother, you were eavesdropping?" Church chastises, but she waves him away.

"The children," Dad begins, emphasizing that awful word in a way that only he could, "were discussing a trip to London over fall break. As you can imagine—"

"London? Oh, yes, we have a flat in Hyde Park. That sounds like a lovely way to spend break."

I realize two things in that moment: Church's mother is beyond nice, and she's also beyond privileged. She doesn't know the meaning of the word *no*.

"While I'm not opposed to Charlotte exploring the world one day, now just isn't the right time," Archie explains, finally turning and coming down the rest of the stairs to stand next to Mrs. Montague.

"If it's supervision you're worried about, David and I are more than happy to go with them. Charlotte will be well-taken care of. Now, look what I've brought for you." She drags the zipper down on the garment bag and whips out a white dress, flashing it for the whole room to see.

"What … is it?" I ask, feeling my throat close up on a ball of raw emotion. I know perfectly well what that is.

"It's your wedding dress!" Mrs. Montague says, draping it across her arms and holding it out to me. "It's the same one I wore when I was seventeen years old." She sighs and looks up at the ceiling, like she's already caught up in a vivid daydream of David Montague as a young man.

"It's bad luck for a groom to see the dress before the wedding," Church says, looking slightly paler than usual. Elizabeth Montague waves his concerns away.

"That's ridiculous. Your father and I picked this dress out together. We eloped to Paris with it." She sighs again and fans her face. "Do you think you two might want to get hitched in London? We could borrow the abbey!"

"The … abbey?" I ask, noticing that Church is giving his mom a look similar to the ones I give my dad when he's being completely over the top. Just, his mom goes over the top in a whole different way.

"Westminster Abbey," she says, like *duh.* I choke on my own spit, forcing Spencer to rub and pat my back to help me clear my throat.

"I thought only royalty could get married there?" I manage to get out as Dad stands dumbfounded and speechless near the staircase.

"We have friends in high places," Elizabeth says, and then she chuckles like it's no big deal.

"Mother, that isn't even a remotely realistic option," Church begins, but she quiets him with a click of her tongue.

"Oh shush, Church. Here you go, darling. What do you think?"

She hands the dress over, and I take it reverently, staring down at the beaded bodice and then looking back up at her face. I'm dating her son, sure, but … I'm also dating four other boys. *What the hell am I doing here?!* Elizabeth looks so excited about the prospect of her son marrying me in this dress; she believes in old-school, love at first sight stuff. What happens if this doesn't work out?

"Mrs. Montague …" Dad starts, looking at the offending dress like he'd rather burn it than watch me get married in it.

"Try it on," she encourages, flapping gloved hands at me, and then reaching up to adjust her hat.

"You don't have to, if you don't want to," Church

says softly. I lift my gaze up to him, and then pan it across the rest of the boys. They're all just … staring at me. Everyone's staring at me. Someone's trying to kill me. How did I even get here?

"Of course she wants to," Elizabeth says as I shuffle in the direction of the downstairs bathroom in a daze. Voices start up behind me as I slip into the restroom and close the door behind me, putting my back up against it. I flick the fan on, so I don't have to hear what they're saying.

"What am I doing?" I wonder, looking down at the admittedly beautiful sweetheart neckline of the dress. It's white, sure, but when I tilt it into the light, there's the faintest pink sheen to the shimmery fabric. It looks old, too, and not just Church's mom old, but like an antique. If both her and my engagement ring came from the antique store, then did this, too?

Slipping out of my school uniform, I drop the dress over my head and stand staring at myself in the full-length mirror near the door.

The dress is fitted at the waist, with straps that start wide on the shoulders and taper in near the bodice. The beadwork on the top is delicate, twisting into floral motifs that swirl together across the front and sides, toward the back and the loose ribbons that hold the corseted back together. While the bodice is form-fitting, the skirt is full, a satin top layer over several layers of tulle.

Looking at my reflection is like looking at a stranger.

Where's the bronze-skinned surfer girl? How about the dorky boy in glasses?

Instead, I find myself looking at someone completely different. And it's not just the dress, is it? It's just life, catching up to me.

Slowly, I push open the door and shuffle into the foyer.

Elizabeth slaps her hands over her mouth while my dad turns a shade of red that hasn't yet been identified in nature. He looks like a vat of cranberry sauce.

"Charlotte," Spencer breathes, his jaw tightening as he looks me over. "You're beautiful."

"So cute," Ranger murmurs, closing his eyes against the sight, a slight pink color tinging his skin.

"You look … good, Chuck," the twins say, blinking in surprise, like they're not quite sure how to react.

The only one who stays silent is Church.

"Well, son, don't you have something to say to your bride?" his mother chastises, giving him a very pointed look.

Those amber eyes are locked on my face, but I'm having trouble discerning what, exactly, it is that Church might be thinking. Is he disappointed in me? Do I look like the bride he's always wanted? Why am I feeling so freaking self-conscious all of a sudden? Slowly, carefully, he opens his mouth to speak.

I cut him off.

"I … need to grab something," I say, and Church pauses, giving me a curious sort of look.

"Grab something?" Spencer echoes as I move over to the door and slip my feet into a pair of rainboots. "What do you mean grab something? From where?"

"Just … from my room," I say, fully aware that I'm not quite thinking clearly. If you've ever seen the movie *The Proposal* with Ryan Reynolds and Sandra Bullock in it, you'll get it. They have a fake engagement, and she runs. And she runs because she … loves him. That, and she doesn't want to hurt his family.

"Charlotte Farren," Dad warns, but I'm already pushing open the screen door and hiking the skirts up as high as I can get them. "What on earth are you doing?"

I start to run down the path, the wind blowing blond curls around my face.

"I'm Sandra Bullocking!" I shout as I zip past a cluster of other students, working on a mycology project—that's fancy talk for mushrooms—and heading straight for the dorms. It's midday, and there are people everywhere, so I'm not all that concerned about the stupid cult or their blood initiation.

I don't stop running until I'm slipping into my dorm room and leaning my back against the door to close it. Only, it won't close all the way because someone's pushing their way in from the other side.

I spin and my wet rainboots slip on the floor, knocking me to my ass as Church steps into the room behind me. He closes and locks the door, looking down at me with a brow raised in questioning.

"Miss Carson," he says, almost like a soft chastisement that makes me wrinkle my nose. "You ran from me."

"I wasn't running from you," I protest weakly, looking away toward the miraculously clean space under my bed. Never in my life have I managed to keep a clean room, but Church tidies it up for us. He says he likes to do it, and I can't decide if he's full of shit or if it really does please his OCD or something. "I just had to get something."

Church squats down in front of me as I reluctantly drag my gaze from the dust-bunny-free zone and back to his aristocratic face. Cheekbones for days, skin like alabaster, a mouth that can make sunbeams but also go sharp as a knife. My heart is already pounding like crazy from my mad sprint across campus, but now I feel like I might pass out.

"You ran all the way over here in a wedding dress and rainboots to grab something?" he questions, and I nod. Words won't come. I'm not sure what to say. I'm not even sure what I'm supposed to be feeling. "Do tell."

"My nightstand drawer, next to the packer penis."

Church smiles and stands up, stepping around me to slide the drawer open and coming up with a small wooden box. It's decoupaged with old magazine photos, just some relic from an elementary school art class. But when he opens it, sliding off the top and peering inside, he'll see it: my mother's hairclip, with all the pearls and lace. She wore it at her own wedding to my dad, when she was just a teenager.

"This?" he asks, coming back around and sitting on the end of my bed. Church leans forward and tucks some of my blond curls back, using the clip to keep them in place. "Tell me about the clip, Charlotte."

"It was my mom's," I say, looking down at my poofy lap. "She wore it when she married my dad."

"You came all the way back here to get it?" Church clarifies again, and I shrug my shoulders, my black rainboots sticking out from underneath the full skirts. "Why?"

"Have you seen *The Proposal*?" I ask, turning to the side to look at him. He's so … perfect looking, dressed in the crisp champagne colored blazer and slacks, his tie straight, his shirt free of wrinkles.

"Just once," he supplies, putting an elbow on his knee and watching me carefully. "Why?"

"They have a fake engagement, too, but at the end, the girl runs away from the wedding."

"And this is what you meant by Sandra Bullocking?" Church asks, and I nod. His smile gets a little wider. "Interesting idea, to turn an actresses' name into a verb. I like the way you think, Chuck." He pauses for a moment to consider my explanation. "So the clip was truly inconsequential then. You *were* running away."

"I was running away to protect you," I say, twisting the fabric around in my hands. "You and your awesome mom, and your really nice dad, and all your sisters …" I pause for a moment, trying to untangle my feelings. "And I did want my mom's clip." My mouth turns down into a sharp frown.

"Come," Church says, standing up and offering out his hand for me to take. I grab on and let him haul me to my feet, brushing off the back of the dress. Hopefully I haven't gotten it too dirty. It didn't even occur to me until now that I could've seriously stained or torn it on the way over here. "Sit with me." He pulls me down onto the bed next to him, holding my hands in his. One of his thumbs lazily traces the surface of the ring. "Is that it? You think that by running away, you'll protect me?"

I look up, from the ring to his face, watching me without judgment, just a hint of concern glinting in his eyes.

"I don't want to unpack … all of this," I say, gesturing at my chest to indicate the strange mix of feelings resting there.

"Why not?" he queries, turning my hands over and

then running his thumbs along the pulse points in my wrists. "Are you afraid you'll hurt my feelings?" I shake my head, shrug, and then nod, just a mess of contradictory body language. "Do you believe I actually have them now? Or am I still a possible psychopath waiting in the wings?"

I snort.

"No, I don't think you're a psychopath anymore. The way you grieved for Ranger in the woods …" I trail off, because neither of us wants to talk about that day just yet. Maybe one day, but not today. "If I were gone, wouldn't you guys be safer? If I left, then the Fellowship would leave you alone." I study Church's face for a moment, searching for clues.

"If we're dealing with any of the families that I currently suspect, then there is no getting away. I could hire you a private security team, but I imagine the Fellowship would want to tie up loose ends. They'd come for you; you'd never feel safe, and you'd never truly be alone."

"But at least you guys wouldn't be in danger," I mumble, wondering why my stupid heart won't stop beating so fast. "And then we wouldn't have to lie to your family about getting married."

Church releases my hands and leans back on the bed, his palms flat against the comforter, ankles crossed.

"You're very concerned with our well-being, aren't

you?" he asks, but I don't know how to respond to that. I am. I'm a million times more worried about them than I am myself. "Are you afraid of getting married? Or maybe you just don't like the idea of marriage?"

"My parents got married when my mom was young. My dad was so in love with her, I thought they'd be together forever. Even when they got divorced, even when she went away to rehab. He *still* loves her, but she doesn't love him anymore."

We sit in silence for a moment before Church gets up and retrieves us a pair of coffees in glass bottles from his cute little mini-fridge. He hands one to me and then sits just a few inches closer than he was before.

"Maybe I thought their divorce didn't bother me, but it does?" I ask, wrinkling up my face. "That sounds pretty pathetic, huh? To be upset about divorce? I mean, half the population has divorced parents. And really, I think high divorce rates are good—it means people aren't taking abuse and shit from their partners anymore."

"But?" Church asks, as I twist the top off my coffee and take a sip.

"But, I guess … if my parents didn't make it? Why would we? Maybe the way I feel about you guys is just crazy teen stuff. Besides, that's another problem with marriage, right? I can only marry one of you."

The smile that takes over Church's mouth surprises

me.

"Only legally, but there are other ways to be committed." I blink back at him in shock as his face takes on this determined edge. "Not to sound like an asshole, but maybe your parents didn't care about each other the way I care about you."

Whoa. Far from sounding like an asshole, his statement floors me. He may as well have admitted that he feels like we're written in the stars or something. My palms get sweaty, and I swipe them on my bedspread to keep from messing up the skirt.

"I …" Words fail me as Church looks up, eyes bright. There's a certainty there, a confidence that I don't feel, but that maybe I should. Looking at him, it truly feels like he has a plan here.

"My parents are still together," he argues, taking the top off his own drink and sipping it slowly. The way he licks the rim of the bottle is most definitely suggestive in nature. He turns to look my way, his amber eyes sweeping over me in his mother's wedding dress. "And maybe, at the time, your father was everything your mother needed—sometimes forever means just for now." Church pauses for a moment and breathes out a small sigh. "But I don't want this engagement to cause you so much pain. I'll go back and tell my mother that the wedding is off; it's clear your dad won't be sending you away again."

"But your mom came all this way to give me the

dress," I start, squeezing a handful of skirts in my fist, struggling to figure out why I feel so reluctant to give it back.

"I can wait and tell her later, if you'd prefer," Church says, watching me with that stoic calm of his. "And you can keep the ring. It's yours, even if you want to sell it and keep the money."

"You picked this out for me?" I ask, and Church nods.

"In the antique store, just like my father picked out a ring for my mother. That's where I went, when I disappeared before your attack in Santa Cruz. The twins told me you were concerned." My face flushes, and I sputter to explain, but … okay, it's true. Church has always been just a tad suspicious, right?

"You were in Nutmeg?" I ask, and he nods.

"Just for a night—I couldn't make up my mind over which ring to choose. And then I took it home to show my parents and ask for their blessing." He sits there patiently, waiting for me to sort out my thoughts again. "I'm glad we were able to get you back to Adamson when we did. But things have changed." Church takes my hand and carefully slides the ring toward the end of my finger.

"Wait," I say, pulling my hand back and adjusting the ring. I feel possessive over it, clutching it against my chest.

He smiles at me again.

"Keep it. But you don't have to wear it anymore."

Our eyes meet, mine searching his for clues.

"You really like me, Church? I mean, I know you said you did at the hot springs, but ... you shouldn't have to be engaged to a girl you don't want."

"Who said I'm engaged to a girl I don't want?" he replies, setting his coffee on the dresser at the end of my bed and turning back to me. He captures my chin in long fingers and studies my face. "I don't typically do things I don't want to do."

"Yeah, but this was just to get me back to Adamson, right?"

"Was it?" he replies, meeting my question with yet another of his own. Church leans forward and kisses my mouth, just so, a soft brush of lips, like the touch of a butterfly's wings. "I like seeing you in my mother's dress, Charlotte Farren Carson."

My breathing quickens, and I struggle to find the words to respond to that.

Church presses his mouth to mine again, and my eyes close of their own accord. Slowly, like he's afraid he might ruin the moment if he moves too fast, he kisses me again. Just like that night on his parent's patio, I find myself melting into his touch, opening my lips for his tongue. My coffee drink falls to the floor and rolls beneath Church's bed, but neither of us cares.

Instead, I find myself lying back in the pillows, his body stretched above mine, lithe but muscular, smelling like lilac and rosemary. His mouth works against mine, relaxing me and bringing sweet sighs and sounds of contentment from my lips.

"It doesn't have to be fake, unless you want it to be," he whispers, his hands sliding up and underneath the full skirts of the dress. Warm palms caress my bare thighs as he settles himself between my legs, kissing each corner of my mouth with the gentlest of touches.

He's holding back. I'm sure of it. But why? It doesn't even occur to me that he might be just as scared as I am, just as unsure, but just as in love.

Love.

That's come up a lot lately, hasn't it?

"You'd actually marry me? The weird, dorky poor girl with a maid for a mom and a teacher for a dad?"

"You know my secret," he says, his face taking on just a hint of sadness. "My biological mother was a maid, too. We're no different, you and me." Church's long fingers tease the waistband of my panties, causing me to suck in a sharp breath. He's avoided touching me for so long, and now I can see why. Each place our skin comes into contact tingles. It's like there are these little bolts of energy darting across my skin. "I'd be honored to marry you—but only if you want me, too."

"I do …" I whisper, but the way I trail off gives him pause. Church stops kissing me, looking down into my face with a sweet mixture of frustration and longing. "I want them, too." It almost hurts to say it, but I know that I have to. It gives me anxiety every day, wondering if there's an ultimatum coming, or an expiration date.

"They're my family, Charlotte," Church says, propped up on with a forearm on either side of me. "They're not going anywhere." He smiles at me and then dips his head to kiss me again. This time, though, there's an edge to it. It's like his personality: half sunshine and half ironclad control. It's a part of who he is, a part of being a Montague.

"There are condoms in the nightstand," I whisper, and Church nods, his eyes hooded as he looks down at me. We kiss again, one of his hands coming up to rest on the curve of my waist, the other slipping beneath my panties. Part of me knows we should take off the wedding dress, but the rest of me doesn't care.

Church dances the fingers of one hand across my clavicle while the other teases the embarrassing amount of wetness between my legs. I'm desperate to touch him, too, but when I drop my hands to his slacks, he grabs my wrist.

With his eyes locked on mine, Church sits up and reaches for his tie, carefully unknotting it and slipping it off. He then takes it and wraps it around one of the spindles on the headboard and then around my wrists, tying it in just such a way that the navy-blue silk holds me tight, but lets my skin breathe.

His own breath catches when he sits back on his heels and looks me over, bound with his Adamson

Academy school tie, and dressed as his bride. Sunlight streams in through the window, coloring Church's honeyed hair with gold as he studies me.

"What are you waiting for?" I ask, sweating and doing my best not to writhe beneath him. But I'm desperate for him to touch me. Desperate.

"I'm savoring the moment," he replies easily, mouth sliding to the side in a devilish little smirk. "If I were a different sort of person, I'd probably take a picture. Maybe even a video?"

"Don't you dare," I growl out, but Church just chuckles.

"I won't. After all, this is just for me to enjoy. If I recorded it, I bet one of those assholes would get ahold of my phone at some point and see the evidence." Church bends down and kisses the side of my neck, making me squirm. "I don't mind sharing, in general, but certain things are just for me. This is one of them."

"You really are an arrogant ass pig, aren't you? And for a second there, I actually thought you were nice."

The nightstand drawer slides open and out come the condoms.

"You thought I was nice?" Church asks, smirking. "That's your mistake."

"Did I really just ... agree to like ... marry you or something?" I ask, but he doesn't answer with words, using his body to fill in the gaps instead. He kisses me deeply, the touch of his mouth cutting right through all the bullshit and going straight for my soul.

I never expected to like Adamson; I most definitely didn't expect to like the Student Council.

And yet, coming here is the best thing that ever happened to me.

Church sighs contentedly and unbuttons his slacks, revealing the hard length of his cock to me. It's not the first time I've seen it—hot springs, remember?—but it's different somehow, now that we're alone, now that both of our intentions have been made clear.

He slips a condom on and then reaches beneath my dress to remove my panties, tucking them into the pocket on his blazer before he takes it off and tosses it aside.

"I can't believe we're doing this," I murmur, as Church pushes the frothy white skirts up around my hips, running his tongue up the side of my neck and then resting his lips against my thrumming pulse.

"Why's that?" he asks, looking down at me.

"Because I wasn't even sure if you liked me for the past year."

"We all have our secrets, Chuck," he whispers, just before he slides into me, keeping himself propped up with one hand and using the other to touch the side of my face. He never stops looking into my eyes, not even as his body's moving inside of mine and bringing tears of pleasure to the corners of my gaze. I try to meet his eyes, but it's so intense, I end up turning away. He turns me back to him, stroking across my bottom lip with his thumb and making me tremble.

When he kisses me again, my eyes close of their own accord and he lets them be, moving his mouth down the side of my neck and encouraging me to lift my chest up to meet the touch of his lips.

It's slow and torturous, but in the best possible way, like a fire stoked slowly and then left to burn. And I'm burning.

"Church," I moan, trying to pull my arms down by my sides. But I'm trapped, and not just physically. My heart's trapped, too, stuck right here in Adamson Academy.

I just hope that doesn't turn into a literal statement.

My body betrays me, muscles tightening, pleasure flooding through me in a wave.

Church cuts my gasp off with a kiss, taking my chin in his hand, owning me with a gentle grip of fingers. He scoots back and then, with another naughty smile, disappears beneath my skirts. I'm still shaking, and I haven't quite recovered yet, but I want more. I *crave* it.

Or maybe I'm just craving him?

Church's fingers curl around my pelvis, holding me in place and giving me a lesson in the alphabet with his tongue.

It doesn't seem to be any difficult task for him to give me multiple orgasms.

Soaked in sweat, I lift my head up to look at him as

he comes up for air, eyes dark with the fervid heat that's taken over our room.

"You've done this before, huh?" I ask, my body quivering as he comes up beside me, lying casually with one elbow on the bed, head resting on his hand.

"Not much, actually. Two girls, one time each. You're more experienced than I am."

"But … you're really good at it," I choke out, breathing hard, my arms burning but that ardent heat in my lower belly burning more.

"I read too much," Church says, gesturing at his manga stack on the nightstand. "Lots of *hentai*," he whispers, putting his mouth up against my forehead. Hentai is Japanese porn, by the way. "The occasional romance. You know what my favorite genre is?"

"Am I about to find out?" I look over at him, still breathing hard, still tied up.

"Bully romance," he says with a smile. "I like to see the bad guys get redeemed in the end."

"And who's the bad guy here?" I ask, cocking a brow as Church sits up and leans over me to grab one of the books, flipping open to a page that's been marked carefully with a bookmark.

"You. You are the bully, Chuck Carson. You knocked my project into the water, and then refused to apologize. When we asked you to help fix your mistake, you acted like we were in the wrong. So, you're the bully in this scenario, trying to regain my trust because you're madly in love with me."

"Is that what's happening here?" I ask, but my voice is too foggy from the double orgasms; I don't sound much like a bully right now. More like a girl who's just trying to figure out how to be an adult.

"*He uses his cock, his tongue, and his fingers to bring me to pleasure over and over again, until I feel like I'm breaking apart. And then I let him put me back together with his body. That's when I knew I belonged to him—fully and completely.*" Church stops reading and lets the cover flip closed, thumbing through the pages absently.

"So you want to belong to me, fully and completely?" I ask, getting a bit of that snark back in my voice. Hah! Take that, Church, big old dominant douche-canoe. "That works for me."

"No, Charlotte Carson. You might be the bully, but I'm the boss." He smiles and hooks his left leg over mine, moving between my thighs and grabbing my ass to readjust my hips. "We're going to recreate every scene in this book, starting with this one. The hero ties the heroine up after their wedding and takes her nice and slow. He doesn't worry about his own pleasure until she's shaking." Church turns his head to the side and looks me over. "This should do."

He covers my body with his own, sliding into me inch by careful inch, so slow that it feels like we might never be fully joined together.

"My little California girl," he whispers against my mouth, moving inside of me until I'm coming again, and then using the shudders of my body to find his own climax.

Afterward, Church unties me, leaving the loose tie around my wrist, and kissing me until the sun sinks low in the sky.

"We just defiled your mother's wedding dress," I whisper against his mouth.

"Yes," he says, our foreheads pressed close together. "Yes, we did."

CHAPTER FIFTEEN

When Church told me that riding in his family's jet would make first class look like a joke, he wasn't kidding. The plane that we end up boarding is at a private airport, just outside of Nutmeg, and it's so tricked out on the inside, it makes my father's house at Adamson look like a dump.

"Fucking rich people," I murmur as Tobias pokes me in the back and encourages me to actually set foot inside what's essentially a fancy little dining area. There are four seats—similar to regular airplane seats but decked out in leather—around a dining table, and just across from a long counter with a wall-mounted TV above it.

"That's right—sometimes I forget you're a peasant,"

Tobias teases as I pause to elbow him in the side. My father, as terrifying as he can be, is no match for the Montagues. I'm going to London, even if he doesn't want me to. "Poor people don't do much travelling, do they?"

My eye twitches as I give the tall, lean form of Tobias McCarthy a scathing look.

"Travel takes money, and billionaires horde it all and don't pay fair wages, so what do you think the answer to that question is?"

"Take a seat, Chuck, and relax," Micah says, scooting around behind me and flopping into one of the spots around the dining table. I grab the one across from him and Spencer slides in next to me. Ranger, Tobias, and Church, on the other hand, take up the sofas in the narrow 'living room'.

I'm still recovering from the embarrassment of the other day, you know, when the others found me and Church cuddled up with a wrinkled wedding dress. I'd just as soon stay over here. *Five for five, right, Spence?* I think, buckling my seatbelt and tapping my fingers on the surface of the table. We're sort of waiting for Elizabeth and David who got caught up making out outside. That happens, a lot, apparently, the Montagues getting lost in each other.

"Champagne?" a flight attendant asks, and I glance Church's way. He gives a slight shrug of his shoulder.

"My parents will likely be on their laptops or gazing

into one another's eyes for most of the flight; they don't care if you drink."

I accept some champagne then, and clink glasses with Micah and Spencer.

"On our way out of the country, and goodbye crazy cult," I mumble under my breath, leaning my head back and taking a long drink. I promised Dad that I wouldn't go to Eric Warren's house, and I intend to respect that.

But Ranger's going.

The others are going to stay behind and watch over me.

It's a crapshoot, but it's worth a shot, right?

At the very least, I get a trip to London.

"Do poor people always wear dirty, mismatched socks with sandals on multi-million-dollar private jets?" Micah asks as Spencer grins. They love teaming up to pick on me. I kick his shin under the table and he makes a face at me.

"They're not dirty! They're just … discolored from lots of use, okay? God. Give me some credit."

"Uh, are sandals with mismatched socks cool to wear to London in winter?" Spencer asks, and I give him a look. "Please don't tell me you're wearing those dirty boy's underwear you like so much."

"They were never dirty," I grumble, poking him in the arm as the Montagues finally board the plane. Elizabeth blows through like a hurricane force wind, a presence to be reckoned with. I look down at the ring and then back up at her, a weight lifted from my chest.

This is never how I saw my life going, but … I like the direction it's taking.

I like being engaged to Church, and baking naked with Ranger, watching gay porn with Spencer (we totally did once), drag racing with Micah, practicing martial arts with Tobias.

"Shall we?" Elizabeth asks, giving Church another kiss on the forehead before settling into her seat.

The flight attendants sit down, fasten their seatbelts, and we prepare for takeoff.

"You look so West Coast," Ranger whispers to me, Tobias, and Micah. I might be wearing sandals with socks, but they're rocking big, poofy sleeveless vests with fur around the necklines, and shorts. "Cold as hell, foggy, drizzling. You guys are ridiculous."

"But the tour guide said he'd never heard someone describe Westminster Abbey as dope AF, right? That's something!" I'm in a good mood now, sipping my to-go tea and enjoying the relative quiet of the countryside as we walk up a curving hill toward Highgate Cemetery. We're getting a private tour today, and I'm beyond excited.

"Oh, that's something alright," Ranger says with a roll of his eyes. He can't deny it though: he likes my goofiness, he *admitted* it.

We've done a full round of touristy things—the Natural History Museum and the British Museum some of my faves—but I'm excited to get away from the crowds for a while and take a breather.

"I can't believe we drove all the way out here to see a bunch of dead people," Spencer says, spinning a black umbrella above our heads as we approach a pair of open gates, one on either side of the road. The part of the cemetery we're starting with is only open to tours, while the other side is open to the public. Regardless, they're both equally creepy, stepped in fog, and perfectly horror movie-esque in appearance.

"Less interesting than dead people," Micah says as we cross the street and Church inquires with the woman in the gift shop about our tour. "Rocks sitting on top of dirt where dead people are buried. Yawn-fest."

"This was the one thing on my list, so slow your roll, dickhead," Ranger says, tucking his hands into his black cargo pants as he studies the brick arch above our heads. "I like this kind of shit."

"No, you *want* to like this kind of shit," Spencer says, turning his phone around and flashing a video of border collie puppies herding ducklings. "But in reality, this is your thing, man. Just accept it." Ranger slaps the phone away from his face and pretends not to be interested, but there's that twinkle in his eyes that he just can't hide.

"This way, my friends," Church says, gesturing us out of the gift shop and to a central courtyard area where our tour guide's waiting. The old man introduces himself and then starts off on a speech about the cemetery. Meanwhile, my eyes are already wandering the tree-covered hill behind him, gravestones peeking out of the shadows.

My neck prickles with unease, and I look around, expecting to see those creeps in fox masks waiting for me next to a mausoleum. There's nobody and nothing there when I search the landscape, but the feeling's pretty persistent as we trudge up the hill, pausing next to certain graves to hear the stories about them.

At first, I'm pretty skeptical, but the further we get into the tour and the cemetery, the more I start to dig it. There's a section of the cemetery called Egyptian Avenue that looks like a set for an adventure film. According to the tour guide, there's a rare type of spider that lives in the tombs here that requires total darkness to thrive.

"But don't worry," he says with a laugh and a wave of his hand, "they can't come out during the day, so you're perfectly safe." I start down the dark hall, lined with tombs on either side, and keep my arms wrapped around myself.

"This so freaking creepy," I murmur as the twins sneak up behind me. One of them pulls my collar back, and the other drops something with *legs* onto my spine. With a shriek, I start tearing my sweatshirt off and flailing around while Ranger curses under his breath, and Spencer steps in to grab my arms.

"Hey, hey, hey, Chuck-let," he whispers as the McCarthy boys snicker at me. I can't exactly see them because my hoodie's pulled up over my face but Spencer stops me from taking it off the rest of the way, tugging it back down again. "It's just a plastic spider this time."

"This time," I groan, sagging in relief and then noticing the rather cool breeze across my midsection. "My bra is showing, isn't it?" I ask, thinking of that scene in *Mean Girls* where the teacher tries to pull her sweater off and ends up taking her shirt along with it. Yep, that's what's happening to me now. "The one with the see-through lace and bows?"

"That's the one," Spencer says, pushing the sweatshirt back in place and then kissing me quick on the lips as the twins high five each other and continue on up the path.

"I'm going to murder those fuckers," I mumble, narrowing my eyes and continuing after them, into this really cool circle of mausoleums that used to surround a giant cedar tree. Apparently, it fell over in a recent storm, but it's still impressive as hell.

Eventually, we end up at the catacombs, stepping into the cool, musty air as our guide uses a flashlight to show us around.

"Right this way," he says, a bounce in his step as he takes us over to a very specific casket and begins to explain the life and times of the surgeon that's buried there. While he's talking, I get that feeling again, putting a hand on the back of my neck and glancing over my shoulder to see if maybe there's an animal peeking out from the shadows or something.

But there's nothing there, nothing at all.

My breathing quickens up just a tad, and Spencer notices. He's attentive like that. I bet he'd make a good dad one day.

I freeze up like a deer caught in the headlights.

"Are you okay?" he whispers, trying not to interrupt our tour guide's enthusiastic speech.

"I'm not having kids until I'm thirty," I blurt, and Spencer gives me the weirdest look known to man before bursting out laughing.

"Aww, Chuck-let," he says, doubling over with laughter as the others glance back to see what all the fuss is about.

My random foot-in-mouth disaster drops my guard for just a little while, making me forget about the creepy feeling.

What a mistake.

We continue our tour through the brick-vaulted

gallery, and then head back to the entrance. I'm in the back of the group with Spencer, trying to avoid his teasing about all the babies he's going to give me, when I hear the sound of a scuffed shoe behind me.

A hand wraps around my mouth, and I'm yanked back into the darkness. The iron gate in front of me is slammed shut by two people in hoodies, and while one of them slaps a deadbolt on the door, the other turns toward me and I see the fox mask underneath his hood.

"Chuck!" Spencer screams as the other boys turn around and spot me being dragged through the darkness. Our poor tour guide looks like he's about to have a heart attack.

The person holding me drags me around the corner and into the shadows as the other two approach, each one taking a leg the way they did before, at the Valentine's Day incident. I'm pulled into the vault, kicking and screaming against a warm, sweaty palm.

They're going fast, too, running full-tilt down the shadowed walkway.

They followed us all the way here, all the way to a different country.

I mean, I knew they could and would follow me, but this? This is next level.

There's a door at the end of the hallway that leads to a set of steps and out into the woods again. I see it all in a blur as the three psychos bounce up the stone staircase and take off into the trees.

Panic is taking over me, but I struggle to fight through it, pulling up memories of practicing with the twins. I'm no ninja, believe me, but I come up with a plan on the fly. The person holding my top half has to keep one hand over my mouth to stop me from screaming, so they've only got one of my arms locked down.

With the other, I swing my fist down and nail my attacker right in the crotch.

Luckily, it's a dude holding me up there this time, and my swing finds purchase. The man stumbles briefly, just briefly, but it's enough that the forward momentum of the other two brings my legs toward my chest, allowing me enough power to kick out.

We come to a bit of a stumbling halt, a tangle of arms and legs on the ground as the boys' shouts for me ring out across the woods.

"This is so not my job," one of the hoodie-dicks growls, and it's definitely a male voice, but not one that I recognize. Trust me: I've heard Mark's irritating little quips enough times to know what he'd sound like.

"Just sort it out," a whispered female voice responds as they try to get ahold of me again. But the second that palm slips off my mouth, I scream. And maybe it's all the, like, orgasms I've been having lately, but I swear I've amped up my screaming game.

The sound echoes across the cemetery as my attacker moves his hand from my arm and back to my mouth. Unfortunately, the group quickly regains control, and we take off again.

We're on our way out an open side gate now, where a limo's waiting, the door open, engine idling. If I get into that car, and it takes off, I'm dead. No ifs, ands, or buts about it.

They shove me inside, and I panic at the sight of another person in a fox mask, but this one isn't wearing a hoodie: he's wearing robes. I kick out my left foot and hit them square in the face, knocking the mask loose just enough that I can see the person's scowling mouth. When I kick out again, I manage to make them bleed before they're grabbing onto my ankle.

The attacker in the fox mask behind me is yanked back with a grunt, and I can see that the boys have finally caught up to me.

"Drive," the bleeding man commands, shoving me out of the way and heading for the door. But if he thought I'd be easy to subdue, he's wrong. I'm not a superhero, but I'm a little scrappy. *Shit, I really should've been Scrappy-Doo for Halloween, huh?*

I leap onto the man's back as he tries to close the door, knocking him to the floor as the limo's tires squeal across the pavement and it starts to take off.

There's a person right there, though, just outside the door. On a whim, I fling my hand out, praying it's one of the guys and not one of the Fellowship assholes. My fingers curl around Tobias' and he yanks me out just as the limo really gets some speed going and disappears up the hill.

Two of my three attackers are fleeing in the opposite direction, the third lagging just slightly behind. Spencer grabs onto the back of the guy's hoodie, but the fabric slips through his fingers and the asshole takes off running.

"Ranger!" he shouts, and then there he is, bursting from the front entrance and slamming full force into the guy. The two of them go tumbling across the sidewalk and into the cobblestone street, coming to a stop with Ranger on top. He doesn't hesitate either, throwing a punch into the side of the man's head that makes a cracking sound. I can hear it, even from all the way over here.

Damn.

My friends are as ruthless as my enemies, aren't they?

Ranger doesn't stop punching the guy until he goes still.

"Alright, that's enough," the twins say, pulling their friend off while Church puts a hand on the side of my face.

"Are you okay?" he asks, and I nod before he turns away and heads over to the downed man, bending low near the guy's face as Spencer grabs me by the hand. I curl my fingers through his and we make our way over.

When the mask comes off, I find myself … slightly

less shocked than I should be.

"Hello Mark," Church says, and the way those words come out of his mouth … I'd be scared if I were Mark fucking Grandam.

"Get the hell off of me!" Mark shouts, but we're not at Adamson right now, and there is no headmaster to save him. There will, however, be plenty of onlookers if we don't wrap this up quick. It's a quiet, drizzly day, but this isn't exactly a ghost town.

"Get off of you?" Ranger asks, his voice this cloud of darkness that makes me shiver. "You just attacked our girlfriend, and you want me to *get the hell off of you*?"

"It was a practical joke," Mark sneers, as if he's got the moral high ground here. I remember that day we went into his room to check the ceiling; he told me, quite easily I might add, that Eugene was in Cancun. But if he's involved in the cult then surely, he knew his best friend was dead. Yet the lie came that easily to him, like it meant nothing. "You have no right to keep me here. I'll start screaming, man."

"Why are you in London, chasing after Charlotte, Mr. Grandam?" Church asks, circling around the pair with murder in his eyes. He's smart enough not to mention the cult. Because if we do, then they'll know that we're aware of their existence. Part of me feels relieved, like maybe I'm seeing the end of this nightmare. *What are you planning on doing with Mark though? Killing him? Tying him up and throwing him into a basement until we can get the rest of this mystery sorted out?*

I realize than that we haven't accomplished anything here—except, you know, for stopping my kidnapping.

"I said *get off of me!*" Mark screams, just as a pair of schoolgirls comes around the corner, pausing as they see the scene in front of them. To be fair, Mark *is* bleeding from the head, and Ranger *is* lording over him like he might very well strangle him to death.

Seeing no choice in the matter, Ranger stands up with a scowl, gritting his teeth hard as he curls his hands into fists.

"We knew you were guilty," the twins say together, standing on either side of me and Spencer, ready to move in if needed. They exchange a look and then nod, turning back to point at Mark. "You killed Eugene."

"What the fuck are you talking about?" Mark asks, stumbling over to the sidewalk and swiping blood from his lip. He pulls out his phone and dials a number, putting it to his ear as it rings and watching us warily.

We've literally caught him red-handed and there's

nothing we can do about it right now.

It's serious freaking torture.

"Yeah, come get me. I'm still at the cemetery." He hangs up as the six of us stand there, watching him like the monster he is. "What? Stop fucking staring at me. Sorry you can't take a damn joke."

"You killed your best friend," Spencer says, his turquoise eyes narrowing. "Or you know who did."

"Seriously, shut the hell up," Mark snaps, and I can see the boys are doing it on purpose to egg him on. "We only came up here because you guys are freaks, and your girlfriend is a freak, and nobody at the fucking academy likes you."

"Nobody believes you followed us up here to play a practical joke," Church says, but Mark's already turning away and marching down the hill. "Who were your friends, by the way? We'd love to know who else was in on this little jest."

A taxi pulls up and Mark gets in, sliding into the backseat without another word, and slamming the door behind him.

"I'm not surprised," Church says, looking back at me, Spencer, and the twins. "But I am intrigued. What does this move mean, exactly?"

"That they're on a timeline?" I suggest, breathing hard, the adrenaline finally fading from my limbs. That was close, closer than last time. What happens next? I'm afraid to find out.

"Let's see if the attacks coordinate with anything in particular," Church says as Ranger looks up the hill behind us, eyes narrowing slightly.

"And who the hell do you think was in that limo?" Spencer wonders as he pulls me close, and the sky opens up into a torrent of freezing rain.

The Montague's 'flat' (that's like, a condo for us 'Muricans) is this sprawling mini-mansion contained within the smooth white walls of some fancy building in a neighborhood called Hyde Park. I don't know much about London, but I hear it's pretty swanky.

I almost choked on my soda when I first walked in here last week.

"My dad'll be here in a half hour," Ranger says, checking his phone and then cursing under his breath. For the last four days, he's been staying at Church's place with the rest of us, but his dad's just come back into town after a business trip, and he's picking Ranger up today.

I'm not the only one with reservations about him going over there.

Church looks away in frustration; he's tried talking his friend out of it, but Woodruff is nothing if not stubborn.

"You sure you're not gonna die over there?" Spencer asks, putting his hands on his hips and looking Ranger over with a sharp frown. "Your dad is actually *in* this cult, like without a doubt. Jenica was scared of him."

"Exactly," Ranger snaps, putting his fingers in his black hair. "And she's dead. So I have to go, if only to find out what happened to her."

"There are other ways," Church says softly, moving over to sit next to Ranger. "We'll explore the tunnels when we get back, find their hidden church. If Jack could sleuth around without getting caught, we'll figure it out."

"And you're assuming you'll find anything of worth while you're there," Tobias starts, and Micah finishes the thought for them.

"Why would your dad keep anything incriminating around? This is pointless."

"I'm going to talk to him," Ranger says, lifting his head up, azure eyes burning. "I'll be careful about it, but yeah, I'm going to ask some hard questions."

Church huffs out a sigh.

"You're impossible," he says as Ranger gets up and impulsively finds his way into the kitchen, unloading some staple items onto the counter. Looks like he's going for a classic brownie recipe. "Tell me what you expect to come out of this with."

Ranger looks around for an apron, and finally scores one in the cabinet on the far end of the room. It's one of those white French maid type ones, and he looks *amazing* when he slips it on, diving into his brownie-making cooldown while we all watch and wait for him to respond.

"Maybe I don't expect to come out with anything," he admits, stirring the batter with hard, fast movements. "I just want to look him in the eye and know that he did it. I want to see what that feels like."

"Trust me," Spencer says, and I wonder if he's thinking about Jack or someone else. "You don't want to see someone you loved after you know the truth. It hurts too much. Let him go."

"I've never loved that man," Ranger says, but that's clearly a lie. The doorbell rings, and he shoves the brownies aside, slamming his hand against the oven to set the temperature as he storms past and heads for the front door. "Don't overcook those fucking brownies. I expect thick, fudgy goodness out of that batter."

He tears the door open as I move closer to see what Eric Warren looks like, curiosity keeping me brave.

The man looks just like his social media picture, like Ranger might in thirty years, but with an unkind streak that isn't present in either his son, or his deceased daughter. She looks just like him, too, and I have to make myself remember that technically, she was his niece.

"Eric," Ranger says as his father looks him over with a displeased sort of glint in his eyes.

"Hello, Ranger," the man replies carefully, his eyes sliding over to the rest of us for a brief moment. That's when I notice it, his split lower lip. My gaze widens, but I'm clearly not the only one who sees it.

Eric is wearing the same injury that I gave the man in the limo.

Ranger's shoulders tighten, and his mouth flattens out.

"How are you?" Eric asks, but not like he particularly cares. More like he has no soul.

"Just fine, Dad," Ranger replies, tossing his apron aside and stepping out the door.

Let's just say, I don't sleep very well those next few nights.

CHAPTER SIXTEEN

The Adamson All-Boys Academy sign is lying on the grass near the edge of the road, and the new one, the one that simply says *Adamson Academy* is being put up in its stead.

"When are they supposed to show up?" Spencer asks, watching the road with a frown fixed firmly in place. Since today is the first day of the quarter, it's time to introduce my new female classmates to the population. Dad has specifically chosen me for this task, and much as I'd like to bail on this, I feel like I owe him a bit.

When I got back from London, I didn't know what to say to him, so I didn't say anything at all. Does he *really* need to know about the attack? Or Mark? I don't want anything to happen to him either.

"Soon," I say, checking my phone and sighing. My eyes swing over to Ranger, standing there with one arm across his chest, his gaze fixed to the woods. He, of course, didn't find any evidence as to his father's involvement with the Fellowship, but that split lip was enough to confirm that he is, in fact, *still* working with them. "Do we know how we're planning on dealing with the Student Council elections? We still don't have a plan."

"We're not going to win," the twins say together, dropping their shoulders in a dramatic sigh. "Why bother?" They hold their hands up and out on either side, effectively giving up. "Besides," Tobias continues, smiling softly at me as the wind tousles his hair around his face. "We have more important things to worry about: like you."

"You can't just give up the Student Council that easily," I say, knowing that it means a lot to them. "We can come up with something."

The sound of the car coming up the frozen gravel drive makes my already chilly skin pebble with goose bumps. There's snow on the ground, and it's freezing cold up here all the damn time. I swear to you, my blood is thinner than everyone else's, and I need a whole two scarves and three jackets to stay warm.

Once the car's parked, the girls climb out and I

greet them with a small wave. There'll be an assembly later, but Dad wanted to give them the chance to start their morning off with a normal routine.

"Hello, Charlotte," Aster says, beaming brightly as she eyes me and Ranger together. "Church, I hope you know that your girl here's got a side thing going with this one."

"We're a polyamorous group, thank you for noticing," he says, but the words might as well be *fuck you and the horse you rode in on.* "It's not like the thing you've got going, slinking around and screwing Mark behind Selena's back."

The quip works and Aster's face flames before she marches around us, crunching through the snow with the other two Everly transfer students behind her.

"That was … reasonably harsh," I say as the twins grin.

"We put condoms in her locker, too." They each grab one of my arms and turn us back toward the main building.

"We figured she might think Selena put them there," Tobias adds.

"Oh, and also, we hate her," Micah adds as we move through the double wide doors at the front of the school. "You know, for running against us when senior year's supposed to be a piece of cake."

"Frankly, between the cult and elections, I'm pissed," Spencer adds, grinning. "So how do we take her down? And what the fuck do we do about Mark?"

"Part of me thinks we should try to win the elections through fair play," Church begins, glancing up at the curved stone ceilings above us. "The rest of me knows that if Mark is involved with the Fellowship, then I'd rather die than hand him my school."

"So, let's do this, our way," Spencer says, sliding his phone from his pocket. "I have an idea."

Showing the girls around on Monday isn't exactly a pleasant task, particularly since one of my boyfriends called Aster out for having an affair with Selena's boyfriend, two of my other boyfriends stuffed her locker with contraceptives, and the silver-haired one is actively plotting against her behind the scenes.

The fifth and final boyfriend decides to wait until our Culinary Club meeting on Tuesday to piss her off.

"You're not coming in my kitchen," Ranger says, standing in the doorway to the classroom with his apron on, arms crossed in front of his chest. His lip is raised in a snarl as he stares down the home ec teacher, Mr. Johansen. Technically, Mr. Johansen's supposed to be our supporting staff member, but I've only ever seen him come by our meetings in passing. At least he gives us all high marks—even I got an A both semesters last year.

"Mr. Woodruff," Mr. Johansen scolds, reaching up to adjust his glasses. "I'm appalled by your behavior. The Culinary Club does not belong to you or the Student Council, much as you might wish it did. Now, move aside and make Aster feel at home here."

With a muscle ticking in his jaw, Ranger moves aside and lets Aster Hayes into the room. She's beaming, red hair frothing around her face in frizzy curls. She even has a light dusting of freckles over her button nose. Thinking of her as a murderer is … difficult.

"I don't like this," Spencer murmurs, eyes tracking her movement through the classroom. Mr. Johansen quickly makes an excuse and disappears down the hall to read his erotica novels. He's always leaving his Kindle on, and always at a questionable scene of dubious character. Old perv.

"Me neither," I hedge as Aster spins, holding her bookbag in front of her, and beaming like a crazy person.

"I was in the Baking Club at Everly," she explains, looking around the room at our glares, frowns, and—in the case of the twins—stuck out tongues. "This is sort of my thing. Thank you so much for having me."

"You know we don't like you," Spencer says as Ranger starts to anger-bake in a whirlwind. "So why the hell are you here?"

"I know it must be tough to have true competition in the elections, but isn't that what politics are all about? Fierce competition, honesty, and integrity?" Aster's green eyes scan the classroom, taking in our cozy reading nook with the alphabetized cookbooks (my work), the gleaming counters, and the fully-stocked refrigerator and pantry. This is our home away from home, y'know? Having her in it feels like a violation.

"Uh, do you follow American politics at all? Because that's pretty much the opposite of how it works." Spencer rolls his eyes and exchanges a long, studying look with the twins. Surely, they're up to no good, but there's also a very good chance that Aster Hayes is guilty, so … fair is fair.

"What are we making today?" she asks, moving over to the cabinets and looking through them. When she goes for the one with the aprons in it, I step in front of her and cut her off.

"This is a private cabinet," I say as Ranger watches stiffly from behind her.

"This classroom is for everyone," she argues, still smiling at me. "But if you don't want me to look in there, I won't. I'd rather we didn't fight. I'm here to be a part of this club."

"Sure thing," Spencer says, but he's not convinced. None us are.

Instead of our usual joking and playing around, the

room is silent while we each work on our own recipes. Sometimes, we work individually, other times we make things together. But with Aster here, everybody stays in their own lane.

"She seems like the type to get us written up, if we were to, say, crack an egg down her back," Tobias whispers, looking across the room at her. I noticed Ranger cringing when she started making substitutions in a recipe from one of the old cookbooks. "You know, that's one of the things we liked so much about you, Chuck."

"Cracking eggs down my back?" I ask, thinking of the plastic spider from the cemetery and narrowing my eyes.

"No, silly, the fact that you didn't get us written up for acting like twat-faces." Micah pops the electric mixer into his bowl as I grin.

"Twat-face. That's a new one, but I like it." I stir my healthy banana-chocolate-oat pancake mix together as I think about that. It never really occurred to me that I could get the guys written up for the things they did to me. That's just not my thing. After all, I've had a headmaster for a father my entire life and believe me, running to him and tattling never did me any good.

Sometimes, we have to face our own problems. And sometimes, those problems turn into blessings.

Toward the end of the day, Spencer finishes his cupcakes and goes about piping fox faces onto them with red icing. He sets the tray down on the island where Aster's working, but even though she looks up, there's no reaction.

"If I didn't think it might get me killed, I'd have put that ugly symbol on all of them," he says, watching the small, short girl put blackberries on the top of her cake.

So, for the rest of the day, we leave Aster alone.

But she isn't going to stick around and ruin Culinary Club for us for the rest of the year.

No fucking way.

The Student Council debates are held in the large auditorium in the rear portion of the main building, this stuffy old theater with enough neoclassical features in its architecture to choke a horse. Since I'm not actually on the Student Council—the assistant position is assigned by the members and not up for election—I sit in the front row to watch the debates, not onstage with the boys.

It's doubtful anybody would show up at these things without being mandated, but, of course, when Archibald Carson has his way, things are bound to get boring. The whole school is in attendance, slumped and groaning in their seats.

"Nice of you to show up," Dad says, pausing next to my seat and looking down at me like I'm the biggest disappointment of his entire life. "I'd almost forgotten that you attended this school."

"That's on you," I quip back, crossing my arms over my unbound chest, and shrugging. "You're the one that said you didn't want to treat me like a daughter anymore."

"That's not what I said," he bites out and then sighs, pausing to run his hand over his thinning hair. "You're misinterpreting my words for your own gain, behavior that's rather childish, especially for a woman who's engaged and planning to marry."

I roll my eyes, but Dad doesn't notice, moving over to the steps on the side of the stage and climbing up to take his position at the podium. As he's hefting his iPad from his briefcase to look at his speech notes (the iPad with the *PAW Patrol* cover, by the way), Aster and her friends appear from behind the curtain, taking their seats on the opposite side of the stage from the boys.

Theoretically, everyone knows that each Student Council position is individual, that there are no party platforms or anything like that. But only theoretically. Either Church will win—and with him, the other guys—or else Aster and her friends will.

The way that room picks up and all eyes flick toward the three new girls in their well-pressed skirts and ties, I have a feeling that the vote is leaning toward

Aster.

With a sigh, I slump in my seat and resist the urge to scroll on my phone. It's painful to watch though, seeing my boys give all the right answers while Mark and his stupid meathead roommate—Gareth, apparently, is his name—goof around.

There has to be some way for us to kick their asses, right?

After the debates, everyone files out and the halls are filled with gossip. People are definitely looking at us in a different way than they used to before. *Student Council only, assholes* just doesn't seem to hold as much weight as it did.

"You said you had a plan," I whisper to Spencer as we watch Mark from across the hall, leaning against his locker and flirting shamelessly with Aster. He doesn't even try to hide it. Like, how does he not know this is all going to get back to Selena? Maybe he just doesn't care? "But you still won't tell me what it is."

"You'll see," Spencer says, but his eyes are bright as he watches our rivals basking in the glow of an adoring crowd. He glances down at me and cocks a brow. "What? It's a surprise! I'm still working on it. I need my dad's help, and we don't have that great of a relationship, so … sort of banking on his guilt to make this work."

"Guilt over what?" I ask, and Spencer makes a bit of a face.

"He left my mom to go live in Paris with his mistress and his other kid, sort of a royal piece of shit." He looks right at me and then puts his hand on the wall above my head, looking down at my face with all due seriousness. "That's why I don't like lies, Chuck. He lied to me, and my brother, and my mom. And then you know what he did? He came *back* and my mom took him back, and guess what? He still lies about the shit that he does, and she doesn't care. Jack doesn't even care." He pauses for a moment, still watching me with those intense eyes of his. "But I do."

"Of course you do," I say, trying to keep my voice soft. "You have big feelings."

Spencer thinks for a moment, and then smiles.

"Yeah, I guess I do?" he says, pausing as a student approaches us warily. "If you're trying to buy from me right now, it's not happening. Not until we win the elections."

"Cheap ass!" Mark calls out, snickering, like we didn't catch him trying to abduct me in London. What a piece of work. He seems to think he's untouchable, but I know better. It's just a matter of time before he gets his. I don't know what the boys plan on doing about it, but they're not going to let it go.

Not a chance in hell of that happening.

By Friday, there's a buzz humming through the school that I can't quite puzzle out. Mostly because nobody likes me. Partially, I blame the boys for that. They've been super overprotective, but considering I'm being hunted by a murderous cult, I don't think that's such a bad thing.

"What is going on?" I whisper as Spencer walks me down the hall, squeezing a stress ball in his right hand. I'm not gonna lie: it's a sperm stress ball. Like, it looks like a giant white sperm. They gave them out for free in health class, and everybody thought they were hilarious. I keep seeing white sperm stress balls everywhere.

"You'll see," Spencer says, grinning as he glances over at me. "Church isn't the only one who can scheme and throw his weight around."

"Meaning what?" I ask as we head in the direction of the auditorium to cast our votes. They'll be tallied up by volunteers from the Adamson staff—including my father, Mr. Murphy, and Mr. Dave—and the winners will be announced at a special ceremony at the end of the day.

Frankly, I'm not all that hopeful, but none of the boys seem concerned, so I've been trying not to let it bother me.

"You're a real hard-ass, Hargrove," a boy in a junior's uniform says, flipping us off as he passes by.

Now I'm *really* curious to find out what's going on.

"Chuck-let," Spencer says, turning and pushing me gently into one of the decorative alcoves that lines the walls of the school. It's this big stone archway that's just deep enough for two people to hide in … I mean, if anyone walks by and glances over, you're screwed, but there's at least some privacy here. We've tested out six or seven of them for, like, research purposes. And obviously at this point, you know that by research purposes, I mean make-out sessions. "Don't you like a little mystery in your life?"

"Do you?" I retort, letting my bookbag fall to the stone floor, so I can put my arms around Spencer's neck. He leans over me in that way I like, one of his arms above my head, his lips curved into a feral grin. "Because last time I surprised you by telling you my dick was actually a vagina, you freaked out." He rolls his eyes at me, but he can't argue that point, now can he?

"This isn't a lie though, just a surprise."

"A surprise that's going to win us the elections?" I clarify, and the grin is back.

"As soon as we do, we're going to rain terror down on Mark and all of his idiot friends. Oh, and that Aster chick, too. Either she's sleeping with a creep or she is a creep herself, I don't know, but I don't like her."

"What are you planning on doing?" I ask as Spencer tucks the sperm-y stress ball into my pocket and I make a face.

"Besides kissing you, you mean?" he pretends to clarify, sliding the fingers of his left hand along the length of my jaw. He cups the back of my head and then moves his other hand to the opposite side, holding me still and stroking his thumbs down my throat. "We can do all sorts of fun things to them. Move their lockers, change their class schedules for next semester, swap their dorm room assignments. Never underestimate the power of petty bullshit. Mark's already like an ugly pimple ready to burst. If we poke and prod, he's going to fall apart, and we'll be able to get him."

"And by get him …" I start as Spencer laughs, low and throaty, making my toes curl in my shoes. A man shouldn't be able to smell so good, by the way. It's making it freakishly hard for me to concentrate.

"Bury him six feet under, in the dead of night, in the old cemetery by the railroad tracks," Spencer whispers, and then he laughs, moving away from me. I grab onto his blazer and yank him back, kissing him on the mouth and opening my lips for his tongue. Several minutes later, we come up for breath, and he smirks. "Your mouth is a good motivator, Chuck-let, you know that?"

"So, the plan with Mark …?"

"We report him—to authorities *outside* of Nutmeg. Shit, we report those authorities, too. There *is* a chain of command for this stuff, you know."

"Won't his ultra-rich family just take care of it the way yours does for Jack?"

"Between the five of us," he says, as students pass by in small groups, whispering about the elections. "We'll take care of it. But we need as much evidence as possible first." Spencer leans in closer, one of his hands traveling down my side and cupping my ass through my skirt. He exhales sharply, like he's seriously holding back right now. "You know I have a thing for schoolgirl uniforms, right?"

"You've never said as much, but I could tell." I grin back at him. "You've fantasized about screwing me in this, huh?"

"Screwing, making love to, fucking, doing it … all of the things."

He nuzzles the side of my neck and makes me go weak at the knees.

"We should really get to the auditorium to vote," I whisper, knowing the others will come looking for us if we don't show up soon. Mr. Murphy walks past us, my eyes briefly meeting his over Spencer's shoulder, but he knows better than to stop or say anything.

"What if we just … made it quick?" he asks as he runs his tongue across his lower lip and I inadvertently mimic the motion.

"Where should we go?" I whisper back, totally getting off on the conspiratorial nature of the moment. My heart gallops like a herd of wild horses, manes billowing in the wind, whinnying softly … Eww. What? Eww. No, that's not poetic or cool-sounding whatsoever. The hell is wrong with me?

"Go?" Spence asks, kissing down the side of my neck as he slides his hands underneath my skirt, palms sliding up my bare thighs. "We don't have to go anywhere. I want to do it right fucking here, where anybody could walk by and see."

"Are you nuts?!" I choke out as his fingers knead the soft flesh of my ass. "We're being hunted by a cult, remember?"

"We better make it quick then, huh?"

He lifts me up and pins me against the wall with his body, my arms automatically encircling his neck, fingers digging into his silver hair. Our mouths meet in a hot, desperate tangle as he presses his erection against me. My lips part in sweet surrender to his tongue, and I can already tell by the heavy weight of my limbs and the flutter of my lashes against my cheeks that I'm giving into him.

"I want to do it without a condom so bad right now," he growls, one of his hands slipping between us to open his slacks. My eyes are closed, my pulse pounding inside my head. I don't have the strength to say no, but at least he does. "But I won't."

"Because Ranger would kill you if you did it again," I whisper and Spencer groans, freeing himself and then digging a condom out of his blazer pocket. I chastised him the other day for carrying them around all the time, but then I did stick several in my bookbag, just in case.

Teenagers are straight-up hoes.

Spencer slips the condom on, letting the wrapping fall to the floor, and then waits for me to hook my panties to the side with two fingers.

His eyes meet mine as he lines up with my opening and thrusts deeps, filling me up and pushing my body into the stone wall with the weight of his own. The pleasure is immediate and intense, releasing a flood of hormones into my body that make me feel both heavy and weightless, all at the same time.

Our mouths find each other again, searching and claiming, as he finds a rhythm that works, grinding me into the alcove with frenzied thrusts. The wall has no give, so each movement sheathes him fully inside of me, taking my breath away. A scream rests in my throat, but I bite it back.

Half the fun is the risk of getting caught, but also … there are few people at this school who I wouldn't lose my shit over catching us like this.

"Oh, Chuck," Spencer moans as he sucks on my lower lip. "You feel so damn good."

His hands cup my ass, holding me up effortlessly as

he moves, my pleated skirt bunched up around my hips. It could be weird to find a school uniform so erotic, but … I fantasize about the boys in their uniforms all the time when I touch myself. Which, you know, is just a little bit more often now that Church and I have finally done it. I'm not so scared of him hearing me from across the room.

"More, Spencer, more," I murmur as he rocks our bodies together, the motion of his pelvis rubbing my clit in a way that makes me think I might actually be able to get off during this little quickie.

My hands scrabble at his back, fingernails digging into the champagne fabric of his blazer, as our lips clash in fire and desperate, primal heat, stifling our moans and grunts from the rest of the school.

"I want you to come with me," I whisper, gathering him close, our breath mingling as we stare into each other's eyes. My body tightens around his of its own accord, an orgasm spiraling through me in a brilliant, blinding wave. Another kiss from Spencer cuts off my sounds of pleasure as he pushes into me, again and again, finishing himself off just a few moments later.

We stay there panting just long enough to hear the soft clapping of several hands.

"Bravo," the twins say, appearing in the alcove behind Spencer's broad shoulders. "That was a fantastic performance."

"*Oh, Chuck,*" Micah mimics, clasping his hands

together and fluttering his lashes. "*You feel so damn good.*"

"I'm going to fucking strangle you," Spencer growls out as he struggles between us with the condom, just barely managing to get it out and off without dropping me.

"Are you both too stupid to live?" Ranger asks, but I can see the pulse in his throat thundering. He liked what he saw, that's for sure. "Chuck is being actively hunted, and you thought a quickie in the hallway was a good idea? You know how vulnerable and oblivious you two looked just now? We've been standing here the whole time, and you didn't even notice."

"*More, Spencer, more,*" Tobias wheedles, his voice high and fluttery.

"I don't sound like that!" I gripe at him, struggling to fix my wet panties, my bunched-up skirt. Spencer ties the condom off and looks around for a trash can.

Magically, Dad appears as if summoned to ruin my fucking life, and Spencer's forced to shove the used condom into his blazer pocket, grimacing as he does it.

"What's going on here? You're supposed to be in the auditorium right now. Or do you not take these elections as seriously as you should?" Dad eyes me and Spencer with a suspicious glint in his blue eyes.

"I assure you, sir," Church begins, taking control as always—a trait I am *beyond* appreciative for. I'm just not the leadership type. "We take our duties *very* seriously." He puts a hand over his chest, and I swear to god, the clouds shift above the school, letting in three gorgeous rays of sunshine through the stained glass above our heads and painting him with a halo. "The Student Council is the heart of Adamson Academy, a prestigious and well-run institution with the finest staff in the country. Today, when we win the elections, I promise you that we'll begin implementing positive change at the student level."

"No wonder he's in all the brochures," I grumble, as Dad narrows his eyes.

"I liked you before, Mr. Montague, but you're pushing your luck now. Get your tardy selves to the auditorium *now.*"

"As you wish," Church replies, but it's said in just such a way that it couldn't possibly be taken as anything but genuine. Somehow, though, I think Church does it on purpose, just to be even more ironic. Dad takes off, and Spencer waits until he gets around the corner before making a face and jogging over to one of the trash cans to drop off the condom.

"Now my pocket's all wet on the inside," he says, and my face heats up with an inferno of embarrassment.

"What is wrong with you?!" I snap at him, grabbing onto his sleeve and shoving him a bit. "Don't say things like that."

"*I want you to come with me,*" the twins chortle

together, and I press my hands over my ears, blocking out their teasing. What I can't block out, however, is my smile.

Especially when, later that day, the announcements are made, and my boys win the election.

Score one for Chuck and her forever crew, and fuck you, Mark. Fuck you.

CHAPTER SEVENTEEN

I'd almost forgotten how intimidating the long table in the Student Council room was, considering I'm now dating every single guy on the other side of it. But when I first came in here, brandishing my new locker assignment, I was nervous.

The room is intended to be intimidating, dimly lit with floor-length beige drapes over the windows. The ceilings are at least twenty feet tall, the bookcases that line the walls just as impressive. There are iron sconces on the walls, two decorative chaises on either side of the doors, and a pair of curved staircases behind the boys, made up of gleaming wood with brass accents. There are only about ten steps on either side, leading up to a second level and a small walkway that wraps the room.

It's seriously way over the top for a high school Student Council, but hey, rich people do horribly ridiculous and disgustingly excessive things all the time. I read about this one politician who claims he's out for the little guys that has solid gold elevators, gold plant pots, and gold ceilings in his home (one of his homes anyway). Serious douche-canoe alert.

Talk about trying too hard; no amount of money could make that guy cool.

"You can't do this!" Mark shouts, gesturing at the boys with his new locker assignment—as far from mine as possible on the Adamson Academy campus. "I've had that locker since freshman year."

I stand to the side, clutching the council iPad, and trying not to enjoy Mark's pain.

Then again, he *did* try to kidnap me in a cemetery, so I guess I'm justified in feeling a bit smug about it.

"We actually can and did," Church says, sitting in his throne, right behind his shiny *President* sign. The other boys all have these languid, self-satisfied smirks going that are about a hundred times worse than the ones they wore when I initially stormed in here complaining about my locker. "We've also just gotten the headmaster to sign off on moving your work duty from the chicken coop and garden, into the kitchen."

"So, you just suck up to your daddy and get whatever you want, huh?" Mark asks, sneering at me.

What I find ironic about his statement is, my dad doesn't do shit for me when I suck up. And Mark's dad bought him a private jet for his sixteenth birthday (the boys told me this). So if anyone is getting favors from daddy, it isn't me.

"Actually, Headmaster Carson, in all of his infinite wisdom, has noticed the tension brewing between us and thought it best if we didn't interact. You'll be washing dishes and helping serve food three days a week." Church taps his fingers on the surface of the table, clearly ready to be finished with this conversation.

"I'm not the fucking help!" Mark roars, and my blood starts to boil. Thoughts of Mom come rushing into my brain and I take a challenging step forward.

"You're right, you're not the help. You're less than the leftover meatloaf that you'll be scraping from pans in the school kitchen. Any one of those people working in there is a better person than you, you spoiled rotten little brat."

Mark starts toward me, but all five boys rise in unison and he stops, fully aware of what they're capable of.

"We've changed your dorm assignment as well," Church continues as Micah, the acting Secretary of the council, scribbles something down on a piece of paper and hands it to me. I pass the notarized dorm assignment form over to Mark, and he gapes at it.

"You're putting me with that loser science geek from first period?" he says, completely aghast, like this is the worst thing that's ever happened to him. He looks up, and I wonder briefly how I thought he was even remotely handsome. Like, I think I was trying to be nice when I said he could be if he didn't have such a rotten personality. In reality, he sort of reminds me of a skunk or a weasel, only with less intelligence and heart than either animal exhibits in the worst of circumstances.

"You tried to murder our girlfriend," Spencer says, sitting slowly back down in his chair and lounging bonelessly in it, like he owns the place. "Don't think we've forgotten that."

"All of this because of some practical joke?" Mark scoffs, getting that cocky swagger back in his step as he approaches the table. "The Montagues might have some sway and influence, but my dad plays golf with the POTUS."

POTUS sounds like the name of a fancy toilet room spray, I think with a small chuckle. Only, I'm not as dumb as Mark, so I know it stands for *President of the United States*.

"So?" Church asks, cocking his head to one side. "What does that have to do with you trying to kidnap Charlotte from a London cemetery? What was up with that fox mask, by the way." Church gestures at his face with his hand. "And who were your friends? Maybe if you gave up their names, we could reconsider the dorm room assignment?"

"My father's going to hear about this," Mark says, gesturing with the page and then spinning on his heel and storming out the door.

I scurry after him, and lock the main office door after he leaves, just so we can have a moment of privacy before our next appointment.

"It's been a week and you still haven't told me how you managed to pull all of this off," I say, stepping back into the room and leaning against one of the statuesque wooden doors that separates this area from the office. "My birthday is coming up, you know, so …"

"Oh, low blow," Spencer says, shaking out his hand like I've slapped him. "Come, take a seat." He taps his knee, and I roll my eyes. But then I go over and sit down on his lap anyway because I'm stupidly, madly, over-the-top, filled-with-glitter, in love with this guy. "You know how my dad owns a pharmaceutical company, right?"

"Yeah?" I hedge, hoping and praying that his dad isn't one of those types who, like, triples the price on EpiPens for no reason at all other than pure profit. But we can get to that later. I figure maybe it's a good thing I'm dating these guys, so I can teach them to check their male and class privilege, huh? Or maybe … maybe I just like them?

"Well, you know how I've been refusing to sell weed to everyone? To get them all psyched to vote for us?"

"You mean blackmail them into voting for us," the twins correct, but Spencer ignores them, clearly proud of his own behind-the-scenes scheming.

"Okay, yep," I say, narrowing my eyes and wondering where this is going.

"Well, I put pressure on my dad to talk to some of the doctors that are popular among the upper class in NYC, the ones that rely on his generosity to supply copious amounts of pills. They cut the prescriptions off for the parents of half the kids that go to this school."

My brows go up.

"Damn, dude, that's hardcore."

"No 'us' on the Student Council, no more celebrity doctors with questionable morals." Spencer shrugs his shoulders. "And I don't even feel bad about it. Why should I? Most of them are like Mark and his family, throwing their weight around all the damn time. It's a lesson that's well-deserved."

"How did you get your dad to agree to that?" I ask, noticing that Ranger looks away sharply at the mention of the word *dad.* His is guilty, that much we know for sure, and as much as he says he doesn't care about his father, it still hurts. I can see it in his sapphire eyes when he looks off into sky sometimes.

"I told him I'd never see him again. I hate his lies

anyway, and it's a chore to be around him. But I guess he must care about me somewhat because he agreed to it." Spencer shrugs his shoulders, also throwing on a bit of a cavalier attitude. One day, I'm going to break these boys down and get to the root of their emotions. And you know what? I hope they do the same for me, too.

"I have to admit, I'm impressed by your scheming," I say, leaning in for a kiss as Ranger grumbles under his breath.

"We have back-to-back meetings all day," he chastises, but I figure he's just jealous and wants a kiss, too. I plant one on Spencer's lips, pulling back before he draws me into that fiery essence of his, and then running down the line to kiss each and every boy on the mouth.

"Oh, that was fun," I say as I hit the door with my back and push it open, spinning out into the office and then doing a triple fist pump and happy shimmy dance where no one can see.

"You've left the door open," Church says, and my face pales as I glance back to see that it hasn't swung properly closed and everyone's just seen me act like a total idiot.

That's … great. Just great.

When Aster Hayes knocks on our door, and I open it, my face is the color of the strawberry-beet jam that the kitchen makes on Fridays.

She smiles at me, but the expression doesn't quite meet her eyes.

Psychopath, I think, but even if that's not true, Aster is up to something.

I just know it.

"She didn't even blow up about any of it," I say as the twins and I fumble through the complicated process of actually trying to make cauliflower mash taste good. I don't even see how it could be healthy at this point; we have to load it up with a crapload of butter to give it any flavor. It's like … tasteless albino broccoli that turns into flavorless mushy white goo when cooked and pureed. "Like, a normal person would be furious. Even used-tampon-face Mark Grandam was annoyed. She creeps me out."

Aster Hayes took every punishment the Student Council laid out with grace and poise, understandably frustrating the crap out of me. Nobody is that calm unless they have something to hide.

"So maybe she's the guilty one and not Selena?" Spencer suggests, looking up from the casserole dish in his hands toward the classroom door. We've been booking it over here after class every Tuesday and

Thursday, just to see if we can't have some time to ourselves before Aster shows up. Despite the punishments laid out by the Student Council, and despite the fact that we've been consistently giving her the cold shoulder, she doesn't seem able to take the hint. "Or, what if we're wrong and there's more than one female attacker?" He goes about putting the dish in the oven as Church raises his head up from his schoolwork, staring at his friend like he's just given him a revelation. "It'd make sense, you know, because I *swear* I saw Selena leaving the Valentine's party with that weird blue-haired girl that Ranger slept with. Then that girl ends up knocked out with no memory of what happened? That's some shady shit."

My mouth tightens into a thin line as Ranger gives Spencer a *dude, STFU* look.

"Kesha." Just that one word, tinged with a bit of apologetic regret as he looks over at me. I don't need him or any of the others to regret the people they've slept with in the past though; I just want them to only sleep with me in the future. Then again, I'm enjoying his attention too much to say anything, catching that sapphire gaze and holding it. "You saw them leave together and didn't think to mention it until now?"

"Well, I was high as fuck, and a little bit drunk, and all I can really remember are Chuck's blue eyes. I'll admit, that night threw me for a serious loop. I'd been considering sucking dick and even swallowing"—he was going to swallow … for me? cue squealing—"and then I met this gorgeous girl that I felt overwhelmingly attracted to …"

"You were going to cheat on Chuck with Charlotte?" I gasp, and Spencer gives me a saucy look.

"You do it with the twins, don't you? Maybe I could've wrangled a pair of cousins?"

"Okay, enough," Ranger says as Tobias and Micah chuckle, using the silicone scraper in his hand to gesture in Spencer's direction. "You saw Kesha leaving with Selena?"

"Pretty sure. And Aster was still inside dancing with Ross. Just saying, we could have two female attackers, and maybe they're not always both present at the same time?" Spencer puts the casserole in the oven as Church rises from his favorite chair, tapping a stylus against his mouth.

"That could explain a lot. Put Mark, Gareth, Selena, and Aster together … Think about that. The lineages match, there's the mention of Libby in Jenica's journal, and every single one of them has given us at least some reason to suspect them." He pauses and puts his palms on the countertop. "The only things that don't make sense are your father"—Church holds up a single finger—"and the business owners in Nutmeg. How do they fit in?"

"You're forgetting the biggest issue with this four-attacker theory," Tobias says, and the twins exchange a look. “We’re missing another body,” they add together, and Church’s eyes narrow in thought.

“Maybe there’s someone else they’ve been stalking here or at Everly?” I suggest, and then we all pause as the door opens and Aster Hayes walks in, smiling her frustratingly perfect smile.

“Have I missed anything?” she asks, taking one of her new aprons off the hook near the door and slipping it on. She wears plain white ones and never bleaches them; I can tell it infuriates both Church and Ranger both.

“We were just about to make a four-cheese casserole,” I say, trying to force my lips into a smile and then pushing the cookbook across the counter.

Now that Spencer’s brought it up, I can’t stop wondering: is there another victim on this campus that we don’t know about?

Worse.

One that we won’t know about until it’s too late …

Nutmeg’s Main Street isn’t exactly the boardwalk back home, but I like coming here on the weekends. All the shop owners—even the ones who don’t like Church’s family—are nice. It probably helps that the guys are all loaded, and whenever I say I like something, they buy it for me.

"You don't have to buy my affection, you know?" I say, sitting with the boys in their favorite booth near the front window. I play with the metal straw in my chocolate shake and pretend like I'm not purposely avoiding looking at the email in my inbox that says *An Important Message from Bornstead University*. I'm not the only one who has one, by the way. We all do.

"We don't have to, but we like to," Micah says, shrugging his shoulders. "And you *are* really poor, so I figure every little bit helps."

"Oh, stuff your face," I grumble as I glance over and watch Merinda sprinting from table to table. *Is this place as far in the red as the antique shop?* I wonder, looking back at Church. He said he'd tell me the story at some point, but I have yet to hear it.

"And stop stressing so much about this stupid university," Spencer says, putting his elbows on the table and resting his chin in his hands. "You know we're not going anywhere without you, Chuck."

"I don't want to hold you guys back because I slacked for the first two years of high school. That's not fair."

"Do you fully appreciate how rich we are?" Tobias asks, but not like he's bragging, just like he's stating a simple fact. "If there's one, meaningful thing our privilege can buy, it's going to be an education for you."

"We've always planned on staying together after high school anyway," Ranger says with a sigh and a roll of his eyes, like he can't believe he ever subscribed to something so stupid. It's all a front, of course. He loves these guys as much as I do. Just … I don't think he wants to suck their dicks. Only difference between us. "We were sort of tossing around the idea of traveling first, but school is important, too. So open the damn email and stop stressing yourself out."

"Maybe I need an apron, a good breeze across my backside, and a tray of colorful cupcakes?"

"When we get back to Adamson, I'll naked bake the crap out of some lavender-vanilla cupcakes. I'm also more than happy to bend you over that counter again and fuck the shit out of you." Ranger taps the screen of my phone with a blue-painted fingernail as Church sips his coffee and the other boys groan. "But only if you open this damn email and put us all out of our misery."

"Actually, I was more interested in the story of Nutmeg and the Montagues—"

"We all got in," the twins say, interrupting me and pausing with their forks paused halfway to their lips, a glistening bite of cherry pie perched on the tines of each. "We already checked with our Mom."

"We got in?!" I scream, standing up so suddenly that I dump my entire chocolate milkshake into Church's lap. My hands clamp over my mouth, but he barely reacts, taking another sip of his coffee before setting the mug carefully down on the table. "Church, I'm so, so, so, so sorry …"

"Don't be, my sweet little bride," he says, flicking his eyes up to mine before he smirks. Ranger and Micah slide out of the bench seat and Church follows, dripping milkshake everywhere. "Our apologies, Merinda."

"Not a problem," she says, as I struggle between wanting to freak out, and wanting to help clean up.

"I've got it," Ranger says, taking the rag from Merinda and shaking his head at me. "Just do it. Go freak out or scream or whatever it is you need to do."

"Really?" I ask, my eyes filling with tears. I'm about to get all blubbery and start snotting everywhere. Is that a word? Snotting? Because it really sounds like one that'd get used a lot … "We got into Bornstead U? All of us?"

"We're in," Tobias says with a laugh as I hold my arms up above my head and squinch my face up, screaming internally since it's not considered polite to shout in the middle of a crowded diner. I fist-pump hard and then turn to slap a strong high five with Spencer. "And guess what? Your tuition is covered."

"I haven't applied for any student loans yet," I say, and the four boys still sitting around the table give me looks. "What? I mean, just because we're dating, I don't expect you to—"

"We're paying for it," the twins say together, taking bites of their pie and then holding their forks up in an X, effectively cutting me off from what I was about to say. "Don't argue with us. It's happening."

"You really think I'd sit by and watch you rack up student loans like that?" Spencer asks, looking over at me. "What sort of asshole do you take me for?"

"I need a minute," I say, holding back tears as I slip under the table and crawl out the other side, my shoes squeaking on the floor as I run outside and throw my back against the sun-warmed wall next to the front door. "Yes!" My voice echoes down the street and several people turn to look at me. I don't care though. The only thing I care about right now is reveling in this moment. It's hard to say how many strings the guys pulled behind the scenes—because Bornstead U is a seriously competitive university—but I did work really hard to turn things around. I've got A's in all my classes currently. First time this has ever happened for me.

I do a ridiculous little jig for the guys' enjoyment, and then throw open the doors to the diner, my chest swollen with pride.

"I'm a future college student," I tell some random Adamson students near the door. I don't really know who they are, but the way they murmur *Student Council lackey* under their breaths shows that they know who I am. When all four of the boys at my table turn to look at them, the students change their tune real fast.

"Go check on your milkshake-laden boyfriend, college student," Ranger says, and I bounce over to the unisex bathroom, pushing in the door to find Church cleaning chocolate off of his crotch with a wet rag.

"Do you need help with that?" I ask, but when I reach to take it from him, Church just leans in and kisses me hard on the mouth.

"Please don't. I'll get a hard-on, and then we'll end up doing it in this bathroom, and Merinda will never forgive us."

My cheeks flush.

Last night, Church and I may or may not have gone at it again in our dorm room. It became a bit of a game to try to stop groaning and moving when Nathan popped by for the nightly room checks. Pretty sure he knew what we were doing, but screw him. He's just as shady and close-mouthed as the asshole librarian.

"Your parents … they don't care if the shops here make any profit, do they?" I ask, and Church looks up with a smile, tossing the rag into the sink. His champagne colored slacks are soaked in the crotch, and it really, really looks like he peed himself, but since this is all my fault, I decide not to say anything.

"They don't."

"Because …" I lead, gesturing with my hand for him to continue the story.

"Because they're both billionaires in their own right?" he suggests, and I give him a look. "Because they met and fell in love in Nutmeg, Chuck. My mother went to Everly and my father to Adamson. They kept seeing each other at all the coed events—the Halloween party, the Valentine's Day dance, the bake-off. This town is the setting for their love story; they want it preserved."

"That's the reason they want to own everything?" I choke out, and Church sighs, like his parents are the most ridiculous people on the planet.

"That's the gist of it, yes. They let the shop owners run their shops the way they always have, they pay them fair salaries, and they don't care if the store is in the red. That's why I've never asked them to give the diner back to Merinda. I know this place wasn't making any money before we bought it."

"And by fair salary …" I start, and Church smirks.

"Merinda drives a Beemer, Chuck," he says, and I snort. Am I that obvious? I mean, socioeconomic inequalities really bother me, but that's not the point. Ugh. Did I just say socioeconomic inside my own head? I wouldn't have even been able to spell that word back in Santa Cruz, let alone use it in an independent thought.

"Well, shit, maybe the other shop owners want to sell their places, but can't."

"Because of the tunnels," Church agrees. "The

Fellowship doesn't want my parents to get ahold of those buildings, just in case."

"So that means there really must be something down there worth hiding, huh?" I ask, and Church nods, just once, but the gleam in his eye … that scares the crap out of me a little.

No way in hell is my future husband going down in those tunnels, with or without my other, you know, future husbands.

Not over my dead body.

Oh. Ow. Ouch.

Bad metaphor.

Over my living body.

They're not going into those fucking tunnels over my very much still alive body.

Not a chance.

CHAPTER EIGHTEEN

Winter break rolls around, bringing with it my eighteenth birthday. All the boys have already had theirs, but none of them particularly cared to make a big deal out of it. We cooked and baked together, had little parties with candles in the Culinary Club dining room. And I put together small but thoughtful gifts for each boy. Spencer, Ranger, Tobias, and Micah got sex on their birthdays, but poor Church didn't since we hadn't quite gotten to that stage of our relationship yet.

Next year though, it's on.

"Happy birthday, Charlotte," Dad says at breakfast that morning. He asked me to come up for breakfast—just me—so we could talk. He even made French toast and scrambled eggs, adding bottles of hot sauce and ketchup next to the maple syrup. My gift is a beautiful frame with my acceptance letter to Bornstead U inside, printed on cardstock, the words embossed in navy blue. Yep, that's a definite gift from the headmaster right there.

"Thanks," I say, smiling and then setting my fork down next to my plate. "Pretty sure neither of us thought I'd live to see this day, huh?" I joke, and Dad's face pales to an awful ashen shade. "I just meant, I thought you might kill me … like, metaphorically speaking. Also, my bad, I shouldn't have made a death joke with a cult on the loose."

"Charlotte," he snaps, eyes darting to the door. To be fair, he has a reason to be nervous.

Last night, I sat down and wrote out a list of all the minor but creepy incidents I could remember from last year.

1. that day the window above the sink was open and I heard rustling in the bushes

2. the large dark figure on Halloween—Mr. Murphy insists this wasn't him

3. the candle wax in the girls' dorm and the missing Jenica picture

4. the strange sounds in the foliage outside the girls' dorm

5. the creaking sound of footsteps in the upstairs of the girls' dorm—although this easily could've been

Ranger

It's very clear that the Fellowship's initiates have been stalking me for quite some time.

Dad exhales sharply, reaching up to rub at his temples. He seems to realize what he's doing, forcing his hands into his lap and making himself smile at me.

"Your mother sent some gifts as well. I put them upstairs on your bed."

"Awesome, thanks," I say, wondering how long I have to sit here before I can call the boys to come get me. It's not that I don't want to spend time with Dad, just … we love each other, but we don't have a ton to say to each other, if that makes sense. "Are you … going to be okay with seeing her on Christmas with Ian there?"

Tomorrow, we're hopping on a plane back to California to see my mom and aunt. Monica, too. But Mom's already dropped about three thousand subtle hints about Ian being at her house on Christmas day. I just hope Dad can handle seeing them together.

"Ian Dave is a good man," he says, looking like he'd truly enjoying punching the librarian's face in.

"Him and Nathan, right?" I ask, tilting my head to one side, like maybe I'll be able to figure my dad out if I look at him from a new angle. "You seem to trust them both, but I'm really struggling to understand why."

"I'm not at liberty to answer your questions, Charlotte. You know that I would if I could."

I don't bother to argue with him. He's an impulsive rule follower. Doesn't make him a bad guy, but it also just seems so stifling to live life so rigidly. I don't want to live a shallow life like my Aunt Elisa, but I also don't want to live in a box like my father.

"You'll at least let me fly on the Montague's jet, right?"

"Charlotte, I frown on that sort of excess. There's nothing wrong with our economy tickets." *Nothing wrong with economy tickets except for cramped knees and people with smelly socks who take their shoes off, screaming babies, and people smacking you in the face when they put their seat back. But sure. Okay, boomer.*

"Alright, then." I stand up, slipping my phone from my back pocket and shaking it for emphasis. "I'm going to call the guys to come and get me."

Before I head out to the front porch to make the call, I pause next to Dad's chair and put my arms around his neck, giving him a spur of the moment squeeze. None of the boys have intimacy issues like I do. I think I'm starting to learn from them. It's okay to give hugs or say *I love you* every once in a while. That stuff doesn't make you weak or vulnerable, it makes you stronger.

"Archie's well-meaning, but he doesn't understand me at all," I tell the guys as we walk back to the dorms, the breeze kissed with the frosty promise of new snow. "Guess that's the thing about most parents, huh?"

"Unfortunately, my mother understands me too well," Church says, looking up at a few tiny snowflakes that are drifting down from the gray sky. He's got a thick scarf wrapped around his neck, the rest of him bundled up in a wool coat. "She wants me to purchase a place near Bornstead U for us to live in." He looks very pointedly in my direction. "Or would you rather live in the dorms?"

I stare at him like he's sprouted antennae.

"Your mom wants you to buy an—I assume—absurdly expensive place to live … or else we can live in tiny, little shared dorm rooms that are probably gender specific, strictly binary, and filled with Ikea furniture?"

Church laughs as Spencer smirks and gives him an *I told you so* sort of a look.

We push open the door to the boys' dorm, the massive fir tree in the corner decorated with lights and glittery glass ornaments. Luckily, most of the students are leaving for break tomorrow, so the building isn't as empty as it could be. I'm just glad the guys are going to join me in California for at least part of the holiday. Each of them has separate plans to meet up with their families at some point during the two-week period, but I'll always have at least one person with me at all times.

Because … cult stuff.

Not because I'm madly in love with them or anything.

"Is it just going to be me and Church …" I start, trying not to be ungrateful but hoping beyond all hope that the other boys will live with us, too. I'm still not exactly sure what's going on with all of us, but I like what we have here. It's our own little family in the making.

"Are you crazy?" the twins ask from either side of the group. It always impresses me how they're able to talk in unison, even when they're fairly far apart. "We'll be there."

"We'll be there," Ranger agrees, pausing at the bottom of the stairs and giving Spencer a look. "Don't worry about that." He looks back at me as I stand there with my hand on the railing, waiting to see what they're up to. "We have something to do right now, but we'll be back. Micah." He joins them and the three of them peel away from Church, Tobias, and me.

My heart starts to pound right away, and I have to scrunch up my face to hold in my excitement.

They're totally planning birthday shit for me.

I just know it.

They've all told me *happy birthday* already, and I've gotten a few random gifts: like a set of fancy pillows from Church, some high heels that look like cakes from Ranger (the Shoe Bakery store is my new obsession), a new laptop from Spencer, and a stack of admittedly cute clothes from the twins.

But that's not it.

I could tell those gifts were more diversion than anything else.

"Don't ruin this surprise," Tobias says, pointing at me in warning, his mouth curving up into a smile. "We worked hard on it."

"Surprise, what surprise?" I ask, flouncing up the stairs to my room before he can answer.

Because I know them too well, and I know that whatever they give me, it's going to be good.

"Charlotte, wake up," Tobias says, gently shaking my shoulder. As I crack my heavy lids, the first thing I see is him smiling at me.

"What time is it?" I ask, glancing toward the window above my bed. It's dark out, but that doesn't mean anything. It's winter in Connecticut. Shit, it's probably like three in the freaking afternoon.

"Almost six," Tobias tells me, sitting on the edge of the bed next to me. I must've gotten so hyped up waiting to see what the guys were planning that I wore myself; I don't even remember falling asleep. With a yawn, I sit up, stretching my arms above my head. Tobias watches me, his attention sweet and tender, his expression softening the sharp lines of his face. "Are you ready, Chuck the Micropenis?"

"For what?" I ask as he stands up and holds out a hand for me to take. Some of my hair is plastered to the side of my face with drool. If this is my birthday wish coming to fruition, then I'm not properly dressed. Drool-covered faces and romantic birthday endeavors don't exactly go hand in hand. "Can I brush my hair, do some quick makeup, and change my dress?" I ask, but Tobias just laughs and pulls me into the hallway. I notice the attic door is open, the wooden ladder dropped down to the floor above us, where my old room used to be.

"Don't worry: we've checked and rechecked that attic today. You'll be safe." He curves his hand around mine and tugs me up the staircase, then waits with his hands on either side of the ladder as I climb up.

There's a ton of junk up here, but nothing fun like at the antique shop. Instead of glass clowns and secret bookcase doors, there are a lot of old bed frames, mattresses, and broken chairs. Yawn-fest.

"The roof access is up here," Tobias says, showing me over to one last set of stairs. As I climb each step, my view of the sky beyond the open door gets better and better, until I'm standing out on the roof, surrounded by stars.

"Wow." The word comes out in a whisper as Tobias joins me, leading me around the corner and onto the part of the roof that faces the woods behind the school.

The rest of the guys are there, dressed in warm clothes, and waiting on a blanket mound that's spread across three different mattresses. They must've dragged them out of the attic for us to lay on. *Stargazing,* I think, without even having to ask. I mentioned offhand to the twins that I wanted to do something like this, and here we are.

They listened.

It means more to me than I can say. My throat closes up and tears threaten at the corners of my eyes as Micah comes over with a bundle of sweaters, scarves, and mittens, bundling me up against the cold.

"You used to be such a badass, Chuck," he teases, pulling a hat down over my head. For now, the sky is clear, but I can see clouds moving in and threatening to cover the school. We're going to get a buttload of snow, huh?

"I'm still a badass," I grumble as I look around at the scattered candles, the champagne chilling in a bucket, and a tray of chocolate-covered strawberries on an old nightstand. There are even white lights strung up from the flagpole to the raised portion of the roof, where the exit is. They've clearly put a lot of work into this.

"What happens if the Fellowship finds out we're up

here?" I ask, imagining a bunch of robed cultists pouring out the door and onto the roof, surrounding us. They could throw me off the building, be done with me once and for all.

Tobias kicks the door closed and yanks on the handle to show me that it's locked. He then lifts up a set of keys.

"All of these open the roof door. We took them from pretty much every staff member on campus, including your dad, Eddie, even Nathan. And don't worry: we told the headmaster we'd be up here with you tonight. He didn't seem to like it, but he agreed to it."

"He … did?" I ask, blinking in surprise as I turn back to Spencer, Church, and Ranger.

"He did," Tobias confirms as the twins each gently take me by the elbow and lead me over to their kick-ass mattress setup. Looks like it takes at least three queen-sized beds to house us all for a sleepover. Not that I think the boys are all going to sleep in one big bed with me. *Not yet,* my mind snickers, and immediately starts to scheme. Hashtag goals, am I right?

"Take a seat, Chuck-let," Spencer says, patting the spot next to him. Happily, I crawl onto the mattress and lie on my back, my head on one of Church's fur-covered pillows, my gaze on the dark sky above us. The stars are so bright up here, I can even see the swirling brilliance of the Milky Way.

Spence covers me up with a blanket and then lays

down beside me. Ranger crawls in on my other side, with Church next to him, and the twins on the other side of Spencer.

For a little while, we all just lay there in silence, staring up at the sky.

"This is one of the coolest things I've ever done," I whisper, not wanting to break the quiet perfection of the moment. I'm not even mad when one of those stupid owls hoots in the distance.

"I'm not sure that I've ever stargazed before," Micah says, his voice contemplative. He hesitates for just a moment before he adds, "Happy Birthday, Chuck."

"Happy birthday," Church adds, sitting up and grabbing the champagne bottle by the neck. He pops the cork—very likely that dad doesn't know about this part of the plan—and then pours us each a glass. "To Chuck," he says, and we all raise our glasses, clinking them together.

I salute the sky and then down my own drink, handing the glass back to Church, so I can snuggle into Spencer's side.

"We have plenty of food if you're hungry," Ranger says, still sitting up and holding his champagne in one hand. "We cooked a feast for an army." He nods his chin in the direction of a table, laden with those silver serving trays that caterers always seem to use, the ones with the little flames underneath to keep the food warm.

Damn.

They really put a lot of work into this, didn't they?

My pulse pounds out an excited rhythm as Spencer puts his arm around my waist.

"Good, because I can eat for an army."

"Just let me know if you want one of these fucking strawberries," Ranger adds, hooking a thumb in the direction of the tray. "Because I'm feeding them to you —personally."

"Oh, you want to feed me now?" I joke as Spencer chuckles beneath me. "Is that your new kink?"

"Fuck off, Carson." Ranger sets his glass aside and lights up a joint. He passes it to Micah first, sending a white tendril of smoke curling up into the still air. "I bet if we get high enough, we can stay here all night and talk existential theories about stars."

"Or other things," Tobias suggests, like they've all got a certain subject in mind that they've been planning on bringing up. Right away, alarm bells go off and I start to wonder if this might be about our relationship.

I sit up, accidentally elbowing Spencer in the side and making him groan.

"What other things?" I ask, hoping I don't sound too much like a crazy person.

Several of the boys exchange looks as Spencer uses his elbows to prop himself up, a blue-green scarf tucked underneath his chin.

He told me he was okay with me dating the twins because he was confident that I'd pick him, that they were no threat. All along, I felt like he was hoping I'd choose him at some point. So maybe that's it, why we're here? After all, it wasn't realistic for me to expect them to share forever, right?

"We wanted to talk to you about your engagement to Church," Tobias starts, but he's smiling at me, one knee casually propped up on the mattress, his breath fogging in the cold air. "It's not fake anymore, it's real, so we need to figure out where we're going with all of this."

My eyes widen, but I don't interrupt; I want to hear what they have to say.

"You know that Tobias and I always planned on sharing a girlfriend or, one day, a wife." Micah pours himself another glass of champagne and then knocks it back in one swig. "But we didn't want to share with anyone else."

"I didn't want to share at all," Ranger says, glancing at Church. "But that's not how things are working out."

"How do you mean?" I ask, struggling to control my racing heart. If this goes from the best birthday ever to the worst, I swear, I'll flip one of these mattresses off the roof and into the trees. *Good luck getting that out of the canopy, Eddie.*

"We're all in agreement that we like how things are going with you," Church says, and then he smirks.

"That sounded fucking clinical. What I mean is, we all like you, and that doesn't seem to be changing."

"We figured since we were going to the same college anyway, that we should just … make a mutual agreement," Tobias tacks on, ruffling up his hair like he's concerned he might be messing this up.

"We don't want you to date anyone outside of this circle," Spencer continues, finally sitting up the rest of the way and watching me from turquoise eyes. He's struggled with jealousy the most out of anyone, so I'm curious to see where this conversation is headed. "But we won't date anyone else either. Just us, and you."

"For how long?" I ask, and Spencer's gaze softens.

"For as long as you want. We'll always be friends, Chuck-let," he says, gesturing at the other guys. "We'll always be family—you included. If there's romance forever, then we're okay with that. If there's not, we can rearrange things and figure it out when the time comes."

"What are you saying?" I ask, looking back at Ranger.

"We're saying we like our crew as it is, so let's stick with it. No other guys, no other girls, just us." He gives me a look and then sighs, stealing the joint from Micah as he goes to pass it to Spencer. "We're saying that unless something changes, we want to make this our thing."

"We're not going to pressure you, or just wait

around for you to pick. We're here, for the long haul." Spencer exhales and then reaches up to touch the side of my face with a gloved hand. "That's the biggest part of your birthday present, Chuck. We're committing to this." He taps the ring that Church gave me. "All of us, and you, for as long as you'll have us."

"You're not jealous?" I manage to whisper, slowly losing my capacity for human speech. I'm floored. Beyond floored. Pulverized. Crushed. Splatted. But in the best way possible. This is all I want, for us to ... be like this. Now and forever. If things change, we'll figure it out, but for now, at least, this is real.

Spencer shrugs his shoulder, but then he smiles at me, a real, true genuine sort of smile.

"Maybe a little, but I figure that's normal, right? If I wasn't jealous, would I even be human? My point is, I'm saying it's not relevant. I'm doing this for you." He pauses and thinks for a moment before correcting himself. "With you."

"With you," Church agrees, and then he pours another round of champagne. The boys clink their glasses with mine a second time. "Till death do us part," Church toasts, and we all murmur it in reply. What that means, exactly, I'm not sure. Hopefully it doesn't end up being quite such a literal statement before the year is over.

That's as far as I get before my eyes swell with tears, and I have to shove a chocolate strawberry in my mouth to hold back some ridiculously girly crying. Not that there's anything wrong with girly crying. I just … don't want to cry right now, I want to smile.

I want to be happy.

"Before we forget," Tobias says, rising from his seat and grabbing a pink garment box from behind the table of food. It's tied with a white ribbon, and decorated with a bouquet of pink, purple, and red flowers. When I open the card on the top, it just says *Courtesy of the Student Council.*

"What is it?" I ask, and Micah gives me a hard look.

"Chuck, open it." He grins as I untie the ribbon and pull the lid off.

Inside, there's a gorgeous pink gown with white lace on the shoulders. Tobias pulls it out for me and stands up, so he can hold its full, glorious length out for me to see.

"We had this custom made," Church says, looking at me and not the dress. "It was a group effort this time. I know I can be pushy with these sorts of things."

"It's fucking gorgeous," I say, standing up and touching my fingers to the delicate lace, the full skirt, and the ruched bodice. "What's it for?"

"This isn't just your birthday present, it's your …" Ranger pauses and grits his teeth like he's in pain. "God, the word is too stupid for me to say. I can't do it. Somebody else take a crack at it."

"Promposal," the twins say in unison, and I grin,

throwing my arms around Tobias' neck, and then giving each of the other guys a hug just like it. "So, will you go to prom with us?"

"I accept. Yes on all accounts," I tell them, brimming with energy and excitement as I help Tobias put the dress back in the box. "Any chance I can also get a group snug under the stars?"

"A … snug?" Micah asks, tilting his head to one side.

"Snuggle, idiot," Tobias says, shoving his twin onto the mattress. "And of course, you can. That's what we brought all this stuff up here for."

He crawls in on Spencer's other side, Ranger on the far end. I'm in the middle with Micah on my right, and Church on his other side.

We take turns passing the joint back and forth, the Milky Way galaxy sparkling in the sky like a painting.

Did I just get a reverse harem ending?

Yeah, yeah, I think I just did.

I just hope that this really is the happy ending to my story, and not a blip in a horror film set on a course for disaster.

The pot makes us all a bit drowsy, but after a few ours

of smoking and napping and talking about stars (and aliens, lots of alien talk up there), we force our asses up for some food. Because if there's one emotion that can take control over drowsiness when you're high, it's that feeling you get when you know you have the munchies.

"It's not fair that everything tastes so much better when you're stoned," I groan, pressing my back against Tobias as we cuddle in the blankets and try to gauge just how long it's going to snow before the weather chases us off the roof and back inside the warmth of the dorm.

"It's totally fair," Micah groans, falling back onto the mattress. "I look forward to that part of being high. Otherwise, I'm not sure I'd even bother."

We polish off most of the food, quickly giving into the thick white blanket of snow that's soon covering the roof. Most of the stuff we just leave out there to get later, but everyone grabs a pillow and we head back inside.

The attic door is, thankfully, still open and we all manage to get down the ladder and tuck it away before Ranger closes the hatch behind us.

"Snacks for the room?" he suggests with a shrug, and I grin.

"Most definitely. I hate being high without constant access to food. Like, we just ate, but I'll be ready again in ten." I take Ranger's hand and we head downstairs, the other four boys following behind us. We haven't even turned the corner to the kitchen when we hear the sound of footsteps, followed by the slamming of a door.

There's a shout and a grunting sound, like there's some sort of fight happening outside the kitchen. The twins exchange a look and then take off, pausing near the side door and looking out at a very bizarre scene.

It's Nathan, the night watchman, subduing Eddie, the janitor.

Eddie has a weapon of some kind—a knife, I think—that Nathan deftly wrestles from his grip, spinning Eddie around and then pinning his arm against his back before he drops him to the ground completely. Nathan very clearly has martial arts training, beyond just that little bit of karate that showed up on the background check Ranger ran.

The men are arguing, but I can't hear what they're saying.

What I do notice are a pair of silver cuffs that Nathan produces, handcuffing Eddie, and then leading him down the path in the direction of the main building.

"Either this weed is crazy strong, or we just saw something interesting."

"Oh, it's not the weed," Church tells me, staring after the men as they disappear around a bend in the path. "But it looks like Nathan just arrested Eddie.

Didn't Jack say something about a portion of the staff being involved in the Fellowship?"

"Do you think we just found one?" Spencer asks, but even Church isn't sure enough to answer that question just yet.

CHAPTER NINETEEN

I'm flying sky-high when I step into the cute, little suburban house where my mom is staying. And that's a metaphor, not a literal interpretation of the flight I just took from New York to Los Angeles. Dad had a flight attendant spill a drink on his shirt which I sort of took as karmic justice. We both could've been on the Montague's jet instead …

"Charlotte!" Mom says, appearing in the tiled front hall in a red dress with a white apron over it. She opens her arms and I set my bags down, so I can give her a hug. Dad's lingering behind me, like he isn't sure he's comfortable here. He insisted on staying in a hotel, but Mom promised there'd be plenty of room at her place and he caved.

She's always had that sort of influence over him. I used to be jealous, but not anymore. It doesn't matter what the relationship is—platonic or familiar or romantic—but some people just click better than others. Mom and Dad click, but apparently not in a romantic way. Dad and I just don't click at all, but we still love each other.

Life is complicated.

"And remind me which of your many boyfriends this one is?" Eloise asks with a girlish giggle that makes me roll my eyes. If she were serious, I'd be pissed, but she just very clearly doesn't understand my relationship with the Student Council. That's cool though. She doesn't have to understand it, she just has to respect it.

I smile and keep my mood upbeat. After all, she's kept herself clean and sober since that incident at Christmas last year. I couldn't ask for anything more.

"This is Tobias," I say as Micah steps around him, this dizzying duplication of beautiful boys. "And his brother Micah."

"Oh, yes, *twins*," Mom whispers overly loud, so that everyone in the room can hear. She also says it in a very suggestive way that makes me wish Dad weren't standing all of two feet behind me.

"The others are busy with family stuff, but they'll be here on Christmas eve."

"I'm looking forward to it," she says, and then holds

out a hand to indicate the hallway behind her. "Let me show you all where to put your stuff."

"This is way nicer than that shithole your Mom was staying in when we last saw her," Micah whispers as we head down the hall with Dad trailing behind us. "How can she afford this?"

"That's why I'm wondering," I start, glancing into the rooms as we pass. One of them looks like a study, but the pullout bed is out and clearly made up for guests. The next is a bathroom, and the one on the end is a huge guest suite with a king-sized bed.

"This is where Ian's parents usually stay when they come into town, but I figured with Charlotte having so many boyfriends—"

"I'm sorry," Dad says, interrupting her and pushing his glasses up his nose to further enhance his signature glare. "Did you say Ian's parents? Is this his house? Because seeing him briefly over the holiday and staying in his home are two completely different things."

"Archie," Mom begins as Mr. Dave appears in the doorway behind Dad.

"Everything okay in here?" he asks, dark eyes scanning us briefly before he smiles. It looks like his face is melting off, the smile's so damn forced. Grumpy Mr. Dave is clearly just clinging to his sanity for Mom's sake.

"Well, actually, Ian," Dad begins, glancing in our

teacher's direction. "I'd just as soon take Charlotte and stay at a hotel. I was told you'd be around for the holidays, not that Eloise had actually moved into your house."

"Wait, you're a school librarian working in Connecticut and you own a house in Los Angeles?" I ask, exchanging a look with the twins. "Because that just doesn't make a whole lot of sense to me."

"This is my parents' place; I'm renting it from them while they're traveling. Yes, I asked Eloise to move in here. Didn't you see where she was living before? It wasn't safe."

"And you'd know all about keeping people safe," Dad quips, his face slowly changing color. I look between him and Mr. Dave, wondering what all this tension is about. Mom, surely, but there's something else, too.

Biting my lip, I think back on the confrontation we witnessed between Nathan, the night watchman, and Eddie, the janitor. Not only is Nathan a secret badass, but Eddie's gotta be working for the Fellowship. A lot of things make so much sense now: the patched hole in Mark's ceiling, the power going off on Halloween, and the door to the tunnels left open in a staff office that should've been locked.

What a piece of shit.

"I'll show you to your room," Mom says quickly, moving over to take Dad's arm.

"Is Charlotte supposed to sleep in here with these … *boys*?" Dad asks, turning the word boys into an insult.

"She's eighteen, and she's engaged to … well, to one of them," Mom argues, her face scrunching up as she tries to get a grip on the situation. One ring, five dudes. It's fine, just don't think too hard about it. "Clearly, they're going to have sex, so why have a fit about it?"

"Clearly?!" Dad chokes, but he already knows it happens. "Not when I'm sleeping right next door, they won't be."

"Don't freak: there's a bathroom in between our rooms," I joke, and the twins snicker, but Dad isn't having any of it. He pulls his elbow from Mom's hands and disappears into the hallway, leaving us alone with Mr. Dave.

"You going to explain why Nathan can disable a man like a trained MMA fighter?" Tobias asks, taking my usual role of blurting out almost absurdly direct questions. I stand beside him in solidarity as Micah sets our bags on the bench at the end of the bed. "Or why you and the headmaster trust him with the key to all the dorm rooms?"

"Nathan and I are coworkers," Mr. Dave says simply, glowering at us now that Mom's left the room.

"Yeah, no shit. You both work at Adamson," Micah says, giving our teacher a weird look.

"We're coworkers in a different sort of way," Mr.

Dave corrects, and then shakes his head. "I shouldn't even be telling you this."

"Telling us what?" I plead, hating that we're so close to solving this mystery, and yet so far away at the same time. "Are you a cop or something?"

"Or something." That's all he seems willing to offer up as he turns and disappears down the hall, leaving me to slump down on the edge of the bed in frustration.

"Don't fret, Chuck," Tobias says, putting his hand on the top of my head. "We all just confessed our undying love and devotion to you. You don't get to be sad."

"I'm not sad." I look up and make sure that he can see in my face that I'm telling the truth. "How could I be, when I have you guys looking after me? Fuck the cult. I just can't wait until this is all over."

"It won't be much longer," Tobias says with a nod and an exhale. He looks up and across the length of the bed to where Micah's standing. "Give Church some time to look into things, and he always figures it out. We're just the brute strength on the force, not the brains."

"Don't sell yourselves so short. You remembered my birthday when I ran into you at the boardwalk last year. You saved my shitty day and turned it into one of my best. Church is good at mysteries, but that doesn't make him better than you. You're all stripes in my rainbow."

"Stripes in your rainbow?" Micah echoes, and then he grabs me under the armpits and drags me onto the bed, pinning me to the mattress with an arm on either side of my face. "Now that's a cute phrase. I could get used to that."

"Say it again, Chuck," Tobias agrees as he lays down beside me, trailing his fingers across my collarbone. "If you do, we might give you something you'll really like, and that your dad will really hate."

"Are you trying to bribe me with sex?" I whisper, pretending to be scandalized.

"Yeah, pretty much," they agree in unison, and I squeal as Tobias grabs me and pulls me close, leaving Micah to jog over to the door and kick it closed.

The lock flicks into place, and we're in business.

"With the list of missing yearbooks from the library," Church begins, glancing down at the iPad in his hand. "Spencer and I were able to find out the names of either Adamson or Everly Academy students that went missing, committed suicide, or were murdered. There's no obvious pattern, no correlation between each incident other than that they only happen every few years."

"Okay, so nothing we didn't already know?" I ask, lying on my stomach on the bed and watching him through the screen on my phone, wishing he were here to sing ironic Christmas carols about snow while the sun beats down on LA like a curse. Mom goes to spin class, and *juices* now, it's weird as hell. The twins sit on either side of me, their backs to me, but each one with a knee pulled up onto the bed, arms wrapped around it.

"Except," Church continues, and he smiles, this sharp, clever little smile that says he knows how damn smart he is, "for the ages of the children in the families with lineage that goes back to the original abbey. If there's a student at either school that matches one of those family lines, then at some point during their enrollment, there's always an incident."

"What about Libby?" I ask, thinking of Selena's older sister. Jack told us it was Rick who killed Jenica, but if our theory holds true, then Libby should've left a victim behind as well.

Micah snaps his fingers before Church can respond.

"The kid in the park, the one that used to work at the antiques shop."

The smiles that curves Church's lips says that he's nailed it.

"I think we've solved our mystery," he says, turning the iPad around and showing off the copious notes that he's taken. "Selena, Gareth, Aster, and Mark are the hoodie-wearing dicks. Eugene and Jared were killed as part of their initiation rites into the Fellowship, and Charlotte is next on the list. The only things we don't know are who the fourth victim is, or why Eric Warren's daughter was chosen by the cult." Church pauses briefly. "Or why Ranger wasn't invited to join."

"What about Mr. Dave and Nathan?" I ask, lowering the volume on the phone, just in case Ian's listening in.

"They've got no records, nothing of interest in their background checks. But the information Ranger got from that private investigator is too clean. Nobody leaves such little evidence on paper. My guess would be that they're cops, FBI, something like that."

"What are they waiting for then?" I snap, getting irritated and digging my fingers into my hair. "Eugene and Jason are dead. Are they just waiting for me to be next?"

"I imagine they have to be careful about how they collect evidence or how they approach the Fellowship. Otherwise, their lives could be in danger. That, or the members might scatter or cover up their trail."

I nod, but I'm starting to get frustrated anyway.

"We'll see you in a few days then?" Tobias asks, and Church nods. My heart flutters a bit at the idea of seeing him again. Ranger and Spencer, too. Being apart from them sucks.

"You will," Church says, and then he pauses, like he's thinking about telling me something. "Sleep well and keep each other safe."

He hangs up before I get a chance to say goodbye, and I exhale, blowing hair up and out of my face before I sit up. Spencer's been with his dad all week, as per his bargain for the help in the elections, so he hasn't been able to talk much. And I've gotten all of three texts from Ranger which is worrying me.

"Come on, Chuck, cheer up," Micah says, turning and mimicking my pose so that he's laying side by side with me. "I'm really enjoying this chance to see how the other half lives."

"The other half, huh?" I say with a skeptical brow raised in his direction.

"It's quaint, the life of a peasant," he says, trying to keep a straight face, but his lips twitch and give him way. I shove Micah in the shoulder and stick my tongue out, sitting up next to Tobias.

"You'll see how quaint a peasant can get if you keep pushing it."

My phone buzzes in my hand, and I look down to see a surprise text from Church.

I forgot to say, I love you, I read, just before Tobias slips the phone from my hand.

"I love you?" he asks, quirking a brow. "You guys are saying I love you to each other now?"

My cheeks flame, but I shrug nonchalantly, pretending I'm too cool to care.

"Yeah, I mean, I love you guys, too. No big deal."

"You love us?" they repeat, exchanging a long look before turning back to me.

"Get her?" Tobias asks, and Micah nods.

"Get her."

They grab me before I can make a run for the bathroom, and they don't let go until Spencer's knocking on our bedroom door the next morning.

There are no gifts the boys could get me that could top their declaration about wanting to be together. I mean, they try like hell though, and I'm not one to turn down gifts, especially when they come in the form of designer shoes and handbags that Monica would almost literally kill for.

She'll be here for dinner later, but for now, I'm just enjoying a brief reprieve from my parents and Mr. Dave, hiding out in the living room while the adults disappear into their respective bedrooms for a break from the festivities.

It's pretty obvious we have things to talk about, too. I knew it the second I saw Spencer's face this morning.

"We went into the tunnels," he says, leaning forward on the couch next to Micah and balancing his elbows on his knees. He breaks the ice before I get a chance to even realize I'm about to be dropped into cold water.

"You did *what*?" I ask, wishing he wasn't too cute to strangle. "You meaning who, exactly? When? And why the fuck wouldn't you tell me about it?"

"Spencer and I went in," Church says, looking sorry after the fact. "But Ranger was with us on video chat the whole time, in case something went wrong."

"I don't care, I'm still pissed," I say, but then again, I'm also curious as hell. "Did you find anything down there?"

"Nothing but more tunnels," Spencer says with a roll of his turquoise eyes. "Whatever Jack was talking about, hidden churches or what the fuck ever, we have no idea. We never even saw anyone else when we were down there."

"They might just use the tunnels for transportation. Could've been coincidence that you just didn't stumble into anybody else." Tobias looks to Church for confirmation, but he just shakes his head, like he doesn't have this answer yet either.

We're close though, oh so freaking close.

"I learned a little bit more about my dad," Ranger says finally, speaking up and then sighing like he's exhausted. "From my mother, of all people. She got drunk and weird, and then started telling me that she'd left my dad once, briefly, when Jenica was like, eleven, and I was two. We stayed with her weird relatives in Spain who have ties to the Catholic church. She had us baptized while we were there, and she said when she decided to go back, and he found out, that Eric flipped and beat her."

"Holy shit." The words escape my mouth before I can stop them, and I cringe in apology to Ranger. He's staring down at his hands though, like he's daydreaming about beating his father up.

"Anyway, I know it sounds stupid, but you know how into rituals and shit these cults are. I figured maybe we were looking at our reason, why my father hasn't invited me into the Fellowship, or why Jenica died. It's a stretch, but I figure we should at least consider it."

"It could very well be," Church says with a shrug of his shoulder. "You have to be extreme to consider blood sacrifice a normal part of growing up, so it is possible that they saw the baptism as problematic."

"I'm just hoping that wasn't my mom's not-so-subtle way of warning me, you know? Like maybe she knew about the Fellowship at some point and is wondering if I know, too."

We all go quiet, considering. The mood's heavy now and not particularly festive.

"Okay," Ranger says, slapping his palms against his knees. "I'm done with this shit for now. I'm not letting some nutjobs in fox masks ruin my Christmas. Now, we bought you all of those boardgames, Charlotte, so pick one and I'll get ready to kick your ass."

"She's truly awful at videogames, so that shouldn't be hard," Micah says with a grin, but I'm not worried. They've all admitted their knowledge of boardgames is limited—more of a *peasant* activity, or so I hear—and I'm confident that by the end of the night, I'll have their balls in my hand.

That's … not totally metaphorical either.

CHAPTER TWENTY

The quiet lulls me into a false sense of security when we get back to Adamson after break. For weeks, everything is blissfully normal. It's what I've been looking for, been wanting for so long that I let myself get lost in it.

It feels good to have friends, even better to have friends who happen to be lovers, my schoolwork is sorted, and I have a plan for the future. When winter finally leaves and spring kisses the campus, our problems start up again with a bang.

And end that way, quite literally.

"Here, Charlotte," Ranger says, still the only one of the group who regularly calls me Charlotte (as opposed to Chuck, darling, Micropenis, and so on), "take this."

He hands over a box full of frilly aprons, and I grin. To Ranger, these are just as important as butter, sugar, and flour. He can't bake without them. "Spencer can carry the mixers downstairs when you go."

"Aye, aye, captain," Spence says, picking up one of the pink KitchenAid mixers and escorting me out the door of the Culinary Club classroom and downstairs, to the massive industrial kitchen that feeds the school and its staff three square meals a day, seven days a week.

This year, the Northeast Academy Baking Competition is being held on our campus. Last year, it was at Everly. And before that, I hear it was held in New York City, in the giant skyscraper that houses North York Preparatory Academy.

It's a pretty simple affair: the judges hand over a category, and we bake what we can in the allotted time with the ingredients given, and then our desserts are judged. There are three categories in total, and the highest score wins a ten-thousand-dollar donation to the charity of their choice.

Again, with rich people and the game of donating. Like, all the sponsors could just as easily have sent checks to the charities, but it's also kind of fun, so I'm not complaining.

That is, until we get downstairs and I see that blue-haired girl from last year. Kesha. The one that Ranger slept with. She spies me from across the room and waves.

I turn away quickly and pretend to be busy folding and refolding the aprons.

"She's coming this way, isn't she?" I ask Spencer, and he checks over his shoulder to look.

"Yep. Ex-girlfriend incoming."

"Never an ex-girlfriend because I didn't date," Ranger says, slamming a box of cooking utensils down on the stainless-steel counter next to me, his cheeks heating slightly as he glances my way. "Charlotte's my first girlfriend."

"Okay, bro," Spencer says, turning around just as Kesha nears our station, dressed neatly in the white blazer and black tie of Everly All-Girls Academy. She fiddles with the tie for a moment as she looks Ranger over and then turns her attention back to me.

"Good to see you've come out of the closet, so to speak," she says, trying for a genuine smile. "I'm actually here with Selena and Hana. You probably don't remember us all from the Valentine's Day dance last year …" She tucks some electric blue hair behind her ear, and I decide it really bothers me that she likely uses the same hair dye as Ranger. What can I say? I'm a jealous asshole.

"I remember you three from the dock," I say with a nod, glancing over at Ranger as he narrows his eyes.

"Speaking of, do you remember passing out on the lawn outside the dance hall?"

Church and the twins appear with more boxes,

laying them out on the counters and unloading mixing bowls, measuring cups, whisks, and spatulas. They glance our way but keep their distance, like they can guess what Ranger's up to over here.

"Yeah, I remember," Kesha says, her brown eyes crinkling up at the edges. "I mean, I don't remember how I hurt myself, just that Selena found me and brought me inside." She gives Ranger a suspicious sort of look. "Why? What does that have to do with anything?"

"Do you even remember how you got outside? Look, I know it doesn't mean much to you, but something happened to us that night, and we're just trying to get to the bottom of it." Ranger softens his voice up just a bit, and I see Kesha's cheeks fill with color. This time, it's my turn to narrow my eyes.

"All I remember is going outside to get some air ..." she starts, trailing off, like maybe this isn't the first time she's tried to recall what happened that night. "Actually, Selena had slipped out the door just before that, and I figured if she was going to sneak a cigarette, then I might as well, too." Kesha looks up and shrugs. "But that's it. I remember stepping outside and then nothing."

"And Selena?" Ranger pushes, but then the girl in question is sashaying her way over to us with a smile.

"Hey Charlotte," she says, giving the boys a more skeptical expression. "Does Church want to throw me into a wall again? Or am I okay to be here for the competition?"

"I have your dress," I offer up, trying to break the tension. "I didn't mean to hijack it from you for so long."

Selena returns her attention to me, plastering a smile onto her lips that makes me realize that while Church struggles with his emotions, his smiles aren't fake like that. This is most *definitely* not a pleasant sort of smile.

"No worries. I can get it afterward. Do you want to meet me in the dorm lounge or something? Mark's taking me out later, so I'll definitely be around."

"Actually, I can't," I say on impulse, just before she moves off. Selena pauses and blinks back at me like she can't believe I'd have the audacity to refuse. "I'm staying with all five of these idiots tonight, and we're sort of doing a movie thing."

"Maybe just before or just after?" she suggests, but I'm not liking the vibe I'm getting. We obviously don't have a ton of evidence to implicate her, but what we do have is strong. Plus, she's sort of giving me the creeps right now. She's being far too pushy.

"I'll be stuck with them from now until Monday, at least." I give her a dramatic wink, hoping to clear the suspicion from her eyes by acting like a pervy dork. Doesn't work. She tosses her hair over shoulder.

"Fine. I'll send a courier at some point next week,

and you can leave it with them."

"Thanks for understanding," I say, forcing a smile before Selena heads back over to her side of the kitchen.

"What was that about?" Church asks, as I shiver slightly

"She's guilty," the twins say in unison. I glance back at them and find them nodding in unison. "We knew it."

"If she's here, then they're all here, all four of them. That's when something bad is going to happen. Imagine if she caught me alone in the dorm lounge. At least if she thinks I'm going to be with you guys all weekend, they're less likely to try something."

"Good call," Church says, as the announcer blows his whistle and instructs us to line up at our stations. We're given our first category, and the kitchen explodes into chaos. Fortunately, we do this so often that it's practically mechanical at this point, leaving me with enough energy and focus to watch Selena instead.

She, of course, doesn't do a damn thing wrong, but I have that feeling on the back of my neck the same way I did when I was at Highgate Cemetery. I'm not getting caught off guard this time.

Ranger nails all three rounds in the competition, just like we knew he would, and we choose a local animal rescue as our charity. On our way back to the dorm later, we run into something interesting.

Mark and Selena, arguing in the woods.

"There's no point, *Mark*," she snaps, yanking her wrist from him. "It's not going to happen tonight."

"Okay, damn, that's literal," I whisper and Spencer slaps a hand over my mouth, just before Selena continues on, pacing away from Mark and then back again. We're all standing at the edge of the path, along the line of trees, looking in at them.

"You want me to sleep with you, when I know for a fact you're sniffing around Aster's tail?"

"Nothing's happened between us," Mark pleads, but his voice is like oil—far too slick for his own good. "We've just gotten close is all. We spend a lot of time together, and she's here, you're there …"

"I'm being punished for staying at Everly then?" Selena demands to know, scooting away when Mark reaches out for her.

"You're not being punished, Selena, but you know it would be easier if you were here. Everything would be easier. Like tonight, or even this weekend. It wouldn't matter what she was going." I glance over at Church, and he returns the look. What Mark's saying could mean a whole lot of different things, like maybe he's talking about Aster? Somehow, though, I feel like that last part is about little old me.

"It's fine," she says, gesturing loosely in his direction. This time though, she finally lets him put his hands on her waist. "Next time I'm here, we'll do it."

"Yeah, we will, all night fucking long," Mark growls into her ear, and I roll my eyes.

"We're running out of time, Mark," she says softly, her voice a deep melancholy.

"I know," he says, as we slowly move away from the spot, their voices fading into whispers. "I know, but we'll get her—I promise you."

CHAPTER TWENTY-ONE

It all started the morning of senior prom.

According to Adamson Academy tradition, Everly hosts the senior proms for both schools on odd years, and Adamson on even years. Well, since this year is an even year, we're having it here, in the big old stuffy ballroom where the academy hosts its fancy-schmancy parent dinner parties and galas. I mean, you have to give them *something* considering the staggering cost of tuition to go here.

As the Student Council—yay, I'm so excited I still get to say that!—we were in charge of not only the theme, but also essentially acting as a prom committee.

Which, you know, being surrounded by rich assholes makes it super easy since they hired everything out.

Need food? Cater it. Want music? Hire a band. Décor? Get an event planner.

"I feel like we're missing out somehow, you know? Like we should be making paper signs and hanging streamers, and struggling to procure some two-bit loser band from the boardwalk."

Spencer gives me a weird look.

"You like doing poor people stuff?" he asks me as my eye twitches in irritation.

"Peasants have their own customs, don't judge," Tobias adds, nodding his head, and crossing his arms over his chest. But it's a judge-y head nod and arm crossing, so I smack him in the arm with my phone. "What? That wasn't even an insult."

"Also, please stop buying me bras and underwear. I have plenty of it," I say, giving both twins and Spencer a look.

"Oh, that's not because you're poor, that's because we *like* buying you bras and underwear," Micah adds with a loose shrug of his shoulders, looking up at the glittering chandeliers above our heads, and the flower garlands made of real flowers. Each one of those probably costs a small fortune, and there are dozens of them. It looks more like a wedding in here than a prom, to be honest.

The colors are based on the Adamson Academy crest —navy-blue and champagne—and the round room is divided into sections. There are tables to the left of the door, with vases bursting with floral arrangements, tealights waiting to be lit, and plush chairs wrapped with large navy ribbons that hang from the backs.

"You know, since there's only going to be one of me, and five of you tonight," I start as Spencer lifts a questioning brow in my direction. Church is busy sweeping the room with the event planner and discussing small details, while Ranger discusses the arrangement of sweets that we've baked just for tonight's occasion. "If you want to dance with any other girls, that's okay."

"That's okay?" Spencer echoes, looking at the twins, and then putting a palm on the top of my head. "Are you nuts? It might be okay with you, but it's not okay with me. I don't want to dance with any other girls."

"Yeah, but," I start, and the twins smack their hands over my mouth, one twin's on top of the other.

"Nope," they say together as Micah leans in to look at me.

"You don't get to make all the rules. We get some say." They let go of my mouth as I glare at them. "First rule, you don't date other boys. Second rule, we don't date other girls. Third rule, we do this until it stops working for us. Weren't you there on your birthday when we discussed all of this? Or do you have another secret you want to tell us? Perhaps an identical twin hidden out there somewhere in the woods?"

"Oh," Tobias says, snapping his fingers and gesturing excitedly. "That'd be a good plot twist—a secret identical twin, living in the tunnels beneath the school, who leads the entire cult after Charlotte, so she can kill her and claim her life."

"And then one day, we wake up and the snarky Charlotte we know's been replaced with this weird, uptight, stone-faced girl—like a female Church—and one by one, we slowly go missing—"

I cut Micah off before they can get too deep into their ridiculous plotting.

"No talk of cults tonight, we promised," I say, looking up at the glossy banner that's being hung across the back of the stage, with the academy logo and the year of our graduating class.

Jesus, I'm like, not ready.

My hands fist together in my skirts, but Spencer stops my nervous fidgeting with a hand over mine.

"You okay, Chuck-let?" he asks, and I glance his way, letting the passion in his eyes calm me down. The year is flying by, but I have a lot to look forward to. I'm just … nervous about the change is all. And I know we still have three months of school left, but senior prom is sort of a big deal. We've just finished midterms, the quarter is over, and I've somehow managed not to get anything less than a B.

It's a miracle.

I'm pretty sure the universe likes to laugh at us all

and keep its own perfect balance though—if something seems too good to be true, it probably is.

"I'm okay. I'm excited to wear my way-too-expensive dress and dance with five kick-ass boyfriends while my dad glares at me from the punch table."

"Doesn't that sound nice?" Spencer says, sweeping one arm around my waist and using the other to grab my hand. He pulls us into the middle of the dance floor and even though there's no music, he spins me around like we're at one of Church's parents' fancy parties.

My laughter ringing out in the large room is the only tune there is.

Too bad that later on that night, it'd be my scream ringing through the room instead.

Now that the girls' dorm is officially open and occupied by only three students, it's the perfect place to put all of our visitors from Everly. I'm not happy about it. Hell, I wasn't happy about it when they started construction back up on the place and took away my sanctuary. Then again, now that the boys aren't committed to making my life a living hell, I've got plenty of other places that are just as good, like the

Culinary Club classroom.

That means that I'm the only girl getting ready in the boys' dorm, sitting with my mirror on the dresser at the end of my bed and doing my makeup while Church gets ready in Ranger's room. They have their doors open, and the hallway is teeming with people, so I figure I'm safe in here with the door locked and my phone by my side.

The custom dress the boys gave me sparkles from inside the closet, like a jewel winking at me from the shadows. To get my makeup worthy of such an outfit, I've spent the last two hours watching YouTube videos and trying to modify my usual routine.

Gold sparkly shadow for my eyes, dark falsies for my lashes, and a pink lipstick that matches the color of the dress. My hair's too short to put up, but I tame the ringlets and tuck the left side back with my mother's clip. The pearlescent white color of it goes well with the lace at the top of the dress.

"Are you done in there yet?" Ranger asks, rapping his knuckles against the door.

"Almost!" I call back, standing up quickly and pausing the music on my phone. The dress is a little hard to get into by myself, and I know I'll need one of the boys to tie the pale pink ribbons on the back, but I want to be as ready as I can be before they see me.

I step into it and pull the stiff bodice up, slipping my arms into the short lacey sleeves. I'm fully prepared for some bedroom action tonight, with my pink panties over the top of my garter belt and thigh-highs. Monica would be proud of me. Speaking of, I take a quick selfie and send it to both her and Ross. I'd video chat them, but they're both huge gossips, and it takes forever to get off the phone.

Glancing over my shoulder, I can see that the sun's already on its way down.

It's time to go.

Slipping my heels on, I move over to the door and open it to find all five boys waiting in their suits. They've each chosen their own color, like they did the night we went to that fancy restaurant with my mom.

"Damn," the twins say together, exchanging a look before Tobias turns back to me with a smile and presents a crown, woven through with fresh flowers. "We figured five corsages was a little much," he adds, placing the crown on my head.

"And a crown wasn't?" I joke, but I'm flushed from head to toe as Spencer comes around behind me to get the laces on my dress. He cinches me in, his fingers teasing the bare skin of my back as he leans close to whisper in my ear.

"You look good in this dress, but I bet you look better out of it."

"Perv," I grumble, but I can't hide the goose bumps on my bare arms.

"Five corsages might've been too much, but one

should do," Ranger says, offering one up to me. It's made up of pink roses, baby's breath, and a glittering cupcake pendant that gets me all choked up and shit. I've never been good with emotions, but I'm trying to work through my intimacy issues. How can I not, with the five of them looking at me the way they are?

He slips the corsage on as Church, dressed in a stunning white suit, watches from the back of the group. He tries to stand back, to be the leader, and I appreciate it, but I want him to have some fun, too.

"Let's get down there before Mark and his loser friends eat all our cupcakes," I say, trying to keep the mood light as I hook my arms with Church on one side and Micah on the other. It's hard to forget though that Mark isn't just a bully and an asshole—he's part of the Fellowship of the Divine, the pieces of shit responsible for Jenica's death, Eugene's, and Jared's.

No, Chuck, no, no cult talk tonight, I remind myself as the guys walk me down the stairs like a princess. I really feel like one in that moment, too, much like I did the day they took me to the fairy-tale suite in Disneyland.

My dress sweeps the stairs as we move down them together and tears sting the corners of my eyes.

"You okay, Chuck?" Micah whispers, but I can only nod because I never expected anything like this to happen to me. And I don't just mean the plethora of dick (see, I'm deflecting to humor because I have a problem accepting my own emotions). The Bornstead University acceptance letter kept me company the whole time I was getting ready.

"Totally fine," I choke, but the words are high and reedy, and Micah chuckles at me, putting his head up against the side of mine for comfort.

"You'll be alright," he says, and my eyes tear up even more.

Dad's waiting at the bottom of the stairs, like a proper father on prom night. To say I'm surprised is an overstatement. Usually, he's a headmaster first and a father second. Maybe discovering that his only child is being hunted by a vicious, wealthy, powerful cult has shifted his life views a bit?

He takes a picture of me with his phone, no warning, just a flash in my face that has me blinking back stars. Yep, yep, okay, he's definitely in dad mode tonight.

"Charlotte," he says, looking half-pleased at seeing me in my dress and half weirded-out that I have five boyfriends to take to prom. I mean, I've never been an overachiever in anything in life: lower than average grades, passable surfing skills, a karaoke voice that's beyond forgettable.

I guess the one thing in life I've decided to overachieve is the boyfriend thing. Pretty sure I'm nailing this shit.

Oh, and also, I have awards in blurting

embarrassing crap, and acting like an asshole without meaning to. Those are my other rare talents.

"Dad," I say, trying not to get choked up again. "You came."

"Of course I came," he says, a bit of that blustery headmaster voice in his tone. "You're my only daughter. Besides, I promised your mother I'd get pictures for her. Why don't you *kids*"—unnecessary emphasis on the word *kids*, but that's okay—"scoot a little closer together."

Spencer, Ranger, and Tobias stand on the step behind me while I stay in the center with Church on my left and Micah on my right.

My heart is beating so loud, I can barely hear my dad when he tells us to smile.

But I do, I smile big.

He takes several pictures with the group, and then makes the boys rotate, so I have one couple photo with each.

"Thanks, Dad," I say, and we look at each other for a moment before he finally turns away. Our relationship is improving, but it's not perfect. And that's okay.

"I'll see you at the dance," he says, disappearing out the door and heading down the path ahead of us.

Before we step out the door, Spencer grabs the white wool coat I got for Christmas from my mom and slips it over my shoulders. The night is cool, but it's obvious that spring is on its way, keeping the frosty bite out of the air.

Students stream around the side of the main building, heading for the propped open door that leads into the ballroom. Already, I can hear music playing, loud pop songs that used to be my jam back home. I mean, I still like them, but I'm starting to experiment with other genres, too. Church always puts on classical music when he's studying, and it's starting to grow on me.

We head inside, and it's like entering another world.

There's an arch of fresh flowers above our heads, a professional photographer with a full-sized gazebo to the right, and servers bringing drinks to the round white tables.

There's one in the very front, next to the dance floor, with a sign on it that reads *Reserved for the Student Council.* Someone's added *sit here and we'll beat you up* in red on the bottom, probably the twins or Spencer.

"I have to say, with all that money you rich people horde and refuse to pay in fair wages to your workers, you sure know how to put together a nice party."

"Aww, thanks, babe," Spencer says, putting a hand to his chest. Yep, the irony's completely lost on them. He grabs my hand before I even get a chance to sit down and pulls me onto the dance floor, like he did earlier today. Nobody else is dancing yet, but that doesn't stop the turquoise-eyed boy I fell in love with from spinning me around in a completely and utterly unpracticed sort of way.

"You're not the best at this, are you?" I whisper, leaning my head against his chest and breathing in his scent. He smells like temptation, but temptation that's been given into, indulged. The spicy mix of his cologne is twisted up in his own unique scent, something indescribable but irreplaceable. Between the feel and smell of him, the strings of rose lights lit up with gold bulbs, and the sway of our bodies, I feel dizzy. But in a good way.

"I'm not a dancer, not like Church," he says as I lean back and look up into his face. "And, apparently, neither are you." I slap him in the chest with a palm, and he flashes one of his naughty grins at me. "We could take lessons together though. Bet you'd like that, huh?"

"Bet *you'd* like that," I retort, and he shrugs, dressed in a charcoal gray suit and purple tie that makes his eyes seem even more vibrant than usual.

"Bet I would. I'm certifiably obsessed with you, Chuck-let."

He holds up my hand and encourages me to do a quick spin as the music comes to an end, and my father gets onstage to make an introductory speech. Typical Archie. He lives for speeches and assemblies and award ceremonies. Pretty sure that when he realized he couldn't attend them anymore, he decided to become a headmaster so he could host them.

Spencer and I take our seats just before the servers come around and take our dinner orders. *Dinner orders.* Like we're at a restaurant or something. There are only a few choices on the menu, but damn, it's all swanky stuff.

"Why am I so surprised by all of this when we're the ones that planned it?" I ask, tapping a fork against my lips. There's not a girl at that party who doesn't walk by and look at me sitting at a table full of hot dudes without some sort of reaction.

"Because you're a shitty assistant, and you never pay attention?" Micah asks, but he softens the blow of his words with a grin. The twins are wearing different colored suits tonight—Micah in red and Tobias in black—and I have to say, they make a very pretty picture together.

"I am a shitty assistant, aren't I?" I ask, grinning as a server pours sparkling apple cider into our glasses. I'd love a little champagne right about now, but … I glance over to find dad standing at the edge of the room, entertaining a few of his favorite students. Eventually, someone'll spike the punch. Happens at every high school event I've ever been to.

"You really, truly are," Tobias says as I grab some of the sparkly little stars that are spread across the surface of the table and flick them at him. "But we liked having you there."

"Definitely a prettier sight at that desk than Ross was," Ranger says, his suit a deep blue that's almost black. It suits his sapphire eyes and razored rock star hair. He sits with his arms crossed over his chest, eyes scanning the room for trouble. And by trouble, I definitely mean Mark. Or Selena. Or Gareth. Or Aster.

Ugh. Too many villains to keep track of.

"You're not trying to look into cult stuff right now, are you?" I ask, giving him a harsh stare that he returns with narrowed eyes. I point at him, and his mouth twists to the side in a guilty smile. "You are! No more. No more detective stuff. This is our senior prom, and we only ever get one of these, and I didn't go last year at all because I was in Santa Cruz—"

"Okay," Ranger says, leaning forward and putting his hand across mine. "I've got you, Charlotte."

"We could all use a break, I think," Church agrees, pulling a flask out of his suit jacket and offering it surreptitiously to me under the table. I flick a glance in dad's direction as I unscrew the cap, swigging some of it, and then passing it to Spencer. "And now that we know that Mr. Dave and Nathan are working on the problem, we have our solution."

"I can't wait to see those psychos get put in prison," I say, looking up at a paper star lantern above my head. Now, I totally remember procuring these babies for the prom. They remind me of that night on the roof, and I just can't seem to help myself. I'm a hopeless romantic.

"Or in the ground," Ranger suggests, but even though Micah snorts, it's very clearly *not* a joke.

Our food comes, and I have to say, it's off the charts good. I ordered some sort of phyllo wrapped chicken thing with a salad and a twice baked potato, eating until I'm stuffed, and I feel like my magic fairy dress might very well burst open at the seams.

"Okay, enough food for Charlotte," I say with a groan, pushing the plate back and slumping in my chair.

"Hopefully not so much that you can't dance?" Micah asks, giving me a saucy little look that reminds me of that day in Santa Cruz, when we went racing in his Lamborghini.

"Um, hell no. Isn't that what tonight is all about?" he stands up and takes my hand, pulling me away from Spencer and Church and into the gyrating throng in the center of the room. I have to say, he's not much of a dancer either, but he knows how to move in a way that keeps me very, very interested.

"Hey," Tobias asks, leaning over the back of his chair to stare at us. "Are you two dancing or fucking? Because it looks like the latter, for sure."

"You're just jealous, dickhead," Micah retorts, sweeping me away again. He keeps me with him until we're both sweaty and panting, collapsing into our chairs at the table. Every few songs, I switch up which dance partner I take out on the floor with me, grabbing small breaks in between to catch my breath.

"Are you sure you can handle five of us?" Ranger asks as he spins me around, and I try to decide if he's really talking about dance, or he means something a bit more … lascivious. Dancing with five different guys, I can definitely do. But if he means five of them in bed at the same time … then he's going to have to wait a while.

At least until college, right? That sounds like an experimental college thing to try.

"I'm sure," I say, enjoying him as a strong lead on the dance floor. As he escorts me back to the table, I hear the screech of a chair and look over to see Selena leaning over Aster's table. She whispers something to the other girl, and they exchange a venomous sort of look. It's got to be something to do with Mark. Selena hits Aster's drink over, spilling liquid all over her dress, and then storms out the door.

As soon as Mark sees, he's up and out of his chair to go after her. When Aster tries to catch up, grabbing onto his sleeve, he yanks his arm away from her and disappears.

It's pretty damn obvious in that moment which girl he's picked.

"That was painful," I snort, shaking my head and looking back at the guys. But frankly, I couldn't care less about their disturbing love triangle. I'm just starting to get pumped for the night, like maybe I'll dance until the freaking sun comes up. "Tobias, shall we?"

"We shall," he says, rising to his feet and taking my arm before he stops to glare at his brother. "And I'll show you how it's done."

Instead of just grinding our bodies together—which I liked a lot, by the way—Tobias takes it slow, putting his hands on my hips and sliding them up toward my ribcage. He leans in and kisses the side of my neck, our bodies moving at a much slower pace than all the other dancers around us. But oh my god, it's hot.

We're in the middle of a huge group of people, but he's touching me like we're in bed, alone. Fortunately, the crowd is thick enough right now that Dad can't see us. If he could, he'd probably burst a vein in his forehead. I mean, I'm eighteen now, so there isn't much he could do to stop me.

The song ends, and Tobias and I stand there breathless for a moment, separating only when an entire new song has passed.

"Shall we get a drink?" he asks, offering up his arm. I take it, always pleasantly surprised by the muscles in his arm, and move over to the refreshments table to grab some punch. It's been spiked, that's for sure, but none of the administrators have noticed yet. I'm okay with it though; it's nice to have a little bit of a buzz going. The edges of reality blur a bit, making the golden lights seem like stars above our heads. Couples are still slow dancing as Tobias and I stand there and sip our drinks, glancing at one another, and then popping a pair of miniature pink cupcakes into each other's mouths.

"Let's dance again, before any of my asshole friends try to steal you away again," he says, grabbing my hand and pulling me back into the glittering crowd. One of his hands finds my waist while the other grasps my hand, drawing me back into the magic of the evening.

We've only been dancing for a few minutes before I start to notice people sagging into their chairs, or even pausing to sit down on the floor in pools of silk and satin.

"What's going on?" I ask as Tobias groans and releases my hands, stumbling back and landing on his knees in front of me. "Tobias?" I lean down next to him just before I start to feel it, too, a heavy drowsiness washing over me that makes me sway in place.

All around us, couples are collapsing to the ground. Here and there, a person or two seems completely unaffected by it, but that's the exception, not the rule. Even most of the staff members are swaying or falling over.

"What …" I start, lifting my gaze and searching the room for the rest of the boys.

A sound behind me, like stone scraping against stone, draws my attention around to a girl in a yellow prom dress … and the awful, grinning visage of the Fellowship's fox mask. She's standing in the black void of a doorway that wasn't there before.

Another hidden door, like the one in the antique shop, I think before she takes a step toward me.

"Catch for us the little foxes," she whispers, grabbing my wrist and yanking me into the tunnel with her.

Cold water drips onto my forehead, waking me with a start. For a second there, I'm convinced that I drank too much at prom and ended up with a hangover. That's it. Everything else, that was just a nightmare.

But then I blink myself fully awake, staring up at a ceiling that's painted with bizarre imagery, people in robes, in masks. There's a lot of blood. Oh yeah, a hell of a lot of blood in that art. *What in the actual fuck?* My pulse starts to race, and I struggle to sit up, but my arms and legs aren't budging. Turning my head to the right, I can see that my wrist is tied in place. In fact, both of my wrists are bound. Both ankles, too.

Candles flicker from metal torch stands, evenly

spaced around the circular room. We're very clearly underground here; there are no windows, just murals painted to look like them. The ceiling is chiseled stone, as are the walls, and I'm pretty sure the thing I'm lying on is made of rock, too. It's cold against my bare shoulders as I shift slightly, testing my bonds and blinking through a thick haze.

What happened to everyone at the dance? I wonder, suddenly more concerned for the boys than I am myself. Tobias was barely responsive, last I remember.

"Hello?" I call out, my voice echoing in the empty chamber. There's nobody here that I can see, but clearly, I didn't tie myself up on this stone altar.

Altar.

My mind flickers to Jason Lambert, drip, drip, dripping blood from his curled fingers.

Shit. Looking around again, I spot a table draped in assorted items. There are ties, and bouquets of dried flowers, old t-shirts, barrettes, framed photos … including the one of Jenica that went missing from the girls' dorm. It's all gathered there together, trophies of dead students collected into a glittering shrine.

Uh-oh.

The sound of a door opening draws my attention to the opposite side of the room, away from the raised stone dais and toward a group of people, dressed in black robes and fox masks. Just like that day in the woods when Spencer and I were running for our lives.

Fear flashes through me, ice-cold and definite.

The Fellowship of the Divine might have the creepy cult cliché thing going on, but it's not funny. It's not funny at all. It's *terrifying.*

The people file into the room without speaking, walking down a narrow path with pools of dark water on either side. There are statues sticking out of the water, draped in moss, faceless monsters watching over their procession. Stalactites hang from the ceiling, and crumbling white columns dot the room here and there, little hints of neoclassical architecture that remind me of the auditorium.

The cultists start lining up against the walls around me, the sound of their footsteps echoing in the oversized chamber. Another cool droplet of water hits me in the forehead, leaking from the stone above me.

This, this is where the tunnels lead. *I wonder if this place floods when it rains, too?*

I blink a few more times, and then pull against my restraints, the flouncy pink dress fluttering as I move. But even if I weren't tied up, I'm not sure I could get out of here. They must've drugged the food and drinks with … something. *At least that means that everyone else is okay, right?* Because even in that moment, it's not about me. It's about my dad and the boys.

Exhaling sharply, I try to focus on what's happening without letting panic set in. Whatever drug they've given me must be dulling my emotions because I'm not freaking out. I'm scared, but … not panicked. *Think, Charlotte,* I snap at the dulled edges of my brain. *If you don't, then you're dead. That's it. No college, no future, no more happy moments and stolen kisses and sweet nothings whispered in the dark.*

Shit, that was markedly better poetry, huh?

Too bad I'm not exactly in a position to appreciate it.

One of the robed assholes moves to the front of the room, several others fanned out on either side of him. A student dressed in a suit appears first, his mask firmly in place, and kneels down before the dais.

"I have caught for you a fox, a little fox that plundered the vineyards," he says, and I know right away that it's Mark's voice speaking from behind the mask. Arrogance drips from every practiced word. That, and I can smell a turd sandwich from a mile away.

The people around the room begin to chant, their voices echoing off the stone walls and bouncing back at me as I struggle to climb out of my mental fog.

"And the fox's name?" asks the man at the front of the congregation, his voice sparking just a hint of recognition in me.

"Eugene Mathers," Mark replies smoothly, lifting off his mask and rising to his feet. He pauses just briefly to look over his shoulder, his ugly mouth curving into a smirk. That gets a bit of a rise out of me.

If Charlotte Carson is anything, it's ornery, and seeing him look so smug? It just pisses me the hell off. He turns back to the front of the room and steps forward, holding his mask over his chest.

The next person to appear in front of me is wearing a scarlet dress, her red-orange hair frizzing out from behind the mask. She doesn't even need to take it off for me to know who she is. She kneels down, just like Mark did, but with a touch more humility.

"I have caught for you a fox, a little fox that plundered the vineyards," Aster Hayes repeats, pulling off her mask and rising to her feet in a mess of silk and tulle.

"And the fox's name?" the leader asks, without a hint of emotion coloring his words. They're talking about dead kids here, and they don't give a fuck about what they've done. It's all a game to them, like it has been from the start. The boys had said, if one of these families wanted me dead, they could hire someone to do it. That's not what this is about. This is ritual, sacrifice, and tradition.

"Jason Lambert," Aster replies easily, making my breath catch. So, she was the female attacker all along—at least one of them, anyway. That means she danced with me on Valentine's Day, and then tried to kill me on the same night. How messed up is that?

She takes her place next to Mark as the third hoodie-wearing dickhead comes up to the stage, kneeling on the hard stone in his tux.

"I have caught for you a fox, a little fox that plundered the vineyards," the boy says, and even though I know I've heard that voice before, I'm having trouble placing it. It's got to be Gareth though, right? Our detective work was solid.

"And the fox's name?"

I know before he even speaks that it's me. I'm the little fox. My eyes close tight, and I wish with everything I had that I wasn't lying here, helpless, drugged, hoping and praying for a miracle. But truly, am I even going to get out of this? There are dozens of people in here, *dozens*. We're very clearly underground somewhere. Where, I'm not sure, because the boys ventured into those tunnels and found nothing.

Jack though … he said he'd seen it, this underground church, so maybe …

"Spencer Hargrove," the boy says, and my heart shatters to pieces. Spencer?! My head whips around, but I can't find him anywhere. That is, until I force myself to sit up as far as possible, straining against the ropes, and find that there's another altar opposite mine. All I can see from here are a pair of shoes, but my worst fears are confirmed when the boy pulls off his mask and I see Gareth McConnell's stupid, ugly face. Yes, I've been reduced to petty insults, so sue me. I'm under a lot of freaking stress here.

"Make it right," the leader says as another of the

members approaches with a knife and hands it to him. On the hilt, I can see that symbol, the one that was on the stone that I found on my windowsill. Who it was that put it there, I may never know. But clearly, this has been in the planning stages for quite some time.

Gareth moves around the altar where Spencer lays, passed out and unmoving. He pauses with his hands on the knife, the tip pointed down at my boyfriend's chest.

"Spencer!" I scream, my voice ripping through the cavern, cutting right through the dull chanting of the other members. Nobody pays me any attention, not even as I struggle and continue to scream. "What do you need him for when you have me?" I ask, but already, there's another person moving down the center of the room in a golden dress.

She takes her place in front of the dais, blond hair pulled up into a bun at the back of her head.

"I have caught for you a fox, a little fox that plundered the vineyards."

"And the fox's name?" the leader asks again.

"Charlotte Carson," Selena McConnell says, rising to her feet and removing her mask. She glances back at me, but her face is devoid of any emotion whatsoever.

"Make it right," the man in charge repeats, and Selena is handed a knife that's identical to the one in her brother's hands. "The McConnells have disappointed the Fellowship this year. Your sister did not make these sorts of mistakes."

"Yes, sir," Selena agrees, her voice cold and not nearly as submissive as Aster's.

She moves around the altar and takes her place beside me. This time, the knife is pointed directly at my own chest.

The chanting picks up in both speed and volume, but I'm sort of out of ideas here. Tied up, drugged, terrified ...

"Wait," I whisper, but Selena isn't listening to me. She's watching the men on the dais for her cue. "You haven't killed anyone. It's not too late for you to back out of this. You haven't done anything you can't undo."

"For two centuries, our families have guarded this sacred place," the man onstage begins, holding out his hands to indicate the large room. "And we've been rewarded with wealth beyond imagination, success in our various businesses, and the unbreakable ties of the Fellowship. In short, our vineyards have and always will be in blossom. But the world is greedy, and we must work diligently to keep out those who would take from our bounty."

The man waves his hand in Spencer's and my general direction.

"This year," he continues, "we welcome four new initiates into the fold with open arms. But to be a true member of the divine, sacrifices must be made. A pact of blood is unbreakable."

"Catch for us the foxes," the crowd around us

murmurs, and I can feel it in the air, the crackle of violence.

Selena and Gareth raise their knives up high as I watch helplessly, my heart beating out of control. No ninja moves are going to get me out of this one. No amount of training with the twins is going to get me out of this.

The sound of a door being thrown open draws the attention of almost everyone in the room, including Selena, her knife poised above me. Everyone but Gareth McConnell. His knife flashes down in a hint of silver, and a scream tears from my throat. I'm about to see Spencer murdered right in front of me.

One of the robed assholes steps forward, disrupting the unbroken line, and grabs the weapon from his fingers in a flash, spinning it around and leveling it on him.

"What the hell?" Mark growls as Spencer's rescuer reaches up and pushes his mask up, knocking loose his hood and revealing a head of honeyed hair.

It's fucking Church.

"Put the knife down, Selena, or I'll kill your brother," he says, his voice a jagged splinter of ice. No part of me has to wonder if he's serious. Selena just stares back at him, dumbfounded, and then moves away from me. But she doesn't drop the knife. Church slices the bonds on Spencer's arms and legs before moving over to me.

"How did you even get down here?" I ask, but Church is too busy scanning the room to answer. And Spencer, well, he's still not awake. I stumble over to him, fully aware that we're not saved just yet. This is a reprieve, at best.

"A Montague," the leader says from behind us, a certain note in his voice that says that messing with one of Elizabeth and David's children isn't such a good idea. "Subdue him, but don't kill him."

Mark is the first person to step forward, like he's been waiting for his chance to get at Church all along. The thing is, I'm pretty sure Church has been waiting for this moment, too.

"Here." He hands the knife over to me as Mark heads his way. I hesitate, but only for a second. I know that Church can hold his own against the king of the foot-uh-bra-lers? Pretty sure I'm still missing the point of that name.

"Spence," I whisper, pushing the silver hair off of his forehead. He's breathing, but just barely. Either he ingested more of whatever it was that put us to sleep in the first place or else he hit his head on the way down here. Looking up, I finally see what the commotion at the door is.

It's a person in a robe and mask, speaking frantically with several other members. After a moment, one of them pulls away and takes off running toward the front of the room, robes flapping.

Something's happening; we just need to hold on. I let myself believe that because, why not? Where's the harm in hope?

"I need you to wake up, Spencer," I whisper, tapping the side of his face with my palm. It occurs to me then that in all the fairy tales, the prince wakes the princess up with a kiss. Pretty sure my brain is broken from whatever I've been drugged with because that's all I can think about in that moment, kissing Spencer.

True love's kiss, right?

I lean down and press my mouth frantically to his, the room disappearing around me for a minute. Swear to god, it happens (again, probably the drugs), but for a split-second, that's all there is. Just me and Spencer.

He startles awake beneath my lips, and I pull back, my frightened eyes looking into his.

"That … that actually worked?!" I choke out as he sits up suddenly, conking our foreheads together and cursing.

"Where the fuck am I?" he asks, glancing over just in time to see Church putting Mark on the floor, a knee against Mark's back, one of the jerk's arms twisted behind him. Several other members are rushing forward to help, and I know it's just a matter of time before they've got the three of us trapped.

"Secret cult meeting, no time to explain, but you and I," I point back and forth between us, "we almost just died. Like, knives meet chest." His eyes widen in surprise as I rush to finish my explanation. "Yeah, I know it's insane, but—"

"Chuck, down!" Spencer yells, pushing my head down toward his crotch in a way that would've really pissed me off if we'd been in the bedroom. Selena's knife swipes through the air where I was standing, and I stumble back, right into the arms of another cult member.

Just like it did in the cemetery, my practice sessions with the twins come rushing back, and I go completely limp, leaving the person behind me to hold my full, deadweight. Ugh. Deadweight? That's exactly what I'm going to be if I can't come up with a plan.

The person holding me drops me to the ground, and I roll. I'm just operating on instinct here, but it seems to work, putting some space between me and the nearest cult members. *They are so going to pay for dry cleaning this dress,* I think as I struggle up to my feet and find Spencer holding Selena against his chest, back to front, her arms trapped by his. Unfortunately, she still has the knife. Spencer's bleeding from his cheek, but it doesn't look too bad.

My attention switches over to Church, holding off three cult members while Mark and another robed asshole lie on the floor in front of him. His eyes catch mine for a brief moment, just as the leader heads my way. I turn and head for the altars, throwing myself up and onto one in a flurry of pink lace. Before I can catch myself, I slip off and land on my ass on the other side, knocking the breath out of me.

They need you for their ritual, I realize, struggling to my feet. *Selena has to kill you, or it doesn't count.* That means nobody else can kill me, right?

It's a risk, but I'll assume that risk.

What else is there?

I reach down and twist the fabric of my skirts up into a knot, tying the drees up and out of my way. My heels are already long-gone, probably lost as Selena dragged me down the tunnels. I duck down and throw my body forward, into the narrow space between the two altars, ending up back on the other side as cultists rush around it to grab me.

Don't think too hard about this, I tell myself as I grab onto Selena's hand and pry the knife from her fingers. Before Spencer lets her go, I hit her as hard as I can in the face. Some of the boys might've taken it a bit further and used the knife, and even though I *know* it'd be better for me to stab and disable Selena, I can't do it. That's just not me.

"Come on!" I tell Spencer, grabbing onto his hand. "Church!" I shout, and then I start to run toward the exit. I know he'll follow us. He stands a better chance of breaking through the crowd and coming our way than we do going to him.

The door to the tunnels is closed again, locked from the inside, and there are people all around it. I swing the knife at them as I approach, and they scoot back, falling into the pools of deep, black water on either side.

Spencer throws a hard punch at one of the members who approaches us. Spence doesn't have any formal training like Church or the twins, but he's scrappy as hell. Just like me. Pretty sure Spencer and I are the most similar out of all the guys.

Church appears from behind us, using the force of his body to knock aside several of the cultists.

"The door," he says, voice as sharp as the knife in my hand. I shove up the wooden bar that's blocking the door and yank it wide, revealing the curved walls of the tunnels and a seemingly impenetrable darkness.

"Let's bail," Spencer says, snatching a torch from the wall before we take off running together, the knife held pointing down and at my side. Hey, I still remember those stupid safety videos my dad used to make me watch about kids who run with sharp objects. Never thought they'd be referencing a cultist's knife, but hey, it works.

Footsteps and shouts sound behind us, but either nobody's got a gun or else they know they can't risk shooting without killing one of us. Spencer and I, they need for their ritual, and Church, well, Church is a Montague.

"Where are we going?" Spencer asks as our feet splash through the water and I feel my chest get tight with old memories. It better not be raining today. I mean, the sky was clear when we walked from the dorm to the main building, but you never know with my luck.

"I have no idea. This place wasn't on any of the maps." Church comes skidding to a stop, putting out a hand and just barely preventing me and Spencer from tumbling over the edge of a cement walkway and into deeper water. He reaches out and takes the torch from Spencer, lifting it high and looking around. Behind us, the tunnel looks much the same as the one we were trapped in before. But when he turns back around, I can see that the wall across from us is a solid, smooth cement with some sort of warning sign attached to it. "Because this isn't a part of the tunnels," he murmurs.

"We're in the sewer," Spencer adds, finishing Church's thought. He takes the torch back and looks down one side first and then the other. The sound of approaching footsteps makes my heart pound as I look back into the darkness and find a sea of torches coming toward us. "This way."

We head down the walkway together, the cement pathway just wide enough for the three of us to run abreast.

I'm panting, my feet screaming from the scrape of the pavement as I pound down the sewer tunnel barefoot. We've got a bit of distance on the others, but not a lot. And now that we've seen what we've seen, we're not getting out of here as easily as we have in the past.

"Here!" Spencer calls out, skidding to a stop next to an automated door. He licks his lips as he touches the pin pad. "Eddie's in charge of all this stuff, right?" He pauses, breathing ragged and uneven as Church takes the torch and glances over his shoulder. The other torches aren't far behind us. "The twins and I have spent years breaking into every shed, every storage closet on campus." He exhales and tries a combination, cursing when it doesn't work. And then another.

"We may need to run," Church says, watching the bobbing lights as they get closer.

"No, I've got this," Spencer says, plugging in another pin code and then fist pumping hard when the door unlocks. "Did you see that, Chuck?" he asks, turning to me with sparkling eyes.

"Yep, yep, you were cool as fuck, now *go*." I shove him through the door and Church follows, yanking it closed behind us. More than likely, the cultists already know the code, so they won't have much trouble following us. This doesn't buy us much time at all.

Just inside the door is a small command center, probably to do with the water and sewer systems, but we ignore it—none of us would know how to work anything anyway—and head for the ladder against the wall.

We climb out, into the woods behind the school.

Where, exactly, we are, I'm not sure but that's okay. We've been here before, and we survived right?

Spencer takes all of thirty seconds to look around.

"I know where we are," he says, and Church gives him a look.

"You're sure?"

"I'm sure." Spencer takes my hand and we move into the darkness of the trees. Just a few minutes later, we're coming up on the fountain and the pond, the spot where the boys and I ended up falling after we escaped the tunnels.

We've just barely passed it, headed in the direction of the storage shed where we found Ranger beneath the grate, when several of the cultists appear from the trees. Their white fox masks smile at us in the darkness as Selena steps up between them, Gareth by her side.

"You're ruining everything for me," she says, holding another knife, the strange rune-like symbol carved into the hilt. "This is my destiny."

"Sorry to be such a disappointment," I say as she rushes me, along with several of the robed cultists. Gareth goes for Spencer, while Church is overwhelmed with a good half dozen attackers of his own. Selena swings her knife at me as the other cultists chant, still standing in the shadows near the trees, like ghosts, like specters.

The knife is aimed toward my chest. On reflex, I hold up my own knife and her blade glances off it, making sparks. She's in a rage now, her yellow dress dirty from dragging down the tunnels. They must've taken an alternate route to cut us off like this.

We dance around in a circle, knife to knife. Neither of us are experts, so the playing field is fairly even, but it's scary as hell. Sweat pours down my face as I swing my own knife in defensive arcs. I don't want to cut her. I don't want to see her skin bleed. But I'm running out of options, aren't I?

Pink and yellow princesses, knife-fighting in the woods.

The east coast is so weird, you guys. What would my California friends say about all of this?!

Hella fucking lame, bro.

Selena's dark eyes are focused on me, her mouth pursed in a thin line as she presses her height advantage against me, forcing my back against a tree. When she goes for it, putting her full bodyweight into the knife, I drop low and tackle her. Her blade wedges in the tree trunk, tearing out of her hand as we fall to the ground in a glittering sea of skirts and lace. My crown, which has miraculously stayed in my hair this whole time, is torn off and tossed as Selena claws at my face.

"Women are supposed to *fix each other's crowns*, you bitch!" I hit her in the face, just the way the twins taught me, cracking her across the jaw. She pushes me up and rolls us over, the extra weight she has on me giving her an advantage. We struggle over the knife, nails raking one another's skin and drawing blood. It hurts, oh it fucking hurts, but I push the emotion back.

I'm fighting for my life here. There's no such thing as too much to bear.

"Hah!" Selena shouts, wrenching the knife from my fist and bringing it down hard. I buck, throwing her off-balance just enough that the blade hits the grass instead of my throat. As she struggles to right herself, I shove her back, giving myself just enough room to crawl free. My eyes are on that knife in the tree as I struggle to my feet, petals falling from the corsage on my wrist.

A grunt draws my attention to the left, and I see that Spencer's bleeding from his arm, clutching an oozing wound as he grits his teeth and backs a step away from Gareth. He doesn't have a knife to fight back with.

There's no hesitation as I grab the blade from the tree, ripping it from the loose bark and launching myself at Gareth. He turns at the last second, hesitating briefly—probably because I'm not his mark—and then bringing his own weapon up to defend against mine.

The force of my lunge knocks the blade from his hand, but my triumph is short-lived.

White-hot pain explodes across my vision as I stumble and fall, my body going numb as my hands hit the damp dirt of the forest floor. *What just happened?* I think as a boy screams my name. It might be Spencer, could be Church. My brain isn't working so great right now.

I've been stabbed.

CHAPTER TWENTY-TWO

I'm hauled back by my hair and thrown onto the ground. Someone's gotten blood all over my pink dress.

"Finally," Selena breathes, squatting over me, her dark eyes not without emotion. "I'm sorry, but blood is the only pact that can't be broken." She brings her knife to my throat, but I'm not done fighting yet. I grab Selena's wrists, fighting against her much stronger grip. But my body must be running high on adrenaline because I'm able to keep her off of me until two sets of arms grab her on either side and drag her backwards, shoving her and sending her flying.

The McCarthy twins are here.

"Charlotte," Ranger says, lifting me up and pulling me back against his chest. "You're bleeding."

"I think …" I start as my vision swims and I have to blink several times to stop the forest from spinning. "She stabbed me." I put my hand on my lower back and lift it to my face, staring at the bright ruby red of blood.

"Jesus Christ," Ranger growls, hauling me up and into his arms as Micah and Tobias circle Selena, trying to take the knife from her. The other cultists seem loath to interfere with me and Spencer, but they have no problem going for the others. Several of them descend on the twins, and as impressive as their skills are, as impressive as Church's are, they're all humans. They have limits.

"Ranger," a man says, and I recognize that voice as the cult leader's. He steps forward, out of the shadows of the trees, and lifts his mask up. Ranger's body stiffens beneath me as I blink through the fog in my vision and try to make sense of who it is that I'm seeing.

It's Ranger's dad, Eric.

"Stay the fuck away from me," Ranger growls, backing us up until we're pressed against a tree. "I knew you were involved. I *knew* it, but … Jenica … How could you?"

"Blame your mother for that. She didn't want you or Jenica involved in the Fellowship. She took great lengths to defy me, running off to Spain the way she did."

Ranger's eyes are wide, his jaw clenched tight. He looks down at me then and it's fear that fills his expression. My hand reaches up to touch the side of his face, smearing blood.

"It's up to each initiate to choose the person to complete their pact. Rick chose Jenica; there was nothing I could do. If she'd been a part of the Fellowship …"

"Then she'd be a murderer instead of a victim? No thanks." Ranger pulls me close, his gaze shifting over to Spencer, Micah, Tobias, and Church. The latter three are being wrestled to the ground by dozens of cultists. The former is still facing off against Gareth, but at least neither of them have knives. That is, until Selena passes one of the recovered weapons back to her brother. "Call this shit off and maybe I won't testify against you in court."

His father smiles, but it's not a pretty smile.

"Son, our traditions are centuries old. When the Fellowship first began, we even had the blessing of the church your mother's so fond of. The wealth and success of our families depends on these traditions. Don't tell me you haven't enjoyed your privileged childhood?"

"I enjoyed my sister," Ranger says, his heart racing against my palm as I lay my hand over his chest. I'm not even sure why I'm doing that, touching him so reverently. Things are getting fuzzy, I won't lie. "And I enjoy my girlfriend. Let me get her to a hospital."

"You know I can't do that," Eric says as several of the cultists approach and grab Ranger, dragging me from his arms as he does his best to fight back.

Someone lays me on the forest floor and steps away, leaving me with Selena and her knife, and nowhere to go.

I'm going to die here tonight?

I turn my head to the side and find Spencer and Gareth locked in a battle for their lives, the knife inching toward Spencer's stomach. Selena comes for me again, kneeling down with the blade in hand, taking advantage of the blood loss that's making my limbs feel heavy.

With the very last of my strength, I reach up and snatch my mother's hairpin, shoving it into Selena's eye and making her scream. She falls back, and I push up to my feet, shaking like crazy. I throw myself into Gareth, knocking him away from Spencer.

I collapse to my knees immediately, but I've given Spencer the opportunity he needs to take the knife. He shoves it through Gareth's shoulder as hard as he can and comes for me.

"Chuck-let," he whispers, looking back to see the other boys struggling against a horde of cultists. There must be … over a hundred of them now, filling the clearing. We've bought ourselves a few extra moments, but that's it.

It's over.

Spencer picks me up, just like Ranger did, but our backs are to the side of the rocky hillside that surrounds the fountain. There's nowhere to go. Selena is sobbing and holding her hands over her eye while Gareth bleeds. Nobody moves forward to help them. I get it, it's part of their ritual. But this isn't going to last forever.

Mark appears out of the crowd, Aster by his side.

"If you want something done right, you have to do it your fucking self." The two of them come for us, but I've got no fight left, and Spencer can't do much while he's holding me. The rest of the cult streams around us, blocking us in with a wall of robes and masks. The other four boys are on their knees, held by four or more cultists each. "Gareth, stop being a little bitch. It's just a flesh wound."

Gareth's pulled the knife from his shoulder, not the smartest move in the world, but it seems that Mark is right. He doesn't collapse to the ground, and he's not spurting blood, so it's likely Spencer missed any critical veins or arteries. And even though Selena's eye is red and swollen, a bit of blood marring her cheek, she's up and on her feet just a few seconds later.

The four of them surround us, dragging me from Spencer's arms as he screams.

Mark, Aster, and Gareth hold him back as Selena sets me down and takes the blade one, last time.

The sharp edge of the knife presses up against the skin of my throat, and I close my eyes, hoping that it happens quick.

I can't bear to hear the sounds of the boys around me, calling out my name.

"Everyone freeze!" a voice calls out as dozens of people in vests and masks surround us. Selena grits her teeth, shaking above me in pain or fear or adrenaline, I'm not sure. "Nobody move. Put your weapons down."

Selena stares at me, her eyes glittering with a fanatical light, her arm drawing back with the knife clutched tight in her hand. She swings at me, going for my throat, but a single shot rings out in the clearing and her arm goes limp, body slumping forward over mine.

The knife drops from her hand to the ground, but I'm too far gone to really register what's happening.

A moment later, hands are dragging Selena off of me, and I'm looking up into Ian Dave's face. He has an FBI badge hanging around his neck.

"You'll be okay, Charlotte," he says as the boys rush to my side. "You'll be alright."

The last thing I see before I pass out is the Student Council, looking at me like I'm the only thing in the world that matters.

And that, that's a good last memory to have.

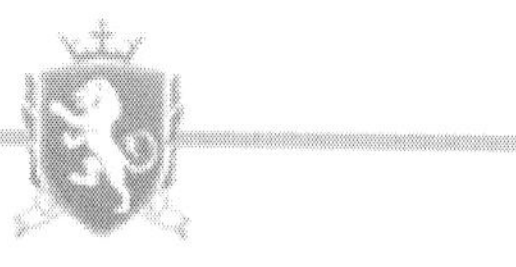

After the main character in a book dies, there's always some purple prose shit, a bunch of flowery fluff about a life well-lived, or all the wonderful lessons the person learned before they passed.

Me, I dream about riding a unicorn, seated behind Ranger Woodruff while the twins march along on either side of us. We come to a castle, where Church is the prince, and Spencer is his handsome silver-haired husband …

Not a very sophisticated death knell, is it?

"Charlotte," a voice whispers as I struggle to blink through the image of Church and Spencer making out on a dais, crowns on their heads, robes trailing out behind them … Oh, dreams are fun, aren't they? "Charlotte."

My eyes open and I find myself looking up at the tear-stained face of Archibald Carson.

"Dad?" I say, or at least … I *try* to say it. Instead, a weird, choking sound comes out before I start to cough. Dad offers me up some water, and I struggle to sit up. He sets the cup aside and helps me get situated in the pillows before he offers it up again. I drink deeply, water spilling out of my lips and soaking the hospital gown I'm wearing. "Where am I?" I whisper, and Dad's face softens.

"You're in the hospital, Charlotte," he breathes, just before the door flies open and my mother appears, blubbering uncontrollably and throwing herself on my bed in a dramatic move that's worthy of some old Southern movie with women in floppy hats.

"Mom?" I ask, putting a hand up to my face as I try to remember what the hell happened and how I might've gotten here. "Where are the boys?"

"In the waiting room," Dad answers for me, tucking some hair back behind my ear. My gaze latches on his. That's seriously one of the nicest, sweetest gestures he's ever done for me. Remember? We don't show affection.

"What happened?" I ask, flashes of knife fights, and fox masks, and billowing robes flickering through my mind.

"Ian," Mom says, lifting her face up to look at me, tears still streaming down her cheeks. *She looks like she's hurting the way I did when I thought Spencer was dead,* I think, and a hot flush colors my cheeks. "He led the sting operation on the Fellowship. He's been working on this for years, you know."

"Ian Dave," I say, thinking of the dark-haired, grumbly asshole of a librarian. It all makes sense now, why he pulled the yearbooks, why he tried to stop us from sleuthing around.

"He's on a special task force that handles cults,"

Mom continues proudly, beaming as she smiles at me.

"He said that he was an investigator," I hedge, rubbing at my head. "Did they catch the bad guys then?"

"Most of the cultists were arrested," Dad says, nodding. "They're combing the woods and the tunnels to see if anyone else escaped. Unfortunately, that girl that tried to kill you is still alive, even though she was shot."

I shift in the bed and then cringe a bit when I feel a pulling sensation in my lower back.

Oh, that's right.

I was stabbed.

I was *stabbed.*

"I got stabbed," I repeat, and then a small smile lights my lips. "That makes me cool, doesn't it?"

"Charlotte Carson," Dad snaps as I glance over at him, realizing in that moment that every asshole thing he does, every barked command and sneer … is because he's my parent. And parents, parents are dicks. Even good parents. Especially good parents. Because sometimes teenagers are rebellious little ass pigs.

"You're sure my boys are okay?" I repeat, just before a light knock on the door interrupts our conversation.

"Come in," Dad says with a resigned sigh.

The door flies open and the twins come rushing in, throwing their arms around me from either side and making me both laugh and grunt with the impact.

"We were sure you were dead!" they howl, rubbing their faces on either side of mine.

My mom chokes on tears and holds a tissue up to her mouth to stifle her sobs. My dad just backs off a few steps, watching over me like a hawk.

"Would you two back off and let her breathe?" Ranger growls, still clearly shaken up by the confrontation with his father. I mean, knowing your dad is part of a crazy cult is one thing, but hearing the bullshit from the horse's mouth? Not easy. "How are you feeling?" he asks me, putting one of his hands over my blanketed feet and giving my toes a squeeze.

"I'm okay," I say as the twins sit on either side of me, releasing me from their maniacal hugging. "Plus, I get to tell everyone I meet from now on that I survived an attack from a rich, powerful cult."

Church's lips turn up into a smile, one that actually reaches his eyes for once.

"I was afraid I'd never get to see you in that wedding dress," he says, making my dad bristle.

"Same," Spencer agrees, glancing briefly Church's way before turning back to me. "I would've died if you had, Chuck."

"Archie, maybe we should let them have a moment?" Mom suggests, giving my dad a look from across the hospital room. His nostrils flare and his face turns that signature color of his, but he relents, moving over to press a kiss to my forehead before he steps out. I notice he doesn't quite close the door behind him, but that's okay. Like I said, parents are dicks.

"Seeing you lying on the ground in your dress, all covered in blood …" Tobias starts, taking my hand in his and entwining our fingers together. "Pretty sure that sight is going to haunt me for the rest of my life."

"You're one tough bitch, Chuck Carson," Micah says, looking down at his lap. I can tell he's trying to be upbeat, but he's still got tears in his eyes when he looks up and grins at me. "God, we hated you so much when you showed up at Adamson. Now we're all, like, clinically obsessed. What have you done to us?"

"I'm like a splinter—once I'm in, you can't get me out without bleeding!" I say, trying to be funny but totally and utterly fucking it up because I'm a shitty comedian. Also, I got stabbed. That's a great excuse for everything now, huh? I can just mess stuff up and say *I got stabbed.* Should work for at least six months or so.

"That's the worst metaphor I've ever heard in my life," Ranger says, sighing like he's releasing a ton of pent-up stress. "After you almost bled to death in the woods? What is wrong with you?"

"I … got stabbed?" I suggest, and he sighs, his face softening up. Oh, well. Damn. I'd get stabbed more often if it'd get me out of awkward situations like this. Could also possibly get me extra Jell-O. They do serve Jell-O in hospitals still, right? "I read once that Jell-O is made out of bone marrow—" I blurt but Tobias shuts me up with a kiss, pressing his mouth against mine and managing to convey every emotion he's feeling with just his lips. "Oh, wow," I say as he pulls back and looks me in the face with those moss green eyes of his. "That … was impressive."

"We love you, Charlotte," he says, and then pauses, like something's just occurred to him. "*I* love you."

"I love you, too," Micah says, drawing my attention back to him. "More than I feel comfortable admitting. Because, you know, I don't want to get committed or anything."

"You're committably in love me with me?" I ask, sniffling. I almost died in the woods. I get to cry.

"Committably isn't a word," Church lets me know softly, and I smile, looking over him, Spencer and Ranger standing on either side. "But also, we're very glad that you're not dead."

"I'm glad you're not dead, too," I say, smiling and then pausing, the expression slipping off my face. "Wait, what happened at the prom after I passed out?" Church watches me from those beautiful amber eyes of his. "And why weren't you affected by the drugs?"

"He spent the whole night drinking that stupid sparkling water, the kind with the corks that the waiters were bringing around, and not eating anything," Spencer says, glancing over at his friend, like they might've had this discussion while I was passed out.

"We're guessing Aster drugged our desserts. Makes sense now why she was so determined to join the Culinary Club."

"And there I was, hoping the punch *would* be spiked," I say with a shake of my head. "Just … not with whatever it was that they gave us."

"Everybody's okay," Micah adds, "but if you thought being the only girl would get you a lot of attention at Adamson, that's got nothing on your status now, as the survivor of a crazy cult attack."

"That still doesn't explain why Church was underground in a mask and robes," I say, grimacing slightly and holding my palms out in an apology. "I'm not accusing you of anything—I've learned my lesson—but … I have to know."

Church sighs and looks down at the floor for a moment, like he's got something he wants to say but isn't sure how it'll be received. When he looks up, there's a devastating amount of guilt in his gaze.

"Ian Dave and Nathan, they asked me to help. The sting operation had been in planning for a while; they knew they were coming for the Fellowship that night, regardless of what happened."

"You … knew all of that was going to happen?" I choke out, thinking of the way he looked down at me as he was escorting me to prom, the way he looked into my eyes. How could he have known what was going on and let us fall right into the trap?

"Not the thing with the drugged desserts or the secret church," he admits, cringing slightly and gritting his teeth.

"You're not a mind reader, a magician, *or* an FBI agent, bro, relax," Ranger chastises softly.

"When Mark and Selena stormed out after their fight, I followed them." Church sighs, like he's tired, too. We're all tired, I think. "After I called Ian, I followed them, then I disabled the cultist who was watching the door they went in through."

"Ian let you follow those psychos?" I ask, blinking through surprise, but Church just shakes his head.

"Not at all. He cursed me out actually, but I wasn't going to let anything happen to you two."

"We're beyond grateful," Spencer says, his expression darkening slightly. How we never figured out he was a mark, too, I don't know.

"The rest of us were lying in our leftover salads," Ranger says with a bit of a growl, and a warm flush in his cheeks. Church gives him a look and smiles slightly.

"Mark entered the tunnels the same way that we went. I was only able to follow at a distance, and without much light. Otherwise I would've recognized earlier that we'd traveled through another door into the sewer system. If I'd only figured that out sooner ..."

"It doesn't matter," I say, thinking of that moment when I was lying on the altar, those creepy psychos chanting around me, the candles flickering. I was certain I was going to die in there. Certain of it. "I'm glad you guys are here. What's going to happen to your dad, Ranger?" I ask, but he just shakes his head.

"I don't care, just so long as I never have to see him again. He and Rick took Jenica from me, and there's no coming back from that. They can both rot in prison for all I care."

I wonder if someday, Ranger's going to think about what really happened, and break down. But if he does, that'll be okay, because we'll be here.

We'll all be here.

"Does this mean we get to enjoy the rest of the year without Aster trying to crash our Culinary Club meetings?" I ask, and the twins grin.

"Told you she was guilty," they say, crossing their arms over their chests.

"You certainly did," I say, grinning back and wishing I could rip this IV out and go home. Only, I'm a big baby and it'd totally hurt, and I'm not dumb enough to mess with medical shit that I don't understand. "So, who's going to be the first guy to bring me a strawberry milkshake from the Jaw Flapper? First one to do it gets to cuddle in bed with me."

"You think we're actually to bother fighting over something like that?" Ranger says, and then pauses. "I better go get you something to eat though."

"Oh, no way, man, that shake is mine," Spencer

says, and they smirk at each other while the twins struggle to push each other back.

"I'll get the shake," Church says, slipping out the door, but not before stopping to smile at me. "And anything else you want. Anything." He steps out and closes the door as I laugh, putting my face in my hands as Dad steps into the room and starts to yell headmaster-y things at the boys.

Ah, life is good, isn't it?

The wind swishes my skirts around my thighs as I stand outside the imposing stone walls of Adamson Academy (formerly known as Adamson All-Boys Academy).

"It looks less like a school, and more like a castle," I say, grinning as I repeat the first thought I ever had about this place aloud.

"More like a church that used to hide a creepy underground chamber for cultists," Spencer says, raising both brows at me. I laugh and bump his shoulder with mine, moving into the hallway to the cheers of the other students. To be fair, I didn't do anything but get stabbed. But senior year of high school? That totally makes you cool.

"For my future bride," Church says, appearing on my left and handing over an iced coffee while Ranger shoves a freshly baked and carefully wrapped muffin into the front pocket of my bag.

"Why, thank you, sirs," I say as I hook my arm with Spencer's.

"And because I knew they'd be trying to butter you up this morning …" he says, reaching into his own bag and grabbing a book. He slips it into mine as I cock a brow at him. Pulling the book out and opening it, I see that it's a manga—a Japanese anime comic—and that it has … it has … My eye twitches. "There's so much sex in this book," I choke out as I try to hand it back to him and he dances out of my way, laughing and folding his arms together behind his head.

"God, Chuck, stop it, I don't want your dirty gay porn mag!"

"Spencer Hargrove!" I chastise as the twins appear, one hand tucked into each of their pockets.

"We warned him not to embarrass you on your first day back," Micah says, and then he glances over at Tobias, and they both smirk.

"We thought you might miss this," they say together, and I realize their other hands were hidden behind them, holding something suspicious behind their book bags. Together, they present the infamous packer penis, right there in the middle of the hallway. And then they toss it to me. It hits me right in the boobs, bounces off, and flies through the air to smack my dad in the face.

"Charlotte Carson," he says as the flaccid penis falls to the floor with a slap. "That's a write-up."

"Wait, no!" I yell, but he's already walking away while Spencer howls with laughter. Ranger and Church are both chuckling as the twins grin and lean in to press matching kisses on either of my cheeks.

"I love you, Charlotte," they both say at the same time, but in their own ways. I don't think either of them even knew it was meant to be a twin thing.

"I love you guys, too," I say, exhaling and lifting my chin. "All of you. Now, if I may, I'd love to have the illustrious Student Council escort me to class."

And, much to my pleasure, they do.

EPILOGUE

The last few months of school are almost too easy. Without the Fellowship to worry about, life is calm. No, no, not just calm, but *good.*

I'm going to Bornstead University next year, and this summer, the boys and I have a trip planned that'll take us around the world and back. It's hard to find anything to complain about. Hell, even Archie and I are getting along alright.

"Do you need anything from me?" he asks, appearing in his 1940s suit, hair slicked back from his face. I shake my head, but he steps into the room anyway, looking me over in my cap and gown with a far-away sort of smile on his face.

"What?" I ask, setting the cap just so over my blond

curls. I've been letting them grow for a while, but I might cut them short before we leave for Paris next week. And yeah, I totally said Paris. Paris, Paris, Paris. Micropenis Chuck is going to see the world! "You're staring at me, and it's weird as hell."

"Oh Charlotte, stop that," he says, coming over and fiddling with my cap so that the tassel falls right into my face. I blow it away with a huff, studying myself in the navy-blue robe, the pink diamond winking back from my finger.

It's nice knowing that I don't have to pick between the boys, that there's no ultimatum, no expiration date for our relationship. We're just going to take things slow, and see what happens. If it works forever, then we'll date forever. If it doesn't, then that doesn't matter either because we're a forever crew. I feel confident that we'll be in each other's lives, no matter what, even if it's just as friends.

But, you know, I don't want to be just friends and luckily, it doesn't seem like any of the guys do either.

"You know I'm only looking at you like this because I'm proud of you," Archie says, and I feel my little icy Grinch heart get all warm-y and shit. Yes, I said warm-y. I'm a shitty poet, so sue me. "You'll always be my everything, Charlotte Farren, whether you like it or not."

I wrinkle my face up, but when Dad turns toward the door, I stop him by throwing my arms around his neck and hugging him tight from behind. He hasn't always listened to me, and I haven't always tried to make things easy between us, but that's okay. Love isn't easy. It isn't perfect. It's not a quiet pond without ripples, but a raging river that cuts through the earth. It might have rapids, but it can carve stone and create the Grand Canyon. That's how powerful it is.

"Your mother's downstairs," he whispers, and I let go, knowing that everything's going to be okay between us. When I marry Church in his mother's wedding dress, Dad will be there by my side. When I choose to commit to the other boys in the same way, I know he'll roll his eyes, but he'll get over it. There'll always be growing pains as our relationship shifts and adjusts, but real love, true love, is strong enough to ride out the storm.

I follow Dad down the steps to find Mom waiting for me in the foyer, a smile on her face as she turns to look at me. Ian Dave is standing nearby, looking a bit nervous and out of place. Dad and Ian regard each other with wary expressions, but when they both turn their attention toward me and Mom, I can see that they each love her in their own way. Hey, if she plays her cards right, maybe she could start her own harem?

"I'm glad you were able to make it," I say, knowing the boys sent her a first-class ticket, just so she could be here today. We hug tight, and I close my eyes, savoring the moment. Mom isn't perfect either, but nobody is. Did she make a mistake when she left me? I think so, but I'm not going to hold her mistakes against her because she's human. She's imperfect, just like me. And I know she loves me the best she can, in her own way.

"So am I," she says, pulling away and smiling softly. She looks better even than when I last saw her, and I have to wonder if Ian Dave has anything to do with it. He might've met her while he was investigating the Fellowship, but I think that what they have is real. Maybe now that he's done at Adamson, they can spend more time together? "Are you ready?"

"I am," I say, taking her hand and leading her down the front steps of the headmaster's house and along the winding path toward the main building.

The boys are standing around the bench at the first curve, that same spot where Spencer waited for me before winter break, kissing me and making me question everything I thought I knew, that I thought I wanted.

"Hey, Chuck-let," he says, as my mom releases my hand, and I go to him, lost in his turquoise eyes and his smile. We kiss, a brief brush of lips that could go on forever. I'd die happy that way, but I would miss the others.

"You look …" the twins start, and for the first time, they mess up their perfect unity by accident.

"Gorgeous," Tobias says.

"Stunning," Micah breathes, and then they exchange a look, and I laugh. Nearby, one of those ridiculous short-eared owls hoots, and I roll my eyes. Sorry, buddy, but the murder-mystery is over, and you don't scare me anymore.

I throw one arm around each of their necks, squeezing tight as the wind blows pink flower petals around us.

"Ready to graduate?" Tobias asks, hooking his arm around my waist.

"I'm ready," I say, planting a kiss on either of their cheeks and trying to step back.

"Oh no, you don't," Micah says, tucking his fingers under my chin and kissing my lips. Tobias isn't about to let his twin get one up on me, so he sneaks a kiss in, too. Meanwhile, my dad clears his throat and shuffles his feet behind us.

"You look cute," Ranger says, and even though he's trying to keep his cool, I can see that bit of pink in his cheeks as he folds me in his arms, giving me one of those signature hugs of his, the ones that feel like they can squeeze all the bad things out and make the world right again. "Too cute for your own good." Before I step back to greet Church, Ranger pulls the neckline of his robe down just enough that I can see one of his grandma's aprons underneath it. "This was Jenica's favorite," he says, and my smile softens up just a bit, thinking of the girl who never got to graduate, but whose brother is more than happy to carry her memory to the ends of the earth. Her spirit lives vicariously in him; I can see it in every smile.

"Are you nervous for your speech?" I ask, glancing over at Church, his blond hair tousled by the wind. He's the valedictorian, after all—no surprise there. But he shakes his head and holds out an arm for me to take.

"Why would I be? I worked hard for the privilege of giving it, didn't I?" He smiles as he says it, softening up some of that arrogant princeliness of his.

"Churchie!" his mom shouts, coming up the path with his dad and sisters in tow. His face pales a bit, but I know that even through all of the embarrassment of them swarming him with hugs and kisses, that he's glad they're there.

And the Montagues aren't the only ones who show for graduation.

Ranger's mother is there, hidden by a big, black floppy hat, looking like the reincarnation of Jenica Woodruff. Spencer's mom and dad are there, but sitting on opposite sides of the room, Jack slumped in a seat on his mother's right side. The McCarthys are there, too, sitting together but worlds apart from each other.

There's a lot to unpack there, between the boys' families and mine.

But we have all the time in the world to do it.

First, we graduate. Next, we travel. Then, we do college.

And all the while, we grow, and change, and love, and make mistakes, and learn.

My dad makes his speech first, ever the consummate headmaster, with Church stepping up to the podium at the tail-end of the ceremony.

"It's been said that our high school years are the best years of a person's life. I respectfully disagree. While I've met fantastic people here at Adamson Academy, while I've fallen in love with a beautiful girl"—he looks right at me, and my cheeks flame as the crowd turns to see who it is that's captured that blinding smile of his—"I think there are no best moments in life. We're all just lucky to be alive, period. And if we're happy here, in this little corner of time, this slice of forever, then that's enough."

The crowd cheers like crazy for him—as they should because, uh, Church is freaking awesome—and the ceremony ends with us holding our diplomas in one hand, and our futures in the other.

"To the Jaw Flapper for ice cream?" Spencer suggests, and we all raise our diplomas in agreement, like knights raising their swords.

"For ice cream, and *coffee*," Church corrects, and I grin.

"Ice cream, coffee, and good company," I agree, and together, we walk down the stone halls one last time, head out into the sunshine, and into our future.

This is Chuck Carson, the secret girl, with her

ruthless boys, her forever crew, signing out.

Peace, love, and pink cupcakes, my friends.

Always remember: hug like you mean it, love with your whole heart, and naked-bake something every once in a while.

Over and out.

The End

ORIENTATION

A Rich Boys of Burberry Prep x Adamson All-Boys Academy

THE FAMILY SPELLS

The Family Spells #1

FILTHY RICH BOYS

RICH BOYS OF BURBERRY PREP, YEAR ONE

FILTHY RICH BOYS

ALL BETS ARE ON ...

USA TODAY BESTSELLING AUTHOR

C.M. STUNICH

Rich Boys of Burberry Prep # 1

SHADOWED

Academy of Spirits and Shadows # 3

SIGN UP FOR
THE C.M. STUNICH

NEWSLETTER

Sign up for an exclusive first look at the hottest new releases, contests, and exclusives from the author.

www.cmstunich.com

JOIN THE
C.M. STUNICH

DISCUSSION GROUP

Want to discuss what you've just read?
Get exclusive teasers or meet special guest authors?
Join CM.'s online book clubs on Facebook!

www.facebook.com/groups/thebookishbatcave

STALKING LINKS

JOIN THE C.M. STUNICH NEWSLETTER – Get three free books just for signing up http://eepurl.com/DEsEf

TWEET ME ON TWITTER, BABE – Come sing the social media song with me https://twitter.com/CMStunich

SNAPCHAT WITH ME – Get exclusive behind the scenes looks at covers, blurbs, book signings and more http://www.snapchat.com/add/cmstunich

LISTEN TO MY BOOK PLAYLISTS – Share your fave music with me and I'll give you my playlists (I'm super active on here!) https://open.spotify.com/user/12101321503

FRIEND ME ON FACEBOOK – Okay, I'm actually at the 5,000 friend limit, but if you click the "follow" button on my profile page, you'll see way more of my killer posts https://facebook.com/cmstunich

LIKE ME ON FACEBOOK – Pretty please? I'll love you forever if you do! ;) https://facebook.com/cmstunichauthor & https://facebook.com/violetblazeauthor

CHECK OUT THE NEW SITE – (under construction) but it looks kick-a$$ so far, right? You can order signed books here! http://www.cmstunich.com

READ VIOLET BLAZE – Read the books from my hot as hellfire pen name, Violet Blaze http://www.violetblazebooks.com

SUBSCRIBE TO MY RSS FEED – Press that little orange button in the corner and copy that RSS feed so you can get all the latest updates http://www.cmstunich.com/blog

AMAZON, BABY – If you click the follow button here, you'll get an email each time I put out a new book. Pretty sweet, huh? http://amazon.com/author/cmstunich http://amazon.com/author/violetblaze

PINTEREST – Lots of hot half-naked men. Oh, and half-naked men. Plus, tattooed guys holding babies (who are half-naked) http://pinterest.com/cmstunich

INSTAGRAM – Cute cat pictures. And half-naked guys. Yep, that again. http://instagram.com/cmstunich

ABOUT THE AUTHOR

C.M. Stunich is a self-admitted bibliophile with a love for exotic teas and a whole host of characters who live full time inside the strange, swirling vortex of her thoughts. Some folks might call this crazy, but Caitlin Morgan doesn't mind – especially considering she has to write biographies in the third person. Oh, and half the host of characters in her head are searing hot bad boys with dirty mouths and skillful hands (among other things). If being crazy means hanging out with them everyday, C.M. has decided to have herself committed.

She hates tapioca pudding, loves to binge on cheesy horror movies, and is a slave to many cats. When she's not vacuuming fur off of her couch, C.M. can be found with her nose buried in a book or her eyes glued to a computer screen. She's the author of over thirty novels – romance, new adult, fantasy, and young adult included. Please, come and join her inside her crazy. There's a heck of a lot to do there.

Oh, and Caitlin loves to chat (incessantly), so feel free to e-mail her, send her a Facebook message, or put up smoke signals. She's already looking forward to it.

Made in the USA
Middletown, DE
11 February 2025

71199127R00266